Air Cadet

The Air Cadets

C.R. Cummings

Also By
CHRISTOPHER CUMMINGS

The Boy and the Battleship

The Green Idol of Kanaka Creek

Ross River Fever

Train to Kuranda

The Mudskipper Cup

Davey Jones's Locker

*Air Cadet

Below Bartle Frere

Bowling Green Bay

Airship Over Atherton

Cockatoo

The Cadet Corporal

Stannary Hills

Coast of Cape York

Kylie and the Kelly Gang

Beyond the Barrier Reef

Behind Mt. Baldy

The Cadet Sergeant Major

Cooktown Christmas

Secret in the Clouds

Mischief at Mingela

The Word of God

The Cadet Under-Officer

Through the Devil's Eye

Barbara in the Bush

The Smiley People

Barbara at her Best

Barbara's Bivouac

Air Cadet

The Air Cadets

C.R. Cummings

DoctorZed
Publishing
www.doctorzed.com

Published 2020 by DoctorZed Publishing

DoctorZed Publishing books may be ordered through booksellers or by contacting:

DoctorZed Publishing
10 Vista Ave
Skye, South Australia 5072
www.doctorzed.com

ISBN: 978-0-6488271-2-2 (hc)
ISBN: 978-0-6488271-1-5 (sc)
ISBN: 978-0-6488271-0-8 (ebk)

National Library of Australia Cataloguing-in-Publication entry

    Author: Cummings, C. R., author.

    Title: Air cadet/ Christopher Cummings.
    ISBN: 978-0-6488271-2-2 (hardcover)

    Series: Cummings, C. R. The air cadets.

    Target Audience: For young adults.

    Subjects: Adventure stories, Australian.

    Military cadets--Queensland--Fiction.

Cover image © Faizal Idris | Dreamstime.com
Cover design © Scott Zarcinas

Printed in Australia, UK & USA

DoctorZed Publishing rev. date: 14/06/2020

**Special Thanks
to the
Officers of Cadets
and
Instructors of Cadets
of the
Australian Air Force Cadets**

This book, while a work of fiction, is dedicated to all the Officers of Cadets and Instructors of Cadets of the AAFC. Your dedication, hard work, and the excellent training you provide make the AAFC a disciplined and efficient youth development organisation that Australia can be rightly proud of. Because you give up your spare time to be volunteers you provide life-changing opportunities for young people. Thank you.

Chapter 1

WILLY'S ROCKET

"You're a mad bugger Willy. You'll blow yourself up," Stick commented.

Willy Williams, 13, grinned back at his friend and shook his head. "She'll be right. It will work this time."

Carefully he adjusted the model space rocket on the home-made launching platform and again checked the angle to be sure it would miss the trees when it lifted off. The rocket was nearly a metre in length, a shiny aluminium tube to which a red nose cone and various fins and control planes had been added.

The third boy, John Rhuddock, bent down to watch. "Just how many match heads did you cram into this thing Willy?" he asked.

"Five hundred," Willy replied. "Plus some sulphur and gunpowder and other stuff."

Satisfied that the rocket was resting firmly on its launcher he began unrolling the fuse which led up into the base. He was a bit doubtful about the propellent mixture. Both his chemistry textbook and the internet had given him various formulae, but he had been unable to obtain all of the correct ingredients. He could, he knew, have easily stolen small amounts during each chemistry lesson at school but the thought of being a thief was not something he wanted to consider.

Stick Morton, tall and gangly, hence the nickname, shook his head doubtfully. "Are you sure it will work?"

"No. But it doesn't matter if it doesn't," Willy replied.

He gestured to the surrounding countryside. It was a Sunday afternoon and the boys were standing at a curve in the Myola Road a few kilometres out of the small town of Kuranda in North Queensland. They were twenty paces beyond the edge of the last patch of tropical rainforest before the Kuranda High School. On three sides of them were open fields sloping away down to either tree lined creeks or the Barron River. The roofs of the High School were clearly visible about half a kilometre away. There was no-one in sight, and very few cars had passed them.

All three boys were actually Year 8 students at a high school in Cairns, 35 kilometres away down on the coastal plain. They were spending the day at the farm owned by Stick's aunt. Willy was taking the opportunity to test his new rocket. He was a bit concerned that it might not fly straight and that it could start a fire. For that reason he had chosen to do the test flight near Kuranda where there was a lot of rain forest and where the grass was damper, rather than at the farm owned by his own uncle and aunt. Their farm was further west beyond Davies Creek. This was in much drier country where a grass fire would be a serious threat to both crops and houses.

Manufacturing the rocket and then smuggling it up to Kuranda had been a major undertaking for the boys. The last thing they wanted was an adult to learn about it. Willy was sure they would make a fuss and veto the experiment.

Now Willy was feeling good and confident. He glanced up at the sky and smiled. *Perfect,* he thought. It was August, Winter in North Queensland. For most of the time that meant clear blue skies. That was how it was at that moment, not a cloud in the sky and a gentle breeze. Gesturing backwards with his hand he said, "You blokes get back under cover while I light the fuse."

His friends needed no urging. They hurried the twenty metres back to the first of the trees on the edge of the jungle. Here the boys took shelter, peering around the trunk of a large tree to watch. Willy smiled at their caution, then took out the box of matches he had taken from home. After a final check that there was no-one around and no cars in sight, he struck a match and applied the flame to the end of the fuse. For a few moments the fuse resisted his attempt to get it alight.

"Come on you bloody thing!" Willy muttered. "Ah!"

The fuse began to splutter and hiss. It was only a thin fuse bought from a hobby shop, but it was now well alight. Willy had done a couple of test burns to check the rate of burning but now he became anxious.

I hope I have calculated the length correctly, he worried.

Pocketing the box of matches Willy turned and began walking back towards his friends. In spite of mental images of explosions and all the physical symptoms of anxiety he forced himself to walk with every appearance of nonchalance.

It's a rocket, he told himself. *It will just go whoosh up into the sky.*

As he walked, he managed to grin at his friends concerned faces. He knew that he had a reputation around the school of being a 'mad scientist' and he liked to play up to it. "It's OK," he commented as he joined them. Even so, he found it a secret relief to get in behind the tree himself.

The trunk of the tree wasn't really big enough to shelter all three but that didn't worry Willy unduly. He wanted to watch the launch anyway. This was his second rocket and the first had been satisfactory as far as it went, but that wasn't far. It had been only twenty centimetres long and had been filled with gunpowder. Even so it had shot up to a respectable looking height during a test firing a month earlier.

I should have arranged for observers to be stationed well out to take angles on the rocket so we could calculate its altitude by trigonometry, he thought.

He had not yet been taught how to do that but knew about it and understood the basic principles. That was Year 11 work and he was looking forward to it.

Stick nudged him. "That fuse seems to be taking a long time to burn down," he observed.

"Maybe it's gone out," John suggested gloomily.

Willy had been thinking the same thing himself but didn't want to admit that his calculations might have been wrong. He shook his head and screwed up his eyes. "No, I can still see smoke coming up," he replied, trying to sound more confident than he felt.

Suddenly Stick grabbed Willy's arm. "There's an old man!"

Willy looked and a wave of cold shock swept over him. An old man wearing dark long trousers held up by braces over a white shirt had appeared on the path along the other side of the road. He was hobbling along with the aid of a walking stick.

Willy swallowed with anxiety. "Bloody hell!" he muttered, "Where did he spring from?"

"I think he came out of that side-track on the edge of the jungle," John replied.

Willy felt his heart begin hammering with alarm. The old man was getting closer to the gap in the long grass where they had positioned the rocket. *Maybe he will just walk past,* Willy hoped.

But even as he thought it the old man suddenly turned his head. He took a quick, alarmed step backwards, then stopped and peered more closely, squinting at where the rocket stood. It was the hissing that had attracted his attention. Once again Willy experienced a stab of doubt about the timing of the fuse.

"Maybe he will keep walking?" he muttered.

Willy tried to will the old man to move away but, to his consternation, the old man stepped even closer to the hissing rocket and took out a pair of glasses. "Oh no!" Willy groaned.

"He'll be killed!" John wailed.

As the old man took another step closer, while putting on his glasses and adjusting them Willy acted. He dashed out from hiding and raced towards him. At every moment he felt stabs of alarm about the fuse.

It should have gone off by now, he thought angrily.

The old man heard him coming and looked around in alarm. Obviously fearing attack he put up his left arm to fend Willy off. Willy shouted, "Get away! It will go off at any moment!"

Suddenly becoming alive to possible peril the old man turned quickly. In doing so he tripped in the knee-high grass and stumbled. Willy was now in a lather of anxiety. He dashed over, grabbed the frightened old man and shoved him away. The old men staggered two paces before falling flat in the grass beside the road.

As the old man went down Willy glanced over his shoulder at the rocket, which was still spluttering and hissing only a metre from him. To his dismay he saw that the fuse was all gone and that sparks were shooting out of the base of the rocket. To his astonishment this was glowing cherry red.

Willy stared at it in horror. "It's going to.."

BANG!

Smoke and sparks enveloped Willy and the next thing he knew he was lying flat on his back in the grass. *Bloody hell! It blew up!* his stunned mind told him. Then he remembered the old man and anxiety took over. Rolling over onto his hands and knees Willy waved the billowing smoke aside and looked around. To his dismay the old man was lying nearby, face down. *Oh no! I've killed him!* Willy thought, the anxiety giving way to genuine apprehension.

Scrambling across to him Willy reached down and took hold of the old man's shoulder and went to turn him over. Suddenly the old man shook his head and shrugged and then snarled, "Get your hands off me!"

Willy sprang back, his heart hammering with anxiety. The old man rolled over and sat up, then glared at Willy. "You bloody young fool! You could have killed me!" he shouted.

Willy could only nod and then a drop of something splashed off his eyebrow. He wiped it away and then glanced at his hand. To his horror it was smeared with blood. *I must be injured,* he thought. Only then did he realise he was hurting in several places and that he was having trouble hearing and that his vision was going blurry.

The old man's expression changed as he climbed slowly to his feet. "Well, it looks like you've gone and hurt yourself."

Willy nodded then a wave of dizziness swept over him and he stumbled and then sat down heavily in the grass. More blood trickled down his forehead and began to drip off the tip of his nose. Stick and John arrived and stood staring at him, their faces a study in ghoulish fascination and concern.

Blackness engulfed Willy as he fell backwards into the grass.

* * * * *

The next couple of hours were hazy for Willy. He dimly remembered lying in the grass with worried faces and mumbled voices with waves of darkness pushing him in and out of consciousness. Through a haze of pain he heard someone say, "Don't pull it out! It might have penetrated his brain."

What are they talking about? Willy wondered. But the throbbing waves of pain told him that whatever it was, it was not good!

Then, during a lucid moment, he realised that there were sharp pieces of metal embedded in his skull and face. He felt hands pull his own away and hold them firmly. Later he certainly remembered thinking he was dying and curiously not being too terrified at the prospect. There had only been a muzzy regret that he had not lived, meaning he had not yet had the opportunity to make love to a girl.

Then there were more serious faces as he was transported by ambulance down the mountain to the Cairns Hospital. Most of the trip he was out to it but a few times he surfaced and noted their progress. After that came the usual hospital bustle and disinfectant smells and people in blue gowns, blue caps and blue face masks.

There was some pain and then nothing for a while. At one stage he returned to a semi-conscious state, or maybe it was a dream? Floating above him was a beautiful girl with the most serene face and ever so kissable lips. For a few moments he thought he was looking at an angel.

I am dying, he decided as the vision blurred and faded. *She is an angel come to take me to heaven.* But then the image came back into focus between waves of pain and he noted the long black hair and a name floated into his fuzzy thoughts. *Petra!*

A vivid flashback scrolled through his mind, the first day of Year 8 at his state high school. He had just had his name ticked off on the roll by the middle-aged lady teacher who was the class 'Form Teacher' and then looked around for somewhere to sit. His anxiety level had been very high as it was the first day and he felt very much the 'new boy' and quite lonely.

Then his gaze had lighted on the smiling face of a person he recognised. *John Rhuddock,* Willy remembered. *He was in my Year 7 class.* He didn't really know John who was a big, dark-haired lad but he had returned the smile.

John had been seated right at the back. He had beckoned so Willy had walked along the aisle between the rows of desks to him. As he arrived John gestured to the empty seat beside him.

"You could sit here Willy," he said diffidently.

Willy wasn't all that keen to sit next to John who he remembered as a bit of a dull plodder, but he did like the idea of sitting at the back and that was the only seat left in the back row. And just across the aisle was the beautiful Dianna. So he nodded. "OK," he agreed.

After sliding into the seat Willy placed his books and pencil case down and looked around to see who else he knew. To his relief there were a few: Scott Tremlow and Roger Dunning and right in front of him black-haired Sonja and big-bosomed, blonde-haired Gillian.

And off to his left front, two rows away was Barbara. At the sight of her Willy's heart leapt. *Barbara Brassington! Oh good!* he thought. Right through Primary School Willy had admired Barbara and the previous year he had developed a real 'crush' on her. *She is so pretty,* he thought, noting the sunlight glint on her bright, copper-coloured hair. For a good few seconds he surreptitiously studied Barbara, noting that she looked to have even longer legs than before.

To his annoyance and secret embarrassment Barbara had become so gangly and long-legged that her nickname the previous year had been 'Giraffe'.

I hope that doesn't stick this year, he thought.

Barbara stood up to adjust her desk and Willy was able to study her more carefully. He noted her freckles and her green eyes and again thought she was very attractive. *And she is just starting to show some promise of womanly shape,* he decided, noting that her hips were just noticeable and that she had developed tiny pointy breasts over the holidays.

They were both a sign of hope and a disappointment for Willy who had already developed a strong preference for girls with large breasts. Having recently reached puberty Willy was now very interested in girls.

And here's another pretty one, he thought, noting a very shapely girl with shiny black hair who had just entered the room. The girl looked very anxious and shy and she hesitated in the doorway while she looked half-fearfully around.

Heavens, she is pretty! Willy thought. Then he looked again and changed his assessment to beautiful.

Mrs Ramsey, the Form Teacher, called to the girl. "Hello! Come in dearie. What's your name?"

The girl walked across from the door to the teacher's desk, or rather glided gracefully, while Willy watched, entranced. Stopping in front of the teacher she replied with a distinct foreign accent, "Plis, my name it is Petra Pantovitch."

Petra, Willy noted. *She is just gorgeous!*

Mrs Ramsey consulted her list and nodded. "Yes, here you are. Welcome Petra. Where do you come from?"

"I from der Ukraine do come," Petra replied, her voice having what Willy thought was a very attractive musical lilt.

Mrs Ramsey looked around the room. "Now, where can we sit you?" she said.

As she said that Willy regretted his choice. *She could have sat next to me,* he told himself while his eyes feasted on her every lovely detail. To his eyes she just looked perfect: nice legs, spotlessly clean and ironed uniform, dainty hands, a nice rounded bosom, slender neck and very kissable lips.

Petra also looked nervously around the room. Then their eyes met, and it was as though an electric shock went through Willy. *I'm in love!* he thought. To his mind she appeared to glow with a radiance that set her apart. *Like an angel come down from heaven,* he thought.

For a fleeting moment her eyes had widened and then she had given a faint smile before her gaze moved on. Willy had been thrilled and began to adore her. But she was not seated anywhere near him. Instead she was placed next to Belinda over against the wall a row in front and two to the right. *Oh I wonder?* Willy began to speculate.

Then the vision faded and he lapsed into blackness. Stabs of pain lanced through like shards of silver glass. Then medication induced sleep took over.

And now Willy was awake and obviously in hospital and instead of an angel or Petra leaning over him it was both his parents. His brother's face hovered in the background.

Both Willy's parents were doctors. Now his mother's anxious face stared down at him. "Oh Willy! What on earth were you up to this time?" she asked, a note of exasperation creeping into her voice.

Willy shrugged. "Just a bit of space exploration," he replied.

His father grunted. "Huh! Another dangerous experiment from the sound of it. What went bang?"

Reluctantly Willy described the rocket and the fuel he had concocted. His mother was horrified and his father shook his head. "Where did you get this crazy idea of using match heads from?" he asked.

Willy felt sheepish but replied: "Mythbusters."

At that his brother Lloyd let out a neighing laugh and then added, "Mythbusters! I saw that. Theirs didn't go bang!"

Willy's father called over his shoulder, "Be quiet Lloyd! Stay out of this." Then he turned back to Willy. "I saw bits of that program too and I clearly heard the presenters say several times not to try this one at home."

It was on the tip of Willy's tongue to say that he hadn't been at home, but he knew his father was genuinely angry. Instead he managed to look contrite and say, "Sorry. It won't happen again."

"It had better not. You need to take up some safer hobby," his father replied.

"What happened to me?" Willy asked, aware of a number of dull aches and sharp pains in his face, chest and left arm.

His mother answered. "You got four pieces of shrapnel in your face:

two in the left cheek, one in the eyebrow above your right eye and a big piece in the forehead. You are lucky you didn't lose an eye," she said.

That gave Willy pause. Only recently he had conceived the ambition of becoming a fighter pilot in the air force and he knew that a damaged eye would mean the end to any such career.

And before it even started, he mused.

His mother went on: "The worst was the huge chunk of aluminium that got stuck in your forehead. It went in right to the bone."

Lloyd chuckled again. "That wouldn't have done any damage. With a skull as thick as his there isn't any room for a brain!"

"Lloyd!" their mother cautioned.

"Sorry Mum, but the crazy ideas he comes up with makes you wonder," Lloyd replied.

Willy winced at a sharp pain in his left side. "So why do I hurt down here," he asked.

"Because you got three pieces of metal in your chest and side and another two in your left arm," his mother replied. "You are lucky you weren't killed."

"I'm not going to die am I?" he asked.

Lloyd snorted and cut in: "Huh! No chance! Only the good die young."

Again their mother frowned. "Lloyd, that will do. No dear, only if an infection sets in. They had to operate on your chest cavity," she said.

Another worrying thought came to Willy. "Is the old man alright?"

Willy's father nodded. "Only a bit of shock and bruising. He didn't get hit by any flying pieces," he said.

"Am I in trouble? I mean, will he take me to court or something?" Willy asked anxiously.

His father shook his head. "No, but the police are involved and will be talking to you," he said.

That was a shock. Willy dimly knew that there were laws about explosives and so on but only now did it occur to him that there might be serious legal consequences. That was also a real cause for concern as he knew that people with criminal records could not join the air force.

Oh bugger! he thought. *I hope I don't go to jail or something.*

His mother looked very worried and said, "So no more playing with explosives or rockets and things please."

"No Mum. I promise," Willy replied.

His mother managed a weak smile and then reached down and took a parcel from her bag. Willy saw that it was a rectangular shape and wrapped in coloured paper like a present. *A plastic kit?* he thought.

It was a present. His mother held it out and said, "You will be here for a day or so, so here is something to occupy your mind."

Willy felt a rush of affection and took the present. Just by the feel he could tell he was right; it was a plastic kit. Tearing open the wrapping he saw that it was one he really wanted. It was a 1:72 scale kit of a model Lancaster bomber of World War 2. "Oh thanks, Mum! I really wanted this one!" he cried.

Willy already had a dozen plastic kit model aircraft, having been given his first one for his 8th birthday. They decorated his bedroom and it had now become something of a family tradition and joke that for both his birthday and Christmas he be given a plastic model aircraft by everyone.

His mother said, "You are not making this here at the hospital. You can make it at home. Meanwhile your father has something to occupy what little mind you appear to have."

At that Lloyd chuckled and murmured something that sounded like 'I told you so!' and Willy blushed. His father reached down and lifted up another present, a book by the look of it. It was. Willy tore off the wrappings and found himself with a copy of *How to make 1:35 scale World War 1 Aircraft Models.* The front cover was decorated with pictures of famous World War 1 aircraft: German Albatross IIIs, the 'Red Baron's' red Fokker triplane and British Sopwiths and De Havillands.

Willy was thrilled and did not try to hide his feelings. "Oh thanks Dad! This looks great." He was very interested in aircraft and flying was the great passion of his life, or had been until he reached puberty a few months earlier. Now girls were starting to rival aviation in his thoughts and daydreams.

His parents and brother went home and Willy was left alone with his thoughts. For a while he just lay there thinking about the train of events that he landed him in hospital and the possible consequences. Then his thoughts wandered onto girls. After a few seconds these focused in on Petra. Willy decided she was the most beautiful girl he had ever seen.

I must get to know her, he decided.

What he actually meant, but had trouble admitting even to himself, was 'pluck up the courage to ask her for a date.' Ever since he had first seen her, he had been trying to do that.

Then his fantasies moved on to images of Barbara: long-legged, red-headed Barbara. But so far Barbara had not even acknowledged that he existed and that irked. Willy was so in awe of her that he had not been able to muster the courage to speak to her either.

That bothered him because usually he had no difficulty talking to other girls. *After I get out of hospital and back to school I will speak to her,* he told himself as he flicked open the book on making model aircraft.

Within seconds he had forgotten about girls and was absorbed. The book only covered World War 1 aircraft but Willy didn't mind. Since he was 9 he had been reading and collecting the famous *Biggles* novels by Captain W. E, Johns and spent hours fantasising that he was up there in the war torn skies over the Western Front in 1917 with his hero and the other pilots of 266 Squadron.

It was already a source of annoyance and regret that the series had been deemed 'politically incorrect' because of some of the racist remarks and opinions voiced in them. These had obviously mirrored the attitudes held when the books were written but were now quite offensive to many. Willy certainly found them distasteful and wished they weren't there either. He also regretted them because they had resulted in the really great flying parts of the stories being censored as well when the books were taken out of print and off library shelves, thus making them hard to collect.

They could have just edited out the few comments that offend people and allowed the books to be on the shelves, he thought. *That's what they did with other books, like Enid Blyton's.*

Only a few months before Willy had been given an hour-long joyride in a Tiger Moth biplane as a 13th birthday present and that experience had profoundly affected him. He had loved every second and the feeling of freedom that the fragile wood and canvas aircraft had engendered made him yearn to fly in one at every opportunity. It had also given him some real experiences to weave into his fantasies and to give a sense of realism to his reading.

Now he studied the plans and pictures of a dozen biplanes and a couple of monoplanes. Willy had four plastic kit biplanes in his collection:

a Sopwith Camel, a Fokker DR1 triplane, a Bristol Fighter of 1916 and a Tiger Moth.

The Sopwith Camel was the first plastic kit he had ever purchased with his own money, and it was now minus its upper wing and with two broken wing struts; the result of being accidentally dropped. The Fokker DR1 triplane—the Red Baron's famous fighter—was also broken and minus its undercarriage and two upper wings, the result of an accident when he was wrestling with Lloyd in a dispute over whose turn it was to wash up.

There were also a Bristol Fighter of 1916 design and a much more recent Tiger Moth that he had purchased himself. They both stood on a bookshelf at home but keeping them intact was always a problem as they were so fragile.

Their upper wings and the struts holding them on are the weak points, Willy mused. He was very aware, from several failed attempts to do so, that plastic kits were virtually impossible to repair once they were broken.

Willy now noted that the models in the books were all constructed out of balsa wood and similar materials and that gave him pause. *Balsa wood!* he thought.

I haven't got any of that. I wonder where you get it? I will have to look in the hobby shops when I get out.

Happily, he settled down to reading until sleep gently overtook him.

Chapter 2

Two days later Willy was released from hospital. It had been a boring and frustrating experience, but he was at least aware that he had been very lucky. The interviews with the police had been really worrying and he was still anxious in case they decided to charge him. He knew that his chances of joining the Air Force when he grew up would be almost nil if he had a criminal record.

Also he had missed two days of school and he regretted that, not because of the academic work he had missed (he found school easy and usually got top marks in most subjects), but because he was now determined to speak to Petra.

The best thing about the time in hospital was that he had been able to read his new book and that had inspired him. *I must make some of these models,* he thought, picturing whole squadrons of model aircraft he could play with. It had been a disappointment to find that none of the plans in the book were for models that could fly. They were just to look at, or to play with.

I will make a whole squadron of these German planes, he told himself. *I will make an all red Fokker triplane for the Red Baron and another for his Number 2. And it will only be partly red. The other planes will be 'Albatrosses'. They will be painted all sorts of colours like they really were.*

Willy particularly liked the 'Albatross DIII'. To him it looked really good with its torpedo shaped fuselage and curved wings. *A really graceful, functional aircraft,* he decided.

His mind moved on to making a collection of British aircraft: Sopwith Camels and Sopwith Pups, plus a couple of SE5As and an FE2. *Oh, and a couple of Bristol Fighters,* he added.

But when he got home, he was unable to do more than draw the plans and make lists of what he wanted. He had no balsa wood or suitable glue or paint. He knew he could just ask his parents and they would get it but after upsetting them he did not like to put them to that trouble. *I will buy it all myself,* he told himself. He was given a reasonable weekly allowance of pocket money and was careful to save most of it.

Wednesday he had to spend at home. Being 13 his mother considered him old enough to be left home alone so she, his father and his big brother Lloyd all went off to work or school. That suited Willy as he liked being alone at times and he was able to relax.

For a time he read. Next, he went on the internet and checked Cadetnet to see if there were any activities he could apply to do. Then he lay and looked at his plastic model aircraft. Most were on four shelves above his head but four were suspended from the ceiling on nylon fishing line. The largest of these was a Sunderland flying boat. Willy had read just enough history to understand their importance in World War 2. Ever since he had read Ivan Southall's *They Shall Not Pass Unseen* he had really admired the men who had flown them.

I must assemble my new Lancaster kit, he decided.

So he set to work preparing. Having plenty of experience with plastic kits Willy knew that careful preparation was half the battle. He cleared his hobby table under the high-set 'Old Queenslander' house and then placed old newspaper on it. Next, he stuck a layer of clear plastic 'Clingwrap' over this. The box was then opened and all the pieces were laid out neatly to one side. Glue, a craft knife, tweezers and fine sandpaper were placed beside these.

Then Willy sat and studied the picture on the box cover and then read the instructions. As he did, he muttered his father's favourite sarcastic comment: "When all else fails, read the instructions!"

Willy also understood that it was important to paint as much of the model as possible before assembling it. He had quite an extensive range of paint, about thirty tiny tins of Humbrol brand paint. He also had suitable brushes and thinner to clean them with. These were all positioned ready, along with a cleaning cloth. Then he began.

Two hours later Willy wiped his paint brush clean, screwed the cap back on the bottle of thinner and then stood up. To his surprise he felt quite stiff and sore and it was a relief to walk upstairs and have a drink of cold cordial and then to find some morning tea.

Refreshed he lay on his bed to study his other model aircraft, and promptly went to sleep.

Two hours later he woke up, his mind and body still under the influence of a dream. During it he had been flying in some sort of biplane, but the wings had begun to come loose and he had tried to land it. Somehow he must have managed this, despite nearly hitting a lot of electrical wires and then he was hurrying along suburban streets in a town that was vaguely familiar but which he didn't recognise. But he did recognise the girl who came walking the other way: Petra.

He was just about to say hello when he woke up. Shaking his head to clear it Willy sat up. Hearing someone in the kitchen he made his way there and found it was Lloyd, home from school. Pleasantries were exchanged but neither had much to say to each other. Lloyd had some afternoon refreshments and then said he was going to a mate's place and went out. Willy made a glass of cordial and went back to his bed.

This time he picked up the book he was reading: *Biggles of the Camel Squadron,* and quickly lost himself in it. Ever since his Tiger Moth flight he had started re-reading the *Biggles* World War 1 series from the beginning, starting with *Biggles Learns to Fly.* After that he had read the whole of *Biggles of 266* in one day, and during the previous week he had started and finished *Biggles; Pioneer air fighter.* The stories provided his imagination with the stimulus to daydream he was a World War 1 pilot, and always doing something heroic against heavy odds.

I wonder if I have the guts to be a fighter pilot? Willy thought as he placed the book aside and lay back to rest an hour later. For a while he daydreamed of heroic flying. But then his mind moved on to including girls in the daydreams, with him rescuing them and them thinking he was wonderful and allowing him to kiss them, or even offering to kiss him.

Willy had very limited experience of girls, not having a sister, and he had never been kissed by one in the way a girlfriend might kiss her boyfriend. Now he tried to conjure up the images and emotions such an experience might involve, using Petra as the girl. To his annoyance he found that Barbara's image kept slipping in.

Not Barbara, Petra! he told himself with annoyance. Barbara was attractive but she didn't have Petra's delicious roundedness or bouncy boobs.

The sound of his mother's car arriving in the driveway instantly derailed that train of thought and left him anxiously checking whether his aroused state was obvious. By the time she had parked the car and

21

come upstairs he wasn't. She kissed him and fussed and then went to make afternoon tea.

Willy went back to reading and daydreaming until a knock at the front door interrupted Willy's thoughts. He heard his mother walk to the door and open it then say, "Oh you want to see Willy? He's in bed. Come through."

Wondering who it could be Willy again checked that his pyjamas were decent and then sat up.

It was John. He looked a bit uncertain but smiled. "Hello Willy. How are you?" he asked.

"OK," Willy replied, glad to see John and cheered up by his obvious friendliness.

"How are your injuries?" John asked.

"Healing," Willy replied, fingering the plaster covering the cuts in his face.

"I heard they had to operate on you," John explained. "You are lucky to be alive, they say."

Willy could only nod and smile. His mother ushered John in and offered him cordial. John very nervously sat on the chair at Willy's study desk, looking around the room with interest as he did. It dawned on Willy that John had never been to his home before. Seeing John studying the aircraft models got Willy all anxious and embarrassed. He didn't want his friends to think he was a little kid who still played with toys.

John looked up with open admiration on his face. "These are great Willy. What type is that?" he said, pointing to his model Sunderland.

Willy was surprised at the question, assuming that all boys knew the names of different aircraft types. But it was plain that John did not know them all, so he named the ones John pointed to. That eased the conversation along and the arrival of cordial and biscuits for them both helped even more.

By the time John said goodbye Willy was feeling much happier and was glad he had come to visit. "Thanks for coming over," he said.

"That's alright. Are you going to school tomorrow?" John replied.

Willy shook his head. "No. Mum said not till next week," Willy replied.

"May I come over again tomorrow?" John asked.

Willy nodded and said yes. John then left and Willy settled back to his reading and fantasising feeling considerably more content.

Thursday was a repeat of that. During the day Willy read *Biggles Flies East* (and wasn't impressed, considering it altogether too far-fetched and unlikely). In the afternoon he went down to the workshop and carefully separated the pieces of his plastic kit from the sprue. Then he used the craft knife to carefully slice off any small lumps and bumps from poor casting of the plastic. The sandpaper was used to smooth any other blemishes. Then he completed the painting of those pieces.

That afternoon John came to visit and he was taken down to the workshop area and shown the model under construction. After admiring it John shyly admitted that he had quite a number of plastic kit models.

"Mine are mostly modern jets. You should come over and see them," he suggested.

On Friday morning Willy's mother again examined his wounds. By then Willy was bored and badly wanted to see Petra. "Can I go to school Mum?" he asked.

"No you may not. Your injuries are still not healed and there are some stitches I don't want pulled open," she replied.

Hearing that got Willy all anxious. "What about Air Cadets tonight Mum?" he asked.

"We will see how you are this afternoon," she replied. "Now you just lie there and take it easy."

Willy nodded and dutifully lay back against his pillows but inside he squirmed. As soon as he had turned 13 a few months earlier he had joined the Australian Air Force Cadets. The AAFC is a part-time volunteer organisation managed by the Royal Australian Air Force and Willy was a very keen cadet.

If I miss any parades the officers might think I am not reliable and might not choose me for promotion, he worried. So far he had never missed a parade and he was very keen to keep that record intact. He had been lucky to get in to this year's intake as they had cut off recruiting for the year the week he had joined. *So I am last and bottom in seniority in the whole flight,* he fretted.

To fill in the day Willy finished painting his plastic Lancaster and then played with his model Wellington, pretending to fly on desperate bomber missions over Nazi Germany. After that he lay and read and fantasised.

23

The arrival home of Willy's parents ended the daydreaming. His mother came to check on him and was pleased with his temperature and the state of his wounds. That cheered Willy up so he asked if he could go to Air Cadets.

"Please Mum!' he added.

"Oh alright! Now go and have your bath and iron your uniform."

In the Williams' household people did their own chores and it had been made abundantly clear to Willy that if he was old enough to join the Air Cadets he was old enough to care for the uniform himself. So Willy checked which uniform was the order of dress for that night and dug out the DPCU trousers and shirt. These were the same blue camouflage pattern as those worn by the Air Force. There was also a khaki felt hat but unlike the famous khaki 'slouch hat' worn by the Australian Army and Army Cadets it was always worn flat and had a dark blue hatband.

That hat needed its brim ironed flat too, so Willy spent half an hour getting ready and then had his tea and got dressed. His mother drove him to the Cairns Airport where the Air Cadets have their depot in the 'General Aviation' section on the western side of the main runway.

Willy loved being an air cadet. Just wearing the uniform was a source of great pride and it all added to his determination to pursue a career in the Air Force when he finished school. He also liked most of the people and among the cadet leaders he had found several role models he secretly hero worshipped.

I will be just like Flight Sergeant Barnett when I am older, he told himself.

Making friends was not one of Willy's best social skills so Air Cadets had helped him there as well, finding people with similar interests. Thus two of his friends were both air cadets: Stick and Noddy.

It was Stick who greeted Willy as he walked across the car park towards the building that was the AAFC Depot. "G'day Willy. How are you feeling?"

"Fine," Willy replied, pleased by Stick's obvious friendliness.

Noddy Parker joined them. "How's tricks Willy? How far up did the rocket go?"

Willy blushed and felt annoyed. "Not high enough," he replied.

Noddy chuckled. "I heard they had to cut lots of bits of metal out of you. Is that right?" he asked.

"Yes," Willy answered shortly, fingering his still tender face as he did.

Noddy leaned closer. "Oh yeah! I can see the marks. Are you gunna be scarred for life Willy?"

Willy hoped not but he just shrugged and said, "They are healing."

"Stick told me all about it," Noddy explained. "He reckons you are lucky to be alive."

Willy shrugged and made a non-committal answer. He didn't really want to describe the incident but found he had to. Then he had to repeat the story five times. First, he had to tell it to others in their section and then to his Flight Commander, Cadet Under-Officer Penrose and to Cadet Flight Sgt Barnett. Then he had to take a note from his mother to the HQ and explain to the WOD (Warrant Officer Discipline) why he could not go on parade or do drill.

This did not save him from being yelled at and told to get on parade by another sergeant in his flight, Cadet Sgt Jason Branch, who was his section sergeant. Another explanation was required. Cadet Sgt Branch, a big, handsome lad in Year 11 at Willy's school listened, hands on hips and obviously not impressed. "A likely story," he commented. Reluctantly he allowed Willy to sit at the back of the parade ground when the unit went on parade for roll call.

For the next hour Willy was able to sit out as the period after parade was also drill, saluting to the right on the march. But it irked him that others seemed to think he was dodging drill because it was hard work. In fact he really enjoyed doing drill and wanted to do it well. So he stood and did some practice on his own as he wanted to be sure he could master the skill but he did not stand in the squad and do all the marching up and down.

There was then a ten-minute break and Willy found himself being both teased and questioned about the rocket incident.

As he talked Willy saw a sneering glance on the face of one of the female cadets, Flora Finlay, a dark-haired Year 8 girl from Trinity Bay State High. Then a corporal in 2 Section, Hughes, made an aside to the cadet next to him. "Bloody drongo!" he said.

That burned Willy's self-esteem and he would have stopped except both Stick and Noddy kept adding details and others kept asking questions.

Cadet Sgt Soames from 1 Section amused the listeners the best by pretending he was talking on the radio. "Crzzz! Crackle, buzz, Houston, we have a problem, crackle, buzz, BAM!"

Willy laughed with the others but also blushed with embarrassment.

The noise attracted the attention of the CO, Flight Lieutenant Comstock. He called Willy over and asked, "What happen to your face Cadet Williams?"

Ruefully Willy described the incident and his injuries. Flt Lt Comstock shook his head and said, "That was a very silly thing to do. I hope you will have more sense in the future."

Oh dear! Willy worried. *He might think I am a person who shouldn't be promoted because they do silly things.* That was very sobering food for thought.

After cadets Willy did not stay to chat. His mother was waiting and took him straight home. After a bath, change of dressings and a supper of hot Milo and biscuits he was put in bed. There he was told not to read so instead he lay in the dark and daydreamed. Once again his dreams soon turned to fantasies in which Petra figured highly. But Willy never imagined doing much more than just kissing and hugging her.

She is a nice girl and it wouldn't be right, he told himself.

Not that Willy didn't want to experiment and find out more about sex, he did. He was right at that age where puberty had exploded in him and his body wasn't entirely under his control!

All night he experienced both dreams and nightmares. When he woke on Saturday he felt better but his mother insisted that he stay in bed. "We don't want a relapse and I am taking those stitches out tomorrow and don't want any complications," she said,

When Lloyd heard this he protested. "Aw Mum! It is Willy's turn to mow the lawn," he cried.

"Too bad! You will just have to make a sacrifice for your little brother," their mother replied.

When their mother had left the room Lloyd walked over and punched Willy on the upper arm. "Sacrifice!" he grumbled. "You silly little toad! You owe me!"

The punch hurt but Willy did not call out. He was past the stage of calling for his mother or father when there was a bit of sibling friction. Instead he decided that staying in bed wasn't a bad idea as it excused him from the usual chores of weeding, sweeping, tidying his room, washing the dog and so on. So he happily lay and read a book and daydreamed.

After lunch, when Lloyd had gone over to a mate's house, Willy got up and went down to the workshop. Here he began assembling his model Lancaster, taking his time and doing it as well as he could.

On Sunday Willy completed gluing the model together. He decided not to put the undercarriage on. *I will hang it up to make it look like it is flying,* he thought. Nor did he put the propellers on. In their place he secured circular disks of clear plastic cut from the top of an old shirt box. These looked like revolving propellers. The propeller bosses were then glued on the front of these. Satisfied with his efforts Willy hung the Lancaster above his bed from a hook he screwed into the ceiling.

That evening his mother removed the stitches. As she pulled the first one out Willy cried in pain. "Ouch! Go easy Mum!"

His mother shook her head. "Hurt did it? Good! That might be a lesson to you to be more sensible in the future."

"Yes Mum."

Monday morning came around and Willy felt rested and impatient to go to school. *I want to see Petra,* he thought. He resolved to make an approach at the first opportunity.

This happened sooner than he expected. When Willy got out of his mother's car at school Petra was standing at the side gate, looking as though she was waiting for him.

With his heart beating with anxiety and hope Willy waved his mother goodbye and then turned and walked straight over to Petra. As he approached he studied her, noting the nice legs, shapely curve of hips and waist and the very nice roundness of her bosom. A pretty face and what looked like very kissable lips completed the whole effect of attractiveness.

"Hi Petra," Willy croaked.

"Hello Villy," she answered, looking surprised he had spoken to her.

Willy's mind raced and his jumbled thoughts seemed to turn to mush. For a second or two he groped for something to say. "How was your weekend?" he queried.

A frown crossed Petra's pretty face and she shrugged. "Ok. Vot happened to your face?"

Surprised that Petra hadn't heard the story Willy told her, conscious that many of the passing students were casting curious glances at them. He tried to gloss over how dangerous and stupid his actions had been and instead made it sound funny. To his relief Petra laughed. When he had finished, she smiled and said, "So that's vy you at school ver not last week."

"Yes," Willy replied. All this time his stomach had been churning with anxiety and now he swallowed and plucked up his courage. "Petra, I'd like to be your friend," he managed to say.

Petra looked surprised and a shadow crossed her face but then she smiled. "That is nice. Ve can be friends," she replied.

Willy gestured towards the school buildings and said, "I'm going to put my bag in the port rack. Want to come?"

"Sorry. I am for someone vaiting," Petra replied.

That cast Willy's hopes down, but he did not give up that easily. "Can I talk to you at morning break?"

"That vill be nice," she replied.

"See you then," Willy answered. With his heart bursting with hope he turned and walked away. Twenty paces on, almost trembling with relief he risked a glance back to see if she was watching him.

To his surprise she wasn't. Instead she was smiling at one of the Year 11 boys who had just arrived—Jason Branch!

Chapter 3

BRANCH

Willy stared in dismay. *Jason Branch! Was Petra waiting for him?* he wondered, instant stabs of jealousy twisting his gut.

Once again he glanced back. He saw Petra smile at Branch and then Branch speak to her. More darts of anxiety assailed Willy as he walked away.

Now very worried that Branch might be Petra's boyfriend Willy again looked back. At that moment Branch looked towards him, a slightly puzzled look on his face. Then he definitely frowned. Willy felt his stomach turn over with anxiety.

Branch must have seen me talking to Petra and he is not happy, he thought.

Feeling slightly sick and also wondering if he had just made a fool of himself by making a pass at Petra when she already had a boyfriend Willy hurried around the end of the first building, and straight into trouble.

He collided with Scranton, a notorious Year 10 bully. Scranton was hurrying the other way with a couple of his cronies. Being the bigger person Scranton regained his balance first. Angrily he lashed out, cuffing Willy on the side of the ear. Then he shoved Willy aside. "Get out of my way you little Year Eight toad!" he snarled.

His left ear smarting from the slap Willy stumbled and almost fell. Recovering his balance he opened his mouth to reply but seeing the look on Scranton's face he desisted. Instead he turned and hurried away.

As he did, he heard one of the bullies laugh then say: 'Mad scientist' and then 'rocket.'

Hearing those comments made Willy feel both embarrassed and pleased. He knew his reputation around the school was as the 'Mad Scientist' and, in his loneliness, had started to act up to the role.

At least I get noticed, he thought.

He placed his bag in the port rack near his first room and then went looking for his friends. Instead he ran into more problems. This time it was three Year 9 boys led by one named Blake. Willy didn't know if that was his first name or his last, but he tried to smile when Blake called loudly, "Hey Willy! Which way is up?"

Willy pointed up and managed a weak grin. At the same time he glanced around to see if any of his friends were in sight. Instead he saw another Year 9 boy join Blake. The newcomer was a fair-haired boy named Andrew who was in the Navy Cadets.

Andrew said something to Blake as he sat down at one of the benches under the end of the building. Blake grinned and then turned and called loudly, "Hey Willy! Willy's wocket it not go woosh?"

Willy burned with embarrassment and he scowled. Then he decided that was bad tactics and forced a grin. One of Blake's mates laughed and yelled, "Willy's wocket it go whoompa!"

The whole group cackled with laughter mixed with some hurtful jeers. Willy burned some more and glanced at them to see if they were going to try to stop him. His eyes met Andrew's and he saw that while Andrew was laughing, he was also smiling and shaking his head. Willy gave a smile and a shrug and hurried on out of their sight.

Later several others teased him and a few questioned him about what happened. By then it was time for class and Willy was looking forward to that. The main reason was to see Petra. His concern now was that she might not have meant what she said about being his friend. But when they met outside the classroom, she gave him a big smile and most of his worries evaporated. Just a niggling doubt about Branch remained.

Willy smiled back and stared at her in wonder. For a moment she seemed to glow and notions like 'angel' and 'goddess' flitted across his mind. *She is just so beautiful. She is the one for me!* he thought. Still smiling he took out his books and chatted to her as they made their way into the room.

He badly wanted to sit beside her but could not muster the courage to ask. *Besides, she sits next to Cynthia and she will have to agree to the move,* Willy thought. *And it might upset John,* he mentally added.

At that moment John was the closest he had to a proper friend and he didn't want to upset that relationship.

So Willy gave John a big grin and moved to sit beside him in his usual seat. Then he looked over to his right to where Petra was seating herself against the far wall a row in front. To his surprise and delight Petra looked around and met his eye then smiled.

Maybe she does like me? Willy wondered. He was unable to believe his luck and felt as though he might burst with joy.

Then he saw Barbara seat herself two rows to his left front and another little niggle of doubt crept in. Firmly he thrust the notion out. *It is Petra for me, not Barbara,* he told himself. But Barbara had a pretty face too, he had to concede.

John was in a very friendly mood and chatted until the teacher came into the room and told the class to be quiet. First lesson was English with Mrs Ramsey. The subject Willy found a breeze, so he was able to quickly do any class work and then devote his attention to day-dreaming or to surreptitiously studying Petra.

Second period was Social Science with Mr Conkey. He was one of the few teachers Willy really admired. It wasn't particularly for his knowledge or teaching skills but because he actually cared about kids, and also he was the Officer of Cadets in charge of the school's army cadet unit.

Mr Conkey set the class to work and then strolled around supervising. When he stood next to Willy he smiled and gave a quizzical look. "I hear you had a bit of a misfortune with your part in the space race Willy," he commented.

"Yes sir," Willy replied ruefully. He managed a grin and fingered the plaster on his face.

"Never mind. Werner von Braun didn't get it right the first few times either and Edison claimed he made ten thousand experiments before he got a working light bulb so keep trying. Remember, the losers fail once and give up. The winners fail many times and learn from their mistakes and keep on trying," he said.

"Yes sir," was all Willy could think of to say.

Mr Conkey then looked serious. "But be safe please. Get your chemistry right. Pay more attention in Mr Feldt's lessons."

"Yes sir," Willy replied. The idea that the teachers might actually talk to each other about students came to him as a bit of a shock. But it was a good idea.

Willy settled back to alternating between working, fantasising and studying Petra. His gaze lingered on her very alluring curves and he admired the softness of her skin, the perky tilt of her nose, the way she moved her hands and head.

She is just wonderful, he told himself.

And then it was Morning Break and his courage was again put to the test. As they left the room they exchanged looks and she smiled but then she took her lunch box from her bag and hurried off with Marcia towards the toilet. Willy was left wondering and churning with anxiety. To fill in the time he got his own morning tea and walked with John and Stick down to where they usually sat under 'D' Block.

A few minutes late Willy noted Petra and Marcia appear. They sat with a group of girls at the other end of the under croft. *Bloody hell! How will I speak to her now?* Willy wondered.

One thing he did not want to do was set himself up for public humiliation by having her turn him down in front of a whole group of classmates. Then he sucked in a deep breath. *Oh well, nothing ventured, nothing gained they say. Faint heart never won fair lady and all that,* he told himself. Summoning up his nerve he stood up and walked towards Petra.

When he was halfway she looked up and their eyes met. Willy smiled on his face but inside he was terrified and he almost faltered in his steps. But then she collected up her food and lunch bag and stood up. To Willy's enormous relief he saw that she was coming to join him. The other girls all looked and he noted a few asides and behind-the-hand whispers which made him blush but he did not stop.

"Hi!" was all he could think to say.

Petra smiled and said, "Ve walk?"

Her precise English with its quaint accent reminded him she was a migrant, but he was so happy he didn't care. "Yes please," he croaked.

So they walked and Petra asked him to describe his rocket again. He did so and she gave a musical trill that sent shivers of delight through him. Then she put her hand on his forearm, sending pulses of desire through him. "I think you are the very clever fellow," she said.

That was balm to Willy's ego and he glowed and admired her all the more.

The pair walked up and down the centre of the school all of the morning break and then met again at lunch time. This time they sat on a seat under a tree halfway down to the oval. By now Willy was hopelessly lost. *I am in love!* he thought. He admired her every word, her every movement and gesture. *She is just so nice and so wonderful!*

Then Jason Branch walked by. As he did, he looked hard at Willy and the resentment or malice in his eyes sent a shiver through Willy. *Have I cut him out?* he wondered. Then another more worrying idea came to him. *I hope he doesn't take it out on me at cadets. He's a 4ᵗʰ Year and a sergeant and I'm only a lowly recruit.*

But by this time Willy was smitten. He told himself that for Petra he would fight fire breathing dragons with his bare hands. It was with great regret that they made their way back to the classroom when the bell went.

She seems to like me too, he told himself as he sat in class watching her. *I wonder if she would let me walk her home?*

But when he put this idea to her at the end of the day as they stood on the veranda Petra emphatically shook her head. "No. Sorry. My mudda... er... mother, she would not be pleased. She say I am much too young for boyfriend," she explained.

As she was only the same age as Willy he accepted this but with regret. *Besides, my mum is coming to pick me up. I need to ride my bike to be able to walk her home,* he told himself.

"What if I walked you part of the way? We could say goodbye somewhere out of sight of your mum," he suggested.

"That is good idea. I think about it, OK?" she answered. With a cheerful grin she turned and hurried away leaving Willy in a daze of hope. For a few minutes he stood and watched her until she was out of sight, his mind filled with delightful dreams.

Only as he turned to go did he realise that John was standing nearby. With a guilty start Willy realised he had been neglecting his friend all day. "Sorry John, just chatting," he said.

"Are you able to come over to my place this arvo?" John replied.

"Sorry, no. Tomorrow. I will ride my bike. My mum is picking me up today. She thinks I am still an invalid," Willy answered.

"Huh, invalid alright!" came Stick's voice from behind him. His pronunciation changed the meaning and that hurt Willy a bit.

Stick then put in another verbal jab. "You trying to chat up the delectable Petra?"

Willy blushed and shrugged. "She's very pretty."

"That's what all the Year 11's say too," Stick commented, sending more waves of jealous anxiety through Willy.

He swallowed and mustered the courage to ask if she had a boyfriend.

Stick smirked. "Only a couple of hundred."

That hurt. Willy angrily faced him. "What do you mean by that? Has she or hasn't she?"

Stick shrugged. "Not that I know of. She has turned a few down. I think she is too stuck up."

That was also hurtful to Willy but was comforting. *She seems happy to talk to me,* he thought.

At that moment his mother arrived so he said goodbye to his friends and got in the car. Only after answering his mother's queries about how his day had been and how he felt did it occur to him that he had not found out where to buy balsa wood. *Tomorrow,* he told himself.

He did, and he found out in a roundabout way. His mother allowed him to ride his bike and accepted his statement that he was going to John's after school so would be home late. At school Willy found Petra again waiting at the gate but this time she waved and smiled and then turned and walked with him.

Astonished and delighted Willy said, "Aren't you waiting for your friend today?"

"Tania? No. She vill OK be," Petra replied.

So she wasn't waiting for Branch, Willy thought, licking his lower lip and biting it with satisfaction. After chaining his bike into the bike racks he walked with Petra to the classroom to dump his bag and they sat and talked until the bell went. The only fly in the ointment was seeing John go past and give them an unhappy look.

When they went to class Willy took the opportunity to admire Petra. *She just looks so nice!* he thought. *She is always well groomed and very well dressed.* Approvingly he ran his gaze over her spotless and brilliant white blouse and the clean and ironed blue skirt. Her sheer beauty and presence almost rendered him speechless with admiration and he found it hard to believe she was actually willing to talk to him.

But she did. After they came out of class, they took their morning tea from their bags and walked down stairs and under 'D' Block. As they reached a seat that had some vacant spaces Petra gestured and said, "You sit here. I must to the toilet go."

Willy smiled and nodded. He put his lunch box down but stood and munched at a biscuit. While he did, he looked around, studying the other students and feeling very pleased with himself.

Suddenly he was violently shoved from behind. A boy's voice snarled, "That's my seat. Clear out, you little shit!"

Willy staggered and dropped his biscuit as he put out his arm to brace himself. Out of the corner of his eye he saw his open lunch box land on the concrete, spilling his cake and other biscuits. With an effort he remained on his feet. Angrily he looked around and snapped back, "Get stuffed! I was here first, you bully!"

But even as he said it Willy wondered if he had made a mistake. The boy who had pushed him was Larsen, a big, red-headed thug in Year 11. Larsen had been about to sit but now he suddenly reached out and grabbed the front of Willy's shirt. Larsen was both much bigger and much stronger and Willy was almost lifted off his feet. Larsen leaned close and snarled at him. "Don't you call me names, you little wart!"

"Let me go!" Willy blustered, fear making him ashamed of himself. But there was anger too and he resented the assault. Stubbornly he pushed back and then tried to loosen Larsen's grip on his shirt.

Larsen tightened his grip and gave him a quick slap to the side of his face. "Or what? If you aren't careful I will stick one of your silly rockets up your arse and light the fuse. Then we will see if it can reach space."

Cackles of malicious laughter sounded and through a mist of anger and tears Willy saw other faces, including Branch's.

Has Branch set him up to do this? he wondered.

At that moment, another Year 11 boy touched Larsen's sleeve. "Hey Red, there's some jerk trying to chat up your chick."

Larsen turned his head to look then swore and roughly shoved Willy away, sending him down hard on his bum on the concrete. For a moment Willy could not see what was happening clearly as tears of pain and shame misted his vision. Then he saw Larsen striding across under the building towards where two Year 9s, a boy and a girl, stood talking. The girl was a big blonde with a very prominent bosom. Willy had often seen her and he also recognised the boy.

Graham Kirk, he thought. Kirk was often in trouble.

At that moment Petra arrived. "Vot he do that for?" she asked, sympathy clear in her voice and face.

Willy struggled to his face, masking his pain and upset as he did. "Just a bully who wanted this seat," he explained.

"Vot he do now? Who is zat?" Petra queried.

Willy stood beside her and watched. "A Year 9 kid named Graham Kirk. The blonde is Ailsa," he explained. By then Larsen and his cronies had reached the pair. Larsen just shoved Graham hard in the shoulder and spoke to him. Willy couldn't hear what was said but the body language made it obvious there was an argument. To Willy's surprise Graham did not retreat but argued back.

He is going to get smashed, Willy thought, glad it wasn't him. Larsen was not only two years older, he was a good head taller, with arms and legs proportionally longer.

Other students began hurrying towards the spot, the word 'fight' being called from all sides. In the process several kicked Willy's lunch box or trampled his cake and biscuits.

"Hoy!" Willy cried, reaching down to retrieve what he could. But he was ignored and the students hurried past. Willy stayed where he was with Petra gripping his arm.

And a fight it was. Larsen placed his clenched fists on his hips and snarled something. Graham obviously gave a defiant reply as Larsen shook a fist in his face and shouted, telling him to clear off!

By then a crowd of spectators was obscuring Willy's view but he distinctly heard Graham say: "No!"

"OK idiot, cop this!" Larsen snarled. He stepped forward, his right fist coming up in a sweeping uppercut.

Somehow Graham dodged the blow then stepped closer and swung his left in a short, hard jab into Larsen's stomach.

Willy cheered. "You beauty! Hit him again!" he cried.

Graham did. Larsen grunted sharply in pain and doubled forward. As he did Graham swung a smashing right cross which landed solidly on Larsen's jaw. To Willy's surprise and delight Larsen went down hard.

Larsen's face suffused with rage. Graham obviously had a chance to hit him as he got up but instead stepped back and allowed the bully to regain his feet. Larsen wiped dirt from his face and rubbed his jaw. Swearing loud threats he rushed at Graham, fists flailing.

This time the punches came too fast for Graham to duck them all. Willy stood open-mouthed, hoping Graham would not get too badly hurt. Graham managed to avoid a couple but one smashed into his nose and sent him reeling. Another landed hard on his mouth sending him staggering back.

As Willy watched it occurred to him that Larsen did not know how to fight and that Graham did. To his delight he saw Graham again punch Larsen in the stomach and then knock him sideways with a right cross to the jaw. By then the combatants were the centre of a ring of chanting, shouting students of both sexes.

By this time the hullabaloo had attracted the teachers and Willy watched as Mr Page, the Geography Master, rushed in and grabbed Graham's right arm just as he drew it back to deliver a knockout punch.

An enraged Larsen attacked. Ignoring the teacher's call to stop he slammed a punch into Graham's chest. Larsen drew his fist back to strike again but Mr Page stepped between the two and blocked the blow with another muscular arm. Then Larsen was also gripped by Mr Conkey.

Larsen shouted angrily and swore at the teacher. "Let go of me! You can't touch me! I'll have you charged with assault," he screamed.

"Go ahead!" Mr Page replied calmly. "Hit me and see what happens to you boy. You'll need more than the police."

For an instant it looked as though Larsen would lash out at the teacher, but his eyes registered that Mr Page was not bluffing. With a wild glare in his eyes Larsen lowered his fist and snarled a few more threats. "Take your hands off me! Teachers aren't allowed to touch students. I'll have you in court."

"Good idea. We can start the process right now. Both of you, to the office!" Mr Page commanded.

As the group walked off towards the office Petra squeezed Willy's arm. "Are you to the office going?"

"Me? Why?" Willy asked in surprise as he surveyed the crumbs and squashed cake.

"Because the bully he you hit," Petra replied.

Willy shook his head. "No. He's being dealt with," he said. He did not want more trouble. After that he was happy just to sit and recover while talking to her. The fight was a big topic of conversation among those who had seen it but it appeared that no-one else in the class had seen the incident involving Willy. That was both a relief and a source of niggling injustice to Willy. But he didn't care. *Petra likes me. She talks to me!* and he found it hard to believe she was actually willing to talk to him.

And she did. She spent the whole of 'big lunch' sitting with him or walking with him. The only complication was when John grumbled a bit when Willy sat next to him after lunch. "Are you coming over to my place this afternoon?" he asked.

That put Willy on a spot. What he really wanted to do was go with Petra, at least as far as she would allow him.

What do I do: go with Petra and hurt my friend's feelings? Or go with him?

Chapter 4

BALSA AND TISSUE

Willy met John's eyes and saw that he looked unhappy. *Damn!* he thought. *What should I do?* But it was no contest really. Petra offered far more than John. Mentally torn Willy bit his lip. *Oh damn and blast it! I haven't asked Petra yet but John has asked me.*

Looking up he nodded. "Yes, I'll come over to your place," he replied. "But I won't be there before about four. There's something I have to do first."

John looked briefly unhappy then his gaze flicked to Petra. "Something or someone?" he said with a grin.

"It's not like that! She's not that sort of girl," Willy replied hotly. To his mind Petra was such a lovely person that anything grubby was not to be considered.

So after school Willy met Petra and together they went to get his bike. Then they strolled along the street, chatting happily and Willy basking in the pleasure of her company and also in the ego-boosting knowledge that other students pedalling by could see them.

To Willy's surprise Petra only lived five blocks from the school. As they got close, she stopped. "I live around the corner. You must not any further come. If my mother she see us then I into much trouble get."

Willy understood that and instantly stopped. "Fine, I am happy with that," he said, although really he wanted to be alone with her because, despite his worship of her, he was a flesh and blood male with hot blood pumping and he did want to try for at least a little kiss.

"See you tomorrow then," Petra said. Then she smiled and walked away. Just before the corner she turned to wave and smiled again. That set Willy's heart hammering and his hopes soaring. He grinned and waved back.

With his spirits high Willy jumped on his bike and began pedalling towards John's. He was so happy he wanted to sing aloud. *I am in love! She is just so wonderful!* he thought.

John's house was only a few blocks away, on the other side of the railway lines in an area with a swampy drain behind it. It was an 'Old Queenslander' on high blocks and in its own large yard with an extensive lawn and gardens. Willy had never been there before so felt quite nervous.

John was waiting for him, his face a mask of obvious anxiety. This changed to a wide smile when Willy appeared. "Come in," he said at once. Willy dismounted and wheeled his bike inside the front gate and left it against the railings on the steps that led up to the front door.

Afternoon tea was provided by John's mother amidst a lot of noise from three younger siblings who went to Primary School. Then the boys retired to John's room.

Willy instantly liked John's room and was secretly jealous. It was larger than his bedroom and had more furniture. John had two big bookshelves and one of these was devoted entirely to his extensive collection of model aircraft, mostly modern jets. And John also had two tables. One was a study bench with a computer for homework but the other was for making models.

Willy's gaze at once noted several model aircraft spread on this table. There were four of them, all to the same scale and with a wingspan of about 20 centimetres. Then a second look revised Willy's ideas.

They are not models. They are only toys, he told himself. "What are these?" he asked.

John picked one up and said, "Gliders," he replied.

Willy noted that it was made of flat pieces of wood with black lines printed on one side. The fuselage and tail were in one piece. The wing was solid and glued across underneath this and the tailplanes were also a single piece and were glued into a slot at the back of the fuselage. On the front was a piece of plastic with a plastic propeller mounted in it. Willy recognised it as a simple version of a Mustang Fighter.

"May I?" Willy asked, reaching forward. As a model builder himself he was very sensitive to other people touching his models.

John nodded and passed him the model. Willy was surprised at how light it is. "What's it made of?" he queried.

"Balsa wood," John replied.

Willy nodded and turned the model over to study the wood. "That is what I need to make some models from a book I was given," he replied. "Where do you get it?"

"Not sure. Toy shops or hobby shops I suppose. I've never bought any. These were little kits that I got for my birthday." He indicated a packet with a coloured picture of a Skyraider on the front.

"I wonder who would know?" Willy thought aloud.

"Stick might," John suggested.

Lying on the desk were gliders that Willy recognised as a Spitfire, 'Messerschmitt ME109' and a 'Focke Wolfe 190'. "How about these; which one flies the best?" he asked.

"Not sure. Would you like to try them out?" John asked.

"Too right!" Willy replied enthusiastically.

So the gliders were picked up and the two boys made their way down the front steps to the side yard. John stood facing back along the lawn and held up the Spitfire. "You hold them like this," he said, demonstrating. Then he threw the glider.

To their delight the glider swooped down and then up over in a sweeping loop before drifting down to a nice soft landing on the grass.

Willy then tried but the result was disappointing. The glider immediately went into a spin and then nose-dived into the grass. Picking it up he tried again, noting as he did that the Spitfire John was throwing would swoop down and then do a complete loop before gliding five more metres to a belly landing.

Twice more the glider spun and crashed. The third time Willy saw that small plastic propeller was broken. "Oops! Sorry!" he said.

John shrugged and indicated the ME109 and FW190. Both had blades missing. "Doesn't matter. I actually think that the propeller might look good when it is spinning but that it generates so much air resistance that it causes them to stall."

"You might be right," Willy agreed. He held the glider end on and squinted along the longitudinal axis. "Can I try a different one? I think the tail planes are out of true on this one."

He didn't want to be critical of his friend's workmanship, but it was obvious the gliders had been hastily stuck together. *They might fly better if they had a wing cross-section like a real aircraft,* he thought.

At that moment a voice called from behind them. It was Stick and with him was a Year 9 boy with lots of freckles and glasses. They had just arrived on their bikes.

"What ya doin' Johnno?" Stick called.

"Flying planes," John replied. "Come and have a go."

Stick and the Year 9 boy both hurried inside. Stick indicated the boy with the glasses. "Steve. He's in Year 9. Steve, this is Johnno and that's Willy Williams."

Willy got all embarrassed. He didn't like meeting people. But his mind had worked. *Stephen Bell. He's in the same class as Graham Kirk,* he remembered. "G'day," he mumbled.

Stephen looked at Willy then nodded. "You are the Mad Scientist who blew himself up on the way to the moon aren't you?"

"Yes," Willy admitted, feeling both pleased and peeved at the same moment.

"Bloody moon!" Stick cried. "I thought he was heading for heaven when the bloody thing blew up."

They all laughed but Willy mentally winced. Then Stick annoyed him even more by saying: "I saw you trying to chat up Petra the Peach this afternoon. Any luck?"

Willy shrugged and smiled. The last thing he wanted to do was discuss his romantic hopes with others.

Stick chuckled and went on: "Boy! Look how red he's gone. It must be true. Well, good luck. That's a peach worth plucking, if you get my meaning! Plucking, get it?" At that he nudged Stephen and chuckled again.

Willy managed a smile but inside he resented the insinuation that he was after Petra for sex. "She's very nice," he replied as the other boys picked up a glider each.

Stick then shook his head. "Be careful Willy, or you'll be sorry."

"Mind your own business!" Willy snapped back.

"Yeah well, don't say I didn't warn you," Stick retorted. He then flung the toy glider and went racing after it as it spun into a garden bed.

After several minutes of playing Stick hurled a glider so hard it zoomed up and landed on the roof. "Oh bugger!" he cried. "These things don't fly very well."

John looked upset but then he shrugged. "They are only cheap," he replied, obviously nettled by Stick's actions.

Stick then upset him more by saying, "Steve's got some really good models that glide like a beauty."

Willy's interest perked up. "Have you Steve? What are they made of?"

Stephen nodded. "A couple are plastic, but the really good ones are made of balsa and tissue paper," he replied.

"Tissue paper?" Willy queried, intrigued.

"Yeah. You make the framework out of balsa wood and then glue tissue paper over it. It is the same technique they used back in World War One when aircraft frames were made of wood and canvas was stretched over it," Stephen explained.

Willy nodded his understanding. "And this balsa wood, where do you get it?"

"Mine came in a kit. There were flat sheets of it in the box and the pattern was printed on it. You just cut the pieces out or it was already cut to the right size," Stephen replied.

"But you can just buy Balsa wood?" Willy asked.

"Yeah."

"Where?"

Stephen frowned. "Hobby shops and craft shops, I think. I don't buy it like that, but I have a friend who does. He makes model ships and things with it," he answered.

"Could you ask him please?" Willy requested.

"You can ask him yourself. He is in my class: Graham Kirk," Stephen replied.

"Graham Kirk!" Willy ejaculated. "I saw him have a fight with that bully Larsen today."

They all had and for the next few minutes the boys discussed the fight and then bullies at their school. "They give us Year Eights hell," Willy grumbled.

Stephen laughed. "Good thing too! Otherwise you would get too big for your boots. Anyway, come and see me under 'F' Block at morning break and I will introduce you to Graham, if he isn't off having another fight over some girl."

There was more laughter and the group broke up. It was time for Willy to go home by then, so he said his farewells to John, collected his bike and set off with Stick and Stephen. They both lived in the same suburb, so they stayed together most of the way.

When they reached Stick's street Stick said, "I've got a lot of model aircraft too. What about coming over to my place tomorrow to have a play?"

Willy really wanted to spend his time with Petra but had to say yes. Then he and Stephen pedalled on. As they did Stephen admitted he had an extensive collection of plastic kit model aircraft as well as the balsa and tissue ones.

"You can see them if you like," he offered.

"Thanks, but I had better go to Stick's first," Willy answered.

Stephen accepted this and agreed to introduce him to Graham the next day.

He was as good as his word, much to Willy's annoyance as he was walking along with Petra during the 'Little Lunch' when Stephen and Graham stopped them.

Stephen smirked at Petra and bowed. "Hello pretty one. My name's Stephen."

Petra looked both surprised and anxious but then she smiled. That both surprised and peeved Willy who had expected her to rebuff Stephen's smarmy approach.

"My name is Petra," she simpered back.

"A lovely name for a beautiful girl," Stephen replied, bowing again.

That annoyed Willy even more but he held his tongue while the by-play continued. Stephen then turned to Willy and gestured to Graham, who had been watching this with wry amusement. "Graham, this is Willy, the Rocket Scientist."

The boys shook hands and Willy explained why he needed balsa wood. Graham nodded and named the craft and hobby shops where balsa and other hobby products could be purchased and gave their approximate prices.

Willy was a bit surprised. "That's fairly expensive," he commented.

Graham shrugged. "Balsa is a fairly rare wood. It is very soft and light and it only grows in South America," he replied.

For several minutes the boys discussed balsa and its uses and then Willy mumbled his thanks and managed to get Petra to keep walking. As they walked away, he was further bothered when she looked back and waved.

"I like your friends," she commented, sending little tingles of alarm and jealousy through him.

Then Willy noted John sitting on his own nearby. *Gosh, he looks pretty miserable!* he thought. It dawned on him that John was lonely. *Me spending every minute with Petra mustn't help,* he mused. But that just left him feeling torn and a bit resentful.

That afternoon after school Willy again walked with Petra as far as the corner before her house. By this time Willy was feeling quite confident that Petra really did like him and that he had no competition. He ached to take the relationship further, to take her out and to get to hold her—to kiss her!

From there he made his way to Stick's. Stick also lived in a high block 'Old Queenslander' set in its own extensive yard. There were two other bicycles leaning on the fence, so Willy placed his there as well and made his way up to the front door and knocked.

Footsteps sounded in the hallway and a moment later a girl came out into the front room. She was short but curvy and dressed in a High School uniform. *Year 7?* Willy thought. For a moment she studied him then her freckled face dimpled into a smile of welcome.

"Hi! I'm Marjorie. Are you here to see Stick?"

"Yes I am. I'm Willy," Willy replied.

Marjorie placed her hand over her face and giggled, then indicated that Willy was to follow her. He did so, noting that Marjorie had white, pudgy legs and a fairly big bum for such a little girl. *But she's got big boobs for a Year 7 kid,* he noted.

Stick was sitting with John and Stephen in what was obviously Stick's bedroom. Marjorie looked in and called, "Willy!" then giggled and turned to make her way into a room opposite.

Willy blushed at that giggle because he felt sure Marjorie was associating it with the term 'willy' as a nickname for a boy's penis. *Silly little girl! But I suppose with a brother like Stick she might have seen one,* he decided.

From the room opposite came the word 'willy' again and then more giggles. There were obviously other girls there as well and Willy blushed some more. Willy tried to ignore it and focused on saying hello and looking around.

The boys were examining a really good plastic kit model of an F18 jet fighter and when Willy got to hold it and look at it closely he had to admit it was very well put together and the painting and detailing were superb. A niggle of jealousy upset him but then he complimented Stick on his work. "It is very good, Stick," he said.

Stick smiled and shrugged then pointed to his other models which were placed on shelves and on top of cupboards or hung from the ceiling. Again Willy experienced a stab of jealousy, but he hid this and sat to chat and study the models.

Marjorie and two other Year 7 girls came out of her room and poked their heads into Stick's. Stick scowled. "Clear off you chicks!" he growled.

The girls did, but not before looking at each of the visiting boys in turn. They then hurried to the front door whispering and giggling. Again Willy blushed as he was sure the girls were discussing him.

Marjorie returned and looked in, interrupting the boy's conversation. "You didn't have to be rude to my guests," she said to Stick.

"Stop sticking your ugly face into my room," Stick retorted.

Marjorie poked her tongue at him, looked directly at Willy and withdrew to her own room. But she did not close her bedroom door and from where Willy sat he could see into it. To his surprise he saw that Marjorie was undressing.

Has she forgotten we are here? he wondered. *Heavens! She is stripping right off! What should I do?*

Willy watched in pleasant but embarrassed surprise as Marjorie peeled off her skirt and shirt. *Maybe she doesn't know I can see her?* he thought anxiously, wondering if he should call out.

But then Marjorie glanced over her shoulder and her eyes met his. She gave him a mischievous grin and then reached behind to unclip her bra. *She knows alright!* his shocked mind told him. Anxiously he cast a glance at his friends to see if they were looking but they were all listening to Stick who was holding up a large model airliner.

It dawned on Willy that Marjorie was deliberately undressing where he could see her. *But out of sight of her brother and the others,* he decided. *Bloody hell! They are nice boobs.*

This last because she had now removed her bra and after holding her arms across her front for a few tantalising seconds had taken them away and cast the bra aside. With a mouth going rapidly dry from lust Willy stared at her lovely shape.

Bloody hell! They are nice set of bouncers for a kid her age! he mused. Unable to tear his eyes from the sight he licked lips that had suddenly gone dry. To his dismay he felt himself becoming aroused.

Willy had thought she would stop at that and could only sit and stare like a bird mesmerised by a snake as she slid off her knickers. In the process he was granted a full view of her ample buttocks.

Marjorie then bent and picked up a towel and wrapped it around herself before turning and walking to the door. There she paused to give Willy another impish grin before she strolled out into the hallway and along it. Now the other boys also saw her. John gaped and Stephen stared and blinked though his glasses.

"Bloody hell!" he muttered.

Stick looked up and then shook his head. "Don't pay any attention to her," he commented. "She's just a bloody little tease. She's always running around in the nuddy."

Stephen looked amazed. "What do your parents say about that?" he asked, his eyes riveted on the now empty hallway.

Stick shrugged. "Oh, she doesn't do it when they are at home."

John shook his head in disbelief. "Does she let you see her?" he asked.

Stick nodded. "Yeah, sometimes. She can be a bit of a pain."

Willy saw him blush and guessed that there was more to the story but he did not dare ask. The notion of anything going on between brother and sister he found quite distasteful.

To his relief the conversation moved back to model aircraft but the whole time his real focus was on the sound of the shower and what Marjorie might be doing in it. Secretly he hoped for another look, but when Marjorie came back she had the towel wrapped around her and this time she closed her bedroom door. When she re-opened it ten minutes later, she was dressed in T-shirt and shorts.

By then the boys were leaving although Willy found he wanted to stay. As the boys made their way out into the hallway Marjorie came and stood in the doorway of her room.

Bloody hell, she is nice! he thought, eyeing her bosom.

Then he felt ashamed of himself for having such thoughts about a Year 7 kid. *She is years too young for that sort of thing,* he told himself. But when she met his gaze and gave him a cheeky smile he grinned back and found himself thinking he would like to visit Stick's some more! *She must be only a year younger than me,* he thought.

But by then a visit to Stephen's had been agreed on for the next afternoon so all he could do was hope for an invitation on another day.

It was only when he was pedalling home on his own that Willy remembered Petra. That caused him a spurt of shame. *How could I be so disloyal?* he thought. But then memories of Marjorie's nude form flooded his mind and he found them hard to drive out. To ease his conscience he told himself that Marjorie is different.

Petra is not like that. She is a really nice girl, a good girl and there is a difference between true love and lust.

But for a 13-year-old boy whose erotic fantasies were now fuelled by such real images he found the line hard to define and that night he lay in bed enjoying alternating daydreams of being a hero for Petra and being rewarded by a gentle hug and a polite kiss and by fiery fantasies of being naked with Marjorie and of doing all the incredibly rude things he had seen on the sort of X-rated videos that Lloyd and his mates sometimes watched when the parents weren't home.

The inner conflict of fantasising about seeing Marjorie and imagining what might follow versus his self-image of being in love with Petra and of staying loyal to her tormented Willy all the next day. Along with that went the embarrassing realization that he actually had very little control over his own body as he experienced several involuntary erections which took some hiding from other people.

His embarrassment was greatest when he was actually with Petra. *I don't want her to get the wrong idea. I don't want her to think I am only interested in sex. I love her,* he told himself. But he did want to see Marjorie again!

So it was to his regret that it was to Stephen's, not Stick's that he made his way after walking Petra close to home yet again. Stephen lived in Mooroobool in an old, timber and fibro house on low stumps. It was set in a nice yard with a car port on the left and inside was very pleasant and comfortable.

After introductions to Stephen's parents, both of whom were teachers, the boys were led through to Stephen's bedroom. It was smaller than Willy's and only contained a bed, table, chair and wardrobe. But like his bedroom and Stick's it was full of model aircraft. They hung from the ceiling and were placed all over the bookshelves and on top of books and in corners. Most were plastic kit models and Willy studied them with jealous interest.

Then Stephen took out his balsa and tissue model. It was an Auster high wing monoplane and was 25 centimetres long and with a 30 centimetres wingspan. The tissue paper was white and the thin balsa framework was visible through it.

They all got a chance to hold it and Willy was amazed at how light it was. When John was given a go, he used his forefinger to try to turn the plastic propeller set in the nose.

"Does it fly?" he asked.

"It is only powered by a rubber band," Stephen explained. "But it flies really well."

"Can we see?" Stick asked.

So the boys trooped out to the front and Stephen stopped on the concrete front porch to the front gate. Kneeling down Stephen carefully wound the propeller round and round until he was satisfied the rubber band was fully tensioned. Then he placed the model at the back of the porch and lined it up with the steps and the concrete path leading to the front gate.

Stick was sceptical. "Is that a long enough take-off run?" he queried.

Stephen nodded. "Yes. And it should clear the fence and land on the road," Stephen replied.

Willy doubted that but watched with interest as Stephen let go of the fuselage and the propeller at the same instant. The propeller became a blur and the model began to move forward. To Willy's delight it quickly picked up speed and then took off. The model kept climbing until the rubber bands unwound and the propeller stopped. Then it began to glide down.

Just when Willy thought the model would plough into the fence it swooped up and then gently drifted down to a wheels-up landing out on the bitumen a good 25 metres away.

"That was bloody great!" he cried, running with the others out to retrieve the model. Stephen picked it up and checked for damage. Stick then reached out for it. "Can I have a go?" he asked.

Stephen shook his head. "Sorry. It took too much effort to make it and models like this are pretty fragile."

Willy admired the model and said, "That was really good Steve. It flies like a beauty."

Stick pouted and shrugged. "Huh! I'll bet I could make one as good as that."

"Go ahead and try," Stephen replied with a grin.

Willy said, "Did you buy that as a kit Steve?"

Stephen shook his head. "Not this one. I got the plans for this one out of an old encyclopaedia at my granddad's. But you can buy kits like this."

"Let's make one each and see whose is the best," John suggested.

Chapter 5

TROUBLE

Willy felt a sudden surge of excitement.

Yes, a competition! he thought happily. He had seen model aircraft fly before but never close up and they had never looked like ones he might be able to make himself. The challenge really appealed to him.

"Are we going to judge the models on how well they are made or on how well they fly?" he asked.

"Both," Stephen replied at once.

John looked a bit worried. "Do we have to make them from nothing or can we use kits?" he asked.

"Have to be kits," Stephen replied.

"Why?" Stick queried.

Stephen shook his head and took his glasses off to polish them. "Because you wouldn't be able to find the plans on the right scale to make them and trying to draw your own would be a real challenge."

Willy agreed with that. The concept of having to 'scratch build' including drawing his own plans to the right scale had been his first big worry.

Stick gestured to Stephen's model Auster. "So what scale do we use?"

"This one is a 1:20 scale," he replied. "I reckon anything about this size will be fine."

"Does it have to be made of balsa and tissue paper?" John asked.

Stephen nodded. "Yes, or it isn't fair. You can buy plastic kit rubber-powered models that you just snap together, and I've seen some made of solid balsa and also from polystyrene but there is no skill in that."

Willy nodded. "I agree. We can make the others for fun or for experience at building or flying but the competition has to be as equal as possible."

"What sort of planes?" Stick asked.

Stephen shrugged and replaced his glasses. "Whatever you like but it has to be rubber-powered. That means propeller driven, so no jets."

"And only single-engine," Willy added.

"Can we pick ones we like then?" Stick asked.

"Yes," agreed Stephen.

John looked worried. "How much do these things cost?"

"Not too much," Stephen replied, naming the cost of a model he had seen the week before.

"And when do we have this competition?" Willy asked.

Stephen picked up his Auster. "Let's look at a calendar," he suggested. He led the way back inside and the boys crowded around a calendar above the kitchen bench. Here Stephen ran his fingertip down the calendar and stopped at the September school holidays. "What about the second week of the school holidays," he suggested.

"That's a long time away," Stick objected.

Stephen shook his head. "No it's not! It is only four weeks or so and it will take that long to make a proper model."

Having spent an entire week just painting and assembling a plastic kit Willy could only nod in silent agreement. But John still wasn't happy.

"Why the second week?" he asked.

"Because I have to go to cadet camp in the first week," replied Stephen.

Willy was surprised. Somehow he had never associated Stephen with anything military. "Cadets?" he cried. "Are you a cadet too?"

"Yes," Stephen admitted, looking embarrassed and shamefaced.

"Army cadets?" Stick asked.

Stephen nodded. Willy was intrigued. "Stick and I are air cadets," he explained, gesturing to the others.

"I know," Stephen replied. Willy half expected Stephen to tease them in the way army cadets often made derogatory comments about air cadets, but he didn't. Instead Stephen said, "So how come you lot haven't got a camp in the school holidays?"

Stick, who had been an air cadet the longest, replied. "We are only 'First Years' and our G.S.T. camp was in June. Only the older cadets go to camp in September, for advanced training or specialist stuff like flying courses or survival training."

"G.S.T.?" Stephen queried.

"General Service Training," Willy answered. "There are three levels: Basic, that's us, Proficiency for 2nd and 3rd Years and Advanced for the senior cadets."

"What do you do on them?" Stephen asked.

Willy shrugged. "Basic service knowledge, like how to wear your uniform and who to salute," he said.

"And aircraft recognition and fieldcraft," Stick added.

Willy nodded, "And navigation and radio work."

"And we do lots of drill!" Stick added with a moan.

That irritated Willy. He wanted air cadets to sound really good, better than army cadets. "And we get to study aircraft and the theory of flight and in Advanced we can learn to fly."

"Our Third Years get to fire rifles," Stick put in.

"Our First Years do that!" Stephen retorted. "I will fire a Steyr at camp."

That shut them all up for a moment and Willy felt some jealousy. Then he commented, "We get to fly in aircraft."

"What sort?" Stephen asked.

"We flew in a 'Hercules' during our G.S.T. Camp in June," Willy replied. It had only been a 30-minute flight around the RAAF base at Garbutt in Townsville and he hoped Stephen would not ask for such details.

Luckily, he didn't and the conversation moved back to discussing dates. Finally they agreed that Monday 4th October would be the date.

With that settled Willy made his way home, luckily only a few blocks, and he at once took out several reference books on aircraft and began leafing through them.

What type of aircraft will I make? he wondered. His initial idea was a Sopwith Camel but he understood that his choice might come down to what was available in the shops at that time. *I might make a couple and submit the best one as my entry,* he considered.

Friday at school started well. Petra met him at the gate and they sat together and talked for half an hour. Willy felt very hopeful that their relationship was moving onto a solid foundation and he resolutely pushed intruding thoughts and images of Marjorie and Barbara out of his mind.

In class he sat next to John and did his work without effort. But when the bell for Morning Break went, he hurried off to be with Petra again, to the annoyance of John who wanted to talk about model aircraft.

At the end of a very enjoyable Morning Break, during which Petra had laughed at his jokes and even nudged him and put her hand on his forearm, Willy went to his next class. This was English with Mrs Ramsey. John was waiting at the door and after saying goodbye to Petra Willy walked in with him.

After placing his books on the desk Willy sat down, still chatting to John. As he did a stab of piercing agony shot up through his left buttock.

"Arrgh!" Willy cried, jumping up and reaching behind to feel for the cause of the pain.

It was a drawing pin. Willy pulled it out of his shorts and held it with his left hand while rubbing his bum with his right. Tears of pain and mortification formed in his eyes and he was hotly aware that every student in the room was staring at him, including Petra.

John leaned over to look. "What is it?" he asked.

Willy opened his left hand to reveal the drawing pin. "A thumb tack, on my chair," he replied, holding back the tears by an effort of willpower.

"What the? I wonder who put that there?" John said as he moved to sit down himself. Then he stopped and looked down. "Bloody hell! Here's another one on my seat."

Willy looked down and saw a second drawing pin lying point upwards on John's chair. For a moment their eyes met and then he bit his lip. "Someone put these here deliberately," he muttered.

The arrival of Mrs Ramsey ended any chance to pursue the matter at that moment. Rather than make a fuss Willy sat down and placed the tack on his desk. John also sat down, driving his thumb tack hard into the top of the desk.

"Who the bloody hell put these here?" he said again.

Yes who? Willy wondered.

He glanced around the room and in doing so saw nothing suspicious. But his gaze did meet Petra's and she gave him a sympathetic smile. That didn't help as it just reminded Willy of his humiliation and he burned with shame and anger.

Putting these pins here was a deliberate act, he mused. *Which means I, we, have an enemy.*

That was a very shocking thought. A secret enemy! *But who and why?* Willy was at a loss to explain it. *If it had been just me I would have assumed that it was put there by someone who was jealous over Petra. But John had one as well so what have we done to make someone want to give us grief?* he wondered.

Still angry and brooding over the incident he tried to settle to his work, but the pin had really hurt and a nagging pain persisted and paranoid anxieties began to swirl in his head.

At lunch time, while they walked down to the back oval, Petra asked him what had happened. Willy described the incident and then speculated on who might have done it.

Petra was amazed. "You the secret enemy have you think?" she said.

"Must have. Why else would it happen?" Willy replied. It was too unlikely for them to be the target of a random prankster.

There was no answer to the question, but Willy began to surreptitiously study all the people he could see to try to detect anyone who might be keeping them under observation.

If I do have a rival he might strike again, he decided.

With that worrying thought he went to his next class, Geography with Mr Conkey, taking good care to check his seat before sitting on it. John did likewise and the boys again discussed who might have placed the pins on their chairs.

"It's a real worry," John said. "We will have to keep our eyes open."

Willy agreed and felt even more concerned. What he now puzzled over was the question of whether the secret enemy was a person in the class or someone else. *It would be easy for an outsider to slip in and place the pins during a break,* he decided. The school rules forbad students to be in the classrooms without supervision by a teacher during breaks but this was an upstairs room and if there were no teachers in the building it would be easy to do.

So, was it just a random attack by a practical joker? Or did someone know which chairs John and I usually sit at? he pondered.

Willy bent to his work, his mind still busy with anxiety. Suddenly he was struck in the right ear by a flying object.

"Ow!" Willy cried, dropping his pencil and clapping his hand to his ear. As he did the cause of the sharp little pain became obvious: a paper plane had struck him. The paper plane, a classic dart design, had fallen onto his desk. Willy's eyes noted the probable direction of flight and he found himself meeting the smiling eyes of Stick who was grinning at him.

Then Stick's eyes flicked to Mr Conkey and so did Willy's. Mr Conkey, along with most of the students, had turned to see what had caused the outcry. Willy instantly used his right hand to brush the paper plane off the desk onto his lap.

Don't want to get my mate into trouble, his racing mind thought. Passing notes by 'air mail' was a common occurrence, when the teacher's back was turned.

Mr Conkey frowned and met Willy's gaze. "Yes Willy? What's the problem?" he asked.

"Just bumped my knee on the desk sir," Willy replied, reaching down to rub at his right knee.

Mr Conkey looked doubtful but only nodded and turned back to the board. Willy glanced at Stick who theatrically wiped his brown and gave a 'thumbs-up'. Willy now unfolded the paper plane and found it did contain a note.

Are we going to look at model planes after school? it read.

In his pursuit of Petra Willy had forgotten that plan. Now he looked up and nodded to Stick, then glanced at Petra, who was also looking at him and smiling. *I will walk Petra home first, then meet the others,* he decided.

Carefully he printed: I will meet you at the shops. There is something I have to do first.

Then he checked the folds on the paper and waited until Mr Conkey was looking away. With practised skill he sent the plane skimming over the heads of Bert Lacey and Roger Dunning. They both looked up in alarm and Bert turned to frown but Stick caught the plane and quickly read the note.

Stick grinned and then wrote another note on the wing of the paper plane. He then waited until Mr Conkey had turned away before tossing it back. It was off line and both Roger and Bert had to duck. To catch it Willy had to half stand and reach across in front of Dianna.

As luck would have it Mr Conkey chose that moment to look around. "Williams, bring that projectile here," he called.

Bugger! Willy thought. But he wasn't unduly concerned as Mr Conkey was usually fairly easy going. So he stood up and walked along the aisle. As he did he glanced down at what Stick had written and got a jolt that annoyed him.

Stick had written: Do you mean someone?

Willy felt a sharp spurt of resentment at the taunt and he badly wanted to scrunch the paper into a ball so no-one could read it, least of all a teacher. But there was no help for it. Mr Conkey held out his hand and Willy handed the paper plane to him. Then he stood and anxiously watched as Mr Conkey unfolded the paper plane and read the various comments. Once he raised his eyebrows, but he kept a straight face. Then he met Willy's eyes.

"Are you the manufacturer of this missile?" he queried.

"Yes sir," Willy replied. "Nobody else in this class has the skill for something as hi-tech as this." His answer pleased him as it kept his mate out of trouble (Not done to dob on a mate!) but at the same time was revenge for the hurtful comment.

"Is that so?" Mr Conkey replied in a dry voice. He casually crushed the paper into a ball and looked around the room. The students all grinned, except Stick, who put his head down and pretended to work. "Well, if that is the best the air force can do we are in trouble. There must be more airworthy designs than this one."

"Yes sir," Willy replied.

"Get on with your work and no more paper planes in my class," Mr Conkey snapped.

"Yes sir," Willy replied. Thankful that no painful consequence was to follow he turned and made his way back to his seat, scowling at the smirking Stick as he did.

That afternoon Willy again walked Petra home. Thinking that their friendship was developing very nicely Willy was tempted to ask her to sit next to him in class. He was even more thrilled when she several times touched him as he talked, either placing her hand on his forearm as he wheeled his bike or nudging him with her elbow when she laughed at one of his jokes. In both cases it sent little electric shocks through him and got him aroused so that he became flustered and worried.

I don't want her to see anything like that! he worried. *I don't want such a nice girl to be offended or get the wrong idea.* And he knew he was a hypocrite because each night now he fantasised about doing very rude things with a nude Marjorie!

After farewelling Petra near her home Willy rode his bike to the shops to meet up with John. The plan was to look at model aircraft kits and to buy any that seemed suitable. After locking his bike into the bike racks Willy stood near the main entrance and looked around for John.

Instead he spotted Jason Branch. Branch did not see him but went walking into the shopping centre. Willy watched him go and thought, *Cadets tonight. I hope I don't wear any grief over Petra.*

When John did not appear after five minutes Willy decided he might be already inside so went in and made his way to the Toy and Hobby shop. John was not there either so Willy began browsing along the aisles, studying the models available.

His first impression was of how limited the range was and then of the wide variety of technical 'gadgets' available. He was dismayed and astonished to see numerous different types of motors and radio control appliances. The huge array of radio-controlled drones, mostly quadcopters and similar machines, also dismayed him. Willy was quite familiar with such things, had even owned a couple of toy ones, but had an irrational prejudice against them as not being 'real' aircraft.

After looking at the number and variety of models available for a few minutes Willy shook his head. *They all look a bit complicated and expensive. It is just as well we are making rubber-powered models.*

But there were only two available, and both were plastic. One was an ME109 'Messerschmitt' fighter and the other a Mustang. Willy didn't particularly like either, but he picked up the ME109 box and began reading the notes on the outside.

While he was doing that John appeared at his shoulder along with another boy from their school: Scott Tremlow. "Hi Willy! Where have you been?" John asked.

"Just being nice," Willy replied. "Hi, I'm Willy," he added, this to Scott.

"G'day. I'm Scott. I'm in Eight C."

Willy nodded. "I've seen you at school."

"You are the mad scientist trying to make guided missiles," Scott added, causing Willy to grin but also blush with irritated embarrassment.

Scott now reached up and took down the Mustang box. After studying it for a few minutes he said, "This looks pretty good. Is this for the model aircraft competition you guys are having?" he asked.

John nodded and said, "Yes." Then he looked at the shelves and said, "Is this all there is?"

Willy nodded. "Looks like it."

"What's that one?" John asked.

"An ME 109," Willy replied, handing the box to John. "You can have it if you like."

"But there are only these two. What will you use?" John asked.

Willy shrugged. "I will go to another shop or buy a kit on the internet. It's OK. You have it if you want it."

"You are sure?"

"Yeah. I want a Spitfire," Willy replied.

"Thanks," John replied, looking quite emotional as he did.

The boys studied a few other models and again Willy noted the size and cost of the true flying models, the ones designed to have motors and radio controls.

I might try them once I have a better idea what I am doing, he thought.

The boys paid for the models and then strolled around the shopping centre, discussing models and eyeing the girls. Willy happily entered into this game, until he remembered Petra.

I shouldn't be looking at other girls, he rebuked himself.

A few minutes later the three boys reached the entrance to the shopping centre. By then Willy was feeling very happy and had begun to daydream about being with Petra. And then he saw his bicycle. The front tyre was flat.

Oh no! he thought, moving quickly to check. There was no doubt. The tyre had no air in it at all.

Scott and John joined him. Scott said, "Have you got a puncture Willy?"

"No, my bicycle has!" Willy snapped back as annoyance took the place of dismay. But then his eyes took in the fact that the valve was missing. He reached down and fingered the empty fitting. "Someone has unscrewed the valve," he said.

John bent to look and then met his eyes. "Your secret enemy again maybe?" he suggested.

Chapter 6

SUSPICIONS

Willy felt his stomach churn as that horrible idea took hold. *Secret enemy!* he thought, appalled that anyone might not like him. With that thought uppermost he looked up to check who might be nearby.

And there, only 25 metres away and just mounting his bike, was Jason Branch. Branch had his back to them but as he started to pedal away he glanced around and saw Willy. For a moment their eyes locked but then Branch looked away and he rode off.

Is it him? Willy wondered. *His actions certainly looked suspicious, and he doesn't like me because of Petra,* he thought. That was worrying stuff with cadets scheduled that night.

But the problem now was how to get home. There was no shop in the shopping centre that sold bicycle parts and the nearest was a long way away. One option was to phone his parents and get them to pick him up. The other was to walk. Rather than try to explain things to his parents Willy opted to walk.

John and Scott walked with him for a block but then said goodbye and went their own way. That left Willy to trudge along alone, brooding about who his enemy might be. And pushing a bike with a completely flat front tyre was hard work, as he quickly discovered.

It was a tired and footsore boy who arrived home just on dusk. In answer to his mother's anxious queries about where he had been Willy merely commented that his bike had a flat tyre. She accepted this and he went to his room and threw himself on his bed to brood some more.

Will I go to cadets? he wondered. The possibility of Branch being his enemy and of persecuting him he found quite daunting. But then his stubborn streak asserted itself. *No. If I don't go he wins,* Willy told himself. So he prepared for cadets and hid his hurts and worries from his parents.

His mother drove him to cadets and it was a very anxious boy that climbed out at the depot. And his anxieties were justified. Branch did have it in for him, or so it seemed. First, he rebuked Willy for poor drill and then he criticised his uniform. Willy kept his face neutral and made polite, "Yes sergeant," answers. He knew he had not spent as much time or care on ironing his uniform as he usually did so he told himself the criticism was probably justified.

Then Branch seemed to take every opportunity to rebuke Willy for every little thing, incorrect drill mostly but twice for answering Noddy when he started talking to him in class.

During the break Willy took Noddy aside. "Stop talking to me during lessons Noddy," he said.

"Why, what's the problem?" Noddy replied.

"Because Branch is looking for any excuse to pick on me," Willy answered.

"Why would he do that?" Noddy queried. "What have you done to upset him?"

Reluctantly Willy replied, "He fancies Petra."

"Oh ho! Petra the Peach eh!" he cried, so loud that every cadet nearby glanced towards them. One of these was Branch and Willy saw his facial expression change to a scowl.

"Stow it Noddy! You don't have to embarrass me," he snapped.

Noddy chuckled and seemed unabashed. "I see! Oh well, may the best man win," he said. Then he chortled again and winked at Willy and nudged him. Willy was annoyed but decided to let the matter drop.

There were no further incidents that night and Willy began to relax. During the dismissal parade the CO, Flight Lieutenant Comstock, spoke to them. "We have been invited once again to take part in the annual Tri-service Drill Competition. The competition will be in Mareeba in October. 106 Squadron are the hosts this year and they haven't won it for nearly ten years, and I am told they are training really hard. Remember that we have won it for the last four years in a row. Each unit is requested to provide a drill team of twelve cadets. Over the next few weeks anyone interested in trying out for the team is to put their name down on the list on the squadron notice board and we will choose twenty and train them. The best fifteen will be selected. That will give us three reserves."

I might try for that, Willy decided. Despite what Branch said, he thought his drill was pretty good. After dismissal parade he stood waiting, talking to Stick about model aircraft until he was picked up.

That night Willy's fantasies were all tinged with mild paranoia as he mulled over the unpleasant incidents of the last few days. *Is Branch my secret enemy?* he wondered. *Or maybe not so secret.*

Saturday morning brought chores: pets to wash, groom and feed; washing to be done including the cadet uniform; rooms to tidy and vacuum and a lawn to mow. Willy actually wanted to go to another shop to look for models, but there was no time before lunch and he knew those sorts of shops were mostly closed on Saturday afternoon and Sunday.

To fill in a boring weekend Willy played 'Red Baron' and 'Battle of Britain' on his computer. He particularly enjoyed the simulated war flying with the biplanes. *I really like Sopwith Camels. I wonder if I would have been good enough to be a fighter pilot in World War 1?* he mused. And by good enough he not only meant the quickness of hand and eye and the flying skill but the necessary ruthlessness to press the trigger and send other men to their death.

It was sobering stuff and after a while he eased off it into fantasies of flying that involved rescuing beautiful maidens from peril, notably Petra. For hours he daydreamed, building her image and worshipping her.

On the Sunday afternoon his mind shifted to studying illustrations and photos of aircraft in some of his books. In one of them he found a cut-away drawing of a Sopwith Camel and another of its great rival the Fokker DR1 triplane.

This is how Stephen's model Auster is built, he thought. *I wonder if I could draw some plans to scale and make my own model?*

The hard part, he decided, would be getting the balance right. The actual shape and dimensions was a simple measuring task. *I probably can,* he decided.

And then it was Monday and he could hardly wait to get to school to see Petra. But first he had to repair his bike. Luckily his father was very efficient and there were spare valves in the storeroom under the house, so he was able to insert one and then find a pump to inflate the tyre.

I'd better take a spare valve and a pump in case it happens again, he decided, slipping these items into his school bag.

At school his heart shot up instantly, along with his hopes when he saw Petra waiting for him at the bike racks. She beamed and jiggled happily, adding to Willy's mounting excitement. To his dismay he began to get aroused and he broke into an anxious sweat and tried to will it to go down. The reaction bothered him a bit as he did not want to offend Petra, or get teased by others who might notice. So, shielding himself with his school bag he greeted her cheerfully and they strolled to the classroom together.

In the classroom John had not yet arrived. Willy and Petra strolled in to where Willy sat. Petra then placed her books on John's desk. That surprised Willy and he looked up at her.

Petra smiled. "I sit with you yes?" she asked.

For a moment Willy hesitated, knowing John would feel hurt. But it was no contest really and he nodded and smiled back. Petra slid in beside him and pressed her knee against his leg, sending his heart rate pounding and causing him almost instant arousal.

And John was hurt. It showed on his face the moment he walked into the room and saw what had happened. He came and stood over Petra.

"Hey, that's my seat!" he cried.

Petra smiled back. "You with Marcia may sit," she answered sweetly.

John cast Willy a hurt look and then huffed over to plonk himself in the empty seat at a desk on his own over to the right front.

By then Willy was torn. He was delighted that Petra had come to sit with him, but he was fearfully embarrassed and afraid that he might be told to stand up for some reason, in which case his aroused condition would become obvious to all his peers. He was also both proud and flustered by the looks he and Petra got from the other students and from the behind-the-hand sniggering and gossip that resulted.

Well, they think we are an item now, he thought.

The next concern was that one of the teachers might not approve of the arrangement and move either him or her. To his relief the only consequences were a few raised eyebrows when teachers noted the situation. For the remainder of the lesson he sat in a state of near bliss, happy emotions churning in him.

When they went out for morning break so keen was Willy to sit with Petra that he almost ran to the toilet. Feeling relieved he then hurried to re-join Petra under 'F' Block.

But as he came around the corner, he was almost hit by a paper plane. It skimmed past his face and landed on the concrete path. A glance showed that Scott had thrown it. Stick and Noddy stood near him, both with paper planes in their hands. Mixed feelings of shame and guilt caused Willy to hope they could not tell what he had been doing. He forced a grin and continued on.

But Scott called, "Willy, pick that up and throw it back."

Silently cursing Willy nodded and stopped to pick the paper plane up. After glancing around to check that no teachers were watching Willy did. He was then called on by Noddy to get his and return it. Willy did this, aiming to try to hit Noddy with it. In this he was unsuccessful, the poorly made paper plane curving well off course.

Nearby were a group of Year 9 boys, and the paper plane flew close past them. Standing at the end of a table was a Torres Strait Islander named Luke and Willy heard him say to his friends: "Not me mon. No way! You wouldn't get me in that sea at night, not even if the ship sank from under me!"

Then Luke glimpsed the paper plane and turned, first frowning and then grinning. "Why if it ain't the great rocket scientist!" he cried.

Navy cadets, Willy noted, recognizing Andrew Collins and his mates.

One of them, Blake, laughed and then called in a jeering tone: "Is that the best the air force can do Willy? You should try adding an engine."

A boy named Simmo also laughed but then called: "No, a rocket motor. That would really make it go boom, I mean zoom!"

They all laughed some more. Willy burned at the teasing comments about 'Airey Fairies' and 'Space cadets' as he bent to pick up the plane. As he did Andrew Collins said, "Willy, there is a teacher over there. You had better take your paper planes out of sight in case you get into trouble."

Willy looked and saw it was Mr Walsh. *He's a mean bugger,* he thought. Nodding he called: "Thanks" to Andrew and hastily turned to his friends. "Teacher!" he hissed.

Scott, Stick and Noddy took one look and quickly hid their paper planes. Willy hurried over to them and handed Scott's back to him. Then he remembered Petra and looked around. Almost immediately he saw her and his heart turned over with anxiety. She was staring at him and even from 50 metres he could see she was frowning.

During the next few seconds Willy was assailed by a mix of conflicting emotions. Part of him wanted to be with his friends but there was also a strong urge to be with Petra. For a few moments he dithered, wrestling over what to do while his friends chattered away.

They will tease me if I just leave, he thought.

There was also that gnawing desire to be accepted, to part of the group and that held him for another minute.

But then he shook his head. *Hell hath no fury,* he reminded himself. So he muttered, "See you later," and turned away.

As he did Scott called, "Where are you off to in such a hurry Willy? Our company not good enough for ya eh?"

That hurt but Willy ignored it and started walking towards Petra. Noddy then commented to the others, "Willy's 'willy' is controlling him at the moment."

"What do ya mean?" Scott queried.

"He's smitten by Petra the Poke," Noddy replied.

Both the comment and the insulting insinuation about Petra caused Willy to burn with hurt but he made himself keep walking. It didn't help when Scott called after him: "Give her one for us Willy."

She's not like that! Willy burned to shout but instead he ground his teeth and kept walking.

When he joined Petra she did not help. "You look ver angry," she commented. "Vot vos those big boys teasing you about?"

"They are navy cadets and they were teasing me for being an air cadet," Willy replied.

'Kadet? Vos ist zat?" Petra queried.

Willy was astonished. *She doesn't know I am an air cadet!* he thought. But he was even more astonished when he discovered that she knew nothing about the AAFC at all. So he set out to explain.

She listened for a moment and then frowned. "Does zat mean you in the military must be ven you are older?"

"No. Being an air cadet is a purely voluntary thing," Willy explained. "It doesn't give us any obligation to serve in the armed forces when we grow up. But I plan to join the air force anyway. I want to be a pilot."

"A pilot?" Petra queried, her accent making the word hard to understand.

"Yes, you know, a person who flies aeroplanes," Willy said.

Petra nodded and her face went blank. "Oh yes. One of my mother's friends der pilot is. He and some of his friends zey come over sometimes," she said.

That statement puzzled Willy. It was on the tip of his tongue to ask what her father thought of that but then decided it might not be a good idea. Instead he just nodded and to change the subject he said, "Do you have any brothers and sisters?"

Petra shook her head. "No," she said in a very wooden tone.

Now Willy felt he just had to ask so, moistening his lips, he said: "What does your father do?"

Petra's face went even harder. "No father," she muttered.

Willy felt a chill of anxiety. *You have walked onto some thin ice here Willy my boy,* he told himself.

In an attempt to again change the subject he asked Petra if she had ever flown in an aeroplane. To his relief she mentioned that she had, and they were able to discuss what types of aircraft and where the flights had been from and to. He was then able to steer the conversation onto what places in Australia she had been to (Only Sydney and Cairns) and her mood slowly thawed.

The period after lunch was Social Science and Mr Conkey took the class to the Library to do research for their next History assignment. Once there, Willy and Petra stood between two shelves and talked quietly. To Willy's delight Petra snuggled against him and the message his heated, pounding brain seemed to be telling him was that she wanted to be kissed or hugged. To his dismay he became fully aroused again.

Greatly daring, Willy touched Petra's hand with his and then, when she smiled, he took hold of it. It felt so warm and smooth and wonderful that his heart hammered so hard he feared it might burst. Then she pressed against him and placed her head on his shoulder. Her hair tickled his neck and face and he could scent her delightful smell.

Oh, I hope no teacher sees us, he fretted, knowing that such fraternisation was forbidden by the school rules.

But it wasn't a teacher who interrupted them, it was John. He chuckled and cried out, "Oy! Oy! What's this then?"

Willy looked over Petra's head and gave a wry smile and tried to hide his irritation at the interruption. "Don't dob John," he requested.

"I won't. Look what I've found Willy. It is a book on how to make paper planes," John replied.

Willy forced himself to be polite and to look. It looked to be an interesting book and he agreed to look at it later. John nodded and turned away, then hurried back. "Here comes Miss Sims," he whispered.

Just in time Willy released Petra, realising he had his arms around her but not remembering putting them there. The pair pretended to be studying book titles and then moved apart, going in different directions. They met up again in the next aisle after the teacher had passed. Petra giggled and looked so desirable that Willy just reached out and drew her to him. She came willingly and this time they kissed.

For a few seconds Willy was completely overwhelmed by the surge of emotion and passion and then he kissed her again. Only then did he realise that he was pressing hard into her stomach. Not wanting to offend her he tried to ease himself back. But she clung tightly to him and he had to just hope she would not notice.

That kiss went on and on, Willy rapidly losing control. Where it might have ended, for his hands were starting to roam over her back, hips and sides and his mind was moving to more passionate things, he never found out because two of the girls: Barbara and Karen, interrupted them.

Barbara tapped Petra's shoulder. "Come up for air Petra. Mr Conkey is coming," she said.

Reluctantly Willy let go and eased himself back. Petra seemed to float in his vision like a picture of angelic loveliness and his heart pounded with love.

"I love you," he whispered.

Petra's eyes went all misty and she would have melted back into his arms except that Mr Conkey was now in the room. Willy met Barbara's gaze and noted a quizzical, half-amused look in her eyes. *Barbara is nice,* he thought.

But there was no more kissing. Mr Conkey called the class to sit at a group of tables and the lesson continued. Willy slid into a seat beside John, hoping that nobody had noticed his horny condition.

At lunch time Willy sat with Petra down at the far end of the oval. They held hands and pressed against each other, but it was too public for pashing and there seemed to be always a teacher on Playground Duty (Miss McLeod, not to be trifled with!).

After lunch Willy and Petra sat together in English. Once again, they kept touching and Willy kept getting aroused. It took a real effort to concentrate on the schoolwork. Pausing to think Willy looked up. He noted John was busy folding a paper plane. It was not the usual triangular dart design but had cantilever wings folded to stick out from near the nose and there was a swallow tail.

John glanced around and met Willy's eyes. Grinning he held up the paper plane. After a check at what Mrs Ramsey was doing John turned and launched the paper plane into the air. To Willy's astonishment the paper plane flew better than any he had ever seen. It glided easily over and landed on the floor near him. Just in time to avoid the teacher's gaze Willy scooped it up and hid it.

After studying the complex folding pattern Willy waited for a safe moment and then threw the paper plane back. This drew a shake of the head from Petra and a frown from 'Miss Goody Two-shoes' Brianna on his left.

The game developed. Willy felt challenged so he took out a sheet of A4 and made a triangular dart, measuring and folding with particular care to ensure symmetry. This he threw across to John. The dart flew well enough, but Willy saw that it had to be thrown hard to make it fly and that it tended to spin.

To Willy's annoyance John took out his scissors and cut two slits in the back of each wing. Then he folded small ailerons. *Or are they elevators? What do you call the flaps at the back of a delta wing that doesn't have a separate tail?* Willy wondered. After adjusting one flap to face up and the other to face down, John threw the dart back. The effect was to make it rotate rapidly. It flew past Willy and crashed on Brianna's desk. She brushed it onto the floor and gave Willy a disapproving look.

I hope she doesn't dob, he thought, noting Mrs Ramsey now looking at Scott's work. The making and throwing of paper planes continued, each throw more daring than the last. Willy half expected to get caught but wasn't particularly concerned. *Mrs Ramsey is a good sort. She won't make too much of a fuss,* he thought.

Then Stick and Scott joined in. And it was Stick who made a bad design with poorly folded wings that flew off course and landed near the front of the class. Mrs Ramsey saw this, and both Stick and Scott were cautioned. As soon as Mrs Ramsey's back was turned Willy grinned at Stick and made throat cutting motions. Undeterred Stick made another plane.

But then the bell went and the day was over. Willy was glad as that meant he now got to stroll with Petra. But first he got a shock. On reaching the bike racks Willy saw that his front tyre was again flat!

"Damn!" he swore as a sick feeling of hurt swirled through him.

Instantly he looked around, hoping to catch a glimpse of the person who did it. *Where is Branch?* he wondered. A hard look in all directions revealed that there was no sign of him.

Petra took hold of Willy's left arm and put her other hand to her mouth in dismay. "Oh dear! Who might that have done?" she cried.

"I don't know," Willy answered, his mind clouded with suspicions as he tried to work out who disliked him so much. But Branch's was the only name he could really dig up. *Those Year 11 bullies wouldn't do this. They would just thump me,* he reasoned.

At that moment John arrived from behind him. John stood beside them and looked down. "What's happened Willy? Has someone let down your tyre again?" he asked.

"Yes, and taken the valve again," Willy replied.

To his dismay he found that it upset him so much he wanted to cry, and it took an effort of willpower to keep the quaver out of his voice. He saw that the enemy had again taken the valve by unscrewing it.

"What will you do now?" John queried.

Willy shrugged and took off his school bag. "Luckily I have a spare valve," he replied. He took this out and held it up.

Petra squeezed his arm and smiled. "Oh Villy, you der very clever fellow are!" she cried.

That was balm to Willy's ego and hurt feelings. He smiled and bent to screw the valve back in.

"How will you pump it up?" John asked.

"I brought a bike pump too," Willy answered.

Again Petra cried her praise and Willy felt much better. He took out the pump and screwed it to the valve then set to work to inflate the tube.

This was soon done and as he tested the pressure with his thumb John said, "Are you coming over this afternoon?"

"I would like to," Willy replied. "I will just walk Petra home first."

John nodded and smiled but Willy sensed a bit of resentment in his response. To appease John he said, "What if we go to another shop to look for more models?"

John brightened at that and agreed. The friends parted and Willy walked Petra home. After a reluctant farewell to her he pedalled over to John's. The boys had afternoon tea and then he and John rode their bikes to another shopping centre. After locking their bikes, not without some trepidation on Willy's part, they went inside and walked around looking for models. They didn't find a suitable one but once again Willy noted that there were both electric motors and petrol engines for use in model aircraft. And the prices of some of the kits staggered him.

"Flying radio-controlled models is a sport for adults with plenty of time and money," he commented.

"We could make our own maybe?" John suggested.

"Worth a try," Willy agreed. "What will we do now?"

"I will just buy another spare valve," Willy answered. He had been thinking about that and worrying that someone might even then be tampering with his bike. So he bought three.

In case they take the valves from both tyres at once, he thought.

John nodded approval. "That is good planning," he applauded. "Now what will we do?"

Pleased by John's praise Willy gestured along the arcade. "Let's go to the Newsagent. I saw some magazines on model aircraft there and they might help.

So the boys made their way to the nearest Newsagent and browsed the shelves. Willy quickly found what he wanted, after having to resist the temptation to linger at the 'girlie' magazines with their photos of naked females.

Willy purchased *Radio Control Model News* and John bought an American one titled *Fly RC*. Leafing through the magazine as he walked along, Willy said, "I had better get home. I was in trouble for being late the other day."

"I hope our bikes are OK," John added.

Yes, thought Willy as a spurt of anxiety surged through him. *I wonder if our enemy has struck again?*

With that concept nagging at him, he hurried towards the front door.

Chapter 7

I TOLD YOU SO!

When he reached the door Willy strained his eyes to check his bike as soon as it came into view. To his relief it appeared to have nothing wrong with it. In a happier frame of mind he rode back to John's and then made his way home.

At home he lay on his bed and read the model aircraft magazine and was astounded. He discovered that there were hundreds of different types of engines for models, both electric and petrol powered. There was also a bewildering array of servo motors and switches and so many different types of radio control consoles that he quickly gave up.

This is a lot more complicated than I thought, he mused.

A knock on his door attracted his attention. It was his father. "Have you done your homework?" he asked.

"Not yet, Dad."

"Then do it, or no TV or computer games. And put that magazine away so that it doesn't distract you."

"Yes Dad. Hey Dad, do you think we could build a radio-controlled model aircraft?" Willy asked.

"I don't know. What's involved?" his father asked.

Willy had to hide a smile. *Dad is so easy to hook!* he told himself. He held up the magazine. "Have a read of this."

His father took the magazine and withdrew. Willy reluctantly then sat at his laptop and worked on his homework until dinner time. After dinner he completed the homework before settling to draw rough plans of various aircraft. But it was the Sopwith Camel that kept edging into his mental list of favourites. *I will try to make one,* he decided. So he made up a list of items he would need before going to have supper.

While he drank his Milo Willy was pleased to note that his father lay on the lounge sofa reading the model aircraft magazine. *Good, I might get some help now,* Willy told himself. *My name should really be 'Wily'.*

The next morning at school Willy met Petra as usual but then they got drawn into a discussion about a shipwreck Andrew Collins and his sister

Carmen had been diving on that weekend. Willy now learned that both Andrew and Carmen were qualified open water divers. The thought of going down under water out in the ocean caused him to shudder.

I wouldn't be game, he thought.

Then John butted in. He had his book on paper planes and a folder of A4 sheets. He insisted Willy try to make one. Reluctantly Willy did. While he was folding it Scott, Stick and Noddy joined them and got involved. Soon all of them had made paper planes and began throwing them.

Roger came past on his way to join his friends and a paper plane thrown by Noddy almost hit him in the eye. "Ow! Watch what you are doing you lot!" he growled.

"Don't walk across the runway then," Noddy retorted.

Roger made a face and then added, "You lot will get into trouble if you aren't careful."

"Piffle!" Noddy cried. But Willy glanced around as throwing things, even paper planes, was banned by the school rules. There was no sign of any teacher, so he set his paper plane flying. To his gratification it flew really well, looping the loop before landing softly on the grass. He started walking over to pick it up.

Noddy now picked up his plane, a fairly roughly made delta dart, and he threw it with all his might. The paper plane went off spinning and swooping in a curving flight. Willy followed its flight with his eyes and was astonished, amused and dismayed all at once when Mr Page, the Senior Geography Head of Department, walked around the corner and was struck full in the chest by it.

Noddy gasped, his face registering his horror. "Oh bugger!" he cried. Then he turned and bolted.

Mr Page grabbed at the paper plane, saw what it was and then crumpled it in his fist. Anger mottled his face. "Who threw that?" he shouted.

Noddy was gone, off behind Andrew, Roger and their mates. Willy shook his head and then realised he had no paper plane in his hand. John and Scott both had planes in their hands and Stick was even then in the act of throwing his, his right arm drawn back.

Mr Page glared angrily. "Don't you throw that Morton. Now, who threw this one?" he demanded to know.

Nobody spoke. Mr Page looked from one to the other. Scott slid a paper plane behind his back in an attempt to hide it. Mr Page looked at Willy. "Did you throw it Williams?"

Willy shook his head. "No sir. That is mine there," he replied, pointing to the paper plane on the grass.

"So who was it then?"

Willy stayed silent bit broke into a sweat. Mr Page glared and then said, "Was it a friend of yours?"

"Can't say sir," Willy replied.

"Or won't?"

"Won't sir," Willy replied. Now he felt anxious and did not want to get into trouble. Petra moved beside him and looked worried.

Mr Page looked at the others. "And none of you will say either?"

Silence.

At that Mr Page pursed his lips together and then nodded. "That's fine. Loyalty and moral courage are wonderful qualities. You will all bring me an essay on loyalty at lunch time, five hundred words, and none of your usual spelling mistakes. Now stop throwing paper planes in the school grounds and get to your class," he said.

Willy sighed with relief. A 500-word essay would only take him half an hour and he knew he could write it during other lessons without any difficulty.

Stick wasn't so happy. He scowled at the teacher's back and muttered, "Bastard! He didn't have to do that."

"Yes he did," Willy replied. "He couldn't just do nothing."

"Oh easy for you!" Stick snapped.

Willy could only shrug. He knew that Stick had trouble with English and was notorious for not having assignments in on time.

The bell went and they made their way to class. Once there, Willy settled to roughing out his essay while pretending to listen to Miss Hackenmeyer. The lesson was Maths and he could do the calculations standing on his head. More distracting was Petra's presence and her arousing touch.

Then a paper plane drifted across the room when Miss Hackenmeyer's back was turned. Willy watched it land on Barbara's desk. With an irritable sweep of her hand she flicked it off her desk and frowned. Willy looked around and saw Stick grinning.

Silly boy! he thought. Annoying Mr Conkey or Mrs Ramsey was one thing but antagonizing the formidable Miss Hackenmeyer was quite another.

Stick made another paper plane and threw it across to Willy. 'Get the other one off Jiraarf' was the note on it. Seeing Barbara called 'Giraffe' annoyed Willy even though he knew it was her class nickname because of her long legs. So he shook his head. At that moment Samantha bent down and picked it up. First, she checked to see if there was a message on it and then looked around to see who had thrown it. Seeing Willy nod she waited until Miss Hackenmeyer was not looking and threw it back to him. Stick then made gestures to indicate he should throw the paper plane back.

Fearing to be teased as a wimp Willy waited his moment and threw it. The paper plane skimmed low over Bert and Roger, both of whom ducked and then looked around. Roger made a face and shook his head.

During the break between classes Roger, who had been under or in the flight path of a dozen flights by then, stopped Willy as he left the room. Shaking his head he said: "You guys will be sorry."

Willy shrugged and grinned and then went outside with Petra. In her presence it was easy to push concepts like paper planes and consequences out of his thoughts.

Then, after classes started again, Willy got another niggling little shock. He went to pick up his pen to resume writing the essay that was due in about an hour's time, and he couldn't find it. For a minute or so he searched his desk and bag.

Petra watched and then said, "Vot for are you looking?"

"My pen," Willy replied.

"It vos on der desk ven ve went out," Petra answered.

Willy clearly remembered that, but it was certainly not there now. *Has someone taken it?* he wondered. Then the word 'somebody' was replaced by the word 'enemy' and he experienced a little wave of cold. *Is my enemy in this class? Or is it just a simple mistake?* he wondered.

The incident upset and annoyed him more than he had expected. It wasn't as though the pen was worth much, it was just a cheap biro and he bought them by the packet, it was the notion that someone might have deliberately taken it. Once again, he carefully scanned everyone in the class, seeking for any clue as to who the person might be. But nobody was acting in any way that looked unusual or odd and there were at least five biros of the same cheap brand visible in other people's hands.

Oh well, I will just have to have spare pens as well as spare bike valves, he told himself. Luckily, he did have a spare and was able to get on with his work. The essay was completed on time and he could then focus his attention on Petra.

At the start of the lunch break Willy stood outside the classroom and held up his essay to his friends. "Are you blokes coming up to Mr Page now?"

Both Scott and John nodded and showed him their essays. But Stick shook his head and scowled. "I haven't got mine finished yet. I don't know what to say."

John scowled. "Get Noddy to write it. It was his plane."

Noddy went red and glared at John. "Get knotted!" he snapped.

Stick looked at Noddy but Noddy just shook his head. Willy sighed. He wanted to go and sit with Petra but could not see any way out of the situation other than by helping Stick. "Let's go downstairs and help Stick," he said.

So the group made their way down to their usual seats and Willy took Stick's attempt off him and tried to read it. But that was hard going. The spelling and grammar were so poor he had great difficulty working out what Stick actually meant.

"God almighty Stick, this is gibberish!" Willy commented. Shaking his head he began to re-write it. "You other guys go and hand yours in. Tell Mr Page we are on our way," he said.

Scott and John left and Noddy made himself scarce. Willy then quickly wrote a page, finding it difficult not to use the words he had filled his own essay with. *We don't want it to read the same or Mr Page might suspect collusion,* he thought.

After twenty minutes Willy stopped scribbling. He held the two pages out and said, "Here you are Stick. Copy them out in your own handwriting. Now I'm off." With that he stood and walked away, leaving Stick muttering and biting the end of his pen as he settled to the task.

Willy went up to Mr Page's staff room and knocked and then handed in his essay. Luckily Mr Page was busy and just nodded and took it. Sighing with relief Willy turned and hurried back downstairs to find Petra.

The afternoon was easier. Both lessons were in different areas, Science in a laboratory and then Music in the Performing Arts Block. The music Willy really enjoyed. They were learning to sing 'The Volga Boat Song' and he and the other boys all tried to get as low as they could. Then Petra started to sing and the notes were so clear and true that the others just went silent and listened.

She sings like an angel. She is an angel! Willy thought, his romantic notions and emotions flooding through him.

That afternoon after school Willy plucked up the courage to try to advance their relationship another step. When Petra said goodbye just around the corner from her house Willy took her hand and hinted that a kiss would be nice.

Petra understood at once and smiled but then she shook her head. "Nyet... Nix. Er, no Villy. Not here my love. If der neighbours they see they might my mother tell."

"OK, thanks anyway," replied the disappointed but still elated Willy. "I will see you tomorrow. I love you."

Petra smiled back and then turned and walked quickly away. Willy leapt on his bike and pedalled quickly over to John's and the two boys spent the next hour making different designs of paper planes and then testing them in the garden. Willy was amazed at how many variations there were and by just how well some of them flew.

In class the next morning Petra was on the top of Willy's consciousness, until a paper plane drifted across his line of vision and slid to a stop on the floor beside him. The lesson was Maths and Miss Hackenmeyer was busy writing some notes on the board, she being one of the old-fashioned teachers who did not use the room's computer technology.

The plane had come from John and had no note. John just grinned and indicated he should throw it back. Willy waited and then did so, earning a frown from Bert and a wry smile from Roger as it flew low over their heads. Then, as it sped straight for Stick, Scott suddenly leaned out from where he sat in the row behind and grabbed at it. He did not quite succeed. The paper plane was bent and fell to the floor.

While Scott and Stick silently squabbled Willy took out a sheet of paper and began making his own paper plane. He tried to remember the exact folds of the best design from the day before, but the finished product looked slightly different from how he pictured it.

Never mind. It will do, he reasoned.

Then he had to sit forward and work as Miss Hackenmeyer began walking around the room to check people's work. This did not deter Stick. He straightened out the bent paper plane and launched it across when Miss Hackenmeyer was looking the other way. But that didn't work as the plane immediately flew off course and struck Callum. Callum let out a little yelp (He had actually been doing some work for a change).

Miss Hackenmeyer looked quickly towards him and frowned. "Are you alright Callum?" she queried.

"Yes Miss," Callum reassured her. "Just bumped myself."

Willy noted that the paper plane had ended up on the floor under the teacher's desk. There was nothing he could do about it so he just shrugged and continued to work until an opportunity arose to try his paper plane.

Watching Miss Hackenmeyer out of the corner of his eye he raised his right hand and drew it back then threw. To his instant astonishment and then dismay the model did not fly straight but swooped up until it almost hit the ceiling. Then it came down in a rolling dive to do another loop. As it did it skimmed Miss Hackenmeyer's hair. A little gasp rose from the watchers.

The teacher obviously felt the wind of it as she quickly straightened up and looked around, a suspicious frown on her face. Then she studied the class. By then Willy was busy writing, unsure where the paper plane had gone. When he did look up he was horrified to see that it had landed on the teacher's desk!

Oh no! How can I retrieve that? he wondered. The people sitting closest to the desk were Karen and Barbara. *Barbara might get it for me,* Willy decided. But how to attract her attention? She had obviously seen the paper plane land in front of her but both she and Karen had their heads down working.

I will send a note on another plane, Willy decided. *But no fancy designs this time. I will use the traditional design.*

So he took another sheet of paper and began quickly folding it, anxious that his first one not been discovered and hotly aware that Miss Hackenmeyer was getting closer and he needed to get his work done. Worse still she was in a bad mood and several times she snapped at people to stop talking and to get on with their work.

Then Callum and Sean, the class clowns, joined in. Both made paper planes and threw them across the room. Stick, Noddy and Scott all made more and these went flying as well. By then there was an undercurrent of excitement and tension through the whole class and students kept glancing around to see who was going to throw the next one and what Miss Hackenmeyer might be doing.

That she was aware that something odd was happening was obvious from her body language. She began to suddenly lift her head to look around. Thus it was that she saw Callum raise his hand to throw his paper plane.

"Webster! Crumple that up and get on with your work!" Miss Hackenmeyer snapped. "And write out the seven times table fifty times to show me during morning break," she added. Then she looked around the room and added, "Any more nonsense like that and there will be detentions and people going to the office. Now get on with your work!"

Willy hid his paper plane until her back was again turned. Then he carefully wrote on the wing: Barbara, please take my plane off the teacher's desk. Willy.

Petra had been watching all this, first with amusement and now with concern. She nudged Willy with her knee. "You vill into the trouble get," she whispered.

Willy knew that and was quite anxious but nodded but kept on printing on his second paper plane. Then things suddenly got worse. Despite the warning Noddy and Scott both made more paper planes and threw them across at Willy. One hit Petra and another slid onto the floor against the back wall. Callum made a rude gesture at Miss Hackenmeyer's back and then he and Sean made two more planes, and these ended up on the floor at the front of the class.

Willy watched Miss Hackenemeyer, trying to predict her movements. To his annoyance she was standing in the aisle on his left, halfway between him and the front of the room. This put her close to the flight path from Willy to Barbara's desk. *I will wait until she leans forward to check Sylvia's work,* he decided. In preparation he gripped the plane ready to throw.

Then what seemed to be a safer idea came to him and he added to the note: Stick, throw this to Barbara please, Willy. *That will keep it well away from her,* he thought.

Miss Hackenmeyer turned the other way. Willy's hand went up and back. Aiming at Stick's desk he threw. To his relief the plane flew straight and Stick was watching. He grabbed it as it skimmed across his desk. He quickly read the notes, then grinned and nodded. Waiting his moment he readied the plane for the next leg of its journey. Then Miss Hackenmeyer bent down with her back to both Stick and Barbara and Stick drew his hand back to throw the paper plane.

But then Callum was hit by another paper plane and let out a squeak. Miss Hackenmeyer suddenly straightened up. At that moment Stick threw the paper plane. His face told Willy that he knew instantly it was a mistake, but he was a fraction of second too late to stop himself.

The paper plane sped across the room and struck Miss Hackenmeyer hard in the side of the face as she turned to look towards Callum. Horrified, Willy saw her hand go up to her face and then she gasped and looked around in shock.

Oh no! What have I done? Willy thought. Frozen with fright he sat and stared.

Miss Hackenmeyer stepped back, anger beginning to mottle her face. She glanced down and saw the paper plane. "Who threw that?" she demanded.

The whole class sat silent, breathless with anticipation. Willy glanced at Stick, but he was pretending to be working. When there was no response, Miss Hackenmeyer became even angrier.

"Come on, own up! Who threw that paper plane?"

For a few seconds Willy sat in agonized confusion, impaled by the moral dilemma. *Stick threw it but I made it,* he thought. *He wouldn't have thrown it if I hadn't asked him to.* In his heart he knew he had to own up. *This is going to hurt,* he thought.

Chapter 8

WHO IS IT?

Willy began pushing back his chair as Miss Hackenmeyer looked across the room in the direction from which the plane had come.

"Who threw this?" she shrieked, her whole body shaking with indignation.

Still nobody moved so she bent down and picked up the paper plane. By then Willy was standing. He saw her glance at the writing on the wing of the plane. Then she read it and his heart sank lower.

Miss Hackenmeyer glanced at Stick and then towards Barbara. As she did the teacher obviously saw the paper plane on her desk. Then she noticed the others littering the floor. Her lips tightened. Her head turned towards Stick. "Morton, did you throw this?" she asked.

Stick looked sick but nodded. Slowly he stood up. That was too much for Willy. "Miss, I made the plane. I got him to do it," he said.

Miss Hackenmeyer shifted her gaze to meet his. For a fleeting moment Willy thought of the ancient Greek myth about the woman who could turn men to stone with her eyes and he shivered.

After glaring angrily at both boys Miss Hackenmeyer snapped, "Then you are both to blame! I will not allow myself to be assaulted."

That word struck chill into Willy and he gasped. "Miss, it was an accident," he blurted.

"Be silent! Now collect all of these paper planes and then get on with your work. You will be spending your Morning Break on detention. Now pick these things up!"

Reluctantly Willy nodded and bent to pick up one of the paper planes at the back of the room. As he did, his eyes met Petra's and she looked very sympathetic.

Not so Bert. As Willy made his way past him Bert shook his head. "I told you so!" he muttered.

Willy could only nod and agree. For several minutes he and Stick collected all the paper planes, a surprising total of twelve, before he returned to his seat.

Petra nudged him. "Ve not now meet at leetle lunch," she whispered.

"No," Willy whispered back.

Miss Hackenmeyer heard this and swung round. "Stop that whispering! If you can't work quietly then I will separate you," she snapped.

That idea also chilled Willy so he lowered his head and set to work. *Blast Stick!* he thought, but he knew it was his own fault. *I shouldn't have given in to temptation.*

So during the Morning Break Willy and Stick sat at desks outside Miss Hackenmeyer's staff room and did extra Maths. Then it was off to Science with Miss McLeod and he and Petra were separated anyway. It wasn't until Social Science with Capt Conkey that they got to sit together again.

But even when the Lunch Break came Willy could not immediately join Petra somewhere relatively private. Both he and Stick had to show Miss Hackenmeyer the completed Maths problems. So the two boys set out to find her. Luckily, they met her coming downstairs from her staff room.

Miss Hackenmeyer insisted on checking a couple of answers and that got Stick into more trouble. "This is nonsense boy!" she growled, shaking her head. "Go and do it again. I will be on playground duty on the oval. Show it to me there in fifteen minutes."

With that she turned and walked away, out onto the grass quadrangle between the buildings. Stick poked his tongue at her retreating back. Willy shook his head. "Don't let her catch you doing that mate," he commented. "Now let's find somewhere to sit and get these worked out for you."

Willy started walking out of the doorway and along under the building. As he did, he glanced towards Miss Hackenmeyer, now about 25 metres away. Even as he looked a paper plane flashed down from the veranda above. It flew straight and true and struck the teacher right between the shoulder blades.

The blow could not have really hurt but Miss Hackenmeyer spun on her heel, glanced down at the paper plane on the lawn and then at the two boys.

"Come here you two!" she shouted.

"Miss, it wasn't us!" Stick cried.

Willy's mind was racing. *Someone did that deliberately, and they knew we were here,* he thought. The concept of 'secret enemy' flitted across his mind. His first impulse was to run up the stairs behind him to see who it was. He could hear footsteps hurrying away along the upper veranda, but he sensed that the teacher was in such a bad mood that any attempt to run the other way would lead to even bigger trouble.

Reluctantly he and Stick walked out onto the grass. As he went Willy glanced back several times to see if there was a person visible on the upper veranda. But there was no sign of anyone. Feeling quite dismayed and sick he and Stick stopped in front of the angry teacher.

Miss Hackenmeyer glanced down and instantly her anger turned to rage. She bent and picked up the paper plane and Willy noted with dismay that large swastikas had been drawn on each wing with a black felt pen. *On no!* he thought. Over the years there had been other occasions when students had made unkind jibes about Miss Hackenmeyer's German origin and they had really suffered.

Then it got a whole lot worse. Miss Hackenmeyer turned the plane over and Willy saw writing on the undersides.

HACKENMOLL, HITLER'S MISTRESS

Oh my God! This is going to hurt! Willy thought.

He opened his mouth to again deny any knowledge of the paper plane when he saw Miss Hackenmeyer turn the plane over. Clearly printed on it was his message to Stick and to Barbara.

I put that in the bin. Someone has taken it out and thrown it, Willy thought as dismay swirled in his stomach.

Miss Hackenmeyer looked at the notes and then her eyes bored into Willy. "This is yours Williams. How do you explain it?"

"I did make it Miss," Willy replied, licking lips that had gone dry with fear. "But that is one of the planes I put in the bin. Someone has taken it out and thrown it."

Contempt and disbelief showed on Miss Hackenmeyer's face. Her lips curled. "A likely story! Who is this someone?" she snarled.

"I don't know Miss, someone who doesn't like me," Willy replied. The very notion made him feel sick at heart.

"Huh! And why would that be so?" Miss Hackenmeyer grated.

Willy thought it was because of jealousy over Petra, but he did not want to discuss his love life with the teacher. *She's so ugly she wouldn't know what love is,* he thought, bitter at the trap he had fallen into.

For a few seconds pure rage showed on the teacher's face. With an obvious effort she controlled it. "Well you can explain that to the Deputy Principal. I don't have time to deal with it now as I have to go on playground duty. Now wait here while I write a note," she snapped.

Miss Hackenmeyer took out a pen and notebook and quickly wrote a short note. This was handed to Stick. "Take this note to Mr Fitzgerald, and this insulting object as evidence. Make sure it gets there. I will check. Now go!"

Feeling like he was on his way to the guillotine Willy took the paper plane and turned to go. Stick followed, mumbling about it all being unfair. That annoyed Willy a bit. "You will be alright Stick," he snapped. "It is me who is in deep shit!"

The two boys made their way slowly up the Deputy Principal's office. But the much-feared Mr Fitzgerald was busy with other miscreants. "You two wait there until I get to you," he ordered, indicating the long bench seat outside his office.

So Willy and Stick sat down, along with several other mischief makers. As he sat there, Willy brooded over what had just happened and then got quite upset worrying about the trouble he might be in. *I hope my parents don't get called in,* he thought. But it was the idea that someone hated him so much that they wanted to deliberately hurt him that upset him the most. *Who could it be?* he worried.

Stick quickly recovered his spirits and when asked by one of the other boys what he had done began to relate the tale, with suitable embellishments and bravado. He nudged Willy. "Show them the paper plane Willy," he said.

Willy shook his head. He had folded it and put it in his pocket and despite Stick asking several times he refused. Luckily, those boys were called in to Mr Fitzgerald's office soon after and Willy was able to sit and think. As he did he began to cheer up a bit.

Surely Mr Fitz will believe us? Surely, he wouldn't think we are so stupid as to throw a paper plane straight after speaking to Miss Hackenmeyer?

Then Andrew Collins came wandering by. He saw Willy and raised an eyebrow. "What are you here for Willy? Are you in trouble?" he queried.

Willy nodded. "Yes, over a paper plane," he replied.

Stick chuckled. "It hit Miss Hackenmeyer," he interjected.

"Oh silly boy!" Andrew commented, shaking his head but grinning.

Willy couldn't help it. He grinned back. "Stick hit her with it in class," he replied.

Andrew looked at Stick and then back to Willy. "So if Stick threw it why are you here?" he asked.

"Because I made it," Willy answered. Then the memory of Stick's face as he saw the plane hit Miss Hackenmeyer came to him and he chortled. For the next few minutes he related the incident in the classroom but kept the second part to himself.

Too hard to explain, he reasoned.

And it was. When Mr Fitzgerald called him and Stick in a few minutes later Willy did not know how to start. Luckily Stick began to angrily defend himself. "It wasn't Willy sir, or me. Someone else threw it from up on the veranda," he claimed.

Mr Fitzgerald raised an eyebrow. "And why would anyone do that?" he asked.

There was an uncomfortable silence for a few moments before Willy decided that a full explanation was probably the only way to save them. "Because someone doesn't like me sir," he said.

Mr Fitzgerald's eyebrows went up even higher. "Oh yes! Why would that be?"

So Willy explained his theory of jealousy over Petra and the other things that had been happening. He described the classroom incident of the paper planes in detail and then the incident that had landed them there.

Mr Fitzgerald looked hard at him. "Petra, pretty little girl from Russia of somewhere?" he queried.

"Ukraine sir," Willy replied.

"Hmm. Yes, I see. Apart from the fact that you are both too young to be having relationships it sounds plausible," Mr Fitzgerald replied. "Even I don't think you are silly enough to antagonize a teacher, and particularly Miss Hackenmeyer, in such a way. Trying to launch rockets to the moon maybe, but not setting yourself up for that sort of grief."

Willy was astounded that Mr Fitzgerald knew about his rocket and even seemed to know about him. "No sir," was all he could mumble.

"I will accept your story for the moment, but I will need to speak to Miss Hackenmeyer first. That means both of you be here as soon as last period ends," he said.

Oh drat! Willy thought. *That means I won't be able to walk Petra home.* "Yes sir," he replied.

Mr Fitzgerald looked from one to the other. "I will be keeping an eye on both of you. So no more trouble, now get out of here," he said sternly.

Feeling both relieved and peeved Willy fled. Stick followed, and when Willy wouldn't slow down, he called, "Willy! What's the rush?"

"I want to tell Petra what has happened," Willy replied, flushing hot with embarrassment as he did.

"Huh! Her! You'll be sorry," Stick answered huffily.

That stung. "Why do you say that? Petra's a lovely person," Willy retorted.

Stick made a face. "She's more of a moll than my little sister," he replied.

That really shocked Willy. He stopped and glared at Stick. "She is not! She's a nice girl."

Stick shrugged again. "Suit yourself," he said. Then he turned off and went the other way.

Feeling indignant but uneasy Willy went on alone. He just had time to find Petra and explain to her what had happened before the bell went for the end of the lunch break. *She is so lovely,* he thought as he watched the play of emotions on her pretty face. *She is so nice; and I am just so lucky!*

He did not get a chance to sit with Petra again that afternoon as they had PE down on the oval and the girls were put in different teams. But he did get a good chance to watch her. Several times she looked his way and when their eyes met she smiled. Willy felt his heart would burst with love and he happily took part in games he would normally have loathed.

But Stick had sown a seed of niggling doubt and that bothered Willy more than he cared to admit. He resolved to quietly check out who Petra's other friends were. Then the final bell went, and Willy walked with Petra back to the classroom to collect their school bags. As they did, she chatted happily and he had to resist the impulse to take her hand. He just itched to kiss her, to hold her!

"I have to go back to the Deputy Principal's office," he explained.

"I know. Poor boy! It vill be alright," she said.

"I hope so. See you tomorrow," Willy answered.

Petra smiled and once again he had to resist the urge to take her in his arms. *Oh! I'm in love!* he thought. But he did not want to make her worry about him being too possessive, so he waved and turned away, only glancing back to her admire he as she went towards the gate. Once she looked back and waved and he went on with a lighter heart.

He met up with Stick and they made their way back to Mr Fitzgerald's office. Once again, they had to sit and wait until Miss Hackenmeyer arrived. When they were called in Mr Fitzgerald listened again to their story, but this time Willy minimised the 'conspiracy theory' and did not mention Petra by name.

Miss Hackenmeyer looked doubtful but did concede it was unlikely they could have taken out the paper plane, smoothed it and thrown it in the few seconds between when she spoke to them and when it struck her.

In the end she stated that she would be satisfied with an apology and a promise not to make any more paper planes in class. Willy nodded but carefully answered, "I promise not to make any more paper planes in your class Miss."

At that Mr Fitzgerald looked sharply at him. "No, don't be a bush lawyer boy! You will promise not to make any more paper planes in class, and that means all the classes in this school."

"Yes sir," Willy replied, abashed and peeved he had been so quickly caught out.

"Now no more nonsense from either of you! Off you go!" Mr Fitzgerald said sternly.

Willy and Stick quickly left the room and hurried downstairs. Relief was the common emotion. As they came out into the walkway they were confronted by the sight of the school's army cadet unit forming up for its Wednesday afternoon 'Home Training' parade.

It was the first time Willy had really seen the army cadets close up and, in a group, and he was quite amazed at their numbers. *They look like they have more kids than us,* he thought.

Stick indicated the groups of camouflage clad cadets standing in their ranks out on the grass of the quadrangle and snickered. "Mob of bloody noddies," he commented.

Willy grunted agreement but wasn't quite so sure as his roving gaze picked out the faces of some of the cadet leaders. *That CUO over there is Garth Grant and he is my 'House' captain in sport; and the one next to him, Broughton, is the top academic of Year 12. They can't be all dumb,* he mused.

Then his eye caught sight of Graham Kirk standing in the ranks of the second group. *So the rumour is true. He has been made to join the army cadets,* Willy thought. That surprised him because he understood that the Army Cadets, like the Air Force and Navy Cadets was a voluntary organisation. *But then the rumour did say that he was in trouble of some sort and it was either join or get chucked out of the school.*

At that moment, a senior cadet standing on his own at the front of the parade called loudly: "Companeeee, Attteennnn, Shun!"

Willy stopped to watch. *This should be interesting,* he decided.

Stick didn't think so. "Come on Willy, their drill isn't as good as ours," he grumbled.

"Maybe not but I want to see how they do things," Willy replied.

Still grumbling and muttering insults about the army cadets Stick stood with him while the army cadets were marched 'On Parade'. The procedures were basically similar to how the Air Force Cadets did things but some of the words of command and orders were different. The small difference held Willy's interest until the OC, Mr Conkey, now transformed into Captain Conkey, went on parade.

"I like Old Conks," Willy commented.

Stick grunted. "Huh! Just another teacher. They all treat you like you are an idiot," he replied.

Willy had to hold his tongue. *Don't say it!* he cautioned himself. He didn't want to end the friendship. Across his mind slid an image of naked Marjorie and the wicked thought crossed his mind that he would like to see her again.

As though able to read his mind Stick said, "Do you want to come to my place this afternoon?"

"Yes please," Willy answered.

So the friends walked to the bike racks, only for Willy to get another nasty shock. This time both his tyres were flat!

Bloody hell! Who is it? he wondered.

Chapter 9

TEMPTATIONS

Willy stood there, staring at the two flat tyres as a swirl of emotions sickened him. Hurt surprise turned to deep anger but mixed in with both were horrible feelings that anyone should not like him and then a mixture of anxiety and doubt.

Who dislikes me so much they want to hurt me all the time? he worried. It all made him feel very distressed and quite ill.

Stick didn't help. "What again!" he cried. "Who have you annoyed Willy?"

"I don't know," Willy answered, looking anxiously around. But there was only them. The only other people in sight were the distant army cadets who were now marching off to lessons.

"Looks like you won't be coming over then," Stick commented.

"Yes I will be!" Willy answered between gritted teeth. "I have two spare valves."

Stick gave him a look of surprised admiration which made Willy shake his head. It had been obvious to him that if his enemy struck again as the bike had two wheels then at some stage this must happen. He took the valves from his bag and knelt and screwed them in. Then he took out his pump and inflated the tyres.

The two boys then pedalled to Stick's. As they parked their bikes Willy was pleased to note Marjorie poke her nose out the front door. She gave him a smile and then vanished. Stick led the way upstairs. At the front door he called loudly, "Marjorie, are you home?"

"Yes, why?" came the answer.

"Are you dressed?"

"What is it to you?" was Marjorie answered.

Stick scowled. "I have a friend with me and I don't want him to get offended," he called back.

"I bet he wouldn't mind," was Marjorie's cheeky reply.

Willy's imagination filled with images from his previous visit. *I wouldn't either,* he thought hopefully.

But Stick was in a bad mood. "Don't you embarrass us!" he growled. Leading the way inside he turned to say, "Sorry Willy. She can be a real pain sometimes. She's discovered boys and takes great delight in teasing me and my friends."

"I saw her last time," Willy admitted, hoping he would see her again.

He did, but she was wearing shorts and T-shirt, a very tight yellow T-shirt and a very short pair of shorts. Willy couldn't help himself. He ran his gaze over her and thought, *She is very nicely rounded for her age!*

But Stick told her to go away and to leave them alone. Marjorie's response was to poke her tongue at Stick, give Willy a mischievous grin and to scuttle out of sight before Stick could hit her.

Drat! Willy thought. Then he blushed at his own wicked hopes. Then shame at being disloyal to Petra made him feel quite bad and he tried to drive wicked thoughts of Marjorie out of his mind. Instead he began discussing model aircraft with Stick.

When he arrived home that afternoon Willy was surprised to find his father already there. Of even bigger surprise was finding the dining table littered with the plastic parts of a small radio-controlled model.

A high wing monoplane, Willy thought, mildly irritated that he could not immediately name the type. "What's this, Dad?" he asked.

"It's called a 'Champ' and it's for learning to fly," his father answered.

Willy moved over to look more closely at the model. A glance showed that it was mostly a clip together type of kit. A radio control lay on the table nearby. "What sort of motor does it have?" he asked.

His father pointed to a small shiny blue and black cylinder with a propeller attached at one end. "Electric."

"Battery powered?" Willy queried. He had read about them but hadn't made up his mind whether he preferred electric powered models or ones with petrol engines.

"That is the battery being charged there, a three point seven LiPo," His father indicated.

"Can we have a go now?"

His father shook his head. "No. It has to be assembled and tested and then we need somewhere to try it out," he explained.

"We could go to the park," Willy suggested, pointing in the direction of the nearest park.

His father shook his head. "Not necessarily. There are laws and regulations about flying things like this, for safety. I need to check but I think that most of Cairns is inside what is called Controlled Air Space. That is for real aeroplanes."

Willy knew that from Air Cadets and nodded. "So where then?"

"We might go up and see Aunty Isabel and Uncle Ted on the weekend," his father replied.

Willy liked that idea. It was always nice to visit the farm, which was in the Davies Creek area about 50 kilometres to the west off the Kennedy Highway between Kuranda and Mareeba. "Where did you buy it, Dad?"

"On the internet, from one of the hobby shops in that magazine of yours," his father answered.

"How much?"

"Too much for you. The plane was one hundred and fifty dollars and the control console cost nearly the same," his father answered.

That answer dashed Willy's hopes of buying something similar. It was way outside his normal budget. *I will have to do some work and also save up,* he thought. But that immediately introduced a dilemma. He was saving money in case Petra was allowed out on a date and he also wanted to be ready to buy her things like birthday presents. *I will need to watch my money,* he decided.

Inspired by the idea Willy made his way to his room and set to work to draw the plans he needed for a balsa and tissue Sopwith Camel. That kept him busy for the next two hours and involved a lot of careful measuring and mathematical calculations as he converted the diagram he had in the book to the scale he wanted.

Thursday was an easier day. Willy was careful to avoid trouble at school and spent all of his free moments with Petra. He felt sure that their relationship had now moved onto solid ground and he felt elated every time she touched or spoke to him.

She is just so wonderful! he marvelled.

But that afternoon he got another jolt to his ego. On reaching the bike racks with Petra he again found both his tyres flat. And this time he had forgotten to buy two more valves! *Oh damn!* he thought. He burned with embarrassment as he felt sure that Petra must be thinking him stupid.

She was very sympathetic and again squeezed his arm. "Vot for vill anyone do such a thing?' she commented.

"Because of you I think," Willy replied.

"Me!" Petra cried in astonishment. "Vy because off me?"

"I think you have a secret admirer and they are jealous of me," Willy explained.

Petra looked both pleased and worried. "But you not giff me up?" she queried.

Willy shook his head emphatically. "For you I will swim flooded rivers, climb mountains in a cyclone and fight crocs bare handed," he replied before he realised just what a grandiloquent declaration he was making. Then he blushed.

Petra looked astonished and then very pleased. She reached out and drew him to her and then kissed him full on the lips. "You are the vonderful boy!" she said as she released him.

Willy was delighted and embarrassed all at once. At that moment he would have fought any enemy for her but did not say so. Instead he shrugged and muttered that she was wonderful too.

Petra simpered and took his hand and they set off, Willy wheeling his bike. This was fairly difficult but he persevered. After seeing Petra safely home he kept on walking, detouring to the nearest shopping centre to buy more valves.

This time he bought four and that left him with almost no pocket money. The walking had consumed several hours so he was nearly late for tea when he got home. This time he had to explain what had happened and his father just shrugged but his mother frowned.

"Why would anyone do that?" she asked.

That put Willy right on the spot so he shrugged and muttered, "Because a girl likes me and I think some other boy is jealous," he answered.

"Over a girl?" she queried.

"Just a theory, Mum," Willy answered.

"You are too young to have a girlfriend," his mother said.

"Aw Mum! Fair go! A man has to start some time," Willy replied.

His father looked up from the paper and nodded. "That's right young Willy. You need to make women a lifelong study to have any chance of understanding them at all, and even then you'll often be in trouble for either doing something you shouldn't have, or for not doing something you should have. And you won't be told which," he explained

As he said this Mrs Williams turned to him and put her hands on her hips. "Oh is that so!" she cried.

Only then did Willy's father realise that he might have said the wrong thing. "Er, yes dear. It can be. I'm just giving the boy a bit of advice," he muttered.

"That's not the sort he needs. He needs the birds and the bees bit so that he doesn't do something silly and get himself or some girl into trouble," Willy's mother snapped.

"Yes dear. I'll speak to him," his father answered, trying to not grin as he did.

And he did. For half an hour Willy had to sit through a 'father and son' talk which clearly embarrassed both of them on things Willy mostly knew anyway. Except that his father being a doctor made it all a lot more technical and specific.

Anyway, I'm not thinking of anything like that with Petra. She is too innocent and too nice, he told himself. Then he had to try to drive out mental images of Marjorie to stay loyal to Petra.

That evening, after doing his homework, Willy worked on his model aircraft plans, all the while fantasising about Petra, and battling with lustful images of Marjorie and other girls.

Marjorie even appeared in his dreams that night, tantalising him with erotic images and giving him a very restless night. *I must stop thinking about her. It is Petra I love,* he chided himself.

Friday was the school Sports Day. Willy wore a yellow T-shirt, the colours of 'Cook House', and set off happily to school. He didn't mind sports or games but wasn't particularly skilful. What he was hoping for was to get a chance to be alone with Petra.

But she turned up wearing the green of 'Flinders' House and that separated them while the houses paraded and chanted war cries at each other. All Willy could do was smile at her every time he saw her.

Then there was the pleasure of seeing the other girls in their short sport's dresses. *Heavens!! There are some horny looking chicks!* he thought as his gaze roved over the hundreds of girls.

For the next few hours he threw himself into all the activities he could: javelin, discuss, shot put, running, long jump, hop-skip and jump, a long-distance relay and a 400-metre race. Very quickly Willy decided that had not been a good decision. After a hundred metres he was puffed and by two hundred he was gasping and had a stitch.

Petra cheered him on from the sidelines and then ran out onto the track and ran with him, urging him to keep going. "Run Villy, run!" she cried.

The spectators laughed and there lots of calls of 'Willy' and 'Villy' and then 'Will he?' That got Willy burning with annoyance and embarrassment.

Scott shouted, "Use your rocket Willy!" This caused more laughter and a chant went up: "Run Villy, run!"

Scranton's sneering face appeared. "Not will he. It should be can he?" he jeered.

Petra poked her tongue at the crowd but kept running beside Willy. "Come on Villy, I der kiss give you if you vin," she offered.

With that incentive Willy pushed himself and he did win. Gasping and with his heart hammering fit to burst he pushed himself into a last-minute sprint to cross the line just ahead of Luke. As soon as he had been to the teacher who was recording the results, he pulled Petra aside. "What about that kiss?" he whispered.

"Not here! Not vith everyones looking," Petra cried.

But where could they go? Willy thought fast and looked around. He knew they were not supposed to leave the oval. Then an idea came to him. "Come with me," he said.

The pair pushed their way through the cheering, shouting throng to the more open area beyond. Willy then pointed and said, "Behind the swimming pool."

"A svim would be ver nice," Petra answered.

It would too, Willy thought.

He had never seen Petra in a bathing costume and now wished he had. To his relief she trotted happily along beside him. By the time they had passed the basketball courts the crowd had thinned out to almost nothing and apart from a few students walking to or from the main buildings they were alone.

We are a bit conspicuous, Willy worried. But he was bursting with happiness and had to resist the temptation to hold Petra's hand. *She is going to give me a kiss!*

The school pool was built on a mound of earth because the water table in that part of the city was so close to the surface. They walked across past the end of the school's swimming pool outside the safety fence and looked around the far side. Here there was a strip of grassy mound and lawn 75 metres long with a garden bed and fence on the other side. These screened the area from the street. On the other side of the street were houses and buildings.

But to Willy's disappointment the place wasn't deserted as he'd hoped. Sitting on the grass were four people, and two of them were smoking. Even as Willy's mind registered the forbidden activity, he recognised Stephen. Beyond him was Graham Kirk sitting on the mound and facing a plain but busty Year 9 girl with dark hair. Beside Stephen and also smoking was another Year 9 girl, a big, busty brunette who Willy did not know.

The Year 9s all looked at him. Willy saw Stephen and the brunette quickly hide their cigarettes behind their backs. Stephen scowled. "Bugger off Willy! Find somewhere else," he snapped.

Willy did not feel like making it an issue. With a shrug he turned and led Petra back the way they had come. As they came out past the end of the pool, they met Scott. He was hurrying towards the oval. He looked at them suspiciously and said, "Hi Willy! What are you two doing?"

"Just going to the toilet," Willy lied.

To add appearance to his tale he turned left and walked towards the main buildings. After fifty paces he glanced back to check if Scott was watching them. He was but he was also talking to Mr Fitzgerald while pointing across to the far side of the swimming pool. A grim-faced Mr Fitzgerald nodded and headed in that direction and Scott turned and hurried off towards the oval.

The bloody dobber! Willy thought. His first instinct was to run around the far side of the pool to warn Stephen and Graham, but he realised he would be too late. Instead he walked slowly and led Petra to one side to watch from the other side of a garden bed near the main hall.

A few minutes later his suspicions were confirmed. Stephen, Graham and the two girls, all looking upset and anxious, appeared with Mr Fitzgerald. Graham and the dark-haired girl turned and headed for the oval but Stephen, the brunette and Mr Fitzgerald turned the other way and made their way towards the main buildings.

"Bloody Scott, he has told Mr Fitz about them," Willy whispered as he and Petra sat behind the screen of plants.

After they had vanished from view Willy looked around. They were in between two of the long buildings of the Technical College part of the campus and there were a number of nooks and crannies that appeared to suit his purpose. "What about along there?" he suggested, pointing to the nearest one.

Petra nodded, and as they stood up she took his hand. That had an electric effect on Willy, and he began to get aroused. Quickly he led the way along to where a small corner was hidden by some lockers. As he stepped into it he glanced back, and saw Scott walking by towards the main buildings. Scott glanced at them but kept going.

Did Scott see us? Willy wondered. *And will he dob on us?*

For a few seconds he contemplated going somewhere else but at that moment Petra melted into his arms and the temptation was too strong. Hotly aware that he was fully aroused Willy put his arms around her and began to kiss.

I hope she doesn't mind, he worried.

She didn't appear to. In fact Petra hugged him and pressed herself hard against him while returning his kisses. It was wonderful and Willy surrendered to the sheer pleasure of it. Getting more and more heated and aroused by the moment he returned her kisses and hugs with interest.

This is wonderful! he thought.

Then a niggling worry caused him to draw back and to look around. *We really should move,* he decided. *I don't trust Scott. He might be the secret enemy.*

"We had better get back to the others or we could be in trouble," he said. Petra pouted and was reluctant to leave. Instead she kept pressing and rubbing against him

Reluctantly Willy stepped back and took her arms from around his neck. "Come on, we'd better go. If you get into trouble with the Deputy Principal, he might tell your mother."

A look of horror crossed Petra's face. "Oh yes! That be terrible. I be in the real trouble zen."

So they strolled back towards the end of the building. As they reached it Willy let go of Petra's hand and glanced to his right, and got a nasty shock. Scott was hurrying towards him and pointing at him, and ten metres behind him was Mr Fitzgerald!

He did dob! The bloody rat! Willy thought.

Mr Fitzgerald called loudly. "Stop! Wait there you two!"

Willy did, now deeply embarrassed at both being caught and by his aroused state. He was sure that it must be very obvious to both Scott and Mr Fitzgerald.

Mr Fitzgerald stopped and glared at them. "What are you two doing?" he queried.

Willy shrugged. "Just walking around sir," he answered.

"Not the usual 'just talking' eh?" Mr Fitzgerald retorted sarcastically.

Willy blushed but stood his ground. "No sir," he croaked. Out of the corner of his eye he noted Scott hurrying away towards the oval.

Mr Fitzgerald pointed that way. "Get back to the oval and stay in your own house areas. I don't want to see you two together for the rest of the day. Now get!" he growled.

Willy and Petra did. As they hurried towards the oval Willy said, "Phew! At least he didn't order us to the office. Sorry."

"That's alright. Good ve not in the trouble but pity ve have to stop," Petra replied.

Willy could only agree, and his heart hammered faster as his hopes shot up. "Some other time then," he suggested.

"Yes please," Petra replied.

I'm in luck! Willy thought ecstatically as he headed for his own house.

But there was also a score to settle. *Scott, where is he?* Willy wondered.

Chapter 10

ENEMY

Is Scott my secret enemy? Willy wondered as he went looking for him among the crowd.

He found him with John and Stick. They were watching the Year 11 girls doing long jumps. Scott saw him coming and looked like he wanted to sidle away except he was hemmed in by the jump and the supervising teachers.

Both Stick and John greeted Willy normally but then went silent when they noted Willy's stance and face. Willy stopped close to Scott and placed his hands on his hips. "Did you just dob on us Scott?" he demanded.

Scott looked uneasy and his gaze flicked right and left as though he was seeking a way out of it. "No," he muttered.

Willy snorted his disbelief. "You did so! I saw you pointing at us!" he cried.

Stick and John both stood watching and others turned their heads, their attention attracted by his tone of voice. Willy didn't care. He was deeply angry, and memories of the flat tyres and long walks stirred his anger. "Did you let down my bike tyres and steal the valves?" he queried.

"No. I haven't touched your bloody bike," Scott replied.

"So if it wasn't you, who was it?" Willy snapped.

"You said it was Jason Branch," Scott cried, his nervousness very evident.

That brought an instant change to the situation. From nearby came Branch's voice. "Who's saying I did what?" he demanded to know.

Branch shouldered his way between Stick and John and confronted Willy and Scott. "So, who's accusing me of things?" he snarled.

Before Willy could speak Scott gestured to him. "Williams is. He claims you have been letting down his bike tyres."

Branch turned to glare at Willy. His lip curled derisively. "Letting down you bloody tyres! Why would I do that? Why should I bother with a little First Year wart?" he said angrily.

That question really put Willy on the spot. There was no way he was going to make a public statement of his suspicions that his secret enemy was attacking him out of jealousy over Petra. So all he could do was shrug and mumble.

Branch stepped forward. "Is that what you've been saying Williams?" he asked.

Willy defiantly met his eyes but even as he did the thought crossed his mind that Branch was not his secret enemy. "I did," he replied.

"Why?" Branch snarled, bunching his fists.

"Because you were giving me such a hard time at cadets," Willy answered.

Again astonishment showed on Branch's face. "Giving you a hard time! Bull! I haven't been picking on you, even if you are pretty slack and deserve it. But I will from now on. You turn up at cadets and I will make your life misery," he threatened.

For a moment the two eyeballed each other, both breathing fast and with fists raised. Then Mr Page intervened. "You boys stop that! Jason, get out here and rake this sand," he called.

Branch gave Willy another hard glare and then turned and walked back to where he had been helping the teacher smooth the sand in the jump. Willy stood there watching him, trembling in every muscle and breathing hard. Inside he felt sick.

If Branch wasn't an enemy before he is now, he thought miserably. The threat about cadets hit him hard.

The anxiety over whether to go to cadets or not that night upset him for the remainder of the day. So ill did Willy become that he started to tell himself that he could tell his mother he was sick and stay home. But that idea stuck in his craw.

That just means I am a bloody coward and he wins, he thought bitterly.

So out of stubborn pride Willy determined to go to cadets. All afternoon at home he hid his anxiety, and even when he was dropped off at the Air Cadet Depot he was able to put on a brave face until his mother drove away. Then he stood in the semi-darkness of the car park and calmed himself, all the while glancing around for Branch.

Yet when cadets began Branch barely glanced at him. He certainly snapped at him a few times over allegedly poor drill, but he did that to most of the cadets and Willy was left baffled and wondering.

Branch says he didn't do anything to my bike. So who did? Who is my secret enemy? he wondered.

During the evening Willy noted several cadets writing on a list on the squadron notice board. Out of curiosity he went over to look and saw it was a sheet for people to nominate themselves for the drill squad. Willy quickly added his name to the list.

As he did Branch walked past. He stopped and looked. "Huh! Fat chance Williams. Your drill is so poor it looks like it is being done by a spider that has been stepped on. You can't even stay in step with yourself," he commented in sneering voice.

Willy bristled at the insult, knowing he was much better. Restraining the impulse to reply he just nodded and walked away. *I'll show him!* he told himself. But he realised it might not be that easy. The sergeants would undoubtedly be asked their opinions on who should be selected for the team. It was a worry, but Willy determined to try.

On Saturday the family drove up to the farm at Davies Creek. Uncle Ted and Aunty Isabel were Willy's favourite relations and he always enjoyed trips there. But this one was even more enjoyable. His father brought the radio-controlled model and Willy got a chance to fly it several times. He also learned more about how such models were controlled.

His father pointed to the control console. "We are using three radio channels at once here. One is controlling the motor. The next is controlling the elevators and the third is controlling the rudder and ailerons," he explained.

Willy understood all of that having long since mastered the theory of flight. Now he set his mind to grapple with the functioning of the radio-controlled electro servo motors that moved the control surfaces on command. So when his father set the bright yellow model on the concrete floor of the big machinery shed facing out over the back paddock his own finger itched with the desire to be the one doing the controlling.

That first flight was a bit dodgy, but Dr Williams got the model to take off and Willy's heart lifted with it. "It flies great, Dad!" he cried. But then it was heart in mouth for a few minutes while his father struggled to keep control and then managed to turn it round and bring it back for a rough but safe landing. His father made several experimental flights before allowing Willy a go.

"Start slowly and increase the motor speed bit by bit. I will hand launch, that's how the book recommends starting. You try to fly her straight and level. No fancy stuff and if she looks like stalling level out and increase revs," he said.

Willy first tried moving the controls while his father held the model steady in front of his eyes. Only when his father was satisfied that Willy understood which way to move the control joystick and buttons did he nod and say, "OK, give us half revs and I will launch."

Willy did so and a moment later the model went flying slowly forward. It just had airspeed and began to lose height, so Willy cautiously increased the engine speed. But he was a bit too anxious and pushed the 'throttle' too far. At once the model went zipping forward, its electric motor humming loudly. Before Willy could work out what to do the model ploughed into the ground and went cart-wheeling along.

Feeling sick at heart at possibly having broken his father's model Willy ran over to it. His father and Lloyd joined him, and Uncle Ted called encouragement from the shade of the big shed.

The model wasn't broken but it needed a bit of adjusting and the propeller seemed to be slightly out of true. Willy looked anxiously at it and then at his father. "Can I have another go, Dad?"

"Yes. You need to try again to get confidence. Half revs and get ready," his father answered.

This time the model buzzed forward and Willy got the speed right. But instead of losing height it went into a sharp climb. Willy tried to correct but instead overcorrected. The model went into a steep dive and before Willy could move his fingers it had ploughed into the ground nose first. A cloud of dust flew up and a yellow wing went flying.

Oh no! I've bust it this time! Willy thought unhappily.

He had. The propeller was obviously bent on its shaft and the wing would have to be reglued.

Lloyd punched his arm. "You little toad! I wanted a go too," he cried.

Their father intervened. "That will do Lloyd. Accidents are bound to happen. It is my fault for not buying two or three of these things so we all had one to learn on. Now bring the model and we will go and have morning tea and then see if we can fix it."

They could. It took a couple of hours of careful work but by evening the model was flying again. This time Lloyd was given a go and to Willy's delight he crashed it a couple of times, giving him a chance to retort. Luckily, the model wasn't broken in either crash and Willy's father had several more flights. The battery had to be changed and the old one put on a charger. Willy was then given a go. This time he asked if he could take it off from a standing start on a 'runway'. That worked. He pointed the model out of the shed and set it going. It lifted off before it reached the edge of the concrete and then Willy had the pleasure of flying it around the bottom paddock for nearly ten minutes before he brought it back and landed it.

That wasn't quite as successful as he cut the power a fraction too soon and the wheels touched down on the rough gravel of the driveway instead of on the concrete. The result was that the model pitched up on its nose and then ended up upside down.

Lloyd jeered. "Ah ya dumbo! Crashed it again!" he called.

Willy hurried over to the model, hoping it hadn't been damaged. He was lucky. It hadn't been. It was a very happy boy who carried it up to the house as the sun set.

That night, when lying in his bed Willy read a book about the very earliest exploits of aviators back in the early years of the 20th Century. That set his imagination working, and after the lights were switched out he lay in the darkness and fantasised about making himself a wood and canvas biplane powered by the engine from a motor mower. Then he pictured himself taking to the air in this frail contraption, struggling through increasingly worsening weather to rescue Petra.

Except that Petra turned into a naked Marjorie in his dreams and he woke feeling both very aroused and very guilty at being so disloyal.

Sunday was a repeat with two flights for each of them. There were fewer crashes as their skill and understanding increased, and it was with real regret that the flying finished and the family packed up to go home. Best of all his father mentioned that he would buy several more models they could all have one to fly.

"And my friends too?" Willy asked.

"Yes, and your friends," his father agreed. Willy was delighted and thought he had never been happier.

But back at home Willy had to complete homework before he was allowed to work on the plans for his rubber powered model. Even though he had now enjoyed the pleasure of powered flying he was still determined to make his own model.

And once again he daydreamed about flying in Wright Biplanes and Bristol Boxkites and fantasised about rescuing Petra. He fairly itched to get to school to see her.

And he did. They met at the bike racks. She gave him a big smile and then asked, "Did you remember to bring the spare walves for your bike?"

Willy nodded. "Yes I did. But I need to buy some more." he added. He had brought money and was thinking of going to the shops that afternoon.

John also wanted to go to the shops. He put this idea to Willy as they waited for the teacher for Period 1. Willy agreed but then went and sat with Petra.

There was no Tomfoolery in class. The warnings had been too stark for that. Instead Willy concentrated on his lessons and on fantasising about Petra. To his dismay he became aroused nearly all the time and then his thoughts wandered to images of Marjorie.

During the morning break, while he was sitting with Petra, Willy saw Stephen walk past towards the office. "Steve, what happened to you on Sports Day?" he called.

Stephen paused and made a face. "Lorna and me? We are in deep shit of course. We have lunch time detention all week."

"What about Graham and the other girl?"

"Mandy? No, they got off with just a talking to," Stephen replied. Then he hurried on to join his friends.

For the remainder of the day Willy concentrated on being nice to Petra and on doing all his schoolwork. John asked if he was still coming to the shops after school, but Willy shook his head and mumbled that he was busy. What he didn't say was that first he wanted to walk Petra home and after that he wanted to go to Stick's. To his own shame he knew he hoped to get another glimpse of Marjorie with nothing on.

In this he was disappointed. She wasn't home and Stick was playing a computer game with Noddy. So Willy sat and chatted until he felt he had been social enough. Then he went home and played on his own computer and worked on model plans.

Tuesday began well. Petra met him at the bike racks and they sat together as much as possible. Classes were just a drag enlivened by the antics of Callum and Vincent during English. Then, while Willy had his head down working, a paper plane landed on his desk. Mystified and slightly annoyed Willy picked it up. It had a note printed on it that read:

WILLY IS A WIMP

The insult really hurt. Willy looked sharply in the direction from which the plane had come but everyone there was apparently busy working. *Who threw this?* he wondered. For a minute his eyes roved over the boys in that direction: Bert and Roger? No. Callum and Vincent? Maybe. John on his own? No. Stick and Noddy? Very possibly. *But I thought Stick was my friend,* Willy thought unhappily. The idea that someone in his class did not like him was a real blow to his ego.

But there was nothing he could do so he crumpled the paper plane and went on with his work, glancing up from time to time to check if anyone was looking at him or getting ready to throw another plane.

I'm getting paranoid, he told himself.

At lunch time Willy sat talking to Petra. As he did, he noticed John and Stick running in circles playing a game with model aircraft. *They have got plastic kit planes,* Willy noted. Knowing that it was against the school rules to bring toys to school he called to them when they got closer. "You guys will be in trouble if the teachers catch you."

Stick shook his head and John just shrugged. "It will be alright."

Willy could see that John held a 1:72 scale model Spitfire while Stick had a 1:72 scale ME109. "Whose are those?" he asked.

"Mine," Stick answered.

The two ran on, circling each other and making engine and machine gun sound effects with their mouths. Willy shook his head and transferred his attention back to Petra.

That set the pattern for the day. After school Willy walked Petra to near her home and then he jumped on his bike (No flat tyres today!) and pedalled over to John's. The two boys then made their way to the shopping centre. With some trepidation Willy locked his bike into the bike racks but a hard look in all direction showed no sign of either Scott or Jason Branch.

No obvious enemy in sight, he thought. But the nagging anxiety remained as he realised he did not really know who his secret enemy was.

At the hobby shop Willy first selected the sheets of balsa wood he wished to purchase. These were three sheets of 2mm thickness each 75 centimetres long and 15 centimetres wide. Another sheet of 1mm balsa and a tube of Tarzan's Grip wood glue completed the list.

Then he joined John, who was looking at plastic kits. John held up a box of a 1:72 scale model of a B17 Flying Fortress. "I might buy this one. I don't have any big four engine planes like your Lancaster," he said.

"That's a good idea," Willy agreed. His gaze then settled on a 1:72 scale Bristol Beaufighter. *I would like one of them,* he thought. Into his mind's eye came the famous World War 2 newsreel taken by Damien Parer of RAAF Beaufighters attacking Japanese ships in the Battle of the Bismarck Sea. "I will buy this one," he added.

John looked a bit jealous but nodded. "A Beaufighter eh? The Japanese nicknamed them the 'Whispering Death' because of all the guns and rockets they carried."

Willy knew that from reading *Biggles in Borneo* but he just smiled and nodded. "They certainly carried a lot of guns," he agreed, trying to count them from the drawing on the cover of the box.

While they were doing this Callum and Vincent arrived. "Wotcha doin'?" Callum queried.

"Buying parts for our model aircraft competition," Willy explained.

"Oh yeah?" Callum asked. "What's that?"

The competition was explained and the boys bent to study the array of models on sale. Vincent picked up a drone. "These are good," he said.

"They are," Willy agreed. From his reading he knew quite a lot about the various types of drones, particularly the ones used for military purposes.

John said, "The army use these for spying on the enemy."

"They do," Willy agreed.

"Do the air force?" Callum asked.

Willy wasn't sure. "Don't think so. But they certainly have U.A.Vs but the ones they have are small radio-controlled aircraft."

"U.A.V.? What's that?" Callum asked.

"Unmanned Aerial Vehicle," John said.

"Uninhabited I think it is," Willy corrected.

That led to a bit of an argument and the problem of words like man not being gender neutral annoyed Callum. He picked up a small toy quadcopter. "Anyway, whatever! My little brother's got one of these. He flies it around inside the house."

At that John laughed. "You should try flying it around the classroom when Hackenmeyer's got us," he cried.

They all laughed at that idea. Callum then pointed to a large drone nearby. "What's that thing called?"

"A quadcopter," John suggested.

Willy shook his head. "No. Quad means four. That's got eight rotors. It must be an octocopter."

Callum frowned. "So what would they call this one with six rotors?"

"A sexcopter?" Willy suggested.

At that Callum burst out laughing. "Sex coptor!" he cried. "That's what you need, you and Petra."

Willy was instantly on the defensive and hurt. "Why do you say that?" he said.

Callum grinned, "Because that's what you two will be doing if you keep on carrying on like you did in the library the other day," he replied.

Willy experienced a rush of erotic memories and blushed. "She's not like that," he said angrily.

"They are all like that, mate!" Callum retorted. "Rape is the wrong man."

That concept hurt and Willy was annoyed that they thought so badly of Petra. "She's a nice girl. She isn't like that," he snapped between clenched teeth.

"Not what I've heard," Callum replied.

"She's not! Stop saying things like that!" Willy snapped, clenching his fists and glaring at Callum.

Callum shrugged and John looked anxious. "Suit yerself!" he muttered.

John ended the incident by talking about how photographers used drones all the time and this led to a discussion on how they were also used a lot by scientists.

"And surf lifesavers," Vincent added.

"What do think of drones Willy?" John asked.

Willy shrugged. "I've got one at home and it's alright," he said. It was only a cheap toy one and he had actually flown it into a wall and was damaged, but he didn't want to admit that.

"We could have a drone race," John suggested.

"No!" Willy snapped. "We will stick to real aeroplanes this time."

That ended the argument and the boys completed their purchases and then walked back to their bikes. Once again Willy felt a spurt of anxiety as he remembered his secret enemy but to his relief his bike was untouched. After placing the Beaufighter kit in his school bag he climbed onto his bike, clutching the balsa sheets in one hand. It was a bit awkward riding with them across his handlebars, but he managed it alright.

After seeing John home Willy rode to his house and parked his bike. The balsa and glue were placed in the workshop next to the plans for his Sopwith Camel and he went upstairs. After tea and homework he went down and set to work carefully tracing the outlines of wing frames and other parts onto the balsa sheets. Then he started carefully slicing the parts out using a razor.

On Wednesday Willy went to school with a light heart, humming to himself in pleasurable anticipation. But to his disappointment Petra was not waiting for him at the bike racks. He stayed there himself, watching for her but she did not appear before the bell went.

Mystified and a little bit worried, he made his way to the classroom but she wasn't there either. Now anxious that nothing had happened to her he sat in his usual seat. But it felt very lonely with her empty seat beside him. A glance showed that John was looking at him. He was also still sitting on his own.

Now I know how he feels, Willy mused.

There was no option but to settle to his work. That kept him busy but not happy. Anxious thoughts slowly morphed into daydreams which in turn became romantic fantasies. Sketches of home-made biplanes were added to notebooks and then the romantic fantasies turned to more sexual ones as images of Marjorie slipped in.

During the morning break Willy sat with John, Stick and Noddy and they discussed model aircraft. Scott was there too but Willy ignored him. As on the previous day John had his 1:72 scale model Spitfire and Stick had his ME109. John gestured to Willy, "Willy bought a new model kit yesterday, a Beaufighter," he said.

Stick looked interested. "Is it any good Willy?" he asked.

Only then did Willy remember that the new kit was still in his school bag. "I think so. I've got it in my bag. I'll show you at lunch time if you like."

So he did. After a period of Maths and another of PE was the lunch break. Willy dug the model kit out of his school bag and carried it and his lunch down to where the others usually sat. Stick and Noddy were there, but not John.

"Where's John?" Willy asked.

Stick chewed a mouthful of sandwich and then swallowed it. "Over at the tuck shop," he answered.

Noddy also swallowed a mouthful of food. Then he crumpled his lunch wrapper and dropped it on the ground before wiping his hands on his shorts. "Let's see this model kit then," he said, holding out a hand.

Willy reluctantly handed over the cardboard box. For a minute or so Noddy studied the coloured drawing on the lid and read the information on it. Then he levered the lid up.

The rough way he did this annoyed Willy. "Careful Noddy! Don't tear it!" he called.

Noddy just shrugged and bent to study the hundreds of plastic parts. Willy took the lid back off Noddy and held it.

Suddenly the lid was whisked out of his hands. Willy looked up in surprise. Two of the Year 10 bullies stood there: Scranton and Carstairs. Willy felt his heart rate shoot up with what he liked to think was anxiety rather than fear.

Scranton looked at the picture on the cover. "What's this Williams? Are you still a little kid who plays with toys?" he said sneeringly.

"Plays with himself more like!" Carstairs added, reaching out for the box. Noddy looked up at him in astonishment but kept hold of the box. Carstairs scowled. "Give it to me shitface!" he snarled.

Noddy tried to move the box out of his reach. But then Scranton suddenly grabbed the box. Noddy tried to pull it away and said no, at which Carstairs hit at him with his other hand. Noddy ducked, but in the process the box was torn and tipped up. The hundreds of tiny pieces cascaded onto the concrete.

Willy felt his fear being replaced by rage. Angrily he stood up and tried to push Scranton away as he moved to step on the pieces. Scranton pushed back and glared at him. In an attempt to save his model Willy decided to risk a kick in the face. Quickly he stepped around Scranton and bent to try to pick up the pieces.

As he did Carstairs moved to block him and in turn raised a foot to stomp on the small parts. Then another person blocked Carstairs and pushed him aside. Willy looked up and saw it was Andrew Collins.

Carstairs looked at him astonishment, then snarled, "What the buggery are you doing? Mind your own business."

"Leave them alone," Andrew replied evenly. His body language indicated he was willing to stand his ground. Both Scranton and Carstairs turned and adopted threatening gestures.

By then Willy had stood up and now he raised his fists to support Andrew. With obvious reluctance both Noddy and Stick stood up as well.

Carstairs snarled, "Bugger off Collins, before we rearrange your ugly face."

Andrew tensed but ignored him. Instead he turned to Scranton and said, "Give Willy back his box."

"Get stuffed! Make me!" Scranton retorted.

Andrew placed his fists on his hips and faced Scranton, then said to Willy, "Willy, pick up the parts before they get stood on."

"You'll get stood on!" shouted Carstairs angrily. "Leave 'em where they are Williams, or else."

Another person came and stood beside Willy. It was Stephen. He took his glasses off and put them in his pocket, then stood blinking at Carstairs, plainly taking sides and ready to fight. That action really sent Stephen up in Willy's estimation. Then John arrived and joined Willy. He also had a plastic model aircraft kit which he tucked under his arm.

There was a tense stand-off for a minute and then Andrew said, "Give back the model kit Scranton."

Scranton glanced around and licked his lips nervously, then tossed the box at Noddy. "Here! Take yer stupid toy, little boy!" he cried. Then he quickly turned and walked away.

Seeing he was left alone Carstairs quickly retreated as well. "We'll get yez later," he threatened.

"I wouldn't advise it," Andrew replied. He then turned and pointed down. "Pick up those pieces quickly," he instructed. Willy and Stick at once knelt to do so. Andrew bent down to help and said, "What is it a model of Willy?"

Willy showed him the picture on the lid. "A Beaufighter," he answered.

"Have you got many plastic models?" Andrew asked.

"Yeah, about a dozen," Willy replied. Then he gestured towards John. "John here has got hundreds. They are great!"

"I think that is all," Andrew said, his eyes scanning the concrete for any more tiny parts. "Are many broken?" he asked, studying the pieces piled in the box.

Noddy shifted a few with his fingers, then shook his head. "Don't think so. Most are still attached to the sprue."

"You shouldn't bring models to school," Andrew commented.

John nodded and said, "That's what I told them. Stick had one broken last week."

"I like them," Stick defended.

Willy nodded. "I didn't mean to. It was in my bag from yesterday," he explained. Then he looked at Andrew and Stephen and said, "Thanks."

Andrew smiled and he went on his way. Stephen turned to the others. "Are you guys still making rubber powered models?" he asked.

"Yes," Willy assured him. "These are just for fun." He then explained the radio-controlled model his father had brought.

John sniffed. "Easy for you! Both your parents are doctors and they've got plenty of money," he said.

"They are for all of us," Willy replied, sharply conscious that he had touched a nerve.

Noddy now spoke. "I am still going to bring my model plane to school tomorrow. Those bullies don't scare me."

Willy liked the idea but not the notion that they would be breaking the school rules about toys. "We could get into trouble from the teachers," he commented.

"Ah, ya sook! What a wimp!" Noddy jeered.

Stick took up the challenge. "I'm game. I'll bring a model."

"Me too!" Scott added.

That stung Willy's pride, but he did not reply. Feeling more hurt than he cared to admit he turned and walked away, struggling to hold back tears. He took his model kit and put it back in his school bag. As he did, he kept an eye out for Scranton and his cronies. When he returned to the spot he found the others were all gone. Instead of looking for them he went away to mope on his own. Shrugging philosophically he walked around, thinking hard about life, love and secret enemies.

That got him fretting about his bike, but when he went to the bike racks after last class he was relieved to find it undamaged. There was still no sign of Petra, so he rode home feeling quiet hurt and lonely.

Chapter 11

LITTLE DISASTERS

The implied insult to his courage was the reason why the next morning Willy carefully placed one of his 1:72 scale model aircraft, a Spitfire, in a plastic lunch box with balls of tissue paper to protect it from accidental damage. He knew it wasn't wise, but he was so upset by the jibe about his courage he felt he had to take the risk.

And he wasn't the only one who brought a model. John had one and so did Stick. Willy learned this when he got to class after waiting for Petra. When she didn't appear, he was downcast but tried to put a brave face on it.

Feeling very left out and isolated Willy sat alone in class and worked. John came and sat with him during History and Willy was grateful for that. When lunch time came, he took his model aircraft from the lunch box and joined the others.

Noddy was holding a 1:72 scale ME 109 and Stick had a FW 190. Willy turned to see what Scott had and saw it was a Hurricane. Deciding that he needed to make peace he said, "That looks good Scott."

Scott nodded and smiled. "Better than these others," he replied.

"Oh I like that!" Noddy cried.

"Ours are better," Willy said, a flash of anger at Noddy's comment the day before sparking him. On an impulse he held his model Spitfire as though it was flying and dived it at Noddy's plane. "Cop this! Tata-tata-tata-tat!" he yelled.

Noddy sprang up and twisted his model away then tried to swing it around to point at Willy's. Stick and Scott at once joined in and within a few seconds the boys were running in circles, their models pretending to dive and shoot at each other. Willy knew they were being silly, that the ruckus could attract a teacher's attention, but he was in no mood to stop so he kept on the 'dog fight' game.

During a pause during which they were all catching their breath Andrew Collins walked over. "You kids will get into trouble if a teacher sees you," he warned.

Noddy curled his lip and shook his head. "We can run faster than them," he replied.

Andrew smiled and said, "And what about Scranton and Carstairs? Can you run faster than them?"

The mention of two of his known enemies caused Willy to hastily look around. So did Noddy. "Scranton? Is he here?"

Andrew shook his head. "Haven't seen him but you kids should be more careful." Then he looked at the model in Willy's hand and said, "That's a Spitfire isn't it Willy?"

"Yes, it is," Willy answered. He liked Andrew and was pleased that the older boy had remembered his name.

Andrew then admired the other models. He handed Stick back his FW 190 and again cautioned them. "Keep an eye out for the bullies, and the teachers. See you later."

He strolled away and the boys at once resumed the game. But as he dived his model onto the tail of Noddy's ME109 Willy happened to glance to his right. *Mr Page!* he thought, noting the Senior Geography teacher coming towards them through a throng of students. "Stop! Stop! Quick, hide! Mr Page is coming," he cried.

The others glanced around and then fled. All four raced off around the nearest corner and kept going until they were several buildings away. Here they gathered behind yet another corner and Willy leaned over and peeked back.

Noddy nudged him. "Any sign of him?"

"Can't see him," Willy replied.

Whereupon the game resumed. Once again, they chased around in circles, yelling excitedly and pretending to fire multiple machine guns as they did. The sound effects had the inevitable consequence of attracting attention, in this case the wrong sort. Willy found his path blocked by Mr Conkey. He came to a gasping standstill and whipped the model behind his back.

Mr Conkey waited till all four boys had stopped running and yelling. "Stop the nonsense you boys," he growled. "It is unsafe. No running on concrete. You might trip or knock someone over."

"Yes sir," Willy muttered, still holding his model behind his back.

Mr Conkey made a face. "And you can stop the farce of hiding the models. I saw them. So show me them," he ordered.

Reluctantly the boys did so. *I hope he doesn't confiscate them,* Willy thought, knowing that the school rules allowed that. Then parents were phoned to come and collect the items.

Mr Conkey looked at each model in turn. "And you put these together yourselves?" he asked.

"Yes sir," they chorused.

"They are quite good, but they are also banned under the school rules. Toys lead to unsafe activities, jealousy, fights and theft, and then tears. So go and place them on my desk in the staff room and collect them after school. Move!"

Relieved they moved. When they knocked on the staff room door and Mr Hamilton queried what they wanted there were a few anxious moments but most of the teachers who were working at their desks just smiled and went on with their work when they saw the boys placing the models on Mr Conkey's desk.

Feeling better Willy went off with his friends to sit and chat for the remainder of the lunch hour. "Could have been worse," was the general consensus. "It could have been Old Buggermaster!"

They all agreed with that. *At least this way we get our models back and the parents aren't called in,* Willy mused. He went off to his next lesson feeling much better. After the last period he went with the others to collect their models. Mr Conkey lectured them again and then let them collect them.

Willy then walked with his friends to the bike racks, only to discover that his secret enemy struck again. Once again both his bike tyres flat, but this time not only were the valves gone but the tyres and tubes had been slashed.

Willy stared at the flat tyres and swore. Then a sharp bout of distress made him feel both ill and angry. A quick glance in all directions revealed no-one apparently looking or gloating over his troubles.

John and Stick were sympathetic, but both said they had to be home early so could not help him. They took their bikes and rode off, leaving a very upset Willy standing there.

For a few moments he contemplated phoning his parents and getting a lift, but then stubborn pride took over and he decided to walk. It was a decision he regretted half a dozen times as he had to walk kilometres to the nearest shop that sold bike tubes and then he had wait while the man there took each wheel off and replaced the ruined ones. That exhausted Willy's available funds and also added to his sense of grievance.

Once again it was late when he finally pedalled home. This time his parents demanded an explanation. Rather than lie Willy admitted he had a problem. When his parents learned that his bike tyres and tubes had actually been cut they were both horrified.

"That is criminal damage! That is a police matter," his father cried.

His mother nodded. "Have you told the school?" she asked.

"No Mum," Willy replied. So far his parents did not know about the paper planes and he did not want them talking to the school in case they found out.

But that hope faded immediately when his mother shook her head and said, "Well, you will tell them first thing tomorrow. Make sure you do. I will check."

"Yes Mum," Willy agreed.

That evening he did his homework and then sat and worked on his balsa model. That at least took his mind off his bigger problems. But it introduced little problems of its own. Willy found he had trouble cutting accurately along the ink lines he had traced and marked. Also when he tried to cut long, straight 'stringers' of balsa the blade of the scalpel would sometimes veer off and follow the grain of the wood, cutting diagonally across the piece and ruining it. In the end he had to cut a third more than he had planned to get the required number.

I hope Petra is at school tomorrow, he thought as he drifted off to sleep after another bout of daydreaming.

She was, but even though she smiled she did not look happy. Willy raised an eyebrow and said, "Are you alright Petra?"

Petra nodded and forced another smile. "Yes, thank you. I the very well am," she replied. But her lower lip quivered slightly, and he felt sure something was wrong.

"Have you been sick?" Willy asked as he tried to think of a policy to gently probe to find out what was really wrong.

"Yes. Sick," she agreed.

She certainly did not look well. Her face was pale and she shivered from time to time. "I am alright now," she assured him.

With her beside him Willy's spirits lifted. He began to chat happily, describing the clash with Scranton and Carstairs and the progress on his model. She listened and smiled from time to time but said little. But when he told her about his bike tyres she was horrified.

"And have you the office told?" she asked.

"Not yet," Willy admitted.

"Zen you do it now," she said.

Reluctantly Willy agreed and they walked to the main office. There Willy had to wait his turn until Mr Fitzgerald was free. Petra sat with him and when he was talking to the deputy she stood nearby.

After listening, Mr Fitzgerald glanced at Petra. "Last time you were in trouble you had a theory as to why this person might be targeting you. Is that right?" he asked.

Willy glanced towards Petra and then wished he hadn't as Mr Fitzgerald also looked at her. "Yes sir," he admitted.

"You might be right. Well, the closed-circuit TV might give us a clue. Let's go and look and you can show me where your bike was parked."

He led the way into the office and Willy had to point out his bike on the monitor. But ten minutes of fast forwarding the previous day's recording did not solve the problem. During the day nobody entered the bike racks area and after the last bell there were just too many students all moving at once or blocking the direct line of the camera. Willy saw a number of people he knew but none of them was a person he considered an enemy.

Having drawn a blank Willy returned to Petra and they made their way to the classroom as lessons had now begun. Again they sat together and that cheered Willy and also got him very aroused when Petra touched him with her knee or hip.

It would have been a very enjoyable day if the nagging worry about his bike being interfered with hadn't continually bothered Willy. To try to prevent this he went to where he could see the bike racks during the breaks. Petra was happy to stand with him after he explained why he wanted to be there. But he saw no-one acting suspiciously.

During the lunch break at school on Thursday Stephen and Stick stopped to chat. Stephen said, "I've bought another rubber powered model if you guys would like to come and watch it fly this afternoon?"

Having no other plans, Willy agreed. *But first I will walk Petra home,* he thought. Then the image of his slashed tyres came to him and he shook his head in anxiety. *If I haven't been sabotaged again!*

He hadn't been. To his great relief, his bike was untouched and he was able to wheel it along while walking with Petra. Once again, he wished they could hold hands or kiss but he did not push the issue.

"See you tomorrow," he said at the corner.

Petra nodded but had to obviously force her smile. That bothered Willy but there was nothing he could do about it, so he set off on his bike for Stephen's.

The model was a Japanese World War 2 Zero. It was about 40 centimetres long and was a dark green colour with the red roundels of Japan on wings and fuselage. When Willy came around the corner near Stephen's it was flying out across the street and it looked really good. Stephen, Stick, John and Noddy were there and went running after it.

Willy parked his bike as Stephen wound up the rubber bands and then placed the model on the bitumen road. Then he released the propeller and then the aircraft. The red plastic propeller become a crimson blur and the model rolled forward quickly on it black wheels and after about a 5-metre run it lifted off and climbed very gracefully to about head height before the propeller stopped. It then glided down to a good landing.

That was good! Willy thought, though not without a twinge of jealousy. He hurried to park his bike and join the others and was then astonished to find that the model was actually made of polystyrene. It was very light but surprisingly strong.

Stick was first to the model after the next flight. Despite Stephen's protest he picked it up. "Can we have a go?" he asked.

Reluctantly Stephen agreed. "Just be careful. I don't want it broken," he said.

Stick wound the propeller until Stephen stopped him. "It is tight enough. You will break something if you wind it too tight," he said.

Stick did a good job, despite Stephen standing beside him with twitching fingers and an anxious look on his face. The model did a good take off and flew right out across the street. Then John wanted a go. He also made a good job of it so Stephen allowed Willy to try.

Willy was very careful and his flight gave him a little thrill. The model lifted off nicely but then there was a gust of wind that caused it to yaw and turn to port. For a moment Willy feared it would hit the fence, but it actually got caught in a rosebush. Luckily no harm came to it so Stephen allowed Noddy to have a go.

Noddy chuckled as he wound up the rubber band while walking back across the street to Stephen's. Once there he set the plane down on the driveway and aimed it out into the street. As he did Stephen said, "Wait Noddy. Wait for this car to go past."

But Noddy didn't. He released the model and it went whirring forward, lifting off and then flying straight out across the road. Stephen swore and ran after it and Willy stood, hand to mouth watching. To him it seemed that car and model must meet but then the model skimmed over the roof of the car. Willy saw the car driver jerk back and the car swerve before driving on. The model landed as light as a feather in a flower bed across the street.

Stephen picked it up. "You bloody nong, Noddy! You could have caused a crash!"

"Aw, sorry!" Noddy replied.

Luckily, the game wasn't over as Stephen allowed Stick another go. That went well so John was given a chance. His flight went very well, despite the wind catching it. Then the model was handed to Noddy.

Noddy began winding vigorously. Stephen watched with mounting concern. "Not so hard Noddy it might…. Bloody hell!"

Something had gone snap inside the model. Noddy looked foolish and then quickly passed the model back to an angry Stephen. Willy stepped closer to look. He saw that a small bamboo rod which had been passed through one side of the rear fuselage to protrude out of a small hole on the other side had vanished inside. When Stephen tried turning the propeller there was a clattering, scrunching noise inside.

Shaking his head with annoyance Stephen unclipped the nose cowling and slid the propeller and its mounting off the model. A twisted skein of long rubber bands followed and then the small bamboo rod. It had snapped.

Noddy looked at it. "Oh that's nothing much," he said.

Stephen glared at him. "It is! It is what holds the other end of the rubber bands. Without that it doesn't work."

"You can easily fix that," Noddy replied defensively.

"Maybe," Stephen answered. "Oh well, sorry you blokes but that is it for a while. Let's go in and see if we can fix it."

The boys all made their way into Stephen's lounge room and he organised cordial and biscuit before sitting down with a Stanley knife and a bamboo skewer from the kitchen. He cut a rod of the required length and then began the tricky job of tyring to reconnect the rubber bands to it inside the model. Willy moved to help.

"Let me hold it for you," he suggested.

Stephen did. Then he concentrated on trying to slide the rod through the four dangling loops of rubber. After a few tries and a bit of swearing this was accomplished.

Noddy saw this and rubbed his hands. "Oh good-oh! Let's have another go."

Stephen shook his head. "Not today. I've got to get my homework done."

"Aw!" Noddy cried.

Stephen was adamant. "Thanks for coming over. Maybe next week after school."

"Why not tomorrow afternoon?" Stick queried.

"Because I'm supposed to go to a cadet bivouac," Stephen replied.

That got Willy's interest. "Cadet bivouac?" he enquired.

Stephen nodded. "Yeah, but I don't really want to go."

Willy was astonished. To him any cadet camp was a desirable activity and the weekend field camps called bivouacs he really liked and wanted to take part in. "Why not?"

Again Stephen shrugged. "Because I don't really want to be in the cadets," he answered.

To Willy that was also unbelievable. For him Cadets was the most important thing in his life. *Or almost,* he thought as a vision of Petra flitted across his mind. "So why are you?" he queried.

"Parents made me," Stephen answered shortly.

He said this in such a frosty tone that he quite discouraged Willy from asking why. Instead he asked, "Where are you going?"

"Place called Davies Creek. West of Kuranda, off the road to Mareeba," Stephen replied.

At the mention of Davies Creek Willy's interest was sparked. "My uncle and aunt have a farm near Davies Creek," he said. What he really meant was he was jealous and wished he was going on a cadet bivouac too. He had only ever done one and that had been just an introduction to living in the field and basic fieldcraft and he really wanted to do more challenging things. "You army cadets do lots of bivouacs don't you?"

"We do," Stephen replied, "About one a month."

Noddy sneered. "Air cadets have better bivouacs," he said.

"Do not! Mob of softies!" Stephen retorted.

"Do so!"

The argument built for a few minutes before Stephen's father appeared from the back of the house. "That's enough you kids. It is time you went home. Stephen, you go and do your homework."

The other boys stood and made their way out. As they mounted their bikes on the footpath Noddy said, "I'm going to take another model plane to school tomorrow."

Willy shook his head. "Not a good idea Noddy. We are in enough trouble already," he said.

"Huh! What's wrong with you? Are ya gutless?" Noddy jeered.

The jibe hurt but Willy could not think of any crushing re-joinder. Feeling quite put out and lonely, he mounted his bike and made his way home.

Do I have any real friend? he wondered. Then he sighed and shook his head. *But I certainly have enemies!*

Chapter 12

SCOTT

The following morning Willy met Petra as soon as she arrived at school and they sat together until the bell went. By now most other students just ignored them, accepting them as an 'item' and not really worthy of gossip. Willy was only vaguely aware of this but his ego was massaged by the sometimes jealous looks they attracted from others.

But first period was Science which Petra did not study so they parted and went their separate ways. He did not see her again until morning break and then only briefly. "I the cake in der oven haf," she explained, gesturing towards the Domestic Science block.

As she walked off, Stick sniggered. "Let's hope she hasn't got a bun in the oven! Haw! Haw!" he commented.

The insinuation really stung Willy. "She's not like that!" he snapped.

Stick curled his lip. "They're all like that mate, especially her," he retorted.

That hurt even more. "She is not! She's a good girl," Willy replied.

Stick shrugged. "Not what I've heard," he muttered. With that he turned and also walked away.

So Willy found himself upset and alone. As he strolled around looking for someone to talk to, he met Noddy. Noddy was all chatty so they discussed the model Zero of Stephen's.

As they did, Willy noted Stephen in the distance. He was talking to Graham Kirk and to two Year 10s: Wally Dru and Derek someone. Gesturing towards them, Willy said, "I wonder why Steve had to join the army cadets?"

Noddy looked and curled his lip. "I heard he was in big trouble with the police," he said.

"Oh yeah? Why?" Willy asked, his interest now aroused.

Noddy shrugged. "Don't know the details but I heard a whisper he was involved with some gang of Devil people who used to meet in the cemetery at midnight and they used to... used to do things like witchcraft."

"Black magic you mean?" Willy asked, both fascinated and horrified.

At a subconscious level he was superstitious but did not like to admit it, not even to himself.

"Yeah. An' they used to get drunk and do things ter girls and stuff," Noddy added, his tone indicating jealousy rather than condemnation.

"I heard something about that, but that was last year," Willy replied.

"Aw, I dunno," Noddy replied. "But I did hear there was some sort of gang fight and some kid got shot," he added.

Willy had also heard that rumour. He now pointed to Graham. "I heard Kirk was made to join the cadets too," he said.

Noddy nodded. "Yeah, but that was for fighting. I heard he was given the choice: join the cadets and do as he was told or be expelled from school."

"Not something to do with girls?"

Noddy shook his head. "Not that I know of," he replied, half regretful.

Then it was off to English and Willy was able to sit next to Petra and he quickly lost interest in school gossip and instead set about adding to it by surreptitiously nudging her under the desk and by holding hands while he daydreamed.

After school he quickly made his way back to the bike racks and was relieved to find that his bike had not been tampered with. Petra smiled and squeezed his arm and that restored him to good humour. Happily, he walked her to near her house and then made his own way home.

Being Friday it meant Air Cadets, so he prepared his uniform and then did some more work on his model. This led to a little disaster that upset him more than he cared to admit. By now he had assembled the fuselage section and to test the propeller he attached the rubber bands to the rod in the rear section of the fuselage and then to the small hook at the rear of the propeller. Then he began winding the propeller to put tension on the rubber bands.

Before his astonished eyes he saw the stringers of the fuselage suddenly begin to bow until it assumed a banana shape. But before he could let the tension off the rubber bands the whole rear section of the fuselage suddenly crumpled. The thin balsa stringers just bent and snapped.

Willy stared at the wreck in dismay. Dismay turned to blazing anger and all his pent-up anxieties and frustrations welled up. Then he lost his temper. "Hours of bloody work! All for nothing!" he cried.

He flung the wrecked model hard onto the bench, causing more damage. That action was instantly regretted, and his fury subsided as quickly as it had come.

Oh bugger! What a waste! he thought.

Then the tears came and he hoped his brother hadn't heard him. Slumping down in the chair he stared at the ruined model and pondered the nature of life. But as he calmed down other thoughts came to him, including his father's advice that there was opportunity in every adversity and set back.

Suddenly it dawned on Willy that in fact he had been given a good turn. *If that had happened when I had covered the fuselage with tissue paper and painted it and put the wings on it would have been an even bigger disaster.*

It was now obvious to him that the fuselage needed strengthening. But how? *If I use materials that are really strong the plane might become too heavy,* he thought.

In the end he decided to compromise by adding three ply 'girders' inside the fuselage. So he found an off-cut of three ply and weighed it with his hand. *Will it be too heavy?* he wondered.

He didn't know and decided the only way was to try it. But then it was time for tea and cadets. He went to cadets anxious that Jason Branch might give him a hard time, and he did. At the start of the second lesson the Cadet Warrant Officer, Discipline, WOFF Mathieson, called on all cadets who had put their names down for the Drill Competition to move to the parade ground for selection and training. Feeling very conscious that he was only a new recruit Willy made his way there.

Branch had also put his name down for the Drill Team and when he saw Willy he sneered and curled his lip. "What are you doing here Williams? Piss off! We don't want any First Years to bugger things up for us."

Willy burned with embarrassment as every head turned to look. But he stood his ground. "The notice said that there had to be First Years in the squad," he replied.

"Crap! Bugger off!" Branch snarled.

But WOFF Mathieson stepped between them. "That will do Sgt Branch. Cadet Williams is correct. There have to be two of every year level and also at least two girls. Cadet Finlay here is only a First Year too. Now stand there as marker. The remainder, form up in three ranks, move!"

Branch was obviously not happy but apart from flashing Willy a hostile glance he did as he was ordered. With his heart beating from the emotional aftermath of the confrontation Willy took his place in the rear rank.

Then the drill began, with two officers and the adult WO(D) watching and assessing on the sidelines. Determined to prove Branch wrong Willy tried his hardest. For thirty minutes the squad marched up and down and did dozens of drill movements, several of which Willy had not yet been taught but which he managed to do after watching the others.

After the squad was fallen out at the end of the period Branch just sneered at Willy and moved off to be with his friends. Willy was left trembling and anxious and wondering if he would be chosen for the team. *I suppose Branch will take it out on me now,* he thought as he went to the next lesson.

But, to his relief, Branch did not seem to notice him and from then on Willy found the evening a very enjoyable experience. Adding to the enjoyment was learning that there was to be a squadron weekend in October at which there was to be the judging of models. The models were to be in several categories: flying models, plastic kits, dioramas and were to cover both kit models and scratch built. The activity was to be conducted in conjunction with the Tri-service Drill Competition and would be at Mareeba. Willy listened with growing interest.

That sounds like it will be a great weekend. I must go to that, even if I don't make it into the Drill Team, he thought. Still hoping to be accepted into the Drill Team as well he logged on to Cadetnet, found that activity now listed, and clicked on the 'Nomination' button.

On Saturday Willy had very little time to himself. There were the usual family chores and then they went visiting relatives. It wasn't until late in the afternoon that he was able to get back to model making. After some thought he set to work on his theory of strengthening the fuselage. But first he had to dismantle the broken one. This turned out to be harder than he expected, and in the process he broke several more of the stringers and then discovered that the circular frames were mostly no good. By the time he had cut out the dry glue and pieces of stringer stuck in the notches around them they were weakened or the notches too big.

So he had to start making more and he quickly discovered that he was running short of the balsa wood he required. This was 2-millimetre sheet and he had only enough for three frames and he needed six new ones. Cursing his luck he made his way upstairs for tea.

Sunday was a bit better. In the morning he sat in the workshop cutting out new frames and then thinking about how to make stringers that were strong but light. His father gave him some clues by telling him to use girder construction. "Like engineers use to design 'I' beams of steel."

Willy made a couple with the thin strips placed together longitudinally but with the top and bottom strips at right angles to the main 'beam'. This seemed to work but after a while Willy lost interest and sat alone brooding. Girls fleetingly occupied his mind but most of the time he worried about who his secret enemy was, and why he did not like him.

What have I done to him? he wondered. In his mind he ticked off a list of friends to eliminate them from his suspicion list. But that only depressed him more. *I don't really have many friends,* he thought unhappily. It was borne to him that most of those he associated with weren't really friends at all. *They seem to laugh at me more than with me,* he thought.

That was an unpleasant thought and he was left feeling dejected and very lonely. *How can I get some real friends?* he fretted.

He was in the middle of a 'good fit of the dejections' when his father came downstairs and asked him if he would like to go for a drive to watch some powered aircraft being flown by the local model aircraft club. Willy was both interested and also shy. Despite feeling a bit anxious about meeting strangers he nodded and put down the model part he was holding.

An hour later father and son were standing in the sun beside a grass airfield near Gordonvale. About twenty vehicles were parked along the verge and four portable shade structures dotted the edge of the field. Willy estimated there were about thirty or forty people there, mostly middle-aged men. There were also dozens of model aircraft of seemingly every size and colour.

That got Willy out of the car and interested. But in such obviously expert company he felt very self-conscious so when his father said hello to several adults he just stood back and gave polite nods and one shy handshake to a grey-haired man who was introduced as the president of the club.

For the next three hours Willy sat and watched with a mixture of envy and awe. That most of the club's members were real experts, both in constructing and in flying the models, was quickly apparent. There were so many different model aircraft that Willy had trouble noting them all and he certainly could not decide which he liked the best. A model gull-wing Corsair with a wingspan as wide as a person's outstretched arms held him enthralled while it swooped, zoomed and climbed. It was then outdone by a petrol-powered Mustang fighter that flashed past and then rolled, swooped and did pretend strafing attacks.

Next, an immaculate model of an AT6 Texan did some quite dramatic aerobatics and then rolled to a stop only a few metres from Willy. A yellow and white painted Hangar 9 Sundowner then outperformed it but at a slower speed and with much less fuss.

Luckily, there was a public address system so Willy was able to follow what was going on. He was excited to watch a 'scratch built' twin-engine model of a De Havilland Comet, 1930s vintage, which flew fast and low and then circled the field looking magnificent.

Scratch built, Willy thought. *That is what I am trying to do with my Sopwith Camel.* It seemed to him to be a much nobler concept because of the much higher level of skill required.

But he still enjoyed the kit models and even the plastic 'snap togethers'. There were even a few electric powered models amid the roaring, growling petrol motors. But these seemed to be the poor relations in the pecking order of the club and they certainly lacked the noise and drama of the petrol-powered ones. So when Willy's father had a short go with their 'Champ' Willy felt quite embarrassed. And there was no way he was going to have a go with all those experts watching!

There were even a few drones, but the general feeling was that they weren't quite the thing and Willy agreed with that. Somehow, they seemed to lack the romance and drama of the 'real' model planes.

Even if they are very much safer and easier to fly!

But it was still a very enjoyable and instructive event for Willy and he went home happy and full of new ideas, as well as very sunburnt.

At breakfast on Monday Willy sat dreaming about what he would say to Petra when they met when his thoughts were diverted by his father who was reading the morning paper.

"It looks like some of the cadets from your school have been heroes," his father said, holding the paper for Willy to see.

Willy looked and saw a headline which read: HEROIC RESCUE BY ARMY CADETS and under it were two photos. One was of the remains of several burnt-out vehicles including a smouldering fuel tanker and the other was of two cadets being given First Air by a paramedic. Closest to the camera was Graham Kirk and beside him sat Stephen.

Good old Steve! Willy thought.

He had never thought of Stephen as being particularly brave but when he read the account of how they had helped an army warrant officer named Howley to rescue people from the burning vehicles he revised his estimate.

At school he saw both Graham and Stephen across the quadrangle. Graham had his hands bandaged and was looking embarrassed while Stephen was smiling and talking.

For a few moments Willy watched and then experienced what he knew was a real stab of envy. *I wish I could do something heroic,* he thought. *That would make Petra really love me.* But those sorts of thoughts got him anxious, worrying about how he would react if it was a real life-threatening situation. *Am I brave, or will I turn out to be a coward?* he worried.

Petra joined him soon after and asked what the fuss was. Willy raised his eyebrows. "Don't you get the newspaper?" he asked.

Petra shook her head. "Nyet. My mother and me we cannot afford such luxuries," she answered. "Vot those boys do?" she asked. So he told her the story. Her reaction was to sniff and then look glum.

"Are you alright?" Willy asked anxiously.

Petra nodded and perked up. "Yes. I fine am," she replied. But he could see she wasn't. However she would not elaborate, and he did not think it was his place to pry into her family affairs, so they chatted about Graham and Stephen.

During the day Willy had several opportunities to observe that being a hero had a distinct downside. On each occasion he saw or overheard Graham being teased or taunted by others who obviously did not like him. *They are just jealous,* Willy thought. But then he admitted to himself that he was as well.

School life then engulfed him and he found himself very busy working and trying to find time to talk to Petra. After the trouble of the previous week he was careful to be well behaved and he made sure all of his homework and assignments were done. This entailed spending the lunch breaks in the library to do research, an activity Petra was happy to join him in.

After school he walked Petra to near her house and then made his way home. Once there he settled to finishing his homework and then to working on his model aircraft. This set the pattern for the next few days. During them he learned a lot more about making model aircraft from balsa and tissue paper.

He found the new reinforced fuselage to be strong enough for the rubber band to be wound quite tight. That was encouraging. Then he turned his attention to making the wings and at once things went wrong. No matter how hard he tried, the wings warped out of true as the glue dried and the wood dried or expanded according to the humidity in the air. It was all very frustrating and three times he had to strip the tissue paper off the delicate balsa framework to get at the problem.

This involved re-doing parts of the structure. Sometimes this meant cutting out sections of stringers to replace them and several times he had to glue the structure and then clamp it with a vice and books to hold it in the correct shape while the glue or damp tissue paper dried.

The same problem arose with the control surfaces, the tail fin and stabilisers. But he persevered and apart from swearing a lot he managed in the end. By Wednesday evening he had all the main parts complete and was feeling good about himself.

School on Thursday was a normal day with no dramas and a lot of simple pleasure by being with Petra during the breaks. But the end of the day brought the usual tension as he approached the bike racks. To his relief, his bike was untouched and he was able to wheel it along while he walked Petra home.

They had only gone a block when Willy saw Scott riding the other way, a large model aircraft balanced on his handlebars. Willy at once recognised it as the Mustang aircraft kit Scott had purchased a few weeks before.

"Where are you going?" he called.

"We are flying our planes in the park near Steve's," Scott called back. He then leered at Petra and added, "Don't do anything I wouldn't do!"

Willy boiled with anger at the insinuation, but he held his tongue while Scott laughed and pedalled on.

'Vot he mean?" Petra asked.

Willy's mind raced as he tried to think of a suitable explanation. "Oh he was just teasing," he answered lamely. But he found the innuendo upsetting.

How can they think such horrible things about Petra? he thought. *She is so nice.* The words 'pure' and 'innocent' also flitted across his mind.

The incident seemed to sour the afternoon as Petra looked hurt and stopped smiling. That made Willy even angrier. *I will teach Scott a lesson,* he thought.

So once he had said farewell to Petra he jumped on his bike and set off for the park. When he got here, he stopped under a tree to one side to study the situation. There were four boys out in the middle of the park, but he only knew two of them: Scott and Stephen. Still unsure what strategy to adopt, Willy chained his bicycle to the tree, passing the chain through the front wheel and the frame before locking it.

Then he strolled out to join the others, pretending nonchalance but actually feeling quite upset and angry. As he approached them, Stephen placed his Zero on the concrete cricket pitch in the middle of the park and let the propeller go. A moment later the model rolled forward on its wheels, accelerated rapidly and then gracefully lifted off. Willy stared at it with fascinated envy.

The Zero lifted well above head height and then flew for nearly 50 metres before the rubber band fully unwound and it swooped down to a gentle nose-up landing on the lawn. One of the boys, a Year 9 from Stephen's class Willy now saw, ran to get it.

By then Willy was close and Scott was busy winding the rubber band on his Mustang. It looked shiny and new, and even though it was a plastic kit that was just clipped together, Willy still thought it looked good.

Then Scott glanced around and saw him. "Oh hello! Here's 'Rocket Man!'. I didn't expect you so soon. Did Miss Poke-a-lot give you the brush off?" Scott said with a sneer.

Instant anger surged in Willy. He stopped a few paces from Scott and placed his balled fists on his hips. "Don't call Petra names!" he snarled.

Scott sneered. "Why not? She earns them," he retorted. With that he turned his back and continued to wind the propeller.

Almost beside himself with jealous rage Willy stepped forward and grabbed at Scott's arm. "You take that back!" he cried.

"Or what?" Scott replied with a sneer. "Take your hands off me, Williams."

"Not till you apologise."

Scott snorted. "Huh! That'll be the day! Who's going to make me?"

Willy became even more angry and determined. "Me!" he snapped, raising his fists.

Again Scott curled his lip. "Go away Williams, ya stupid jerk! We are flying our planes," he retorted.

That infuriated Willy even more. Being called a jerk was bad enough but his strongly held opinion that 'scratch built' models were superior gave a sharp edge to his tongue. "That's not a plane! It's just a plastic toy. You didn't even make it. You aren't good enough," he shouted. He was aware that he was losing his temper and that the others were all watching but could not seem to stop himself.

"Better than anything of yours, ya little dickhead! Here Boyd, hold this."

Scott turned and passed the model to one of the boys and then came straight at Willy, fists flailing.

Chapter 13

THE SOPWITH CAMEL

Willy had not meant to provoke such a situation, but he gamely stood his ground. Before he recovered from his surprise at the suddenness and the ferocity of the attack, he suffered several hard punches to his face and body. Then he began to duck and punch back.

Scott landed several more punches, one of which split Willy's lip but his blood was up and he was determined to fight for Petra's honour, so he rushed in and returned blow for blow. For a few seconds there was a wild windmilling or arms and fists and both boys landed a few more hits on each other.

Then they stepped apart, chests heaving and fists raised. Willy studied Scott carefully, looking for an opening and was pleased to note that a trickle of blood was coming from Scott's left nostril and that he looked quite wary.

"Apologise!" Willy snarled.

"No!"

At that moment, Stephen stepped between them. "Hey, calm down you two! Stop fighting."

Willy tried to push Stephen aside. "He insulted my girlfriend."

Stephen made a face. "I heard, but it's how she behaves," he answered.

That both hurt and shocked Willy. He had never seen any hint of Petra flirting or misbehaving. "When? Where?" he shouted, raising a threatening fist at Stephen.

"Calm down! It's just something I overheard," Stephen said.

"Who from?"

Stephen shrugged. Then he shook his head and muttered, "Can't remember. One of the Year Twelves maybe," he said.

That hurt but by then Willy had calmed a little. He lowered his fists, wondering what to say. Scott lowered his but still glared at him. Stephen then said, "Anyway, you can settle that some other time. We are testing our planes now."

He gestured to the Mustang. By then the other Year 9 boy, Charlie,

Willy thought his name was, had returned with the Zero. Willy looked at the models and felt a strong desire to have a go, but there was no way he was going to ask and risk a rebuff.

Scott then twisted the knife by saying, "Our models are ready for the competition. Why don't we have it this weekend?"

That annoyed Willy. "But we agreed the second week of the school holidays," he replied. By now he was starting to hurt, some of the blows resulting in bruises and he could taste blood on his lips.

Scott shrugged. "If you've been wasting your time with Petra the Popsy instead of working that's your problem."

Willy again saw red and raised his fists, but Stephen again stepped between them. "That'll do Scott," he said. "We could have a preliminary competition this weekend and that would help us see what we need to do to improve. That would still give a couple of weeks to fix things. How about that?"

Willy thought of his half-completed Sopwith Camel and quickly calculated whether he could have it finished by the weekend. "What about Stick and Noddy?" he asked.

"We will tell them tomorrow," Scott answered.

Stephen nodded. "OK, Sunday after lunch, here," he said. "Now let's see if that thing flies, Scott."

They both turned their backs on Willy, leaving him feeling hurt and insulted. While he stood there with his emotions seething Scott's Mustang had its rubber band rewound and it was placed on the cricket pitch 'runway'. Willy secretly hoped it would crash but instead it took a good fast run and the lifted off without any trouble. It then flew straight for about 30 metres before settling to a bumpy three-point landing.

"That was good!" Stephen cried. "Your go now, Charlie."

Willy just stood and watched, feeling excluded and upset. After Charlie and Boyd had both had goes with the Zero and the Mustang without even a hint that he be given one, he felt near to tears. Reaction set in and he bit his lip. After watching for a few more minutes so that his withdrawal wasn't so obviously a retreat, he muttered, "See you tomorrow," and walked unhappily back to his bike.

It was a very lonely boy who pedalled slowly away, his eyes prickling with tears. *Scott is certainly an enemy,* he thought sadly. Which got him wondering yet again who his friends were.

At home Willy sat under the house and brooded for a while, aware that he had not handled things well but also riven by niggling anxieties. *Why did Scott say those things about Petra?* he wondered.

Then his gaze wandered to the pieces of the Sopwith Camel and he turned to it. After a few minutes he was absorbed by the technical challenges of assembling and testing.

His limited reading had made it plain to him that absolute perfection in symmetry was a key part of any aircraft design and construction, so he carefully measured the pieces he had made, matching them against their counterparts. Then he fixed the fuselage firmly on the table between two marble book ends. That allowed him to glue on and brace the two horizontal stabilisers. For twenty minutes he kept crouching every few minutes to squint at the pair of them, making sure they were exactly horizontal when measured by eye against a ruler placed across the books that supported them, and against each other.

I just hope their fore-and-aft set is correct for trim, he thought, knowing that even a tiny error would result in the model either diving into the ground or pitching up into a stall. Either way a crash would result with probable damage and certain embarrassment. What was clear in Willy's mind was that the model competition was no longer a contest between friends but had become serious rivalry.

The tailplane was then added and again carefully held in place while the glue dried. But by then it was teatime and he had to leave his work and go upstairs. Once there his mother glanced at him a couple of times and he hoped she would not notice his face. A couple of small bruises had now developed and there was a small scab on his lower lip. But to his relief she made no comment.

After tea Willy wanted to return to aircraft construction but his father ordered him to his room to complete assignments and homework. "You've got exams next week. You don't want to jeopardize your future by wasting time playing with toys," he said.

They aren't toys! Willy thought resentfully. But he did as he was told because he understood that becoming a pilot in the air force meant he had to get top marks all the time. *There are thousands of applicants for every position,* he told himself. So he sat and studied and got no chance to work on the model until he arrived home the following day.

At school that day he again met Petra and sat with her. But this time ugly, gnawing anxieties kept him glancing at her. She seemed her normal self, and even when he studied her from a distance he could see nothing in her behaviour to indicate she was anything but a modest and chaste young maiden.

They are just jealous, he told himself.

Being Friday night there was cadets. The main efforts were in preparation for those cadets attending the Courses Camp at Garbutt RAAF Base during the first week of the coming school holidays and Willy was very jealous.

I wish I was going, he thought enviously.

Instead the recruits were kept in classes studying aircraft recognition or on the parade ground improving their marching. During this Sgt Branch several times snapped at Willy, criticising his drill and hinting he was useless, but without actually abusing or putting him down. Willy just gritted his teeth and endured this, certain that his drill wasn't that bad.

He is another jealous enemy, he thought bitterly.

That night as he lay in bed he gave way to self-pity and there were a few lonely tears.

On Saturday morning Willy worked fast to get his chores done. *It is at least is earning me some pocket money,* he consoled himself. But as soon as possible he made his way to the workshop and resumed model construction.

The big job was to glue on the lower wings. Because they had to have dihedral, the upward tilt of the wingtips that helped the stability when flying, he took particular care to ensure that the fuselage was firmly secured on the table and that both wingtips were exactly the same height above the table top. He did this by using two pieces of timber which were the same thickness to rest the wingtips on after he had glued the base of the wing to the fuselage.

Then he had to leave it to dry. His fingers twitching with impatience he made himself stop touching the model and took himself off to play *Stormovik* on his computer.

After lunch Willy began the much more difficult task of gluing on the inter-plane struts and then the upper wing. The struts were difficult to stick on as they had such small ends and, as the glue dried, they kept slowly falling over. They had to be held in position or continually re-positioned so that they were in the correct alignment after the glue was dry. It took over and hour to glue on the four short struts atop the fuselage and then the four larger ones out on the lower wings.

By then Willy had the top wing ready. It was one single piece and was reasonably firm but slightly warped. Very gently he tried to twist the warp out of it, but the crinkling of the tissue paper and a tiny snapping sound warned him not to persist.

I hope it is good enough, he thought, his anxiety adding to his feeling of fluster. He was very conscious that the day was rapidly sliding by and he badly wanted to have a test flight in daylight.

Gluing the top wing on was just as tricky. The problem was that a small dab of glue had to be placed on top of each of the struts and then the wing positioned in its correct alignment on top of them. But as Willy quickly discovered that was easier said than done. Because there were eight struts, he found that by the time he had added a dab of glue to the top of each the glue had gone dry on the first couple.

The only remedy was to make the blob of glue large enough to still be slightly liquid when he finished. But that made them quite large and all were slightly different sizes. Still, there seemed no other option so that is what he did.

Then he found it was very difficult to accurately position the wing on top of those eight struts in its correct alignment. On his first attempt he did not set the wing quite square and had to pull it off before the glue dried.

"Or almost dried, drat it!" he muttered as he noted that two small pieces of tissue paper had ripped off with the wing.

Two more goes and some more torn tissue paper had the wings complete. Willy held the model up and admired it. *It really does look a biplane,* he thought. Then he considered whether to try to add the 'bracing wires' between the wings. *Cotton should be easy,* he mused. *But first the undercarriage.*

He now knew that the undercarriage was both the weakest part but also one of the most important. *Even a little irregularity and the model will not run straight on its take-off run,* he remembered. *And a weak undercarriage can just rip off in a landing on lawn.*

He had purchased the wheels and axle but the balsa struts and braces he had made himself and he now glued the whole assembly together and then turned the model upside down on the table to glue the whole lot on.

At last it was done, and he turned the model right way up and gingerly rested it on its wheels. Seeing it there, ready to fly, sent a warm glow of satisfaction through him. *If I paint it and add some markings it will look really good,* he thought.

With an effort he contained his impatience and allowed another half hour for the glue to dry. But it was sunset by then and in the shadow of the mountains twilight was already setting in. Feeling both stressed and anxious Willy carried his model out to the front driveway, which was the only suitable 'airstrip' he could think of. Gently but firmly he wound the propeller until the rubber band felt taut.

Not too tight, he told himself, remembering how the tension had crumpled the fuselage before. Keeping a firm grip on the propeller he lowered the model to the concrete driveway. He opened his mouth to call his father to witness the first flight. But then he closed it again and shook his head.

No. Better wait until I have proved it flies, he told himself.

Lining the model up so that it would run straight down the driveway Willy waited until there was no traffic in the street and then let the propeller go. To his delight the propeller whirred and became a blur. Then the model began to move, rolling slowly down the driveway. Quickly it picked up speed and just as Willy was gnawing his knuckles with anxiety it lifted off. The take-off was so smooth and so sudden that he could only gape in delighted wonder.

The model biplane climbed until it was about head height and then the propeller stopped. But Willy didn't care. He was ecstatic and stood watching, thrilled by the success of his project. But then his heart gave a lurch as the model suddenly staggered in the air. A light gust of wind had struck it beam on and it lurched and then stalled. Suddenly it swooped down. Willy cried out with anxiety as it looked as though it would dash itself to pieces on the bitumen roadway.

At the last possible moment, the model pulled out of its nose-dive and swooped upwards, missing the asphalt by only a few centimetres. Then Willy's heart again palpitated as the model again staggered and stalled. This time it was too low and too slow to avoid crashing and it ploughed into the front lawn of the house across the street. The model flipped and then landed upside down.

Gasping with anxiety Willy dashed down his driveway and across the street. As he did a car horn blared and there was a screech of brakes. Willy glanced to his left and his heart leapt into his throat in fright. A car had almost hit him and had managed to pull up only a metre from him.

"Sorry!" he gasped as he ran on across to the other side.

"Stupid bloody kid!" shouted the angry driver. The man changed gears and accelerated away.

For a few seconds Willy stood in near shock, his heart hammering and waves of hot and cold coursing through him as the nearness of his escape sank in. Then he shook his head at his own carelessness and moved to pick the model up.

To his relief it appeared to be undamaged. Sighing with relief he began to re-wind the propeller. He glanced at the neighbour's driveway but decided against using it as a runway. *I will hand launch,* he thought.

So this time when he let go of the propeller the model was at arm's length above his head and he carefully threw it forward with a smooth but rapid motion. With the extra height and momentum the model easily flew across the road, swooping up as it did, then stalling and swooping down again, to land heavily on his own front lawn. It then pitched tail up on the grass.

Willy hurried across and then felt his emotions boil. The whole undercarriage had been ripped right off. *The tissue paper has torn off,* he noted, anger and frustration fuelling his emotions.

The tears just came and he tried to stop them and to blink them away. As he did his mother's voice came to him from the front steps. "Time for tea Willy. Stop playing and get upstairs."

"Yes Mum," Willy replied, trying to hide his sniffles. Luckily, she turned away so his pride wasn't too badly damaged. But his emotions still seethed.

The competition is tomorrow! How can I fix this in time? he thought.

After tea he took the model to his room and studied the damage. *The tissue paper isn't strong enough. I need to glue the undercarriage legs to the frame of the fuselage,* he thought. As the tissue paper was already damaged, he carefully cut away small openings and then realised that the more solid parts of the framework underneath did not line up with where the undercarriage legs met the fuselage.

The only solution he could think of was to glue two pieces of balsa across to make a stronger frame under the aircraft, using small pieces of balsa at right angles to hold these firmly to the fuselage frame. Then he glued the undercarriage legs to the cross braces.

But by then it was too late and too dark to test fly the model so instead he drew four 4cm diameter roundels on a piece of white paper. Using a compass he drew two concentric rings inside each and then coloured them red, white and blue with felt pens. These were glued to the upper surfaces of the top wing and the lower surfaces of the bottom wings.

The 'markings' made such an improvement to the realism of the model that he then made two small ones for the side of the fuselage and a red, white and blue flag for the tail fin. He even added registration letters. *Now it looks really good,* he thought as he placed it on his bedside table.

He got an even bigger boost when his father came to say goodnight and saw the model. "That looks really great Willy. Did you make it all yourself?"

Willy nodded, glowing with embarrassed pride. "All except the wheels and propeller," he answered.

Later he lay in bed looking at the model in the half light from the streetlights while he fantasised about being a fighter pilot flying a real Sopwith Camel. *And I will rescue Petra,* he thought. He began a romantic daydream about it, the only fly in that ointment being that images of naked Marjorie kept forming in his mind.

He slipped into a deep sleep which was then filled with dreams about flying. But the images kept changing and he found he couldn't get his jet fighter up through all the powerlines that seemed to be across the runway, which had somehow morphed into his street, and when he heard that Petra was at the front door to see him he couldn't find his pants!

And it was Marjorie who was at the park the next day and not Petra. Willy rode his bike with his model in one hand, a fairly tricky operation and one which nearly resulted in two accidents. But he made it safely and chained his bicycle to a tree before walking over to join the others.

Waiting there were a whole group of people, nine or ten at least, and the sight of such a crowd sent his anxiety level shooting up.

Oh, I hope my model goes OK, he thought, anxiously aware that he hadn't done a test flight after repairing the undercarriage.

Among those present were Scott, John, Stephen and Stick. There was also a friend of Marjorie's a girl called Jocelyn with coke-bottle glasses and a younger girl who wasn't introduced but stood near Charlie the Year

9, plus a couple of boys Willy didn't know. Callum and Vincent were nearby and were flying a small radio-controlled quadcopter, the sight of which annoyed Willy a little.

We don't want battery powered things, he thought. *This competition is for rubber powered models.*

Then Willy noted Jason Branch and another Year 11 standing on the far side.

Oh no! Willy thought. Then he noted that both boys had model aircraft. Branch's was a large red and white plastic one with upturned wing tips and wire undercarriage legs. It was obviously a bought kit model but apart from secretly sneering at it Willy was careful to say nothing.

As Willy joined them and called a nervous hello Scott called loudly, "So you finally made it? We thought you might have gone to spend the morning with Petra the Plum."

That annoyed Willy and but when the Year 11 boy called, "You mean Petra with the nice bum!" he saw red.

For a moment Willy was so angry he almost lashed out but when Charlie and Stick also made comments about her having a nice bum he became quite agitated and confused. He wanted to scream that she was not like that, that she was a nice girl, but all he could do was meet Marjorie's eyes and note her amused smile. With an effort he restrained himself.

Don't react, he told himself. *They are just trying to get a rise out of you.*

So he pretended to ignore the hurtful comments and turned to Stephen. "So what do we do?"

Stephen gestured to the concrete cricket pitch in the middle of the open field. "That is the runway. Each model gets three flights. They get judged on how far they fly, how high they fly and how well they fly," he answered.

"What being judged on quality of construction?" Willy asked, hotly aware that his scratch built but unpainted model did not look nearly as good as the plastic and foam kit aircraft.

Jason Branch snorted. "Huh! Lucky for you we aren't judging how well they are made or that bundle of sticks would be scratched before the first race."

That hurt but Willy managed a smile. Stephen then had Charlie,

Noddy and another boy move to the far end of the cricket pitch. Their job was to bring the models back after each flight. When they were in position Stephen picked up his polystyrene Zero. "OK, I will go first."

The Zero was prepared and then placed on the runway. Willy watched with interest and some anxiety, remembering how well the model had flown on other occasions. And it did this time, flying 45 of Charlie's paces and over Noddy's head.

Then it was Scott's turn and he set his plastic Mustang flying. It went faster than the Zero but did not climb as high and only went 43 paces.

Noddy and Stick both teased him. "Yah! Piece of plastic crap!" Stick said.

He then positioned his model. Willy had not noticed it until then but now saw that it was a glossy plastic Spitfire painted brown and green camouflage on the upper surfaces and with new roundels and a small clear plastic cockpit cover. *It looks really good,* he thought, jealousy surging in him. His only consolation was that it was another bought kit.

The Spitfire got off to a great start. It ran fast and took off well but then it began to bank to port and suddenly went swooping off to nose-dive into the lawn. Being a robust plastic kit this did it no harm, but it only covered 32 paces out across the field from the end of the cricket pitch.

Stephen pointed. "Your go now Willy," he said.

Licking his lips with nervousness Willy moved to the end of the cricket pitch and carefully wound up the propeller. As he knelt to position the model he glanced up and found himself staring at Marjorie's legs.

They are too pale and too pudgy, he thought, *but heavens! Those shorts are short!*

For a moment his gaze dwelt on Marjorie's legs and then he looked up to meet her gaze. She was smiling and had a mischievous glint in her eyes. For a moment he stared, his thoughts racing and then he remembered where he was and bent to his model. After taking a big breath he nerved himself and let go. The Camel went racing along the concrete cricket pitch and then lifted slowly off.

It is too heavy now, Willy thought, noting that it barely cleared the grass at the end of the runway.

Nor did the model climb very high, waist height on the Year 9 boy, before its rubber band unwound and it began to descend. But at least it landed well enough, pitching up on its nose but not tearing off its undercarriage.

Willy would have liked to run out to pick it up but Noddy did so instead. As Noddy walked back he lifted the model into a launch position and called, "Does it glide Willy?"

"No! Don't!" Willy called, but too late.

Noddy flung the model as hard as he could. Then he stood and gaped with astonishment as the top wing just tore off from the air pressure. Willy stared in horror, but the damage was done. The model went into a sharp spiral and crashed to the lawn.

Running forward Willy cried out in anger. "You bloody nong, Noddy!" he shouted. "Now you've broken my model."

Dismayed and upset, he felt tears form in the corners of his eyes.

Chapter 14

TEARS

Noddy just sneered and shrugged. "So what? You can just glue it back on. Anyway, you should have added the bracing wires to stop that happening," he commented.

With rage and hurt flaring Willy glared at him but then turned and picked up his model and checked it for further damage. Luckily, there was none. Charlie brought him the top wing and Willy looked at it ruefully and tried to position it in place. But he hadn't brought any glue and two of the inter-plane struts were missing so he could only shrug and stand there, battling to restrain the tears.

By then the others were losing interest and John called impatiently, "Come on, my go!" The group turned away, all except Marjorie who came to stand beside Willy. "Sorry," she whispered. "It looked very nice."

Willy nodded but was in no mood to be comforted. Sadly, he turned to watch as John flew his model ME109. Being another plastic kit it was strong and well-made but it didn't fly at all well. On the first attempt it veered off the runway and went cartwheeling without even lifting off. On the second attempt the same thing happened.

Willy watched then stepped forward and pointed. "The wheels are too close together and not properly aligned," he said. "Twist that port wheel slightly to starboard and start the run over on the side of the runway."

Jason Branch sneered. "Oh what would you know Williams? This isn't a rocket," he said.

Willy was stung by the jibe and by the mocking laughter from others but ignored it. Despite the laughter John studied his model and then tried what Willy had suggested. Then he wound the rubber band up and let the model go. This time the model raced down the runway, still veering to port but managing to lift off just before it ran into the grass.

The model did not fly very well and looked unstable in the air, but Willy was happy that his friend had got it to fly.

"Well done!" he said.

"Thanks," John answered, giving him an embarrassed smile.

Stephen then had another go with his Zero. Willy watched it zip along the runway and lift off. As it did there was another zipping, buzzing noise and over the top of it flashed Callum's small drone. Loud laughter from their right caused everyone to look. Willy saw that Vincent was controlling the drone. Callum stood beside him grinning and slapping his thigh.

Stephen wasn't amused. "Stop that, you buggers!" he called as he ran forward to retrieve his model.

But Vincent didn't. As Scott tried to line his model up the drone buzzed in and began to hover over the cricket pitch. Scott looked up and shouted angrily, "Bugger off Vincent! Callum, take that bloody toy somewhere else!"

They did, flying the drone off to the rear and around the mango trees. The competition resumed and to Willy's annoyance and disgust it was Jason Branch's model which won hands down. It took off after a short run and then went climbing up to twice as high as any other model had before its rubber band unwound and then it dipped and swooped down in a graceful curve to almost stall and then swoop again, covering 57 paces before settling gently on the grass.

Marjorie clapped and jumped up and down at that and she smiled at Branch and chatted to him and that hurt Willy's feelings as well. *I thought she liked me,* he thought unhappily, surprised by how much it hurt.

When it came time to go home Willy said goodbye and went to his bike and unlocked it. Then he held his broken Camel and its loose top wing in his left hand and ran forward to get his bike moving. As soon as it was, he jumped on and began pedalling.

What exactly happened next he wasn't sure, but as his front wheel ran over one of the many exposed tree roots and bounced up the front wheel came off. To Willy's astonishment he saw it roll ahead. But before he could react the front forks of the bike went down hard and dug into the ground. The next thing Willy knew he was being catapulted over the handlebars.

As he came down the notion of trying to save his model flashed through his mind, but at the same instant he realised he needed both hands to break his fall so he let it go. Even so he landed heavily then rolled onto his back. As he did, he heard a distinct crunching noise and he knew with sickening certainty that he had rolled on his model.

For a few moments Willy lay there half stunned, but aware of loud, jeering laughter. That made him burn with embarrassment. Then hands reached down to help him. Stephen and John, both looking anxious, picked him up.

"Are you OK, Willy?" John asked as he dusted leaves and dirt off Willy's back and arms.

Willy nodded. He was more hurt in his feelings than bruised. "Yes thanks," he muttered.

As he did, he looked back. His eyes sought out his model and then focused on it. His worst fears were instantly confirmed, he had crushed it. The model was so badly damaged it was hard to recognise except for one wing. The rest was just a mangled tangle of tissue paper and broken pieces of balsa.

Jason Branch hooted with laughter and called, "That was good! Do it again Williams, ya clown!"

Others joined in the jeering laughter, including Scott but Willy noted that Marjorie looked sympathetic. He burned with anger and upset. To his added mortification tears welled into his eyes and he was unable to stop them.

To try to hide them he looked down at the smashed model. But not quickly enough. Jason Branch saw them and jeered again. "Ah Williams, ya big sook! What a cry baby!" he called.

Embarrassed anger helped Willy but several big tears still trickled down his cheeks. By then John had walked over and picked up his bicycle wheel and Stephen had knelt to look at the front forks. He brushed grass and dirt off and then frowned.

"Willy, the nuts on this have been unscrewed," he called.

A wave of cold shock swept through Willy as the implications of that hit him. *Sabotage!* he thought. *Someone here unscrewed them to make me crash.* As the emotions swept through him, he walked over and bent to look at the bicycle.

His already battered feelings were further assaulted by Jason Branch laughing and calling out: "Williams is a nut and he's got a screw loose!"

Scott hooted at this and Willy looked up and glared at him. "Someone undid these nuts deliberately," he said accusingly.

Scott stopped laughing and became instantly angry. "Well it wasn't me!" he cried.

Willy's gaze moved to Jason Branch and his Year 11 mates. "Well someone did," he said.

At that Jason also stopped laughing and at once curled his hands into fists. "You accusing me, Williams?" he shouted.

Willy met his angry glare but shook his head and then looked away. *I don't have any proof,* he thought miserably. What really hurt was the notion that his secret enemy must be here, in this group. A glance around showed almost no-one else in the park, Callum and Vincent flying their little drone, a man and woman with a baby on the other side, a man walking a dog a hundred metres away and a group of small boys kicking a soccer ball at the far end. *It must be one of these people here,* he decided.

Still sniffling and shaken Willy helped Stephen to reposition the front wheel. "How do we tighten these nuts?" he queried as he screwed them finger tight.

Stephen then pointed to his own bike. "I've got a tool kit on my bike," he said. He walked over to it and rummaged in a small leather bag slung under the seat.

As he did Willy's mind raced. *Did Steve do this?* he wondered. But why would he? *Does he dislike me for some reason,* Willy wondered. *But he always acts so friendly. Is that all it is, an act?*

It was all very puzzling and distressing. When the bike was repaired John handed Willy back his broken model. "Here's your plane," he said. "Pity, it was really good."

"Thanks," Willy said, taking the model and resisting the impulse to fling it on the ground. Knowing that everyone was watching he again mounted his bike and began peddling. This took some courage as he feared that something else might go wrong. But it didn't and he began riding off along the footpath, pursued by a few chortles of mocking laughter from Branch and Scott.

All the way home Willy's mind felt like a squirming bag of maggots. Doubt and distress kept boiling up so that more tears flowed. These so blinded him that he had to stop and get off. For a while he wheeled his bike, ashamed of his weakness and hoping that people in the passing cars or the houses he passed were not looking. The notion that he had an enemy who disliked him so much he was prepared to risk causing him a serious injury really shook him.

But who? he wondered. Thinking about the detective shows his parents watched on TV the old 'motive, method and opportunity' flitted through his mind. *Stephen certainly had the means,* he thought. But that didn't make sense. *He seemed so friendly. And he admitted he had them. Was that just a cunning double bluff?*

It was all very unsettling, and he switched his thoughts to trying to work out when it could have been done. But that was no good. *There were so many people there and so many walking or running around nobody would have noticed,* he thought. He certainly hadn't, his whole focus being on the aircraft models.

By then he was home and he sadly wheeled his bike in under the house. He dumped the crumpled model on the workbench and slumped down to look at it. Frustration and anger welled up and then the burning memories of his humiliation quickly turned to tears. Now he as alone he began to weep, self-pity and distress fuelling his tears.

A knock sounded on the door frame. Willy gulped and tried to hide his tears. Quickly he wiped at them, but too late. His father was standing in the doorway. Shame at being caught crying caused more distress and more tears threatened to spring out.

His father came into the workshop. "I saw you come home," he explained. "What happened?"

Battling to stem more shameful tears Willy wiped his face, stifled his sobs and told his father. Pride and determination not to be weak while his father was there helped. His father listened and was sympathetic. At the end he said, "So you have a secret enemy who wants to embarrass you?"

"He could have killed me, if that wheel had come off in the traffic," Willy cried.

His father nodded. "Maybe. But I doubt if the person had thought of that. So who do you think it is and what have you done that has set this situation up?"

The notion that it was somehow his fault startled and hurt Willy, but he had to concede he must have done something to make an enemy. But he couldn't think of anything except Jason Branch being jealous over Petra and he didn't want to discuss her with his dad. Instead he turned the conversation to the model. "It's totally wrecked," he wailed the tears prickling again.

His father nodded. "It is, but let's do something that will hurt your enemy rather than just giving up," he advised.

"What's that?" Willy asked.

His father gestured to the broken Sopwith Camel. "Well, the Red Baron has well and truly shot this one down. My advice is to make an even better one and make your enemy even more jealous."

Willy liked that idea. Into his mind flashed an image of a blood red model of the Red Baron's famous Fokker DR1 Triplane. "Yes. I will make the Red Baron's Triplane," he replied.

"Good for you! And we will put an engine and radio controls in it," his father answered.

That gave Willy pause. "I'm not sure if I have enough money for that," he said.

"I will pay for the parts. You make the model," his father answered.

So it was arranged that the following afternoon after school Willy would go to the shopping centre with the best hobby shop and make his selections. His father nodded.

"I will meet you there at four thirty," he said, "Patients permitting. If I am not there by five leave the items for me to collect and pay for."

Willy felt a warm glow of love. "Aw thanks, Dad!" he cried. And then he had to battle with the tears again.

I might have an enemy, but I've got two parents who really love me and care for me, he told himself.

Willy's memory sent him to his pile of model aircraft magazines. He remembered being particularly taken by an article by a man who had made a large powered model of the Red Baron's Fokker Triplane. Quickly he leafed through the pages until he found the picture he sought. Seeing the man holding the model caused Willy to feel distinctly envious.

I can make that too, he thought.

There was then the problem of plans. Noting the pages of plans stapled into the centre of the magazine Willy understood what he had to do. After carefully removing these he used his father's photocopier to make copies. Then he enlarged them until they were approximately the right scale for what he wanted. Then he made more copies and cleared the work bench ready to start construction. Feeling much better he went to bed to fantasise about girls.

The following day at school he told Petra the story when he met her at the gate. She was very sympathetic but could offer no clue as to who the person might be. Chatting they strolled up to the classroom for first period. As they approached the door Willy saw Scott go into the room. At the port rack outside Willy and Petra unpacked their books and then stowed their bags before also heading in.

Just as Petra was about to sit down John suddenly hurried across and grabbed her arm. "Lookout! There's a pin on your chair," he cried.

Willy had been about to sit. He looked and saw an upturned thumb tack on Petra's chair. Then he glanced down at his own and saw another. A wave of shock swept through him. *My enemy again!* he thought. His gaze roved the class and instantly settled on Scott, who was busy talking to Sean. Then Scott looked around and smirked.

It must have been him, Willy thought. "Thanks John," he said as he picked up both thumb tacks. *At least I've got one friend,* he thought.

The day progressed like a normal school day except that at the start of Morning Break Petra got a message to go to the office. Willy gave her a quizzical smile. "What have you done?" he asked.

Petra looked very worried and shook her head. Then she hurried off. Willy was left on his own and when she did not reappear he went and joined his friends. They were busy discussing the model flying competition and Willy could not help telling them how his father was going to help him.

"I am going to make a powered model of the Red Baron's plane," he explained. "And it will have radio controls."

"So you can't fly it in our competition then," Stick said. He looked obviously jealous.

"Maybe we could all try to get a radio-controlled model?" Willy suggested.

"Aw, fair go!" Stick retorted. "We don't all have parents who are rolling in money."

That hurt. Willy frowned and replied, "My parents aren't rich, and they work jolly hard."

Stick made a face. Scott sneered and Stephen looked down and shook his head. Willy was left feeling baffled and hurt. But stubbornly he would not get up and walk away. Instead he sat there and listened to the others chatter on until the bell for the middle session lessons went.

To his dismay Petra wasn't back and he had to sit on his own. That led to him noticing Scott glancing back and then whispering to Sean, then again glancing back to smirk.

It must be him, Willy thought. But he could not think of any plan for revenge so instead he settled to school work.

He did not see Petra until the end of lunch when she joined the class again. She looked very pale and upset. Willy was instantly concerned. "Are you alright?" he asked as she sat down.

She sniffed, nodded and tucked her skirt in under her as she settled on the chair. "Yes," she replied.

"What happened?" Willy asked. He felt he just had to know.

"I to the doctor did go," Petra replied.

"I... er... I see," Willy answered.

He was very curious about what the medical issue was but equally he knew it was bad manners to ask. Then it occurred to him it might be some particular female condition and his mind squirmed with suppositions and prurient ideas, made worse because he knew he was largely ignorant of them. Rather than embarrass her or himself he changed the conversation and then helped her with her schoolwork.

After school he went to walk her home, but she stopped him at the gate. "No plis. Not this day. I vould like on my own to walk," she said.

Baffled and feeling a bit rejected Willy at once agreed. Looking at her beauty and seeing her looking sad made his heart swell with concern and love and he just yearned to embrace her and kiss her. But he managed to hide this and after saying goodbye walked over to where his bike was chained in the bike racks. To his relief it was there, and the tyres had not been let down. Just to be sure he knelt and examined the wheels and various nuts and bolts. Satisfied that the bicycle hadn't been tampered with he mounted and rode off.

Half an hour later he was at the shopping centre waiting for his father. While he waited, he strolled around, admiring the girls and looking in the shops. There were lots of nice girls for him to feast his eyes on. Noting a group of four teenage girls heading towards him, he turned to pretend to be looking in a shop window while surreptitiously studying them.

Gee, they are nice! he thought, noting the short shorts, long bare legs and bouncy bosoms below the pretty, giggling faces. Then he recognised the one second from the right. *That blonde with the big boobs and freckles, she is Stick's sister!*

At that moment their eyes met, and Marjorie's mouth opened in surprise. "Hi Willy!" she called, waving at the same time.

Willy could only gape for a few seconds before blushing and nodding. Then the other girls; Year 7s from the look of them, all stared at him and giggled. Willy blushed some more. For something to say he replied, "You are a long way from home."

Marjorie's face dimpled into a mischievous grin. "Good! Nobody knows us on this side of town," she answered, implying that they could misbehave and not get caught.

The girls kept walking and Willy waved a farewell to Marjorie, trying to act cool and nonchalant although he was really embarrassed. Now that he looked more closely, he revised his opinion of them. *They are only little girls. They are too young for me,* he thought. To be labelled a 'cradle snatcher' as he had heard other boys called would be a real 'shame job'.

To add to his embarrassment the girls kept glancing back and giggling and he overheard the word 'willy' several times and was sure they were being rude. *Marjorie is a real tease,* he thought. *And she's got pudgy white legs,* he added, while trying to suppress the notion that her bosom was so large it looked as though it had been inflated. He failed. *They are big, and she knows it, the little witch,* he thought.

To get clear of the situation he walked quickly off and soon ended up in the hobby shop and went to study the range of radio-controlled powered aircraft models available. To his disappointment there was no radio-controlled model of the Red Baron's aircraft. There were only three kits in the shop: a large plastic Spitfire, a shiny silver plastic or foam Mustang and a balsa kit of a German Feisler Storch reconnaissance aircraft of World War 2 design. It had an electric motor he noted.

He was looking at this when his father came in. "What have you got there, son?" he asked.

Willy showed him the kit. His father took it and read the contents list on the box. "This looks good. Would you like it?" he asked.

Images of the hours spent making the smaller Sopwith Camel flashed through Willy's mind and he shook his head. Instead he pointed to the Spitfire kit. "Could I have that?" he asked.

His father put the Storch kit down and took the other kit. After reading for a couple of minutes he looked at Willy. "This will certainly be easier to assemble," he said. "Are you sure?"

By now Willy had been seized by a desire to have a shiny plastic model that both looked good and which flew so he nodded. His father nodded. "OK. It is a bit big. It's got a wingspan of a metre, but we can get that in the car," he said. His father looked around for a few more minutes and then again picked up the Storch kit. "I might make this one," he said.

That surprised and pleased Willy. His father took both kits to the counter and paid for them then tucked them under his left arm. "See you at home son," he said.

Outside the shop Willy's father turned right along the shopping centre arcade and Willy turned left. He was now feeling both excited and happy. *It will be a good model,* he told himself, even though there was a niggling guilt at it just being a snap-together kit.

Thinking happy thoughts he hurried outside to the bike racks, and came to a shocked halt. The frame of his bicycle was still firmly chained to the bike racks, but the front wheel was gone!

Oh no! My bike has been sabotaged! he thought.

Chapter 15

UNHAPPY

It took a few moments for the full realization to sink in. And then came shock and anger. *Has my secret enemy struck again? Or is it just a random theft by some low life?* Willy wondered.

For a few seconds he crouched and examined the bike but all that he could detect was that the nuts holding the front wheel had been undone and the wheel slipped out of the forks. *I should have put the chain around the wheel as well as the frame,* he told himself. Muttering swear words he crouched among the bicycles and struggled to hold back tears which threatened to come in a flood.

Bloody hell! Who has done this? he wondered. Casting about in his memory he thought about who might have known he was going to these shops to buy a model kit. *Who did I tell?* he thought. *And who might they have told?* Then a name came to him and it was like a blow. *Marjorie! She and her friends are here in the shopping centre somewhere.*

The very idea made him feel ill. *Surely not?* he thought. *I thought she liked me. Is that all just a big front to mask her dislike?*

But he could not think of anything he had done to upset or annoy Marjorie. *Why would she want to hurt me?* he wondered. Willy found the notion that she might deeply upsetting. For a moment he considered racing into the shopping centre to find her and confront her.

Then he shook his head as he straightened up. *What could I say? If she is a friend it might hurt her feelings and make her an enemy,* he told himself. Then it came to him that Marjorie would have few opportunities to go to his classroom to put tacks on his chair or to do things to his bike.

Maybe Stick is my secret enemy and she just did that for him? he wondered. It was all very unsettling and distressing.

And this time there was no hope of walking home. Sadly, he made his way into the shopping centre and found the manager's office, the usual place tucked away down a side alley. The manager listened to his story and then allowed him to use the phone to call his father. Then he told Willy to wait so they could check the CCTV recordings.

When Willy's father arrived half an hour later the manager was able to show him video of the bike racks. But it wasn't very helpful. The camera was set high up and a long way from where Willy's bike was. Willy stared at the blurry grey images and noted that it was a boy who went to his bike and that he wore a bike helmet that hid most of his face.

Not Marjorie anyway, he told himself with relief. Then he pointed to the screen. "That's him," he said.

"Do you recognise him?" his father asked.

Willy watched two replays but had to shake his head. *Is it Scott? Or Jason Branch?* he wondered. But he could not tell.

"I don't recognise him," he admitted.

"But he goes to your school," his father noted.

Willy hadn't noticed what clothes the boy was wearing but now saw they were school uniform. *But who is he?* he wondered.

Willy's father stood up. "Well, that looks like that. Thank you," he said to the centre manager. "Now we will take this to the police."

Willy didn't want to do that, but his father insisted. "This person is making your life a misery and we need to catch them and find out why."

So they went to the nearest bicycle shop and purchased another wheel and nuts and took these out and fixed the bicycle. The bicycle was then loaded in the back of the Range Rover and they drove to the police station.

The police weren't very interested, which didn't surprise Willy. *They must have plenty of more serious crimes to investigate,* he thought. *But at least I now know it is a boy and not a girl.*

At home later the story had to be told to Willy's mother. Lloyd was no help. He just jeered and muttered: "Serves yer right. If yer gunna muck around with that little floosy Petra, yer gunna make enemies."

"It's nothing to do with her!" Willy snapped. "And don't call her names! She's a lovely person."

Lloyd opened his mouth to make a retort but then saw the disapproving look on his mother's face and closed it. Their mother snapped at him, "You keep your horrible notions to yourself Lloyd; and speak proper English. Stop that low class talk."

"Yes, Mum."

Willy should have been cheered by his brother's scolding but instead he just felt depressed. *Maybe people are jealous of me going with Petra,* he thought. *But why don't they like her? She is just so nice.*

To take his mind off such things he took himself down to the workshop and unpacked his new plastic kit Spitfire. It was a beauty and he quickly forgot about girls as he eyed its lovely smooth lines and gleaming coloured surfaces. *I don't even have to paint it or add markings,* he noted, seeing that the RAF roundels and registration numbers and letters were already marked on.

His father joined him and that also cheered Willy. His father unpacked the Feisler Storch model and laid out the bits. There were hundreds and Willy was both impressed and concerned.

"Don't mix them up, Dad," he said.

His father held a piece up. "They are all numbered. All I have to do is follow the instructions and stick the thing together in the right order and Bob's your uncle."

"When can we fly them, Dad?"

"Next weekend if I can get this assembled by then," his father answered.

That was a cheering thought and helped Willy to settle to the task of laying out, checking and then assembling the kit Spitfire.

At school the next day he waited near the gate for Petra but she did not appear. Sadly he made his way to class and sat on his own. *Maybe she is sick?* he decided.

She still hadn't arrived by morning break. That left him feeling very lonely and with a dilemma. *If I go and join the other boys they might tease me,* he worried. But then he decided to go anyway. *Better than just being so obviously on my own,* he told himself.

So reluctantly he went and sat with the other boys. To his relief they barely acknowledged him and there was no teasing. Seating himself at the end he listened and waited for an opportunity to speak. The discussion quickly turned to the subject of flying model aircraft.

Willy did not want to mention his new Spitfire for fear of jealousy and teasing but when Stick turned to him and asked if he was going to get another model he had to nod. "My dad bought me one yesterday," he admitted. "A plastic, radio-controlled Spitfire with a petrol engine."

"Oh lucky you!" Scott said with a sarcastic sneer.

"You can all fly it," Willy replied, hoping to save some shreds of friendship.

John nodded. "Thanks Willy. When will it be ready?" he asked.

"By this weekend. Dad says we can fly it up at my uncle's farm near Davies Creek on Sunday. You can come if you like," Willy replied.

"Yeah, OK," John answered. "What about you Stick?"

Stick nodded. "Yeah, I'd like that. But you might have to put up with my little sister too," he said.

Marjorie! Willy thought, images of her nude teasing flitting across his mind. "Yeah, that will be OK," he answered, secretly hoping he might get more glimpses of her charms. Then he remembered Petra and flushed with guilt.

No, not Marjorie. It is Petra I love, he reminded himself.

To change the subject he said, "What about you Steve? Are you still going on a cadet camp?"

Stephen nodded and blinked through his glasses then scowled. "Yes I am," he answered. "I go the day after tomorrow."

"Thursday?" Willy queried. "School doesn't finish till Friday."

Stephen nodded and looked unhappy. "I know, but Graham Kirk and I have been detailed to be part of the advance party and we leave Thursday morning."

Stick frowned. "Why is that?" he queried.

Stephen shrugged and looked uncomfortable. "We just have to. My parents said so," he replied.

It wasn't a very satisfactory answer and Willy's mind speculated on what the real reason might be. Not wanting to embarrass a friend he did not ask.

But Noddy did. "Is that 'cause you and Kirk are in trouble over that cadet bivouac a coupl'a weeks ago?" he asked.

Stephen gave a nod but did not elaborate. That got Willy speculating even more. He had heard vague rumours about Stephen and Graham going off with some Year 10s to go camping on their own. According to the stories alcohol, marijuana and guns had been involved.

Again Willy tried to change the topic. "How long is your camp for Steve? When do you get back?" he asked.

Stephen did a quick calculation and said, "All of the first week of the holidays. We get back on the Saturday in the middle of the holidays."

"What about doing some flying in the second week then?" Willy asked.

Stephen shook his head. "Sorry. After we had our competition last

Sunday I agreed to go on an expedition with Graham and Peter Bronsky," he replied.

That was a disappointment. They all discussed holiday plans and Willy was left feeling quite jealous and very lonely. It seemed to him that everyone except himself was going off on a holiday trip of some sort. *And I can't go to the air cadet camp either,* he thought. As a recruit he was not eligible for the activities being conducted on that particular camp.

The only cheering thing was that Petra had turned up. She came to class a few minutes late and sat next to him. Not wanting to quiz her about personal things Willy merely smiled and nodded. "You OK?" he asked.

Petra gave him a half smile in return and nodded. Then she put her head down and began to do schoolwork, leaving Willy with the distinct impression that all was not well.

I hope it isn't serious, he thought.

That afternoon he walked her home, noting the army cadets starting their Home Training Parade as he did. That caused him another twinge of jealousy about not going to the camp at Townsville.

That afternoon and evening Willy sat and assembled his Spitfire. His father sat with him and worked on his Storch and they chatted about models and Willy felt much better and tried to hide his feeling of vague unhappiness.

I don't have anything to complain about really, he told himself.

But he knew he was lonely, and he went to bed fantasising about Petra, except his thoughts then turned to Marjorie. *Stop it!* he told himself. *Be faithful! It is Petra you love, not Marjorie!* But to his annoyance images of Marjorie then flitted across his mind, followed by some of Barbara.

Thursday was a good day, or it would have been if he hadn't run into the Year 11 bullies. Petra was at school and sat with him but when they were walking down the steps side by side during the changeover between periods, they met Larsen and Carstairs coming up.

Larsen stopped and blocked Petra's path. Leering up at her he said loudly, "Hi Petra babe! How's your pussy?"

Annoyance instantly welled up in Willy, both at the arrogant blocking of Petra and at the crude imagery. He took a step down, burning with embarrassment and hoping Petra didn't understand the crude innuendo.

"Leave Petra alone," he said, steeling himself for a fight.

Larsen turned to look at him, his lip curling in contempt as he did. "Shut up shitface! I was talking to the doctor, not the disease," he retorted.

Willy flushed but stood his ground. "Don't say things about her," he managed to croak. By this time his heart was hammering with fear and he braced himself for blows.

They weren't long in coming. Larsen sneered and then hit at him while Carstairs shoved him from in front. "Mind yer own business, Rocket Man!" Larsen snapped.

Willy tried to keep his balance but fell heavily on the steps. His head hit the concrete tread and he saws stars. Then Carstairs kicked him in the right thigh. *This is going to hurt,* Willy thought.

But it didn't. A voice called loudly, "Stop that fighting! Get to class!"

Willy recognised the voice of Warwick Grey, one of the Year 12 prefects. To Willy's relief, Larsen drew back from punching him again and looked up. Then he sneered but stopped. Petra then stepped past him and bent to help Willy up.

With his head still spinning from the blow Willy got to his feet and then clung to the handrail and to Petra's arm. She glared at Larsen, "You der bully is!" she snapped. "And do not to me the filthy things say or I to the office report you."

Larsen curled his lip. "You do ya bitch and you'll regret it," he retorted but Willy could see that he was scared and guessed that it was bluster. Larsen and Carstairs then continued on up the stairs, Carstairs giving Willy another painful jab with his fist as he went by. Willy cried out and opened his mouth to protest but then saw both Warwick Grey and Mike Masters standing at the top of the steps. "You two get to class and stop picking on the little kids," Mike snapped at Carstairs.

Little kids! Willy thought, flushing with shame.

But Petra was holding him and she looked all concerned. "Are you the all right Villy?" she asked.

"I am," Willy replied, although in truth he felt a bit dazed. At Mike Master's urging he resumed walking down the steps and by the time they reached the next classroom the spinning sensation had stopped but he had a headache.

Petra looked worried when he mentioned this. "You should to the sick room go and to der office to report zem," she said.

"I'd rather be with you," Willy replied, forcing a smile.

At that Petra gave him a hug, pressing her breasts against him and sending his body into instant arousal. "You are the so sweet!" she said, kissing him on the cheek.

They kissed again at the start of lunch break. This time Willy took the initiative. For the previous hour he had been so aroused he could hardly think straight and he was just overcome by a driving urge to hold her, to kiss her. So as the class began leaving the room he reached across and gently took her arm. She turned and looked at him, smiling quizzically.

"A kiss please," he whispered, glancing at the students leaving as he did. One of the last to go through the door was Barbara, and as she did she glanced back and then gave a knowing little smile that caused Willy a spurt of guilt. *Gee Barbara is getting pretty,* he thought, amending that immediately to 'beautiful'. He could not help noting that her breasts seemed to have developed even more and now really stuck out. Then he turned back to Petra and hoped she hadn't noticed.

"May I?" he asked.

At that she smiled and glanced at the other students. Nodding she stood with him until all of the others had left the room. Then she came willingly to him. To Willy it was heaven. Her arms went around his neck and she pressed herself against him. By then Willy was on fire and he didn't care if she could feel his arousal. That she could was obvious as she squirmed and rubbed her stomach against it and nearly caused the top to explode off his skull.

"I love you!" he croaked when they stopped.

"You are so sveet," she replied, stroking his left cheek and pressing against him.

Willy shivered and the passion swirled in him. *I'm in love!* he thought.

Holding her by her hips he leaned back and stared in wonder, unable to believe his luck. His gaze roamed slowly over her glossy black hair and then her heart shaped face with its oh-so-kissable lips. For a moment her eyelashes fascinated him as did the tiny, downy hairs on her cheeks. He swam in the adoring dark pools of her sparkling eyes and then he looked down and his gaze followed the graceful curve of her neck and shoulders. Then he saw the way her breasts were pushing out the front of her blouse and he trembled. Desire surged in him and he moved to kiss her again.

At that moment, a gravely male voice called from the doorway: "What are you two children doing?"

Jerking back with a guilty start Willy looked towards the door and saw it was Mr Burgomeister, the much-feared Senior Maths teacher. "Nothing sir!" he blurted.

A scowl and then a sardonic smile formed on the teacher's face. "Nothing?"

"Just talking sir," Willy added, hastily taking his hands from Petra's waist.

Mr Burgomeister snorted with disbelief and Willy feared they were in trouble. *Oh, I hope he doesn't send us to the office,* he thought.

Then Mr Burgomeister jerked his thumb towards the veranda. "Just as well you were only talking," he said sarcastically. "Now get out of there! You know the school rules: no students in classrooms during the lunch break."

"Yes sir," Willy replied.

Hotly aware that he was very aroused, and hoping that the teacher would not notice, he glanced at Petra and then hastily gathered up his books and pens and hurried to the door, Petra close behind. After packing their belongings and taking out their lunches under the baleful stare of the teacher, they hurried downstairs.

As they went out of sight of the teacher, Petra giggled. "That vos ver good," she said. "You the so clever are Villy."

"Bloody old grump!" Willy replied. "I can't imagine anyone ever giving him a kiss."

Petra giggled some more and then bumped against him as they walked along under the building. "That vos good," she said with a sigh.

Knowing that she had enjoyed his embraces sent Willy into a transport of delight. "It was," he said. "We should do it some more."

"That vould be nice," Petra replied, sending his hopes even higher.

Willy glanced around and then noted a nearby hallway. It appeared empty. "In here," he whispered, steering her towards the doorway. As soon as they were out of sight of the other students he turned and pulled her to him. She smiled and came willingly, snuggling in and pressing against him. They kissed again but the sound of approaching voices made them step apart.

As a group of Year 10 girls walked past, several cast curious glances at them. Willy burned with desire and embarrassment. Pretending to be just talking, he asked her if he would see her during the holidays. It was something he had been summoning up the courage to ask.

Instantly Petra frowned and looked unhappy. She shook her head. "No. I must with my mother work," she answered.

"Pity," Willy murmured.

He was curious about where her mother was employed but did not like to ask. So he kissed her again and they enjoyed a long, passionate kiss and embrace. Only the approach of more students ended it.

By then Willy was so excited he could hardly contain himself, but he managed to calm his breathing and make himself appear normal when they reluctantly let go of each other and moved out of the hallway.

Chapter 16

HOLIDAYS

One of the approaching students was Barbara and Willy saw her eyes flick from him to Petra and back. A mischievous smile flitted across her face and she quickly whispered to Karen Hart who was beside her.

Karen glanced at them and smirked. "Hi Petra! Hi Willy! Don't do anything we wouldn't do will ya!" she teased.

Willy blushed and Petra poked her tongue at Karen who trilled with laughter. The group walked on, obviously discussing them and Willy blushed some more but was actually glad. To his regret he found he just had to go to the toilet. Having relieved the pain he went to find Petra and sat with her during the lunch break.

While he sat there, Willy noted Jason Branch give him a scowl as he walked past. That reminded him of his secret enemy, and he shook his head. *Air Cadets tomorrow night. I suppose Branch will give me heaps,* he thought. But then he shrugged. *Too bad! Petra is worth a bit of pain.* Then the notion came to him that he had won Petra's affection and Branch had not. That boosted him. *He can be as jealous as he likes,* he told himself. *She is my girl.*

After school he walked her to near her home. Once again, she anxiously asked him not to go any closer. "I not my mother want to see us. She think I too young for boyfriends," Petra reminded him.

So Willy could only nod, mount his bike and go on his way. At home he settled to working on his models and that night he had trouble falling asleep. Heated memories of kissing Petra got him very aroused and then the fantasies melded to include images of Marjorie and Barbara.

Oh, I wish I had more self-control! he thought. *I must learn to stay loyal.*

But he could not control his subconscious and his dreams when he was asleep included a heated but frustrating session with a naked Marjorie. He woke up annoyed with himself and very horny.

His unhappiness increased when he went to school. Petra was not there and she did not appear. Feeling lonely and let down Willy moved to join a group of boys from his class. John was there and so were Stick and Noddy but many were away.

Noddy then infuriated him by saying: "Oh here comes the Mad Scientist. Hey Willy, don't you usually sit with Petra Pants-off?"

"Don't call her names!" Willy snapped. "She's not like that! She's a lovely person."

"That's not what all the Year Elevens say," Noddy retorted.

Images of Larsen and Carstairs flashed across Willy's mind and he seethed. "They are just jealous," he cried. "So shut your filthy mouth."

At that Noddy narrowed his eyes and stood up. "You trying to tell me what to do?" he said.

"Don't say horrible things about my girlfriend!" Willy replied.

"Huh! Yours and everyone elses!" Noddy retorted.

That comment made Willy see red and he raised his fists. Luckily Stick and John stepped between them. "That'll do you two. Noddy, stop stirring the pot," Stick said.

The situation was calmed but Willy was left upset and unhappy. He wanted to go away but stubbornly stayed, sitting with the others and joining in the conversation. But inside he was hurting. *Why do they keep making horrible comments about Petra?* he thought, maggots of doubt starting to squirm in his stomach.

Later in the day Willy had two more unpleasant experiences. Being the last day of school it was a quiet day with at least half the students absent. That meant very little work was done in class, but it also meant that the playground was much more deserted. One upshot of that was while Willy was walking around in the hope of seeing Petra at morning break, he spotted Larsen, Carstairs and several other Year 11s sitting under C Block. They were right beside where he would have to walk.

Willy hesitated at the corner of the building. *They haven't seen me yet,* he thought. A churn of fear swirled in him and he stepped back out of sight. The notion of going another way came to him and he turned and made his way right around the building, keeping it between himself and the bullies.

But it wasn't as easy as that. As he walked around out of sight Willy flushed with shame and despised himself. *Don't be a coward!* he told himself. He resolved not to avoid the bullies on his way back.

So five minutes later he walked back under B Block heading towards

C Block. Ahead he noted the bullies still seated in the same place and his heart sank. Part of him had been hoping they might be gone. Once again fear and apprehension welled up to make his steps falter, but he remembered the shame and self-loathing and that stiffened his resolve.

Biting his lip he straightened up and strode determinedly towards the bullies. As he did his stomach churned and the butterflies 'fluttered'. But it was too late to back out because they had seen him. Pretending to be cool and relaxed Willy strode on, averting his eyes as he did.

That was a mistake as something struck him hard on the side of the face. As he cried out with pain and clutched his cheek, he saw a crumpled cardboard milk carton drop to the ground and heard Carstairs yell: "Got him! Oh good shot Red. Come on Space Monkey, you need to go faster than that."

Willy smarted both internally and externally. Anxiously he glanced at the bullies and saw their smirking, sneering faces close beside him. Luckily, they were still seated but he also noted a couple reaching down to pick up small stones. As Carstairs drew his arm back for a throw Willy told himself to run.

But he didn't. Stubbornly he kept walking, pretending to ignore the bullies. There was a sharp whirring sound and then he had to smile as the stone thrown by Carstairs missed and went flying by. But Willy was careful not to show his feelings to the bullies and now had his back to them.

His emotions were boosted by hearing the other bullies teasing Carstairs for missing. Carstairs called angrily: "I won't miss this time."

Willy badly wanted to run and his body began to tense and flinch in anticipation of being struck but he made himself walk steadily away. There was another whirring sound and a stone the size of a marble flew past, just clipping his sleeve as it did. Better still it went on to strike Anastasia, one of the Year 12 girls. It hit her in the back, and she cried out in pain and turned quickly. Her friends, both male and female Year 12s, did the same.

"Was that you Williams?" Mike Masters demanded.

Willy shook his head. "Carstairs. He is throwing things at me," he replied.

Mike and the other Year 12s headed in the direction of the Year 11 bullies and Willy heard raised and angry voices behind him. But he did not look back until he reached the corner of the building. Chortling with satisfaction he kept walking. *Serves the idiots right,* he thought.

But he didn't find Petra. Later that day he checked with John and Stick about flying models on Sunday and then he sadly made his way home at the end of the day.

Cadets tonight and then holidays, he thought. He wasn't really looking forward to the two weeks. To see if his name had been accepted for the weekend activity at Mareeba, he logged in to Cadetnet and was pleased to see he had been accepted. *At least something is working,* he thought.

And then Jason Branch got his revenge. At Air Cadets that night Branch found fault with every little thing Willy did, constantly rebuking him for poor drill or inattention or other minor alleged misdemeanours. Willy bit his lip and held his temper with difficulty, telling himself that he was the one kissing Petra, not Branch.

But it was over Petra that Branch next taunted him. Having ordered Willy to stand to attention over in the shadows on the side of the parade ground Branch now came and stood behind him. Leaning forward he hissed in Willy's left ear.

"You are a snivelling little weakling Williams," he snarled.

Willy made no answer but kept his fists clenched and firmly against his sides in the position of attention. *He's trying to provoke me to get me into trouble,* he thought. The notion that Branch might be setting him up to be chucked out for striking someone of superior rank or for disobedience crossed Willy's mind.

This idea was reinforced when Branch again sneered at him and hissed, "You might be panting hard over little Miss Pantopoke but you are just a creepy worm."

Willy made no response although inside he seethed and had to resist the temptation to smash his fist into Branch's face. Branch walked slowly around him and continued. "Well, are you poking her? Is she a good root? I hear she is, if you've got the money that is."

Again Willy made no reply, holding his temper with an effort. Branch was not satisfied. "Well, answer me ya gutless little prick," he snarled.

"She's a nice girl sergeant and you have no right to speak about her like that," Willy replied. He was very angry now and was not going to remain silent.

"Oh is that so? Who do you think you are, ya jerk! You are just a worm of a new recruit. Are you being insolent and back answering?" Branch growled.

"No sergeant," Willy replied. With an effort he restrained himself although the urge to lash out, to smash his fist into Branch's face, was all but overpowering.

"No sergeant!" Branch sneered. "You're a weakling and a coward Williams. Now, straighten up. Get those thumbs back behind the seams of your trousers. Head up! look to yer front! Cadet Williams, Riiight... Turn! Leeeft... Turn!"

Willy clenched his jaw shut and did as he was ordered. It was the end of the lesson that's saved him from more. As Sgt Branch told him to go, he hissed, "And I'll be watching you Williams! You'll get what you deserve."

"Yes sergeant," Willy replied woodenly.

He hurried away, his mind seething with frustrated rage at the injustice but then it settled on the thought that Branch was jealous because Petra had chosen him instead of Branch. Hugging that satisfying notion Willy went to his next class.

Later that evening he was again subjected to Branch's withering comments when the twenty who had nominated to try out for the Drill Squad were paraded. "You useless jerk Williams! You haven't got a hope in hell of being selected," Branch muttered.

But there were officers and both the adult Warrant Officer and cadet WO(D) present so he was unable to say more as he was trying out for the team as well. For the next thirty minutes Willy made a maximum effort to do the best drill he could. But this was only a preliminary session and no selections were made.

I hope I'm chosen, Willy thought. *If only to prove Branch wrong!*

Saturday was a day of chores at home. Despite being the first day of the holidays Willy was woken up at his usual time and told to have breakfast and then to get on with his jobs. His father added, "We need to get these model aircraft ready to fly by tomorrow, but we are going to emulate the three little pigs, work first, play later."

So Willy worked; mowing, sweeping, weeding and tidying up. Only after lunch did he and his father move to the workshop and settle to work on the models. There wasn't much for Willy to do but he sat and read the instructions for the petrol motors and radio controls while his father assembled his Feisler Storch.

Once Willy had read the instructions, he asked his father if they could test the motor. "We will look silly if we go up to the farm and it doesn't work," he said.

"Too right!" his father agreed. So he stopped assembling his model and they set the engine of Willy's Spitfire up on a 'test bed' screwed firmly to the work bench. Fuel was added in the recommended mixture and quantities and some of it was pumped into the cylinders. Willy then tentatively used his fingertip to turn the nylon propeller to build up compression. Having watched this done on the flying weekend he was a bit scared of the motor suddenly starting and the blades hitting his finger.

But once he was satisfied, he took a deep breath, imagined he was in his WW1 Sopwith Camel calling 'Switches on!' to his air mechanic and then gave the blade a sharp flick. To his delight and amazement the motor burst into life with a very loud and satisfying roar. The propeller became a blurred disc of white. Blue smoke began to pour from it. Willy watched for a few seconds and then looked up to meet his father's eyes. Father and son both grinned and Willy felt like singing, until his mother shouted from the door.

"What on earth are you boys doing?" she cried.

Willy looked around and was astonished to note that the whole room was now filled with smoke and then he realised that the fumes had a particularly sickly and pungent reek. "Just testing the motor, Mum," he cried, noting that his father was looking sheepish and had obviously been included in the 'boys' category.

His mother shook her head and pursed her lips. "Well it works so turn it off! Next thing we will have complaints from the neighbours or the fire alarms will go off," she snapped.

So Willy reached across and switched off the fuel. The motor roared on for a few more seconds and then spluttered into silence. His mother shook her head and turned away and Willy grinned at his father and he smiled back. "It works, Dad!" he cried. His father agreed and then told him to drain the fuel and to dry and clean the motor and to pack it. He then resumed assembling his model.

Then there were phone calls to confirm that John, Stick and Marjorie were still coming the next day.

It was a happy boy who slid into bed that night. For a while he fantasised about flying and about saving Petra but then his thoughts shifted to memories of Marjorie and he found himself lustfully fantasising about her. When he realised what he was doing, he shook his head. *I shouldn't be thinking about her. She's too young and I am being disloyal to Petra. Petra is my true love,* he told himself.

But it was hard to get images of Marjorie out of his mind and she even flitted through the dreams he had later, being mixed in with semi-nightmares of air cadets at which he was in trouble with Sgt Branch and was late for a ceremonial parade and then couldn't find his hat and his best uniform shirt!

Sunday dawned clear and hot. The family were up at seven and on the way by 8:30. The model aircraft were carefully placed in the back of the vehicles. Both his mother and his father drove their cars and Willy went with his father and Lloyd with his mother. They picked up Stick and Marjorie first and they sat in the back of Willy's mother's car and when John was picked up he travelled in Willy's father's car.

Marjorie wore very tight, very short white shorts and a pale-yellow cotton top with no sleeves. Her only concession to the sun was a wide brimmed floppy straw hat. When the vehicles arrived at the farm and they were introduced to Uncle Ted and Aunty Isabel. Aunty Isabel beamed a welcome but then frowned and said to Marjorie, "Don't you get sun burnt dearie. You should cover up more."

Marjorie shrugged. "I will put plenty of sunscreen on," she replied.

"Good. You don't want to get skin cancers dearie," Aunty Isabel commented.

Morning tea was first on the agenda, taken on the wide front veranda in the shade. It was a hot, still day and Willy noted that the mountains of the Lamb Range which took up most of the southern horizon looked like dark blue cardboard cut-outs through a haze of dust. *Or is it smoke?* he wondered, sniffing at the air. For a September day it was hot and promised to get hotter as there wasn't as cloud in the sky.

Then his focus shifted to Marjorie and when he glanced at her he found she was looking at him. Their eyes met and she gave a mischievous little smile. Willy hastily looked away but when he glanced again a few minutes later he found himself looking into her big blue eyes. *Is she making a pass at me?* he wondered.

It was very unsettling, and he told himself that she was not only too young (Despite that big bosom that was pushing out the front of her blouse) but that he was being disloyal to Petra even thinking about such an idea.

Next, Mr Williams led the teenagers to his Range Rover and the two models and their control packs and other accessories were taken out. As he carefully lifted the Spitfire clear of the back Willy was filled with both pride and apprehension. To him the gleaming model looked fabulous, but he was afraid the others might be jealous. He was also anxious about his flying abilities.

I hope I don't wreck it, he thought.

It was very obvious that there was envy, judging by the Stick's face. Both he and John openly admired the model and both half-reached forward, obviously wanting to hold the model and to have it. Marjorie also admired it and clapped her hands with delight but as Willy glanced at her he did wonder if it wasn't a bit feigned.

The group made their way to the large machinery shed at the back of the cluster of farm buildings. The shed had a concrete floor and the wide doors opened out onto the bottom paddock, 500 metres of short pasture. "We will do our flying here," his father explained.

Willy wholeheartedly agreed. That way they could do all their preparations in the shade and use the concrete floor as an airfield for take-offs with half a kilometre of open ground to fly around. There was a line of eucalypts along both the western fence and the southern, but they were so far away they did not pose any risk.

Willy's father insisted on pre-flight checks on everything and then on ground training. The Spitfires' fuel tank was filled and the engine primed and then Willy knelt and placed the model on its wheels facing towards the open doorway. As he did the other teenagers crowded round and hands began reaching towards the model. Willy found Marjorie jostling him on his left and both John and Stick crowding him on his right.

"You hold the model please John," Willy said. That earned him a grunt from Stick and a small sigh of disappointment. John smiled and moved to the rear and took a firm hold of the model's fuselage. The other two knelt on either side to watch. Very aware of the rivalry he began nervously winding the propeller to build up the compression. And this time the motor did not start at the first attempt.

Feeling embarrassed and slightly flustered Willy checked everything and again built up the compression and then gave the prop a hard flick. This time the motor spluttered and then burst into life, again emitting a cloud of blue smoke from its exhaust.

Grinning with relief and delight Willy stood up and took the radio control pack from his father. His father gestured to the area outside the door. "Do some ground practice first William," he said.

Willy nodded and tentatively moved the throttle adjustment. To his astonishment the engine roared even louder. "Wrong way!" he muttered. Carefully he moved the throttle the other way and to his relief the engine slowed.

Licking his lips with nervousness Willy nodded to John. "OK Johnno, let her go," he said.

Chapter 17

FLYING AND FLIRTING

The model Spitfire began rolling forward. For an instant Willy admired it. Then he realised it was rolling rapidly towards the side of the shed door. Quickly he moved the small control knob to turn the model's rudder to starboard. The model swung, but too far. Now in a bit of a fluster Willy turned the knob the other way. Once again, the model responded almost instantly, and once again he had made the correction too large. The model began to swing around sharply to port.

"Bloody hell! This thing needs wheel brakes," Willy cried as he hastily turned the knob again.

Willy's father smiled. "You get what you pay for. You want brakes but that means a much more expensive model," he said.

John looked at him in surprise. "Are there model aircraft with wheel brakes?" he asked.

"Yes," Willy's father answered. "But they are usually big and expensive models. I saw one a few weeks ago, a B17 Flying Fortress with four engines."

"That must have been good!" John replied, his voice tinged with envy.

"It was, oh well done William!" Willy's father replied as Willy at last managed to steer the Spitfire out of the doorway and onto the bare earth in front of the shed.

"It means a lot more servo motors in the model and that means more batteries and more channels for the radio control console," Willy's father added.

Willy eased the throttle back and then moved it slowly forward again. With more room to manoeuvre in without having to worry about the model running into something he increased the speed and started it on a wide, sweeping turn. "I still wish it had brakes," he grumbled as the model wove a slightly erratic course.

Stick laughed. "Ha! They didn't have brakes on World War One planes."

"This is a World War Two plane, Stick," Willy answered.

"Oh! Is it?" Stick replied. "I always get those two mixed up."

"World War One was mostly biplanes," Willy explained.

Stick frowned. "But they had them in World War Two, didn't they?" he said.

Willy nodded and then bit his lip and concentrated on turning the model to face down the paddock. "Yes, ones like the Gloster Gladiator and Fairey Swordfish, you know, the biplane torpedo bombers that hit the *Bismarck.*"

"Oh yeah!" Stick agreed.

Willy looked at his father. "OK Dad, here she goes!"

His father nodded and Willy pushed the throttle forward and gripped the control levers. The model's motor roared. Blue smoke streamed aft from the exhaust. The model began rolling forward and then picked up speed so fast Willy was astonished, and then flustering to regain control. The model's tail lifted, and he feared the propeller would strike the ground and tip the model on its nose so he pulled back on the stick and the model suddenly lifted off just as it rolled onto the dirt.

A spurt of dust caused Willy to blink and his eyes watered as he tried to see what the model was doing. To his astonishment it was climbing very steeply. But then he saw that it was slowing.

It will stall! he thought.

Quickly he pushed the stick forward. The model hung and then its nose tilted and it went into a screaming dive. With a desperate jerk Willy pulled the stick back again. The controls did not seem to have any effect but then the model's nose lifted and it went into a skidding, swooping climb after narrowly avoiding hitting the ground.

Willy's father cried out. "You are making corrections that are too bold William. Gentle and small."

Willy knew that and he now tried that and to his relief managed to get the model levelled out and flying away from him. Then he carefully put the controls in place to make the model do a wide, banking turn to the left. To his relief it did.

As the model went up and around it was silhouetted against the sky and Willy was rewarded by a view of that famous elliptical shape and he smiled. *The Spitfire is certainly the most beautiful aircraft ever,* he thought.

For a few seconds he imagined he was one of the famous 'Few' flying his Spitfire into battle over England in 1940. But then the need to concentrate on maintaining control took his mind off daydreams and he turned the model so that it missed the shed, zoomed above the tall trees to his right and then flew south across the open paddock.

What will I do next? he wondered. He squinted at the model to check its 'attitude' in the air.

With mounting alarm Willy watched the model get smaller and smaller as it dwindled into the distance. With sweat breaking out on his brow he manipulated the controls, but the model was now so far away and hidden against the backdrop of the mountains that he could not really see what its attitude or heading were.

Then to his relief he saw that he had managed to turn it around and that it was heading back towards them. Then it appeared in silhouette against the backdrop of the sky in the low saddle between Lambs Head and the main part of the Lamb Range and he saw that it was climbing. Quickly he made a fractional adjustment to start it descending and then he changed its course to head towards them.

"Whew!" he said. "I thought I'd lost it then. It didn't seem to be responding and I was worried it might have flown out of range of the radio controller."

Willy's father shook his head. "No, it should have a range of two or three kilometres with line-of-sight," he explained.

John, who had been standing beside Willy on his other side and staring anxiously at the model, now turned to Willy's father. "What happens if radio contact is lost Mr Williams?"

Willy's father smiled and shrugged. "Then it continues on the last course it was set on until it either runs out of fuel and lands or it crashes. It does happen I've heard."

Willy had been half listening, but his main focus was on the now rapidly approaching model and he concentrated on showing off. He put the model into a dive and then back into a zooming climb so that it shot up over their heads. A roll and half loop brought it back down and on an even keel and the then sent it around in a hard banking circle. As it flew around the famous silhouette appeared and again Willy was filled with admiration.

What a beautiful plane! he thought. Something he had read once that a good design was also usually visually appealing flitted across his mind and he could only agree.

John shook his head in obvious admiration as the model again roared overhead and began another circle. "But what happens when there is more than one radio control at work? Do they interfere with each other?" he asked Willy's father.

Willy's father shook his head. "Not usually. They are set on different frequencies or channels and unless they are close together there shouldn't be any interference."

"But things can interfere, can't they?" John queried.

"I believe so but I'm not sure. Some electrical equipment sets up electronic interference. That's why airlines don't like some electrical appliances being used on their aircraft," Willy's father replied.

Stick now spoke up. "I read that in World War Two the British found that electric shavers sent German radio-controlled bombers off course."

Willy nodded. "I read that," he said. Then he concentrated, lower lip firmly gripped by his teeth and tongue in the corner of his mother as he lined the model up to land it. *I don't want to crash it and wreck it, or make myself look like an idiot,* he thought anxiously.

To his relief he managed an almost perfect landing and he manoeuvred the taxiing model to near them and after he throttled back Stick was able to grab it. The fuel was turned off and the motor spluttered to a stop.

Stick looked up from the model. "Can I have a go now please?" he asked.

Willy's father answered. "We will let it cool and refuel it first. We will try mine now and you can all have a go with it."

The Feisler Storch model was placed on the concrete and admired. Then Willy's father took the control panel for it and started the electric motor going. This caused an immediate sensation among the others. Stick cried aloud: "Oh! How quiet it is!"

John shook his head in disbelief. "If you didn't see the prop going you wouldn't even know it was working."

Marjorie bent to peer at it. "Why is it so quiet Mr Williams? Does it use different petrol?"

The boys laughed but Willy's father shook his head and only smiled. "It is an electric motor. There are batteries in there," he explained.

He then did some ground manoeuvring to get the feel of the controls.

The Storch moved much more slowly and was much easier to control. This also applied to its flight characteristics. When the model was lined up facing out the door Willy's father opened the throttle and the model lifted off in less than half the distance the Spitfire had required.

Again there were gasps of admiration and disbelief. Stick shook his head and grinned. "See that! It took off in only a few metres," he cried.

Willy's father flew the model out over the open paddock, making it climb gently as he did. "It is a short take-off and landing design. That was one of its great virtues," he explained.

Willy had seen a real Pilatus Porter do just that and he thought it was a really good design. John stared with a look of hungry fascination on his face. "It was a battlefield reconnaissance machine wasn't it Mr Williams?"

Willy's father nodded. "Yes it was. You've heard of General Rommel?" he asked.

The boys all nodded. Stick answered. "Yes. He commanded the German Afrika Korps which fought our army in the Western Desert of North Africa during World war Two."

"That's the man," Willy's father agreed. "He used one of these to personally fly around the battlefield and then when he needed to speak to his commanders or troops he could land. Because it took such a short run it could land almost anywhere."

He then proceeded to experiment with various manoeuvres, getting bolder as he gained confidence. The Storch was made to climb until it almost stalled. Then it was put through a series of rolls and loops and steep descents before being brought into land.

The model's wheels touched the concrete only ten paces in front of them and Willy tensed ready to jump aside but to his amazement it rolled to a stop within a couple of metres.

"Bloody hell! That's good," he cried.

Willy's father grinned, obviously proud of his performance. He held the control console out. "Who would like a go?"

John at once stepped forward, blocking Stick. "Me please sir," he said, reaching out.

"Just take it easy to begin with. We don't want it busted," Willy's father instructed.

Willy watched with some anxiety while John made the model taxi around and then he lined it up and did a flawless take-off. Then Willy watched with a tinge of envy as John put the model through a series of manoeuvres that were really well executed. "That is great flying Johnno!" he cried.

John gave him a nod and a grin and then sent the model into a few more dramatic manoeuvres. For the next five minutes he flew it around with what appeared to Willy to be quite extraordinary skill. Only when Stick demanded a go and Willy's father backed the request up did he reluctantly bring the model in to a prefect three-point landing.

"Thanks Mr Williams," John said as he handed the controls to Stick.

Stick was not nearly as good, and his efforts had Willy's heart in his mouth with anxiety a few times. Stick got the model airborne alright but then made it climb so steeply it stalled. Only by luck did he regain control just before it was about to dive nose first into the ploughed field. Then he several times turned it too tight so that as it lost lift and then lost altitude.

After a timed five anxious minutes Willy's father instructed Stick to land the model. He turned it back towards the shed but then put it into too steep a descent. Willy realised this and opened his mouth to warn Stick. But he was too late. John cried "Pull up! Pull up!"

Stick did, but with a sudden jerk that caused the model to stall. Luckily, it was only just above the stubble so that when the nose dropped again and it dived into the ground it was not hard. The model flipped onto its back amid a puff of dust.

The friends ran out to it. John was angry. "You bloody nong Stick! You've might have busted it."

"I haven't," Stick answered defensively as he picked the model up and looked at it.

"You could have!" John snapped.

Willy's father intervened. "But he hasn't. You must expect a few accidents when flying models. Now, whose turn is it next? Do you want a go young Marjorie?"

Marjorie shook her head vigorously. "No thanks Mr Williams. Willy can have a go if he likes." She met Willy's eyes and gave him a big smile.

So the controls were handed to Willy. The model was dusted and returned to the concrete apron and he did some tentative experiments at ground manoeuvres. But the motor did not seem to be responding well.

"Something's wrong," he commented to his father.

Willy's father nodded. "Probably low battery. Let's put it on to charge and refuel your plane and they can have a go with that."

Willy wasn't keen on that but had to agree. Because it was his turn, he got a second go with the Spitfire and then, reluctantly, handed the controls to John. Once again John controlled the model as though he had been flying them for years.

Willy was both impressed and a bit jealous. "You are a really good model pilot, Johnno," he complemented.

"Thanks," John replied. He then handed the controls to Stick. "Here Stick, your turn."

Willy's anxiety for his model at once flooded back and several times it appeared that his worst fears would be justified as the model zoomed close to the ground or the trees. But Stick managed to keep it safe and after five minutes landed it without incident. Willy's father then had a go and obviously really enjoyed himself.

The arrival of Willy's mother and Aunty Isabel interrupted the flying. "You boys stop playing and come and have lunch," Aunty Isabel said.

The Spitfire was brought down to land and then placed in the shed. The whole group then walked back around to the farmhouse. Willy was feeling very happy and was dreaming of more good flights. But as they walked along the driveway Marjorie kept bumping against him. The first two times he thought it was accidental but when he glanced at her and she gave him a mischievous grin and bumped him again he realised it was deliberate.

Then she made a point of sitting beside him at the dining table so that their legs touched. Willy was both surprised and a little anxious. This was partly because he did not want the others to notice (especially his parents!) but also because her touch began to get him aroused.

During the meal Marjorie spent a lot of time trying to join in the conversation and she continued touching Willy's leg with her own. This resulted in him becoming fully aroused. *I wish she would stop it,* he thought, perspiring with anxiety that others might notice. It was almost a relief to go back out again for more flying.

The group returned to the shed. The fuel tank on the Spitfire was refilled and the battery level in the Storch checked. As he bent to study the gauge Willy said, "Can I have a go with your model, Dad?"

"Yes son. You can fly mine if you don't mind me and your friends flying yours," his father replied.

Willy actually did but forced himself to smile and agree. First, he offered Marjorie a go, but she shook her head and declined. John at once asked if he could have a turn. Willy nodded his agreement and moved to get the Storch ready. At the same time his model was started up and John taxied it out and set it flying.

Soon both model aircraft were zipping around the paddock. That bothered Willy a lot. "We might have a collision," he commented.

But his father shook his head. "We might, but if they fly at different heights and both go the same way round the risk is fairly small," he replied.

Willy had to accept this and settled to mastering the controls of the Storch. He was very careful in his adjustments to the controls and found it very responsive to even the smallest movements. Soon he developed more confidence and was ready to try some aerobatics. First, he made the Storch climb to several hundred feet and then he put it into a steep dive and then pulled it up into a loop. This worked well, but in the process it flew down below the altitude of the Spitfire and for a few seconds it looked like there might be a collision.

Seeing this Willy jerked the controls to make the Storch do a sharp turn to port but as he did John turned the Spitfire to starboard. Willy's heart leapt into his mouth and his mind raced. *Wrong way! They will collide!* he told himself. Instantly he pushed the stick forward. The Storch dipped its nose and dived. The Spitfire flashed past so close it looked as though its wheels had struck the other model's tail.

There was flutter and then the Storch steadied. Willy sighed with relief and pulled the model out of its dive. "That a close," he commented.

His father shook his head. "Always turn to starboard young William. And fly in the same direction as the 'Spit'. And no more fancy manoeuvres please."

Willy blushed with shame at his mistakes but complied. For several more minutes he flew the Storch around testing it with gentle manoeuvres. Then he landed it and Stick took the controls. The Spitfire was landed and Willy's father took over flying it. Willy stood back beside Marjorie and watched.

After another five minutes Willy had another go with his Spitfire while Stick had a turn with the Storch. Once again, the models almost collided but this time it was Stick's fault as he flew it too close to the Spitfire.

Willy banked the Spitfire away and made it climb but as he did a gust of wind blew dust in his eyes and for a few moments he lost sight of the model. Blinking to see through eyes that were watering but full of grit he saw that it had climbed steeply and was close to a stall. Quickly he eased the rate of climb and then set the controls to bring the model down and around. As he lined it up to land, he noted that it was yawing and wobbling as it approached.

"Getting windy," he commented.

His father nodded. "Yes. Nearly time to stop, I think. Land my plane please Stick," he said.

Willy focused on his landing but at the last moment a sudden gust lifted the port wing and the starboard wingtip touched the ground. Before Willy could do anything, the model began to cartwheel. Willy was aghast and felt ashamed at his blunder and concerned for the model. It flipped and came to rest upside down. The motor spluttered to a stop amid a cloud of dust.

As the dust cloud blew away Willy ran to his model and knelt to pick it up. Marjorie joined him. "Is it broken?" she asked, pressing against his right side as she did.

Willy vaguely noted the body contact, but his main focus was his model. To his relief it appeared to be undamaged. None of the main parts had broken or come loose. He checked this by dusting and then gently tugging at wings, horizontal and vertical stabilisers and undercarriage.

"Seems OK," he commented.

Then he watched Stick bring the Storch in to a good three-point landing facing into the wind. As the model rolled to stop, he experienced a spurt of envy and then a flush of shame at not remembering such an elementary thing. *Why did I try to land with a cross wind?* he thought.

John joined him and studied the Spitfire. "Anything broken, Willy?"

"Just my pride," Willy replied.

"Can I have a go now?" John asked.

At that Willy's father intervened. "No. No more flying. The wind is getting too strong. We will end up breaking something," he said.

"Aw! What will we do now? It's only half past one," Stick replied.

Willy shrugged as he dusted clean the shiny plastic upper surfaces of his model. "We could go home?"

But Willy's father shook his head. "Not yet. After afternoon tea. Your mother is helping Aunty Isabel make mango chutney and I need to help Ted. You could always help by doing a bit of farm work."

Willy felt guilty at that. Normally, when it was just a family weekend, he often did farm work. But now he had his friends. "We could go for a walk maybe?"

His father nodded. "Good idea. Show them the creek or something. But be back by three for afternoon tea."

So the models and accessories were carried to the cars and the friends set off behind Willy as he walked off along a vehicle track beside the boundary fence.

Five minutes later they came to the creek. It was a lovely little creek lined with shady trees and with short grass on the banks. Along much of its length it was only a couple of paces wide and ankle deep but there were some nice little pools of crystal-clear water.

Willy turned right and led them upstream along an animal pad. As they strolled along, they came to a larger pool about ten metres across and waist deep. Marjorie clapped her hands with delight. "Oh! This is lovely!" she cried.

"It really floods in the wet season," Willy explained.

John wiped perspiration from his forehead. "It's bloody hot. Can we go back now?" he asked.

"We could have a swim to cool down," Stick suggested.

Willy shook his head. "Be a bit cold, and we didn't bring any bathers," he replied.

Stick snorted. "Huh! Who needs bathers? We can go skinny dipping."

Willy experienced an instant surge of excitement mingled with apprehension. *That would be good,* he thought, but did he dare?

Chapter 18

THE SWIM

Anxiety over possible unpleasant consequences then sent a chill into Willy's ardour. "What about Marjorie?" he asked.

Stick snorted again. "Huh! She won't mind," he commented.

"I might," Marjorie replied.

Willy felt his heart rate shoot right up. She looked excited and had a mischievous smile on her face. "I wouldn't like to offend her," he said.

Stick sniffed again. "Huh! Be nothing she hasn't seen before," he added, making Willy wonder what went on at the Morton household. He then had a searing flashback of seeing her nude at Stick's. To his dismay he began to get aroused but also hopeful.

"She could always go to another pool," he suggested.

Marjorie sniffed. "I will. Is there another pool further up the creek?" she said. But she did not sound very happy.

Willy was now torn. Part of him badly wanted to see Marjorie swimming naked but he was also feeling quite self-conscious about her and the other boys seeing him with nothing on. "There is a better pool another fifty metres up the creek," he commented. "It even has a rope we can use as a swing."

Stick nodded. "Good idea. Little Miss Tease can swim there and we will go here. Go on Marj, clear out!"

Willy glanced at Marjorie. She met his eyes and made a face and he sensed she was not keen on that plan. *Surely, she didn't want to swim naked with us?* he thought. It was both an exciting and a worrying concept. With a shrug she walked on along the creek.

John stood there, looking quite anxious. "I think we should just go back to the house," he said.

Stick curled his lip. "Why? Aren't ya game?" he taunted.

Willy glanced at John and saw a blush spread across his face and neck. The jibe had obviously stung.

Stick stood on the tiny beach and nodded with satisfaction. "This will be bloody good," he said. He began stripping off his shirt.

Willy looked to check that they were out of sight of Marjorie. Now he really wanted to see her nude and was hoping for glimpses but was quite confused about how he felt about her and about the other two boys seeing him. He saw that the trees and intervening bushes almost completely hid the next pool. With fingers that were now trembling with excitement and fear he began unbuttoning his shirt.

John shook his head. "We should go back," he said.

"You can," Stick retorted. He had now thrown his shirt on the ground and there and then he bent and pulled down his shorts and briefs, to stand naked on the small beach.

John stared at him and blushed some more. "We could get into trouble," he croaked.

"Pigs!" Stick retorted. "Marjorie won't tell, and nobody gives a rat's if we have a swim in the nuddy. Come on you guys. Ain't ya game?"

Willy found his heart was now pounding with a mixture of excitement and fear. Afraid of doing the wrong thing he hesitated. Part of his mind was wondering if Stick was actually gay. A host of comments he had heard over the years about gay people crowded his mind, adding to his anxiety. Lurking at the edge of his own awareness was also the troubling awareness that he felt a strong curiosity to see the other boys.

Stick waded in and then turned to face him. "Come on Willy, let's see what sort of man you are," he called.

Willy could only shrug. He found his heart was hammering and that his lips had gone dry and his hands wet. But rather than face Stick's jibes he took a deep breath and pulled his shorts and underpants down.

As he straightened up and tossed them aside, he was hotly aware of his partially aroused state. Stick stared at him and cried: "Holy mackerel Willy! That's a good prong. That should even satisfy Petra the Poke."

At the mention of Petra, Willy felt a stab of shame at his disloyalty and also a spurt of anger at Stick's insinuation. "She's not like that! She's a good girl," he croaked.

Stick grinned, ignoring his anger. "So why do you spend so much time chasing her?"

Willy wanted to reply that it wasn't like that, but he knew they would not believe him. Instead he waded in as quickly as he could, ignoring the cold. Hotly aware that John was also looking Willy quickly knelt in the shallows.

Stick now called to John and teased him until he also stripped off and joined them. For the next ten minutes the boys swam around the shallow pool. The water was cold but very refreshing.

But Willy was now under real pressure. He still felt very self-conscious about the other boys seeing him naked. *I don't want them to think I'm a queer,* he thought.

His eyes kept flicking to Stick and John and he found their naked bodies fascinating. To his own excited shame he realised that he badly wanted to know as much as he could about sex and studying the other boys provided both information and useful comparisons.

He also noted that John was trying to pretend he wasn't embarrassed, but Willy could tell he was actually very self-conscious.

Stick added to the embarrassment by wading ashore and looking along the creek towards the next pool. Then he pointed and grinned. "Hey fellas, come and have a squiz at this," he called.

Willy immediately guessed that Stick could see Marjorie and he was seized by instant desire to see her as well. But he did not want to appear really interested so he remained in the water till Stick called again. "Come on you blokes! Get an eyeful of this," he urged.

"What?" John asked.

"Sis standing in the sun," Stick replied. "Quick!"

Willy waded ashore and moved to stand beside Stick. John remained in the water. "Has she got any clothes on?" he queried.

Stick shook his head. "Nah! Nude as can be. Quick."

John shook his head in disapproval. "You shouldn't look at your sister," he chided.

Stick snorted. "Huh! I often see her with nothing on. She prances around in the nuddy all the time at home," he answered.

John looked astonished. "What do your parents say?" he queried.

Stick laughed. "She doesn't do it when they are home," he replied.

By then Willy was with Stick and peering through a gap in the trees. To his delight he saw Marjorie quiet clearly. She was standing side on to him on the bank in a beam of sunlight and was patting her hair and running her hands over her body. Marjorie appeared to be singing and dancing and looked very happy and to Willy, the very image of desirable female.

Gosh! She is a nice-looking chick alright, he thought.

John remained in the water, his face stiff with disapproval. "You shouldn't be looking," he said.

Stick just grunted and shrugged and kept looking. That was too much for John. "I'm going to tell her," he said. With that he called out, "Marjorie! We can see you."

To Willy's disappointment, Marjorie at once looked their way and hastily covered herself. Turning her back, she quickly waded back into the pool. Then a wave of shame and embarrassment engulfed him and he turned and waded back into the pool.

As he did, he noted that John looked both scared and disgusted. John quickly waded ashore, covering himself with his hands and trying to keep his back to them as he did. He began dressing, ignoring the water on his body. As quickly as he could he did up his shorts. "I'm going back to the house," he said.

Stick looked anxious. "Don't you tell on us, Johnno," he said.

John paused while picking up his shirt and looked at him with a look of disdain on his face. "I won't! What sort of a mate do you think I am?" he cried angrily. Still pulling on his shirt he hurried away down the creek.

Willy was now very embarrassed. Stick met Willy's eyes. "You won't tell on me will ya, Willy?"

"No," Willy croaked. He now found the situation so embarrassing he just wanted to get out of there. Without a word he strode over to his clothes and began pulling them on. Stick joined him and also began to dress. As he tugged on his pants he called to Marjorie. "Get dressed Sis!"

By now Willy was feeling quite ashamed of their actions. He was also quite worried. *What if the adults find out?* he fretted.

Thus it was a very anxious boy who waited until a now fully clothed Marjorie joined them. He tried to act cool and relaxed but actually his whole body felt like it was full of squirming ants and he knew he was gripped by lust.

Back at the house, the social scene was very brittle. The teenagers all acted as though nothing had happened but to Willy their speech and actions all seemed so artificial he felt sure the adults must realise something had happened. To add to his annoyance Marjorie went and sat beside John, talking to him and touching his leg.

The teasing little bitch! I thought she liked me, Willy thought. To change the subject he asked what they were doing the next day. Nothing much it transpired. The Morton's were going to Innisfail to visit relatives and John said he was working on a new model aircraft.

"Can I come over and help?" Willy asked.

John nodded and a time after lunch was agreed. Then it was farewells, into the vehicles and back to Cairns. And during this Willy had his nose put out of joint again when Marjorie sat in the back beside John while he ended up in the front beside his dad.

Far into the night Willy lay and fantasised about Marjorie. He was so randy he had trouble gaining relief and woke on the Monday morning feeling worn out and drained. But even thinking about Marjorie instantly conjured up nude images of her and got him aroused again. He found it a relief to sit in his room to play computer games.

After lunch he rode his bike over to John's. As he locked his bike inside the front gate, he experienced a spurt of guilt. He knew John was his friend and that he wanted him to come over more often, yet he rarely had.

I will try to visit more often, he decided.

To his surprise, Willy found that John was in the middle of drawing plans for a large balsa model. Turning his head to try to read the plans he asked, "What is it Johnno?"

John blushed. "A World War One SE5," he replied. "It will have an 80-centimetre wingspan." He indicated this with his hands.

Willy was both jealous and impressed. He noted that John had enlarged a set of plans and was now tracing and photocopying each sheet as he completed it. Then Willy's gaze settled on two radio controllers which were sticking out of an old carton. "Is it going to be radio-controlled?" he asked.

John went even redder and nodded. "Yes. I was able to buy these cheap at the markets. There is something wrong with each one and I am hoping I can make one working unit out of two," he explained.

"That's a good idea. You are very clever," Willy complimented.

John's response was to frown and give him a quick glance as though he was checking whether Willy's compliment was some sort of put down. Then he smiled and shrugged. "I hope I can make it work. If I do, I can fly my plane against yours."

"That's a good idea. What sort of power unit are you looking at: petrol or electric?" Willy asked.

"Petrol," John answered. "I was hoping to buy an old second-hand motor cheap."

The boys settled to studying the plans and John resumed work while Willy sat and watched and chatted. John was at the stage where he was calculating the servos and linkages needed to make the control surfaces operate. "There always seem to be a lot more than you think," he grumbled.

Thinking about model aircraft and flying them got Willy's thoughts moving back to the plans for the Red Baron's Fokker Triplane that he had at home.

Flying a brand-new factory-built kit aircraft like my Spitfire in competition against a scratch built one with second-hand parts isn't really fair, he thought. He decided to resume work on the Fokker Triplane.

When he got home that evening that is what he did. He again cleared the work bench and then sorted the scale tracings. Then he carefully numbered every part on the plans. *I will need a motor,* he thought. The real aircraft had been powered by radial engines but a glance at a few model aircraft magazines quickly revealed that these were very rare.

To his annoyance Willy found that his mind would not focus. Every few minutes his thoughts wandered off onto lustful memories and fantasies about Marjorie. Even after relieving the urge the thoughts came flitting back. It seemed that his brain had no control over his body at all. *God I am a weakling!* Willy thought.

But he did want to see more of Marjorie. He had to admit that. *Maybe on Wednesday?* he speculated, remembering Stick saying they would be away until then.

By arrangement Willy went over to John's again on Tuesday. This time Scott was also there, and he and John were dismantling and examining the pieces of a petrol motor John had purchased. Scott's presence was socially a bit uncomfortable, but Willy managed to be polite. *I don't want any unpleasantness as John's,* he told himself.

To take the focus off the social situation Willy bent to study the small motors. Willy knew very little about small engines and he tried to hide this ignorance by looking intelligent and nodding agreement and by listening.

Just handling the metal parts he found a pleasant experience. The metal was shiny and smooth and was slightly oily. Odours of fuel and oil and rubber added to the tactile nature of the experience. *I am sure I can master these things,* he told himself as he turned a motor over and moved one of its cylinders up and down.

John had several magazines with articles on motors and Willy sat back and read these with interest while John and Scott cleaned and reassembled the motor. Then they clamped it to a work bench under the house and John tried to start it. To his obvious embarrassment he couldn't.

Willy's fingers itched to help, and he reached out to try but some instinct held him from asking and he withdrew his hands. Not so Scott. He took hold of the motor and at the same time said, "Give me a go."

Resentment showed on John's face but he politely nodded. Scott did not even notice, absorbed by then with studying the motor. He fiddled and adjusted and then pumped fuel before flicking the propeller. The motor burst into life at the first go and Scott grinned and looked around, obviously pleased with himself. "Easy," he commented.

John gave a sickly grin, but Willy could tell he wasn't happy. John then adjusted the engine speed and the boys studied it as it ran. A sickly stench of burnt fuel and oil filled the room and soon had them coughing. That persuaded John to turn the motor off.

"Well it works," he said. "Now I need to finish the aircraft."

Scott turned to glance at the partly constructed SE5 model. "When do you reckon you will have it finished by?" he asked.

John shrugged. "A couple of weeks?"

Scott nodded. "I will make one too and we could have another flying competition. How about that?"

"Yeah, OK," John agreed.

Scott turned to Willy. "What about you Willy?"

Willy liked the idea. "I am making a Fokker Triplane. I will try to have it finished by then. And I will ask my dad if he can drive us to the farm or somewhere to fly them."

The others liked that idea and, as it was time for Willy to go home, he left soon afterwards and pedalled his bike back there. Then he worked on his model, carefully tracing, marking, cutting and sanding balsa pieces, each of which he numbered.

That evening he broached the subject of another weekend flying competition with his parents. His father smiled and went to a calendar. "I thought we were going to the farm this Sunday?" he said.

Willy nodded. "Yes, but we won't have our models ready by then. We will only be able to fly the kit models already put together. We need another couple of weeks."

His father tapped the calendar with his fingertip. "There is a flying competition in Townsville on the weekend sixteenth, seventeenth of October. That is a week after the holidays. How would that do?"

It would do very well John and Scott agreed, and they were both very keen on the idea of going to Townsville to see other model aircraft being flown. They began making arrangements with parents and most of Wednesday was taken up with working on models.

It was also a time of great frustration for Willy. His mind kept filling with images of Marjorie nude and he became continually aroused. The desire to see her naked again began to develop into something of an obsession and only occasionally did he remember Petra and feel guilty that he wasn't fantasising about her. *She is much too nice to do anything rude like skinny dipping,* he told himself.

The frustration was given a sharper edge by the return of Stick on Thursday. He phoned and invited Willy to his house. Willy was very keen to go although he realised he would have to work harder to finish his model on time. But the thought of Marjorie's curves set his fingers twitching and he quickly rode his bike over to Stick's.

Once there he did get to see Marjorie. She gave him a big smile and was friendly, but she was dressed in T-shirt and shorts. The T-shirt was so tight it stretched over her bosom. This bobbled in a way that made Willy's mouth go dry with desire and he had to wipe sweaty palms on his shorts and lick suddenly dry lips.

But Marjorie had several friends visiting and the girls took themselves off to the shops, leaving the boys to discuss model aircraft and the new competition. Stick looked very keen.

"Would it be OK if I joined in?" he asked.

"I'd like that. Let's ask Johnno. It was his idea," Willy suggested.

So both boys rode their bikes over to John's only to find he was at Scott's. So they rode there and found them flying a small electric powered aircraft in the back yard. The model was one of the old-fashioned types with wires leading from the controls to the port wing tip and then ten metres to a handle that the operator held and manipulated to make the aircraft climb and dive. As the model could only fly in a circle around the operator it had no rudder controls but it was still entertaining to watch, until Scott misjudged and flew it into the lawn, snapping off a wing and ripping out one of the nylon fishing line control cables.

The boys then sat and chatted until it was time for Willy to go home. Once there he sat in the workshop daydreaming about girls in between working on his model.

Then his hopes were sent up by a phone call from Stick. "We are going to the swimming pool tomorrow after lunch. Wanta come?"

"I'd love to," Willy replied, his mind suddenly filled with images of Marjorie.

After that the evening at home dragged. Watching the TV programs his parents preferred and playing endless computer games did not have the same appeal as flirting with girls! It was a horny and frustrated boy who took himself to bed where he then lay for several hours, conjuring up ever more lurid fantasies as he did.

The following morning Willy worked on his model Fokker Triplane. He had all the plans drawn by now and most of the pieces cut out so he set to work gluing together several of the small parts: the horizontal stabilisers and elevators and the rudder. These were placed on plastic 'Gladwrap' pinned onto the plans and as each piece was glued it was also pinned down so that as the glue dried the shape was correct.

As he worked Willy's thoughts kept drifting constantly to girls and he alternately became aroused and relaxed. He found it both stimulating and enjoyable but equally frustrating.

After lunch, and in a state of heightened awareness and anticipation, Willy changed into his bathers, pulled on shorts and T-shirt and with a towel in a backpack rode his bicycle to the swimming pool at North Cairns.

By the time he got there he found he was feeling quite anxious but excited. After locking his bicycle into the racks he made his way inside. He paid and went through to the lawn beyond the kiosk. There he stopped and looked around, hoping to see some friends.

To his consternation there was no sign of any of his friends or of Marjorie and hers. *Have they changed their mind?* he wondered. *Or am I just early?*

Uncertain of what to do he made his way across the lawn to a patch of shade beside a garden bed. He chose a spot where the shrubs hid him from the kiosk but from where he could see the front entrance out one side and the main pool on the other. Here he spread his towel and sat down. As he rubbed on sun cream he looked around, scanning all the heads in the water to see if any of his friends were among them. There were a few teenagers he recognised as going to his school but mostly the people were primary school kids and a few adults with younger children.

Oh, I hope they come! Willy thought. He did not want to waste the afternoon at the pool. He wasn't a very keen swimmer at the best of times. But then he spotted two of the Year 12 girls from his school and he changed his mind. The girls looked so attractive in their bathers that he could only eye them with lustful wistfulness. *They are nice!* he thought.

After a time he took off his T-shirt and then his shorts, but he was fairly self-conscious about his body and memories of swimming naked with Stick got him all hot and anxious. For half an hour he lay and admired the girls he saw and hoped his friends would come.

But they didn't and after an hour, during which Willy swam up and down the pool a few times and admired the Year 12 girls some more, he decided to go home.

A phone call informed him that Stick and Marjorie had not been allowed to come. "Sorry, we had to mow the lawn and weed the vegie garden," Stick explained.

Willy was annoyed but tried to keep it out of his voice. "What will we do tomorrow?" he asked hoping for another opportunity.

"What about my place?" Stick suggested. "And everyone bring some gliders or model planes we can fly in the park."

Willy thought that a good plan. *I might get to see Marjorie again*, he told himself.

That night he fantasised and relived every moment of the swim at the farm. He then fantasised about Marjorie. Only later did he feel niggles of guilt over Petra.

Chapter 19

FRUSTRATION

In fact, Friday turned out to be an anti-climax. Willy got no opportunity to get anywhere with Marjorie as Johnno, Scott, Noddy and Stick were always there. And if they weren't Marjorie's mother, a formidable looking woman with mousy fair hair, freckles and a very big bosom, kept looking in to see what they were doing.

Even walking to the park to throw gliders did not offer any opportunity. And Willy knew that he was confused and torn, and jealous. With something of a shock he realised he was very drawn to Marjorie. Seeing her flirting with Johnno and Scott made him feel quite jealous.

I do like Marjorie, he told himself. It was only then that he remembered Petra and a stab of quite painful guilt lanced through him. *Oh, what have I done?* he thought, remembering how excited he had been when thinking of Marjorie. *How could I be so disloyal?*

Sadly he shook his head and resolved to try to get more control of himself. *And I must be faithful to Petra,* he resolved. To him she was an image of purity and love and he blushed with shame and guilt.

But then thoughts of Marjorie again swamped his mind when they began to discuss what to do on the weekend. Willy wanted to get them all to come to the farm for the two days but none of them was allowed. They all had other commitments on Saturday.

"What about Sunday?" he asked.

As he did, he met Marjorie's eye and she grinned. "Will we go swimming again?" she asked.

"If you like," Willy answered, his heart pounding with hope and lust.

"Then I'd better bring my bathers this time," she answered.

That dashed Willy's wilder hopes but still got him thinking and wishing. "I will check with mum and dad. Who else wants to come?" he asked.

Johnno did. He was continually looking hopefully at Marjorie and half the time she responded but Willy got the distinct impression she was teasing or flirting.

Does she like him? he wondered, jealousy again stirring his emotions.

At home that afternoon Willy worked on his model triplane but with only half his mind. The other half was on girls. Images of naked girls kept swamping his consciousness. Every few minutes, or so it seemed, he got aroused. To his annoyance he found that it was images of Marjorie that dominated.

And to his own shame he found it hard to focus on Petra. He still daydreamed about her and tried to keep his thoughts at the pure love level, but these were quickly pushed aside by the more torrid memories of recent days. Vague guilt at being disloyal to Petra and of 'cheating' on her nagged at him, but the more recent reality dominated and he shrugged such worries aside.

And to his own disgust he found he was itching to be with Marjorie. But there was no chance on Saturday, just household chores and working on gluing the middle wings of the Fokker Triplane together, in between fantasising. As Sunday got closer, he found his imagination dwelling on situations where he and Marjorie might get to be alone.

Sunday morning dawned at last and he woke aroused and itching with lustful hope. As he dressed and packed for the day he managed to suppress or hide this, but his excited anticipation dominated. As one the previous weekend the family took both cars and picked up the other teenagers. Willy hoped that Marjorie would end up his dad's car with him but instead Johnno was picked up first and sat in the back. Then, when they collected Stick and Marjorie, she just gave them an impish smile and opted to go with Willy's mum.

Her smile bothered Willy. *Was that for me or for Johnno?* he wondered.

On arrival at the farm they all had morning tea. During it Willy tried to position himself beside Marjorie but each time he was blocked by John who monopolized her company, getting Willy both annoyed and jealous.

Then it was flying. Once again, they took turns with Willy's powered Spitfire and his dad's Feisler Storch. They all had a go with both aircraft except Marjorie. She just stood and watched and, to Willy's annoyance, seemed to spend more time with John than with anyone. Certainly she seemed to be giving him the cold shoulder.

Lunchtime came and the Storch had its batteries removed and placed on the charger and the group made their way back to the farmhouse. It was a pleasant enough gathering but Willy again found himself blocked out and feeling frustrated. To try to rationalize it he reminded himself that it was Petra he should be thinking of.

The problem was that Marjorie was just there and she kept wriggling, giggling and moving so that Willy could not help noticing her female curves. It was all very frustrating and challenging.

When the group returned to the back paddock to resume flying after lunch Willy was in a fevered state of arousal and envy. He badly wanted to organise another swim down at the creek but did not want to be seen too keen to organise it. So he held his tongue and looked for openings when he might hint at such a thing.

But to his annoyance he never got the chance. His father was the cause. Quite unexpectedly he told them all to wait and walked off to his car, returning a couple of minutes later with several cardboard boxes.

To Willy's surprise his father unpacked a brand-new quadcopter. This was lifted clear and held for them to look at. Willy stared at it with annoyance and frustration that slowly gave way to interest. The drone was about half a metre across and was a middle-of-the-range type that carried a camera underneath.

Willy's father placed it on a bench. "I thought we could all have a go with this," he explained.

"Where did you get it, Dad?" Willy asked, bending forward to study it more closely. He saw that it was made of white plastic and that the rotors had no guards. The blades were of white plastic and about 15 centimetres across.

"At the same hobby shop," his father replied as he unpacked the controller. Associated items like battery chargers were also unpacked. Willy's father then opened the instruction booklet and began preparing the drone to fly. "Remember there are strict laws about who can fly these things and where," he said. "So we are only using it here at the farm, right away from other people or air traffic."

As Willy's father carefully read the booklet and bit by bit assembled pieces and inserted batteries, impatience began to build. Willy began to fidget and wished his father would hurry up.

Sensing this, his father turned to him and said, "There's an old saying William that says: when all else fails, read the instructions. I am saying to you read them first and don't waste time or money. So stop hopping from one foot to the other and go and plug that battery charger in."

Willy did so and two batteries were placed on the charger. Two more were taken out. One was inserted in the drone and another into the controller. This was switched on and Willy was pleased to see lights come on and the screen light up. But still Dr Williams took his time, reading and then working his way through the computer menu on the controller.

Willy saw him call up a map of the area and then he clicked in four points which he set in the memory. Then he studied the menu again before clicking a 'home' icon.

"What's that for Dad?" Willy asked.

"To bring the drone back to its start point if anything happens to the radio controller," his father explained.

Noddy frowned and peered closely at the screen. "What could go wrong?" he asked.

"Plenty," Willy's father replied. "The battery could go flat in the controller or some sort of electrical interference or the operator might just push the wrong button," he explained.

"What would happen if you didn't program it to fly back to the start?" Stick asked.

"It would just fly away until it crashed or until it ran out of power and came down," Dr Williams answered.

Stick pointed to the numbered dots on the screen. "What are those?"

"They are called Way Points. Same as in a GPS," Willy's father replied.

Willy had never operated a GPS but had seen one at cadets so had a rough idea of how it worked. "Like the GPS Navigator in the car?" he suggested.

"Something like that," Dr Williams agreed. He next unpacked the camera and inserted a battery into it. After carefully examining it he had Willy and John hold the drone upside down while he studied how the camera was attached. Willy noted that there were snap catches and a screw fastener. The camera was secured and then linked by a short data cable to the drone.

"That's so it can relay the images back to us through the radio link," Dr Williams explained. He then switched the drone and camera on and the controller screen changed to show a blurred image which then focused to show Stick's shirt. The camera then provided a few minutes amusement while it was tested.

Dr Williams worked the camera controls for a while, making the lens move in and out to change focus and causing the camera to rotate. Nodding with satisfaction, he said: "Now I think we are ready. All stand back and we will get ready for lift off."

To Willy's surprise, his father did not take the drone outside for a test flight but simply set the rotors spinning slowly and then gently increased the revs until it slowly lifted off to hover at head height. Again nodding with satisfaction he sent it up higher and then made it move sideways and then backwards and forwards before getting it to circle inside the shed.

"Good! That all seems easy enough. Let's try it outside," Dr Williams said. He moved the controls and the drone tilted sightly and was flown out of the open door.

After that it was half an hour of fun. Despite his prejudice against drones Willy watched with fascinated interest and then had the pleasure and thrill of being given the controller.

As he brought it in to land, he said in an off-hand voice, "Certainly a useful tool."

He handed the controller to John and then stood and watched with envy as John made it all look easy. Stick and Noddy were next and both showed themselves to be quite competent controllers.

Marjorie was then offered a play and to Willy's surprise she said yes and took the controller. She was a bit hesitant at first and tended to make adjustments that were too bold but then she got the feel of it and carried out quite a creditable mission. Looking very pleased with herself she handed the controller back to Dr Williams who passed it to Uncle Ted, who had been watching sceptically from the side.

By then the boys were all fidgeting with impatience and when John suggested that the other model aircraft might also be flown this was agreed to. Batteries were taken off chargers and fuel added to the ones with internal combustion engines and three models were put into the air at once, with some resultant near-misses and minor dramas.

While Stick was having his second go with the drone Willy stood next him, having reluctantly surrendered his Spitfire to John. The images showing on the screen from the camera were very clear. Willy was not surprised as he frequently saw 'drone shots' on TV news and documentaries.

"This is really good," Stick commented. "If we did an exercise against the army cadets, we could spy on them with this."

Willy looked at Stick with surprise. "I think you will find they know all about drones," he replied. "The army has lots of them and uses them right down to section level." He had read a number or articles in newspapers and magazines about the types of UAVs and drones the army had been using for years and had also read articles on how extensively drones were used in the seemingly endless wars in the Middle East.

And then disaster stuck. Stick saw the Spitfire zooming towards the drone and made a sharp turn to the right, resulting in the drone jinking towards the gum trees which bordered the back paddock.

"Stick!" Willy had time to call. But too late! The drone flew into the tree and then went spinning down to crash in a cloud of dust. The camera image showed the upside-down image of the tree and a strand of the barbed wire fence that surrounded the field.

"Switch it all off Stick," Dr Williams instructed.

"Sorry Dr Williams," Stick croaked.

Dr Williams shrugged and started walking. "Can't be helped. As Napoleon said: you can't make an omelette without breaking eggs! Land all those other planes you lot," he said.

The other models were brought into bumpy landings and they all hurried across the dusty paddock to where the drone lay. Willy picked it up and saw at once that one of the rotors was bent out of alignment. "Oh Stick!" he cried. "You've bust it!"

Stick looked upset and contrite and Dr Williams stepped in to take the drone. "It isn't the end of the world. It can be fixed. But I think that is enough flying for the day. The wind is getting up. You kids park these other models and then go and amuse yourselves while I see if this can be easily repaired. Be back by afternoon teatime." With that he and Uncle Ted walked away.

That was the opening Willy had been hoping for but it was Marjorie who spoke first. "What about going down the creek again?" she suggested.

Stick enthusiastically agreed. "Great idea. We could have another dip," he said. "What about you Willy?"

"Yeah, OK," Willy agreed. "What about you Johnno?"

John looked quite put out. "I suppose so," he said with a shrug.

They returned the model aircraft and controllers to the vehicles and then set off along the track down to the creek. John still wasn't happy. "Did anyone bring bathers this time?" he asked.

Stick shook his head. "I didn't. We didn't need 'em last time. It'll be OK."

A mixture of excitement and anxiety sent a shiver through Willy. "What about Marjorie?" he asked.

Stick snorted again. "Huh! She didn't mind last time," he commented.

"You shouldn't have looked," Marjorie replied.

Stick snorted again. "Huh! And you shouldn't have been prancing around in the nuddy."

"Why not? It felt very nice," Marjorie replied.

Willy glanced at her and felt his heart rate shoot right up. She had a mischievous smile on her face and looked excited.

Willy had a searing flashback of seeing Marjorie nude at Stick's and during the previous swim. He began to get aroused and very hopeful. "We will swap pools. There are more of us and we need the bigger pool," he suggested.

Marjorie nodded. "That'll be alright," she agreed.

Willy was soon very aroused and hotly aware of it. He badly wanted to see Marjorie swimming naked, but he was also feeling quite self-conscious about her and the other boys seeing him with nothing on.

When they arrived at the first pool in the creek Willy said, "Marjorie, you swim here. The next pool is bigger and we have a rope swing there."

"OK," she agreed, adding, "And no peeking this time."

Willy glanced at Marjorie and blushed. She met his eyes and giggled, and he sensed that she had not really minded them seeing her. He shrugged and led the way on up the creek.

John followed, looking anxious. He said, "I think we should explore," he said.

Stick looked back over his shoulder. "Why? We all had a swim last time?" he challenged.

Willy glanced back at John and saw him blush and frown.

As soon as the boys reached the next pool Stick began stripping off his shirt. John went very red and shook his head. "I think I will just explore up the creek for a bit," he said. With that he turned and hurried on out of sight.

Stick turned to Willy. "You don't mind do ya Willy?"

Willy was quite taken aback at Stick's forthrightness. And to his own shame and surprise it came to him that he also was interested in seeing other people naked. But his mouth was so dry with lust that he could only croak and nod.

Stick was not really listening, and he now peeled off his shorts. "Ah! That's better," he said.

Willy could only nod and stare. Then he glanced back to check that they were out of sight of Marjorie. He really wanted to see her nude and was hoping for glimpses but was quite confused about how he felt about her and about Stick seeing him aroused. With fingers that were now trembling with excitement and fear he began unbuttoning his shirt.

Willy found his heart was now pounding and was blushing with shame. Burning with lust and embarrassment he hesitated. Stick waded in and then turned to face him. "Come on Willy, don't be shy," he called.

Again Willy shrugged. He found his heart was hammering and that his lips had gone dry and his hands wet with perspiration. Rather than face Stick's jibes he took a deep breath and pulled his shorts and underpants down. Burning with embarrassment he waded in as quickly as he could, ignoring the cold.

For several minutes the two boys swam around the shallow pool. Then Stick went to the rope hanging from the overhanging branch and swung on it. Then he did it again, calling out loudly and pretending to be Tarzan as he did.

With a loud shriek he let go and splashed into the pool. As he surfaced Stick shook the water off his face and grinned. "Your go now Willy," he said.

Willy was now under real pressure. He did not want to appear weak or afraid but was feeling very self-conscious. But when Stick teased him again, he reluctantly stood up and waded to the rope, hotly aware of his aroused condition.

With his heart hammering furiously and feeling very embarrassed he reached up and grabbed the rope and dragged it ashore, trying to hide himself as much as he could. It seemed that the best course was to pretend he wasn't concerned and to make a joke of it, so he copied Stick, making Tarzan noises as he did.

But as he swung out, he was shocked to have his gaze lock with that of an astonished Marjorie. She was gaping at him from behind a tree at the edge of the pool. Fear and shame coursed through him and he immediately let go and dropped into the water.

As he surfaced Marjorie called, "What are you boys doing? Are you alright?"

Willy blinked to clear his eyes and remained neck deep in the water to cover himself. Then he took stock of the situation. Marjorie was peeking around a tree and she was obviously naked. She giggled and stared at him then repeated her question.

"I could hear you calling out. I wondered if someone had hurt themselves," she explained.

Stick answered. "Just pretending to be Tarzan," he explained.

"Tarzan?" Marjorie asked, her eyes flicking from Stick to Willy. Willy watched fascinated. He was glad he was standing in neck deep water but was gripped by fierce desire.

Stick surprised him even more by saying, "Do you want a swing, Sis?"

Marjorie glanced at the rope and back to him but shook her head. "Can I join you?" she asked.

Stick glanced at Willy and nodded. "Sure, we don't mind," he answered.

"Don't look then," Marjorie said. She waited until both Stick and Willy had turned to look the other way. Willy heard her splash her way down into the water and could hardly wait to turn to see what he could see. He found the situation intensely exciting and arousing and found his heart was beating so fast he was almost hyperventilating.

To Willy's delight he saw that Marjorie was kneeling in the shallow water. Only her head and the tops of her breasts were above water. His avid gaze noted that all of her large boobs were visible as shimmering bumps in the clear water.

Lust hammered in his ears and he stared at Marjorie's head and neck and the pale outline of her naked body in the water. He was hotly aware that she could probably also see a fair bit of both boys. "We aren't offending you I hope," he said.

Marjorie curled her lip. "You aren't. Seen one you've seen 'em all," she replied.

Marjorie then sank back into the water and swam away a few strokes. Her behaviour was a revelation to Willy and sent his excited mind into a whirl of speculation and hopes fuelled by lust. *But she is under age,* he thought, but did not have the courage to say.

Marjorie shrugged and swam away from them and then turned and sat up. As she did her breasts came half out of the water again and the sight set Willy's pulses pounding again.

"Don't you tell, please," she said. "No boasting to your mates."

Willy shook his head. "I won't, I promise," he said, his gaze focused on her breasts.

To Willy they presented a fascinating sight. As a teenage boy he was fascinated by girls almost to the point of obsession and he found their breasts particularly alluring and interesting. His heart began to pound with desire even as his mind was gripped by the great mystery of it all.

He had glimpsed a few breasts before, even had brief glimpses of Marjorie's; and he had seen plenty of pictures of them in girlie magazines and on the internet but these were real. They quivered and moved and they were right there!

Willy noted that Marjorie was coming out in goose bumps and the way her breasts moved as she rubbed at them caused him another surge of lust and he experienced a fierce surge of desire. Willy found the situation intensely stimulating.

This is fantastic! he thought as lust pounded in him.

Then a noise behind him made him look over his shoulder. There was a person there and for an instant Willy feared it was one of the adults. But it wasn't.

It was Johnno.

Chapter 20

GUILT

John stood there, eyes wide and mouth agape as he took in the scene. A scarlet blush began to mottle his face and neck. Then he shook his head and a look of revulsion appeared on his face.

"This is disgusting!" he cried.

With that he turned and almost ran back the way he had come. Willy watched him go, shame now warring with lust. He looked at Marjorie and she met his eyes and shrugged. "He's just jealous," she commented.

Stick began slowly swimming around. Willy did the same, shame and anxiety now replacing lust. "Do you think Johnno will tell?" he asked.

Stick shook his head. "Nah! Johnno's a mate," he said.

Marjorie curled her lip. "And a hypocrite. I'll bet he wants to be here with me too. He's just a jealous coward," she said in scathing contempt.

Willy thought that was a bit harsh and he knew he should defend his friend's reputation. To his shame he did not, but he did realise that his relationship with John might now be quite different.

And it was. When he again met up with him waiting at the end of the track back to the farm John angrily confronted him, his eyes flicking to Stick and Marjorie who were walking up the track nearby. "How could you?" John snapped angrily.

Willy could only shrug. Now that his desire had abated under the impulse of fear, he was a bit ashamed. But he had enjoyed it too and decided he really had no regrets. He shrugged again and remembered a cautionary warning he had heard his father giving to Lloyd the previous year.

'A standing prick has no conscience,' his father had said and now Willy understood with an intensity that could only make him blush as re-awakened lust mingled with embarrassed shame.

"She came and joined us," he defended lamely.

But that seemed to enrage John even more. "Oh how could you! What about Petra?" he cried.

Petra! Willy's mind was flooded with images of her and he

experienced a savage stab of guilt. It dawned on him that not once during the afternoon had he thought of her. But then, to his own shame, he hoped that Marjorie had not heard John as the notion that Marjorie might be persuaded to maybe do other things flitted across his mind and he did not want that opportunity compromised.

Anxiously Willy glanced back and saw that Marjorie was talking to Stick and did not appear to have heard. Then another flash of guilt flamed in Willy as he realised he had been considering deceiving both girls. *Bloody hell!* he thought. *What a weakling I am! What do I do?*

And the guilt returned with a vengeance when he accidentally met Petra the following day. He had spent the morning at home but quickly became bored with computer games and reading so he phoned his friends and arranged to meet them at the shopping centre with the best Hobby Shop. After riding there on his bike and carefully securing it to the bicycle racks with chains through the frame and both wheels with a padlock he wandered inside with his friends.

To his delight, he almost collided with Petra at the entrance to a shop. "Oh hi Petra!" he cried, going over to her.

To his dismay Petra's face registered first puzzlement and then, as she recognised him, horror. "Villy!" she cried. Then she gave a quick shake of her head and gestured for him to go away.

A bit taken aback by this greeting, Willy frowned. "What's wrong Petra?" he asked.

Petra licked her lips and cast a worried glance back over her shoulder. "My mutti," she croaked.

Willy's gaze shifted to the person coming out of the shop behind her. Petra's mother was an older looking version of her. Willy's first impression was that she had been as beautiful as Petra when she was younger, but that now she had a hardness to her that took away from that. Her hair was black but starting to go grey and her face was showing signs of wrinkles and was set in a frown of disapproval. Her eyes noted Willy and then her gaze darted from him to Petra and back to him. Her lips pursed and Willy felt a spasm of anxiety.

Petra's mother came to a stop beside her and she glared at him. She then turned to Petra and rapped a series of questions at her in a foreign language. Petra seemed to shrink and shrivel but croaked, "Speak English mamma."

"I der Englick spik ven I vont!" her mother retorted.

Once again, she flicked a glance at Willy, a venomous glance that again made him think of those stories from Ancient Greek mythology about witches or goddesses who could turn men to stone with a single glance. *Medusa?* he thought.

Petra's mother now pointed at him. "Who dis boy? Who tell you to talk to strange boys in der street eh?" she screeched.

"This is Villy. He just a boy in my class at school," Petra replied, fear showing on her face.

Petra's mother cast him a baleful glance and curled her lip. "You arrange to him meet?" she accused.

"No Mutti," Petra. "I not."

Willy was appalled at her evident fear and distress. "She didn't, missus. It is just chance. I did not know she would be here," he said.

As he did, he saw John, Stick and Marjorie appear further along the shopping mall. That set his stomach into a churning whirl. *Bugger! I don't want Marjorie to see me talking to Petra,* he thought. The guilt rose like bile and his anxiety level went up.

Then the situation got much worse. Petra's mother stepped closer and his vision was filled with her hard, hostile face. Willy's heart hammered with anxiety as she waved her arms angrily. "Vot for you spik to my little girl, eh? You vont to be her boyfriend?"

Willy was struck speechless because by now Marjorie was close enough to hear and had seen him. "No," he croaked, hoping to keep Petra out of trouble although despising himself for being too cowardly to speak the truth. "She is just in my class and I just said hello in passing."

"Zen you keep passing! You clear off and not to my little girl talk!" Petra's mother shouted, waving her fists at him. "I know vot filthy boys like you think! You just her for the sex vont! You not spik to her again."

She then turned to Petra, who had gone very pale and was shaking and obviously terrified. "And you, little miss, you not spik to boys again, you hear me?" With that her hand lashed out and she cuffed Petra on the left ear. Then she grabbed her and shoved her around. "Now ve go! Vork zat vay."

Mother and daughter walked off leaving a shaken and shocked Willy feeling both guilty and embarrassed.

Stick, Marjorie and John moved closer and joined him. John gave him a hard look that made him squirm with guilt and Stick added to his discomfiture by chuckling and saying, "I reckon you need to improve your courting technique, Willy."

Marjorie had a hurt and jealous look on her face. "Who is she?" she asked, her eyes fixed on Petra's retreating back.

Stick answered. "That is the delectable Petra, object of Willy's lustful desire."

Willy wanted to deny that and was annoyed with Stick but all he could do was meet Marjorie's hurt gaze and shrug while squirming with guilt and embarrassment.

Stick then twisted the knife by chuckling and saying loudly to John, "My dad said that first a boy has to get the girl's mother onside. If he does that he's in like Flynn."

John made a face. Marjorie scowled and Willy shuddered. A piece of advice from his own father flitted across his mind to the effect that a boy should look at a girl's mother before getting serious. *She might look a lovely little thing when she's sixteen, but genetics says she will probably look like her mother when she's older. Ask yourself if you want to be married to that!* his dad had said.

But Willy could not picture Petra that way, and he stubbornly clung to his ideal and determined to keep trying. Then his eyes met Marjorie's and he blushed as guilt and confusion flooded through him.

Stick did not seem to notice. "Wot ya doin' Willy, other than picking fights with old dragons, that is," he asked.

Willy shrugged and his mind raced. Wanting badly to change the subject he said, "I was on my way to the Hobby Shop to look at model planes," he answered.

"That's a good idea. Let's do that," Stick replied.

So they did. As they walked along Willy found Marjorie beside him and that made him feel guilty and anxious again. A glance at John did not help as his friend was looking upset and disapproving.

At the Hobby Shop Willy made a big effort to forget Petra. He studied all the types of motors and radio controllers until his friends got restless. "Let's do something else," Stick said.

"What?"

"I'd rather fly models than look at things I can't afford," John commented.

Willy shrugged and felt another stab of niggling guilt. "OK, where?"

"My place?" John suggested. "We could fly my gliders."

So that was agreed. The friends made their way out to the bike racks and collected their bikes. They pedalled as a group to John's. Marjorie obviously wasn't happy and Willy, noting this, turned to her. "What would you like to do, Marjorie?"

"Go to the pool, go swimming," she replied.

That idea sent searing and arousing images through Willy's mind, but Stick laughed aloud and looked back over his shoulder. "You can't swim in the nuddy at the pool Sis!"

Marjorie poked her tongue at him and went red. "Don't be crude," she retorted.

"Tomorrow maybe," Willy suggested.

But Stick shook his head. "Nah! Have to be Thursday. We are going to see Aunty Joyce tomorrow," he said.

That was bad news to Willy as he now badly wanted to see Marjorie's body again, even if only in a swimsuit. Then he remembered he was supposed to be in love with Petra and mentally flailed himself as a disloyal weakling.

One result was that he was quite stand-offish with Marjorie the whole time they were at John's. Flying the gliders and making paper planes was entertaining for a while but the events the previous Sunday had cast a cloud over the group. Willy found it was a relief to say goodbye, after making the arrangements to meet on Wednesday.

At home again he sat in the workshop and cleaned his model Spitfire, his mind busy with images of Petra and Marjorie. He found the tussle between love and lust very vexing and he bit his lip and sighed. Life was certainly more difficult than he wanted it to be!

Tuesday, he spent at home. To amuse himself he played computer games, read and then sat and worked on the top wing of the model Triplane. That gave him a lot of satisfaction, which countered to some extent the frustration and anxiety he was feeling about girls and sex. His thoughts were concentrated on Petra and Marjorie.

To his guilty shame Willy found that whenever he started daydreaming about Petra the images would change to searing memories of Marjorie. That began to annoy him. *Am I one of those weaklings who will cheat on his wife by committing adultery?* he wondered.

It was sobering stuff but did not stop him thinking about Marjorie and becoming aroused.

Wednesday started without any planned activities but while Willy was working on gluing the top wing pieces together a phone call from John invited him over. Willy really wanted to go to Stick's in the hope of seeing Marjorie, but he agreed.

When he arrived at John's Willy wished he hadn't. Noddy and Scott were both there and so was Stephen. Stephen had just begun describing the army cadet camp he had been on during the first week.

That got Willy interested. "How was it?" he asked.

"Really good!" Stephen enthused. "We got to fire the Steyr and watched artillery firing and we visited Lavarack Barracks."

Noddy looked peeved. "You didn't fire real bullets?" he challenged.

"Did so!" Stephen replied. "We were trained one day and then went and fired live ammo on a field firing range the next day."

Hearing that made Willy jealous. When Scott pointed out that Stephen was only a First-Year cadet so how could he be allowed to fire a rifle, Stephen shrugged. "That's the way army cadets are. We all fire the rifle."

"That's not fair!" Scott cried. "Air cadets have to wait till they are Third Years."

Stephen snorted. "That's because air cadets are only a third as good!" he quipped.

The jibe hurt Willy's feelings, but he did not join in the mutual teasing that then erupted as each one tried to put down the other cadet organisation. To end this Willy asked what else the army cadets had done. Stephen then described day and night fieldcraft exercises and day and night navigation exercises and even exercises against other cadet units. Hearing that also made Willy feel envious. "You seem to have done a lot in the bush," he commented.

"We were in the bush the whole time," Stephen replied. "All nine days."

Scott was astonished. "What did you do for showers?"

"They took us by truck to a camp and then back to our campsite again," Stephen explained. "We only had one shower every three days."

"And you had exercises against other cadet units?" Willy queried. That idea really appealed and for a moment he wondered if he shouldn't have joined the army cadets instead.

Stephen nodded. "One night a mob from St Michael's College tried to raid us but we had OPs and patrols out, so we knew they were coming," he explained.

"OPs?" John asked.

"Observation Posts," Stephen answered. "In this case three cadets from our HQ platoon with radios."

"Where is St Michael's College?" Scott asked.

Stephen shrugged. "Down south somewhere, a place called Broadsound down between Mackay and Rockhampton I think," he replied. "Anyway, we ambushed them half a dozen times and some of their noddies got lost. Then one got bitten by a snake and we had to find them in the dark to rescue them."

Willy tried to picture that and shuddered. He hated snakes. "Did the kid die?"

Stephen shook his head. "No Graham and a regular army warrant officer found them, and we got a vehicle to get him to hospital," he explained.

"Graham? You mean Graham Kirk in your class?" Willy queried. *I don't think I like him,* he thought. But he didn't know if that was because of Graham's obvious good looks and physique or because he always seemed to be a hero, or because Marjorie thought he was handsome.

Again Stephen nodded. "Yeah. He and I only got back yesterday. We were kept back to be the rear party. We had to clean up and return all the stores to Lavarack Barracks."

Again Willy experienced a twinge of jealousy. He knew that Lavarack Barracks was the biggest army base in northern Australia, and he was interested.

Stephen then looked around at each of them. "So what have you blokes been doing?" he asked.

Searing images of Marjorie flashed across Willy's mind. He shrugged. "Just flying model planes," he answered. He described how they had been flying the radio-controlled models up at the farm.

Stephen looked interested. "That sounds good. Could we do that do you think?"

"Don't know," Willy replied. "I will have to ask mum and dad. I'll let you know."

"So what are we doing now?" Stephen asked.

Scott pointed to one of John's plastic kit models. "Let's have an air battle," he suggested.

So they did. Each took a model, with John continually warning them to be careful. Then they ran around the yard with the models held in their hands doing pretend aerobatics and dog fights. Then they moved on to making paper gliders and then to sitting and talking.

While they were chatting Stephen turned to Willy. "I would have thought you would have spent the holidays in the company of the delectable Petra," he commented.

Remembering the incident at the shops, Willy blushed. Shaking his head, he said: "Her mother won't let her go out with boys."

As he said this, Willy noted Scott was almost glaring at him. *Is Scott jealous?* he wondered. The memory that he had a particular enemy made him wonder.

Stephen laughed. "Ha, ha! That must be why she sneaks off with the Year 12 boys during school time then," he commented.

Willy felt his anger flare. "She does not!" he cried hotly.

Stephen looked at him in surprise. "Yes, she does, and with the Year Elevens. Why do you think she is nicknamed Petra the Poke?" he retorted.

That really hurt. Burning maggots of doubt writhed in Willy's insides and he flamed red. "She's not like that! She's a nice girl!" he shouted.

There was an uncomfortable silence while Willy glared at Stephen, his hands clenching and unclenching.

Chapter 21

GNAWING DOUBTS

For a few seconds there was a tense silence and Stephen stared defiantly back. Then John gave Willy a sympathetic look and said, "So, what are we doing tomorrow then?"

Willy seized on the opportunity to defuse the tension. "I want to go to the shops to check petrol motors," he replied.

"What for?" Scott asked.

"I am making a model Fokker Triplane and need a motor for it," Willy answered.

Stephen took off his glasses to wipe them. "Are you guys having another flying competition?" he asked.

John answered. "It's a good idea. We were planning to go to Townsville in two weeks' time, if I can get a motor that works," he replied.

"What's wrong with the motor you bought off Scott?" Willy asked.

John shrugged and glanced at Scott. "It keeps conking out and runs very unevenly," he explained.

"I've got a motor I would like to sell," Stephen replied.

John looked interested. "How much? I haven't got much money."

Stephen named a price then added: "Why don't you come over to my place tomorrow morning and have a look at it?"

John nodded and it was agreed. The conversation then drifted until it came back to model aircraft again. This time it was Scott asking if the trip to Townsville was definitely still on in two weeks' time.

"Have you asked your parents?" Willy asked.

"Not yet. I need to check first," Scott replied.

That idea had to be explained to Stephen but when asked if he was interested, he declined. "I'm still grounded by my parents," he explained.

The proposed trip to Townsville to fly model aircraft was the question Willy asked his parents over dinner that evening. His father nodded. "If you like. Who wants to go?"

Willy thought then numbered them on his fingers. "Me, John, Scott and probably Stick and maybe his little sister."

Willy's father looked thoughtful. "We'd need two cars for that, and even then we'd have trouble fitting the model aircraft in as well. Can you go dear?" This last to Willy's mother.

To Willy's disappointment, she shook her head. "No. Sorry. I am already committed to the Orchid Society and I am rostered on duty with the Royal Flying Doctor Service on that Sunday."

Willy's father turned back to him. "That means we can take two others with their gear. What about you Lloyd?"

Lloyd made a face. "I can't think of anything worse! I am going golfing on Saturday afternoon and some mates of mine are having a party Saturday night."

"Party? Where? Who is going? What adults are supervising?" Willy's mother snapped.

While this interrogation went on Willy's father turned to him. "You'd better check with your mates if any other parents can do the trip young William; and remind them we have to camp," he said.

The conversation switched off expeditions and soon afterwards Willy went to do the washing up (His parents did not think dishwashers were environmentally friendly and thought the work was good for him) and then he went to the workshop for a while and sat tracing and cutting out paper to glue on the framework of the wings he had completed.

On Thursday morning he did more of this. After pinning thin plastic 'Gladwrap' to the plans he carefully pinned pieces of the wings to the plans and then glued on the long, thin stringers. By mid-morning he had completed all three wings and after morning tea he was able to cut out more paper.

As he worked Willy thought of John and Scott being over at Stephen's but after Stephen's hurtful comments the day before he really did not want to go over to his house. And the comment still hurt. The suggestion that Petra had sex with the older boys really set his stomach churning until he felt nauseous. Unlike fantasising about having sex with Marjorie or other girls he found he was disgusted and ashamed when his unhappy mind thrust images of Petra doing things with other boys into his consciousness. He was left with a gnawing feeling of doubt.

Surely not? he thought. *And besides when did she have time?* he wondered. But then he had to concede there had been a few days when Petra had been absent. *She said she was sick,* he remembered. But then the ugly suspicion that that was what she would say crept in to set his emotions in turmoil again.

After lunch Willy rode his bike over to John's. John was very glad to see him and said he was more than happy to go to the shop with him. Both boys set out soon afterwards on their bicycles. On arrival at the shopping centre they chained and padlocked their bicycles to the bike racks and then went inside.

As the pair walked along the arcades on the way to the hobby shop Willy enjoyed looking at all the pretty girls. "Holidays are good," he commented. "All the chicks are at the shops and they aren't wearing school uniforms."

John laughed and agreed but gave him an odd look. Being reminded of previous incidents niggled at Willy's conscience but that did not stop him looking.

As he stood admiring a particularly curvy teenage girl a voice hissed in his ear: "She's too good for you Williams!"

Willy looked around and found Jason Branch standing close beside him, a sneer on his face. With him was another youth who Willy recognised was a corporal in 2 Flight.

Keeping his fear off his face and his anxiety out of his voice Willy shrugged. "Bottom of my range I know, but somebody's got to keep them happy."

Branch stepped back, and laughed, the sneer still evident. "Keep a girl happy! You wouldn't know what to do with one even if you were lucky enough to meet an ugly and desperate one that said you could!"

Searing images of Marjorie flashed across the screen of Willy's mind. With an effort he resisted the temptation to boast. The situation was defused by John who turned to the corporal and said, "How did the cadet camp go Hughesy?"

Hughes, Willy remembered. *Lance Hughes.*

Hughes proceeded to talk about the 9-day camp that the AAFC had run at the Garbutt RAAF Base in Townsville and at some field training area inland. For the next few minutes Willy listened enviously to their descriptions of the camp. Hughes had flown in light aircraft and in gliders and had even done a flight to Weipa and back in an RAAF 'Hercules'.

Branch had done even more. As a 'Third Year' he had taken part in a live firing rifle shoot and then done a 7 day Adventure Training Course during which he and other Third Years had hiked and navigated cross-country, paddled canoes down the mighty Burdekin River, been abseiling and learned survival in the bush as well as taking part in a number of challenging tests.

John looked openly impressed. "Did you pass?" he asked.

Branch curled his lip and glanced at Willy. "'course I did! What ya think I am?" he replied.

The two older boys then continued on their way and Willy and John resumed walking. Then they met up with Scott and Noddy. Both were in a silly mood and were busy making comments about all the teenage girls and young women that were walking past. Some of the comments were so loud and so blatant in describing their boobs or legs that Willy blushed and wished he wasn't with them.

To his relief they soon arrived at the hobby shop and went in. To Willy going into such places was like entering Aladdin's Cave and he quickly became engrossed in studying all the toys and model kits. To begin with the boys stayed in a group while they looked at plastic kits. Initially these were model aircraft kits but then each one began to linger or move faster to look at the things that interested them most. Noddy and Scott both started studying the plastic kit armoured fighting vehicles and various toy soldiers. John stayed with Willy then moved on to look at kits of model cars.

Willy took out box after box of plastic kit aircraft to study the cover picture and then to read the information, or at least what he could read among the multiple foreign languages printed there! He quickly decided that 1:72 scale was the preferred scale for model aircraft.

1:35 is just too big, he thought. *They take up too much space.*

For a few seconds he tried to imagine his bedroom with 1:35 scale model aircraft on the shelves and hanging from the ceiling and he shook his head. Then his eye picked out a plastic kit of a German V2 rocket. He reached forward and picked the box up and began studying the picture.

"Hello Willy! Found another rocket, have you?" asked John.

Willy looked up in surprise as John's voice had come from directly in front of him. He saw that John was on the other side of the row of shelves, grinning at him through a gap in the stacked merchandise.

"Yes, a V2. What are you looking at there?" Willy responded, blushing at the memory of his last rocket.

"Model railway stuff," John answered, holding up a box containing a HO Scale model passenger carriage.

Willy then glanced along the shelves to where Scott and Noddy were standing at the model racing cars and Monster Trucks. They didn't interest Willy, so he slid the V2 rocket model box back into place on the shelves and moved to pick up one of a Boeing 747 airliner.

A couple of minutes later Willy reached the section of the shop devoted to flying model kits. A quick survey indicated that the shop had not gotten in any new kits. That was a disappointment, but he still checked each of the kits, even the gliders, in the hope that one of them might appeal.

But they didn't, so he moved to the glass-topped counter section where the shopkeeper was watching. He knew them all by sight now and was quite friendly. "What are you after today, son?" he asked.

"A petrol motor and controls," Willy replied.

"Fuel tank and lines?"

"Yes please."

"What is the model and how big?"

Willy used his hands to indicate the 90-centimetre wingspan of his model. "A Fokker triplane this big," he replied.

The man smiled. "The Red Baron eh? That should be good. What are you making the framework with?"

"Balsa covered with paper," Willy replied, proud that he was scratch building.

The man nodded and turned to lift out a small petrol engine. For the next few minutes he and Willy discussed its performance and the size of the fuel tank and length of fuel lines needed. "Are you mounting the fuel tank in the upper wing?" the man asked.

"Yes," Willy answered. Movement beside him made him glance and he saw that Scott and Noddy were both beside him and listening.

The fuel tank was discussed. John strolled around the end of the shelves and came to stand beside Noddy on Willy's right. He began to make suggestions and Willy looked at two more types of engines.

Then Willy's gaze settled on sets of wheels for model aircraft. *If there is one thing I have learnt it is that you need good wheels for a model aircraft,* he thought. Knowing how hard it would be to make his own wheels and axle he then got the man to lift out several sets and he studied and tested these until he found a pair he thought a suitable size.

I can always paint the wheel hubs red, he thought.

The man offered his agreement on how suitable the choice was then asked if Willy wanted them all wrapped. "You buying now?" he asked, naming what sounded like a very expensive price to Willy.

Willy glanced at John and felt a little stab of guilt at the knowledge that his dad would pay. "No thanks. Just put them all in a box and my dad will come in and pay for them," he said.

That was done and Willy, feeling both happy and embarrassed, led the way out of the shop. Noddy at once began ogling girls, whistling and making comments. "What will we do now?" he asked.

"I'm going home," Willy replied. "I want to finish this model before next weekend. Who has asked their parents if they can come?"

John had and so had Scott but Noddy hadn't. Willy could only shrug and think: *Typical!*

The friends walked through the shopping centre and passed out through the same door they had entered by. As they did Willy looked towards the bike racks to check that his bike hadn't been tampered with. At the top of his mind was the worry that Jason Branch was in the area and he strongly suspected him of the earlier sabotage.

Then he found himself puzzled. *Where's my bike?* he wondered. For a few seconds his mind puzzled over what he could see and then the implication of an empty space next to John's struck him. When he saw the broken chain lying on the bitumen the realization struck him like a bucket of ice water.

My bike's gone! It's been stolen! he thought.

Hurrying over to where his bike had been Willy looked anxiously in all directions, half hoping he was wrong and that he had left it somewhere else. But there was his chain on the ground and he saw that it had been cut. The others joined him.

"What's wrong?" John asked.

"Someone's pinched my bike," Willy replied. Hot tears began to form in his eyes and he struggled to control them and to keep the dismay out of his voice.

Noddy joined them. "Are you sure you left it here?" he queried.

Willy nodded. "Definite. It was next to John's and that is my chain." He bent down and picked it up then examined where the chain had been cut.

John fingered the newly cut steel. "That looks like it was cut with bolt cutters or something," he suggested.

Noddy looked at it as well. "Yeah. Not cut by a hacksaw or anything like that," he agreed.

Again Willy looked in all directions. This time he was looking for Jason Branch as well as for his bike. But there was no sign of either. Again he battled with tears and felt the misery well up. With an effort he controlled himself.

Scott also looked around. "What are ya gunna do?" he queried.

"Go to the centre management and then phone my parents," Willy replied.

"Do you want us to come?" John asked.

"Only if you want to," Willy replied. He did not want to inconvenience his friends but was grateful for the offer.

"I'll come," John answered.

The others opted not to so as they unlocked their bicycles and rode away Willy and John made their way back into the shopping centre.

At the manager's office Willy explained to the lady behind the desk and then was allowed to use the telephone to call his father. His father exploded with annoyance. "Wait there young William. I will as soon as I have seen two more patients," he said.

Willy relayed this information to the lady and at that John shrugged. "I can only wait a bit longer Willy," he said apologetically.

"That's OK Johnno. Thanks anyway. I will see you tomorrow maybe."

John nodded and took his leave. Willy then asked if the shopping centre had closed circuit TV and was told he could only view this with the police and his parents. Willy then asked if the police could be called and the lady reluctantly did so.

As he waited in a small front room, Willy had to fight back the tears. What really upset him wasn't so much the loss of his bicycle but the fact that someone disliked him so much they wanted to hurt him. He did not think it was just a random act.

Who is my secret enemy and why do they hate me so much? he wondered. The only name that came to mind was Jason Branch and the only motive was jealousy over his friendship with Petra. Petra! He realised with a guilty start that he had hardly thought about her for days.

When his father arrived, they waited for a policeman and then Willy took them to the 'scene of the crime' and the policeman collected the chain as evidence and asked a lot of questions. They then went back to the centre management and view the last four hours of CCTV. This revealed a youth who wore a jacket and hid his face with a cloth hat and who had walked to the bike and then cut the chain before wheeling the bike out of the camera's view.

The recording showed the timings and the policeman asked where Willy had been then. That caused Willy to think hard before answering. "Two forty-five. I was in the hobby shop with my friends looking at model kits," he replied. Into his mind came the image of the group of friends all looking at kits.

He asked to see the recording again and this time he stared hard at the youth's image. It was only a back view and the camera was, like many such instruments, mounted too high and too far away to get a clear view. To Willy's disappointment the image did not appear to be Jason Branch. But the person looked tantalisingly familiar. *Who is it?* he fretted.

There was nothing more that could be done so Willy's father drove him home and there they discussed the situation with his mother. She was anxious. "This might be the same boy that sabotaged your bike a few weeks ago," she suggested.

"Yes, Mum."

"I hope he isn't likely to do anything more dangerous," she muttered. Then she looked Willy directly in the eye. "William, have you done something that you shouldn't have? Are you mixed up with some gang or something?"

Willy was shocked and hurt. "No, Mum!" he cried.

"You haven't done anything that might provoke people to seek revenge or something?" his mother asked.

Images of being in the creek with Marjorie flooded Willy's mind and he began to blush. He tried to stop it but knew he was blushing and that made it worse. His mother scanned his face and then shook her head. "That's a very guilty look!" she said. "What have you done?"

Willy flamed with shame and hung his head. "Just... just... we all went skinny dipping up at the farm," he muttered.

"Including young Marjorie?"

"Yes, Mum."

"Did you do anything to her?"

Willy shook his head and felt so embarrassed he wished the floor would open up and swallow him. "No Mum. Just a bit of... bit of being rude."

"I hope so. Oh Willy! For heaven's sake, be careful. I know you are that age, but you must not get yourself or a girl into trouble," his mother cried.

"No, Mum," Willy muttered.

At that moment, the front doorbell rang, and they all looked at each other. Willy's father went to the door and Willy saw a policeman standing there.

Chapter 22

THE DRONE

Willy stared at the policeman and anxiety flooded through him. A second policeman appeared behind the first and looked towards him. Images of Marjorie flooded Willy's mind and he broke into a cold sweat.

Has Marjorie told her mother, he worried.

Willy's father listened to the two policemen for a few moments and then smiled as he turned to face Willy. "Come and look Young William. They think they have found your bicycle," he called.

Relief flooded through Willy and he found he was trembling. After taking a few deep breaths he nodded and got up to move to the door. He followed the policemen and his parents down the front stairs to where a police car was parked in the driveway.

Secured in the boot was a bicycle and a glance showed it to be his. A quick check of the number engraved in it confirmed ownership. The first policeman nodded and made a note in his notebook.

"We found two kids riding it along the street. If they hadn't been doubling and had been wearing helmets, we wouldn't have bothered to stop them. They were very scared and claimed they had just found it thrown into the drain near the shopping centre. We got them to take us to the place and sure enough we also found a brand-new set of bolt cutters lying among the rubbish."

That really puzzled Willy. "So you don't think they stole it?"

"No. Their story checked out in other ways and they were both at home with parents when your bike was stolen. It looks like someone else took it and just threw it into the drain," the policeman replied.

That both puzzled and hurt Willy. *Someone hates me so much they will waste money and throw away a perfectly good bike and brand-new bolt cutters to hurt me,* he thought. It was very worrying. But who?

It was an anxious and upset boy who worked on his model Triplane that evening. In bed he found himself brooding more than fantasising as he turned over in his mind who his secret enemy might be. Jason Branch remained top of the list but now Willy even considered people like Scott or Noddy.

But how could it be them. They were in the shop with John and I all the time, he thought. But then he remembered meeting them after the clash with Jason Branch. *Did they see us arrive and then do something to my bike before coming in and joining us?* he wondered. For several minutes he went over possible timings and scenarios in his head but still did not arrive at any definite answer.

Or is it some person I don't even normally associate with?

Willy's dreams that night were not fantasies about girls but instead were all half nightmares about riding his bike and having to try to watch it every time he got off. In the end he had a dream where he rode along a street that turned into a muddy track up a hill and then vanished in a tangle of weeds behind some vaguely familiar houses, and then his bike was gone and he was walking and he had no shoes on and there were prickles!

During Friday Willy stayed home and worked on his model Triplane. He still hoped to have it finished by the time they went to Townsville, but as he struggled to construct the fuselage he began to have doubts. *I need all those parts at the Hobby Shop,* he thought. But he could not get them until his father went there and paid for them. That was not until the afternoon, so Willy sat and fretted or played computer games. He had been so upset by the bicycle incident that he did not want to be with any of his friends.

It is the not knowing, the ugly suspicions that I find the worst, he told himself as he yet again brooded on who his secret enemy might be.

Then he upset himself by his own impatience. He tried to paste the paper on the top wing of the Triplane, but in his hurry he did not apply it carefully enough and as the glue dried the wing began to obviously warp out of true.

"You idiot, Willy!" he muttered to himself. "More speed, less haste."

There was nothing to do but carefully peel and shave off the paper. In the process he broke one of the stringers. To replace that was a difficult job as he had to cut into the frames it was glued into and prize the pieces out. Even replacing it was hard as he had to make sure it did not pull the wing out of alignment as the glue dried. It ended up a fairly messy repair job.

At least it will be hidden inside when I put the paper on and paint it, he rationalized.

The best thing that day was when his father came home after work and had the new parts for the model. Willy's spirits bounced up and he was happy until he realised that he had to redo more of the structure of his model. When making it he had not allowed enough space for the small servo motors that operated the control surfaces and the holes he had drilled in the frames for wiring or linkages were in many cases in the wrong places.

Downcast by this Willy at first sat and sulked. Then he shrugged and made himself start repair work. *A good learning experience,* he told himself as he set to work to cut out more frames or to measure where to drill holes for linkages or for wires. He even found he needed to add some reinforcing to mount the servos on, and as he added these he began to worry that the whole weight and balance of the model would be upset.

That night he was back to almost his normal self and he resumed fantasising about girls: Petra and then Marjorie in particular. It bothered him that he kept having erotic images of Marjorie and he felt guilty about not being loyal to Petra but somehow he could not bring himself to imagine her doing rude things with boys, which only got him wondering why so many others made hints and suggestive comments about her.

She has never made any hints that she is anything like that, he thought. *So why do they think that way?* Putting it down to jealousy or rejection he made himself picture pleasant and romantic daydreams in which he rescued her from villains who threatened her.

But to his own annoyance and shame he found it was Marjorie he wanted to see on Saturday. Then his hopes were dashed after a phone call to the Morton's rang out and all he got was the answering machine. Shrugging and assuming the family were away for a few hours Willy did his chores and then made arrangements to go over to John's that afternoon.

It was a pleasant afternoon with lots of talk, computer games, reading of aircraft magazines and flying of small gliders but it left Willy feeling a bit frustrated and edgy. His mood was not improved when he made a casual comment about going to Stick's and John shook his head.

"They have gone to the Tablelands for the weekend, to some aunty's," John explained.

That hurt. *How does Johnno know that?* Willy wondered. But he did have to concede that he was not Stick's only friend. There was then the residual jealousy of wondering whether John was having success with Marjorie.

More hurt was to follow when John mentioned that his family were going to Innisfail the next day. That left Willy with no-one to play with, and as he rode his bike slowly home he brooded over the fact that he seemed to have very few real friends.

His loneliness gave a sharper edge to his fantasies as he lay in bed that night and then dominated his mood the next day. To hide it he forced himself to work on his model aircraft and to work at various chores around the house.

At least I will see Petra tomorrow, he thought in an attempt to cheer himself up.

But he didn't. When he went to school there was no sign of her. During the first lesson he sat in his usual chair with the seat next to him empty and his stomach churning with anxiety and doubt. *Maybe she isn't coming back to this school?* he thought.

That was a dismaying notion and fretting over it helped to mask the embarrassment he was feeling when he noted others who appeared to be talking about him.

During the break between periods Willy moved out onto the veranda with the others to collect the books he needed for the next lesson. Usually his class stayed in the same room, which was on the first floor, but for some subjects the students and not the teacher changed rooms. As he dug in his school bag, Willy overheard Callum and Stick talking.

"Give us a go Callum," Stick pleaded.

Willy looked and saw that Callum was holding a small quadcopter. The drone was so small it almost fitted into his hand and the controller was smaller than a small mobile phone. The quadcopter had a white plastic frame and four tiny black propellers surrounded by the frame.

"Not yet," Callum replied. "I want a go myself."

Willy studied the drone, interested in spite of his prejudice against them as not being 'proper' aircraft. Noting that Callum was preparing to fly the drone he glanced around to check who was nearby.

"Don't get caught by a teacher Callum," he cautioned.

"Huh! She'll be right," Callum replied.

With that he touched the screen and the four tiny rotors began to buzz. Willy was amazed. The tiny engines were so quiet he could hardly hear them. Before he could comment Callum increased the revs and the quadcopter lifted up and then hovered above the concrete balustrade.

John and Noddy joined them. "That's good Callum," John commented.

"It is," Callum agreed.

He manipulated the small control levers and the tiny machine buzzed almost silently off out over the grass quadrangle between the main building and the lower classroom blocks. Then he made it fly in a circle before flying it back. As it came back Willy noted that the fuselage had two green headlights that looked like eyes and there was even a 'mouth'.

Callum brought it to a hovering standstill just out of reach and said, "Watch this."

A flick at the screen made the eyes turn to red and the face seemed to change to an angry glare. Willy could only applaud with the others.

John clapped. "That is great Callum. You are very good pilot. Where do you practice?"

"At home," Callum answered. He explained that he flew it around his house and also inside the home. "It is really strong. It just bounces if hits a wall," he explained indicating the plastic frames around the rotors.

"What can it do apart from fly?" John asked.

"Nothing much. It's too small. It could take pictures if you had a tiny camera and it can carry little things," Callum answered. He flew the drone in and landed it then picked it up and turned it over. "See this clip under here," he demonstrated.

Willy studied the four rotors and the plastic frame that protected them if the drone hit a wall or building. Despite his dislike he really wanted to have a go. He was about to ask when Angus called to them, "Teacher!"

The drone was whisked out of sight and the boys made their way to the room for their next lesson.

When they got there no teacher was present, so the class lined up outside. Stick kept nudging Callum. "Give us a go with your drone Callum," he said.

"Me first," put in Vincent.

As Vincent was Callum's mate Callum nodded and handed it to him. The boys then stood in the doorway and Callum held the quadcopter on his left hand while explaining the controls to Vincent. Vincent nodded and assured him he understood and tapped the screen. The motors at once buzzed into life and before Callum could utter a caution Vincent pushed at the tiny control levers with his thumbs and the tiny machine whizzed away into the room.

"Stop it! Bring it back!" Callum cried. Willy, who was watching over his shoulder, saw that the quadcopter was headed directly for the windows on the other side of the room. But Vincent froze and just gaped and the quadcopter buzzed on. If the window had been fully open it would have flown straight out the other side but instead the drone crashed into the glass and fell to the floor upside down, its rotors still spinning.

"Stop it Vince! Stop it!" Callum cried, reaching for the controls. But Vincent was still flustered and fumbled trying to turn it off. Finally Callum grabbed the controller and switched the motors off. He then hurried across the room and picked the quadcopter up.

As he did Willy saw the teacher approaching, Mr Page, their Geography teacher and not one to tempt fate with. So he stepped out and spoke to the teacher, giving Callum long enough to both scuttle back to the doorway and to hide the quadcopter and controller in his pockets.

The next class was followed by morning break and Mr Page just dismissed the class and hurried out. Most of the students left immediately but John asked Callum if he could now have a go with the quadcopter. Callum agreed but Willy thought they were running foolish risks. "I will stand guard and watch for teachers, as long as I can have a go," he said.

This was agreed to and first John and then Stick and then Noddy all got to fly the drone for a few minutes. During this Willy stood at the door so he could look both ways along the veranda but also watch the flying. Then Vincent demanded another go. By then Willy was both hungry and impatient. "My go. Stick, you take over as guard."

Reluctantly Stick did so. Equally reluctantly Vincent surrendered the controller to Willy. He and Noddy then left. Willy placed the quadcopter on the front desk just inside the door and then studied the controls before switching the motors on. Satisfied he understood what to do Willy very carefully tapped the screen and the computer brought the machine to a hover at eye height. Not quite satisfied Willy moved it to above head height. Then he gently moved the controls and the quadcopter began to fly slowly forward. After that it was a simple joy to make it fly in a wide circle and then turn and go back the other way.

Willy was so absorbed in this that Mr Conkey's voice came as a nasty surprise. "What are you boys doing in a classroom during the break?"

Willy glanced over his shoulder and saw that he and Callum were alone. There was no sign of either Stick or John. Callum looked scared and Willy felt a spasm of anxiety. While trying to bring the quadcopter to a hover he turned to answer. "Just... er, just experimenting sir," he answered.

Mr Conkey looked in and saw the now hovering drone. "You know toys are banned at school, don't you?"

"Yes sir."

"Didn't I warn you about them the other day?"

"Yes sir," Willy replied. For an instant he was tempted to point out that the quadcopter belonged to Callum but instead he focused his gaze on the controls and brought the machine down to land on the desk. "Sorry sir," he added.

"Put it away and don't bring it again," Mr Conkey snapped. "Now get downstairs."

"Yes sir." Willy scooped up the quadcopter and hurried to get his school bag. As he and Callum hurried away, he passed the drone and controller to Callum, who muttered, "Thanks."

"We wouldn't have got out of that so lightly if it was any teacher but Old Conks," he commented.

"You are right there," Callum agreed.

Once downstairs Willy left him and went in search of Petra, only to be disappointed yet again. That put him in a bad mood and he went to the next class, Maths B with Miss Hackenmeyer, in a state of emotional down.

In that class he sat next to John and to stay out of trouble he concentrated on the work. He was therefore surprised to hear a low buzzing sound from his left. This was followed by Callum hissing and muttering and by a chuckle from Vincent. Willy glanced across and was astonished to see that Vincent had the quadcopter controller and that the quadcopter itself was flying up across the classroom.

You idiots! Willy thought. *Not in Hackenmeyer's class!*

Callum thought so too as he was angrily hissing at Vincent while trying to snatch the controller back. Vincent's reaction was to chuckle again and to hold the controller away from him.

Thus it was almost inevitable that the disturbance should attract the unwelcome attention of the teacher. Miss Hackenmeyer had been bending over looking at Barbara's work but now turned and glared.

"What's going on there? What are you two boys up to?"

"Nothing Miss," Vincent said, whipping his hands in under the desk.

"Something is," Miss Hackenmeyer snapped in return. "You two are up to some mischief. Now bring out your homework both of you and show it to me."

Willy could only shake his head. The quadcopter had now risen until it was hard against the ceiling. *She must hear that buzzing soon and wonder what it is,* he thought. Through his mind flashed images from the movie 'Eye in the Sky' when a tiny drone was flown in above a meeting of Middle Eastern terrorists. *It will be terror for us if Hackenmeyer hears it,* he thought.

What followed was almost pure comedy. Callum tried to surreptitiously grab the controller, but Vincent bent forward to get his homework book out of his school bag and accidentally blocked him. Then Vincent tried to slip the controller into his bag but missed and it fell on the floor. His response was just to shrug and leave it there and he stood up with his homework book and made his way out to the front of the class. This left the quadcopter still buzzing against the ceiling

Callum cast an anguished glance at it and then followed, going up the other aisle to the front. Willy glanced up, then across at the controller.

I wonder? he thought.

Picking his moment, while Miss Hackenmeyer was squinting at Callum's homework, Willy bent and reached across with his ruler and scooped the controller closer. Snatching it up he straightened up and then cast a quick glance to see if his actions had been detected.

No, she is busy with those two clowns, he thought.

Holding the controller down below the desk and glancing down at it and then up at the quadcopter Willy slowed the rotor speed so that the angry buzzing sound died away but the machine remained airborne. But what to do with it?

Then an inspiration came to Willy. An image from 'Eye in the Sky' gave him the idea. He realised that the chances of bringing it down to desk or floor level without it being seen by the teacher were not good. But just near it was a fan. Being winter the fans were not in use. So he carefully flew the quadcopter down and then sideways until he could just see it hovering above a fan blade.

Another quick glance confirmed that the teacher was still busy with Callum and Vincent, and also that at least half the class were watching and holding their breath. As slowly as he was able Willy let the quadcopter down, his anxiety increased by noting a flashing symbol that indicated that the battery was almost flat. From the angle he was at he could not see the quadcopter properly, so when it went out of sight he slowed the rotors even more. When it did not appear below the fan blade on the other side, he took the risk and switched off the motor. The buzzing hum stopped and it seemed that the whole class breathed a sigh of relief.

Callum had not seen what had happened so when he at last made his way back to his seat, with half his answers marked wrong, he looked quite unhappy. "Where's my drone," he hissed to Roger.

Roger, very conscious that Miss Hackenmeyer had finished with Vincent and was moving to stand up gestured upwards with his head. "On the fan. Willy landed it there."

Callum glanced up and obviously could not see the tiny machine, but he glanced at Willy and nodded his thanks. Vincent joined him and received a scowl instead.

There was a frisson of mild tension for the remainder of the lesson with people continually glancing up at the fan. Willy, in particular, was hoping the drone would not fall off.

After Miss Hackenmeyer had walked out at the end of the lesson the class broke into a loud babble of conversation and laughter. Callum came over to Willy and held out his hand. "Thanks Willy," he said.

"You are lucky she didn't want the fans switched on," Willy replied. That caused a gale of laughter. They all then watched as Callum turned on the controller and tried to fly the quadcopter down. "Uh? Oh No! Flat battery!" he cried.

So the quadcopter remained perched up on the fan blade as the next lesson began. As fate would have it this was Mr Conkey for History.

Once again Willy kept glancing up from time to time, appalled to note that a breeze coming in the top louvres was causing the fan blades to sway gently from time to time. He was even more appalled when he heard a distinct click from Callum's direction, followed by a sharp but short *zzzzt* noise from up on the fan.

Willy glanced at Callum and saw that he had the controller in his hands under the desk and had turned it on. Catching Callum's eye he frowned and gave a shake of the head. Callum looked guilty and nodded, then switched the drone's motor off again.

Above them there was another distinct click, loud enough to attract Mr Conkey's attention. He frowned and looked up. So did Willy, just in time to see the drone fall off the fan. By sheer bad luck Mr Conkey was standing directly beneath it and the plastic toy struck the top of his head and then bounced to land on the floor in front of him.

"Ouch! What the…?" cried Mr Conkey, his right hand flashing up to rub at his scalp. Then he saw the quadcopter bounce on the floor and stop. He scowled and bent down to pick it up. Holding it close he peered at it and for a moment, his face suffusing with rage. Willy thought he was going to dash it on the floor. Instead he pursed his lips and glared at Willy.

Holding the quadcopter out Mr Conkey growled, "Is this yours, Williams?"

Willy shook his head but did not want to dump Callum directly in the poo so instead said, "I put it there, sir."

At that Callum put up his hand. "Sir, it's mine. Willy was just saving me," he explained.

"Saving you?" Mr Conkey queried, his eyebrows shooting up with curiosity.

Willy took a deep breath and stood up. He then made up a story and explained how the drone had been flying around the room when Miss Hackenmeyer had come in and how he had managed to get the controller and park it on the fan blade. As he did, he noticed Mr Conkey's mouth, which was pressed into a thin line, twitch slightly and he even fancied he detected a glimmer of mirth in his eyes.

Captain Conkey understands, he thought.

Mr Conkey managed to resume his stern countenance. He held out the quadcopter. "Callum, take this drone and its controller, I presume it has one, to the office and leave it there. You can collect it after school. And don't bring it again."

"Yes sir." Callum moved out to obey and Willy sighed with relief and sat down, hoping that was the end of it.

Chapter 23

IN DEEP TROUBLE

All in all it was an upsetting day. When the lunch bell went Willy first went to look for Petra but could not find her. That lowered his spirits. Feeling anxious and moody he got his lunch and went to sit with his friends.

As he sat there eating his lunch Willy could not help overhearing some of his friends discussing a diving adventure that some of the navy cadets had experienced during the second week of the holidays. Stephen retailed the yarn, describing how the navy cadets had travelled to Mackay on the Landing Ship HMAS *Tobruk* and done their annual camp there.

"After the camp Andrew Collins, he's that navy cadet in my class, went off with his big sister Carmen, that's her over there, the pretty blonde in Year 10, and some Torres Strait Islanders who are Luke Karaku's relations to try to find some shipwreck near Bowen," Stephen explained.

That got Willy's interest. He had heard that Andrew and Carmen were divers but the notion of swimming around under the sea did not appeal to him. But shipwrecks did. He was even more intrigued to hear that another rival group had been looking for the same shipwreck.

"It was supposed to be carrying a cargo of gold and Andrew's grandfather went missing years ago looking for it," Stephen explained.

John looked sceptical. "Did they find it?" he asked.

Stephen nodded. Stephen nodded. "Apparently," he said. He went on to describe what he knew of the navy cadet's adventure, concluding by adding, "There's a lot more to the story but Andrew doesn't want to talk about it."[1]

Willy glanced across at where Andrew and his friends were sitting and viewed him with a new respect. Then he shivered and shook his head. *He can have that swimming with the sharks and stingrays and so on,* he thought. *Give me aeroplanes anytime.*

Then another horrible thought came to him. *My bike! I wonder if it*

---

[1] There is, and to get the details read *Davey Jones's Locker* by C. R. Cummings.

has been tampered with again To check he excused himself and hurried to the bike racks. After quickly checking he was relieved to note that it appeared quite untouched.

As he was hurrying back from the bike racks Willy went past the Cadet Q Store and noted Graham and his friend Peter both there with Mr Hamilton, another teacher who was also an Officer of Cadets. Willy opened his mouth to make a smart remark to Graham as he passed but at that moment Mr Conkey appeared in the Q Store doorway.

"Hi Graham! How's… er… er ... Hello sir," Willy said.

Mr Conkey looked at him and smiled. "Come to join the better organisation have you Willy?"

Willy snorted derisively and then laughed. Continuing on under B Block his eyes scanned the girls seated there eating their lunch or socializing. He was still hoping to see Petra. Then he noted that many students were looking out towards the quadrangle. Through a gap in the crowd of students Willy saw that his much-feared Maths A teacher, the elderly and grumpy Mr Burgomeister, was standing in the middle of the grass quadrangle and acting in a most peculiar way.

"What on earth's he doing?" Willy muttered.

The teacher was jumping and turning and his arms were flying up in the air. For a second Willy wondered if the teacher was having a fit, but as he came out of the edge of the crowd he saw that Mr Burgomeister was actually swatting at something buzzing near his head.

Callum's bloody drone! Willy thought.

At that he shook his head and wondered what had inspired such silly behaviour. By now Willy was out from under B Block and on the concrete path at the side of the quadrangle heading towards the far end of A Block where he and his friends usually sat. As he hurried along, he kept watching the teacher's antics.

By now these had attracted the attention of hundreds of students and they were starting to gather at the side of the quadrangle and a murmur of comments and chortles of glee were building. As Willy watched he saw the tiny drone buzz in from behind Mr Burgomeister who quickly turned to face it and then swatted at it as it zipped close by. Then the teacher had to hastily spin around to face another buzzing swoop.

The drone flew around the teacher just out of arms reach and the murmuring of the watching students began to swell to include malicious laughter. Two more swoops by the drone and two ineffectual grabs by Mr Burgomeister added to the discomfiture of the teacher.

Willy shook his head. He did not like Mr Burgomeister but this seemed a very targeted attack designed to publicly humiliate the man. *Someone doesn't like him,* he thought. It was also obvious that the teacher was becoming very, very angry.

The drone zoomed in and then suddenly pulled back. Willy saw tiny green eyes on the front of the drone suddenly turn to red and that matched the enraged face of Mr Burgomeister.

Callum's? Willy thought. But where was he? Willy looked around as he walked, seeking the location of the drone operator. First, he scanned the two veranda levels of the main building, which was where he considered was the best location. But there was no-one visible other than a couple of teachers who were observing the action from near the main office.

By then Willy had passed the end of the Manual Arts Block and he glanced to his right and saw a head peek around. *There! Callum for sure,* he thought. He also thought that the teasing had gone on too long to be considered a joke. Mr Burgomeister was clearly enraged and was also puffing and gasping.

He's not a young man. I hope he doesn't have a heart attack, Willy thought.

At that he turned right and walked towards where Callum's head kept peeking out. Callum grinned as he got closer and then Vincent's head poked out just behind him.

Willy glanced back and then, as he approached Callum, said, "Callum, that's enough. The poor old bugger will have a heart attack."

Callum shook his head. "He deserves it. He called me a blockhead and some really hurtful names," he retorted. He glanced down at the controller and manipulated the controls again.

Willy shook his head. "Stop it Callum. You will really get into strife for this."

As he said this, he saw Callum's face change to dismay. "Oh bugger! He's got it!" Callum cried.

Willy glanced back and saw that Mr Burgomeister had indeed managed to catch the drone. Now he was standing in the middle of the quadrangle, chest heaving and face red with rage. Several other teachers, including Mr Conkey and Mr Page were hurrying out to him.

By then Willy had reached the corner. As he opened his mouth to speak Callum thrust the controller into his hands. "Here!" he said. Then he turned and fled. Vincent went with him. Both boys vanished around the next corner at speed. Willy stood there gaping and staring down at the controller. Then he turned to see what Mr Burgomeister was doing and saw that the teacher had been looking hard in all directions and was now staring at him.

Bloody hell! I hope he doesn't think it was me! Willy thought.

Quickly he stepped back behind the corner of the building and turned to leave, only to find his way blocked by a large man in white shirt and tie, the Deputy, Mr Fitzgerald!

"Got you!" Mr Fitzgerald snapped.

Willy froze and for a second went to move the controller out of sight behind his back, but then realised that would make him look even more guilty. So he arrested the movement and stood, heart now hammering as he realised he might be in trouble.

"What's that?" Mr Fitzgerald snapped, pointing at the controller. He had obviously come out of the side door of the Manual Arts building as two Manual Arts teachers had followed him out: Mr Duncan and Mr Case.

"A remote control for that drone sir," Willy answered. He had trouble speaking as his mouth had suddenly gone dry and he found his heart was hammering.

Mr Fitzgerald pointed towards Mr Burgomeister. "Is it for that toy that was annoying Mr Burgomeister?"

"Yes sir." By now Willy was starting to feel cold shock seeping down through him and he was aware he felt like trembling. He sensed this was potentially very serious.

Mr Fitzgerald pointed. "Office!"

"Sir, I didn't do it! It's not mine," Willy protested.

"Whose is it then?"

Willy took a deep breath and shook his head. He did not want to dob on the others but could see that he could be suspended or expelled for the act. "A friend's sir. I'd rather not say."

"Oh would you! Very loyal to your mates," Mr Fitzgerald retorted with a sneer. "Let's go and see what Mr Burgomeister thinks."

Reluctantly Willy turned and began walking out across the grass with

Mr Fitzgerald. As he did, he was aware of hundreds of staring faces and then the murmuring of his name: 'Willy!', 'The Mad Scientist!', 'Rocket Man!' With a sickening lurch in his stomach he realised the school all thought he was the guilty one.

Mr Burgomeister obviously thought so too. "Did you do this to me boy!" he shouted. "Are you responsible?"

Willy flinched and braced himself as the teacher appeared so enraged that he thought he might be struck. Mr Fitzgerald obviously thought so too as he stepped between them. "We will resolve this at the office."

Seeing Mr Conkey there Willy turned to him. "Captain Conkey sir, it wasn't me. You spoke to me a minute ago as I walked past your Q Store."

Mr Conkey looked thoughtful and then nodded. "Yes, you did. It couldn't have been you because the drone was flying at the same time. We saw it just after you left."

Willy felt a surge of relief but then Mr Fitzgerald froze that. "So how come you have the control?"

"I went to stop it and call... er... my friend handed it to me as he ran away," Willy replied, blushing with shame as he realised how silly that made him sound.

"Some friend!" Mr Fitzgerald snorted. "And you want to protect him!"

Willy squirmed with embarrassment as Mr Fitzgerald went on. "So who owns the drone and that control thing?" he demanded to know.

"I.. I'd rather not say sir," Willy replied.

Mr Conkey put out his hand and a visibly trembling Mr Burgomeister surrendered the drone to him. "Is this the one Callum had in class earlier today?"

Willy could only shake his head. "Don't know sir," he replied.

Mr Page now spoke, "That was a good essay on loyalty you wrote for your friends the other day, but you can take it too far. It looks like they have played you for a sucker and left you holding the can, or the smoking gun, or whatever. I don't think you owe them any loyalty at all."

Willy blushed again, more at the implication that he was a simpleton who had been duped than at the accusation. Mr Fitzgerald pursed his lips. "Doesn't matter. We will get them. I think I saw Callum Webster and his mate Vincent lurking there at the back corner of the Manual Arts building so, was it them?"

Willy met his eyes and to his shame had to blink back tears.

Somehow he managed not so speak. Mr Conkey then said, "Come on Mr Burgomeister. You have had a bit of a shock. Let's get you to your staff room."

"But I'm going on playground duty," Mr Burgomeiser replied in a voice that quavered.

Willy glanced at him and was shocked. He now saw that Mr Burgomeister really was an old man and that he was pale and shaking and his breath was coming in shallow gasps.

Mr Conkey was obviously also concerned as he said, "That's alright. I will do your duty. What area is it?"

"Area C," Mr Burgomeister answered. He looked visibly upset to Willy and Mr Fitzgerald obviously thought so as he stepped closer and gently urged the teacher back towards the main building. "Thank you Mr Conkey. Now Les, you need to go and recover. Please."

Mr Burgomeister nodded and started walking unsteadily across the quadrangle with Mr Page on his left and the deputy on his right. Mr Conkey handed the drone to Mr Fitzgerald and turned to go the other way.

Mr Fitzgerald turned his head and gestured. "You go to the office and wait Williams," he said.

So Willy reluctantly followed them, hotly aware that at least half the school was watching.

Up at the main office he sat on the bench outside the deputy's office and tried to make sense of what had happened. It was very clear that Callum had a grudge against Mr Burgomeister but Willy felt used and set up. Mr Page's words seemed to scream in his mind.

Some friend! So was Callum a friend or not? *Or did he set me up?* Willy was very sure he had been pushed into the poo and resented it.

Then another thought came to him: Was Callum his secret enemy?

He was certainly in a position to do some of those things, he mused, images of Callum and Vincent in the park the day his bike was sabotaged flitting across his mind. But if he was, why? *What have I ever done to Callum?* Willy fretted.

While he sat there Stick and Noddy wandered by and gave him sympathetic looks and then, to Willy's surprise, Graham Kirk and Peter Bronsky came and sat beside him.

"What have you blokes done?" Willy queried.

"Nothing. We came to support you," Peter answered.

Willy was so touched he was speechless for a moment. "Thanks. But how?"

He learned that a few seconds later when Mr Fitzgerald appeared with Mr Croswell, the Principal. "What are you boys here for?" Mr Fitzgerald asked Graham and Peter.

Peter stood up answered. "We just came to support Willy sir. It wasn't him flying the drone. He was talking to us at the Cadet Q Store when Mr Burgomeister was attacked. We saw it."

Mr Fitzgerald looked thoughtful and nodded. "Thanks for that. Mr Conkey has already confirmed that. OK, you two go now please."

They did and Willy was then questioned. Mr Croswell then shocked him to the core by pointing out that flying drones without a licence and in the wrong places was illegal. "There are all sorts of laws about who can fly a drone and where and when," Mr Croswell said. "The laws are for air safety and to protect people's privacy and things like that. So, do you have a drone or UAV Licence?"

"No sir," Willy replied, meekly, his stomach churning. He actually felt quite foolish as he had been aware of such laws but had forgotten.

"Does your friend who was flying the thing have a licence?" was Mr Croswell's next question.

Willy shook his head. "I… I ... er... doubt it, sir."

"Take it as a warning Willy. The Bible says: 'By their friends ye shall know them', but I like the modern American saying better: 'If you want to soar like an eagle, don't associate with a pack of turkeys'. I think that's more appropriate in your case, don't you think?"

Willy could only nod and blush. *Pack of turkeys!* he repeated in his mind.

Mr Croswell added, "So choose your friends wisely. Now you can go and no more silly nonsense with flying machines."

"No sir."

Willy fled, a little peeved that Petra had not come to check on him. Now he went looking for her but without success. And everywhere he went he was the object of gossip and comments and he got tired of denying it was him.

To avoid this he went to a corner of the library and sat on his own, brooding over Callum's actions and over whether Petra had left the school and wondering how to find out. He asked Karen but she just shrugged and did not know.

And Petra was not in any of the afternoon classes which worried him even more. There was also anxiety about secret enemies. Neither Callum nor Vincent was in class and he was told they were both at the office.

Good! he thought. *Serves them right!*

When classes finished Willy quickly made his way to the bike racks and found that his bike was untouched.

Feeling somewhat battered emotionally Willy rode home and settled to working on his model triplane. He considered telling his parents about the drone incidents but decided not to.

Lloyd will do that, he told himself. But his brother made no mention, only giving him a few quizzical looks. Willy just shook his head. "It was Callum," was his entire explanation.

Homework and TV then took up the evening and his night was filled with yearning, hopeful fantasies and brooding over whether Callum was his secret enemy.

The following morning Willy went to school early and after chaining his bicycle into the racks went to wait at the gate for Petra. As he stood there, gazing hopefully along the street he experienced waves of emotion: deep anxiety that she might not return, romantic fantasies, worry over what the future might hold for her and for him.

As the time for the bell approached with no sign of Petra Willy became quite nervous and then started to become dejected. *She's not coming,* he thought, misery starting to well up as his hopes melted.

But someone else was. Around the corner came Jason Branch on his bicycle. Willy's initial reaction was to want to hurry away, to hide. But then stubborn pride took over. *I'm not going to let him think I'm scared of him,* he told himself.

So he stayed, merely avoiding Branch's eyes until he got off his bike to wheel it through the gate. Then Branch spoke: "Hello Toadface. How's the guided missile business?" he taunted.

Willy met his gaze but did not reply. Branch just sneered and then pushed his way past. As he did he called back: "Waiting for the Passionate Petra are ya?"

Again Willy did not reply but the comment hurt. *Why do they all say horrible things about Petra? She is the nicest girl I know,* he thought.

Then the bell went and he made his unhappy way to the classroom. Once again he braved the looks of his classmates and the hurt look from John to sit where he normally sat with the empty seat beside him. *She might turn up,* he reasoned. *And I want her to feel I care.*

And she did arrive. Halfway through the second period, with a grumpy Mr Burgomeister in full flight about Maths, there was a knock at the classroom door and there she was. Willy's heart and hopes both leapt and he grinned with pleasure. Petra nervously came in and handed a note to Mr Burgomeister who gruffly told her to be seated and to get on with her work.

Petra looked around the room and then met Willy's eyes. A brief smile flitted across her face and then she glanced around the room again before starting to walk towards him. As she did Willy studied her and was shocked. Her face looked very pale and there were dark rings under her eyes.

She doesn't look well, he thought, pushing out the notion that she also didn't look happy.

When she reached the vacant seat Petra slid into it with the lithe grace that made Willy almost gape in awe. She adjusted and smoothed her dress and placed her books on the desk then looked at him. "Hello Villy. How are you?" she said quietly.

"Good thanks. Are you OK? You don't look well," Willy replied, hiding his true dismay at her appearance.

Petra shrugged but only met his gaze fleetingly. "It is nothing. You are right. I not well am, but it is only the woman thing, you know, zat time of month."

Both Willy's parents were doctors and his father had explained the facts of life to him years before and he had also read up on the subject. But his theoretical knowledge did not encompass the actual anatomical details and he blushed deeply with embarrassment.

"I see," he replied gruffly.

To hide his embarrassment he pointed to the page in the text book that they were working on. Petra glanced at it and nodded then opened her own books and set to work. Willy also tried to concentrate but found himself continually distracted by her sheer physical presence. Then, when her knee accidentally touched his, his body reacted and to his shame and horror he became very aroused.

What bothered him was the notion that Petra was pure and innocent. *She's not like Marjorie,* he thought. And her name conjured up heated images which both fuelled his desire and filled him with contempt for himself at his inability to control his physical being or even his lustful thoughts. *Why am I so weak!* he thought, ashamed of his disloyalty.

Luckily, a combination of willpower and the need to concentrate on the subject to avoid Mr Burgomeister's ire helped restore his body to normal by the end of the lesson. Next was morning break and Willy walked out of the room with Petra and returned his books to his bag while chatting to her about the events of the previous day. To his astonishment she had not heard anything about the drone incidents.

Petra looked around. "So vere are dey, dis Callum and his silly friend?" she asked.

"Not at school. I think they've been suspended," Willy replied.

But that was only school rumour, so he really did not know. As Petra clearly was not very interested, he glossed over the incidents and changed the subject to holidays and about the adventures of Andrew and Carmen Collins.

The pair went downstairs and Willy, out of love and hope, began walking with Petra towards the seats where she and the other girls normally sat. But as they did, Petra became very nervous and gestured towards them. "Er... er... Villy... it vood be best if you not with me sit anymore," she said.

Willy was stunned. Stung by the hurt he cried, "Why? Don't, you like me anymore?"

"Oh Villy, I do. You the very sweet boy are and I like you very much... but... but," Petra replied, a look of deep anxiety crossing her face.

"But what?" Willy asked.

Petra gestured towards the girls seated across under the next building. "You see the girl with the black hair at the end? She my cousin Tania is and if she see me with a boy she tell my mother and I into the big trouble get," she explained.

Willy was shocked but the image of the angry mother at the shopping centre instantly convinced him that what Petra said was probably true. "Yes. I understand," he said. "But can we still be friends?"

"Yes, of course. But ve must the careful be. But just for a bit I must ask you not to be with me," Petra replied.

That sent Willy's hopes crashing. He had been looking forward to spending his lunch times with her and walking her home and even maybe meeting at other times. But now he could only hide his disappointment and agree.

"Of course. Sorry. You let me know when it is alright to talk to you again," he replied.

"Thank you," Petra replied. She then turned and walked away, leaving Willy feeling crushed and dejected.

Worse was to follow. The scene had taken place out in the open between two buildings and there were obviously many witnesses. Willy saw their faces and eyes through the blur of unhappiness. *They will all be talking about us now,* he thought unhappily.

Trying to put a brave face on things and to act as though nothing important had just happened he strolled back to where his male classmates usually sat. But as he approached them, Noddy called loudly: "Hey Willy, she give yer the flick did she?"

Willy blushed and shook his head. Then Scott chuckled and commented to the others: "Maybe she's discovered that Willy's Wocket hasn't got enough push?"

Willy glared at him and was about to turn and walk away when he saw John give him a sympathetic look and move along to make room on the seat.

If I walk off in a huff they will all know it is true and my enemies will tease me, Willy thought. So he moved over and slid into the seat. "She will get into trouble from her mother if she is seen talking to boys," he explained.

John nodded. "Oh yeah! We saw her go right off at the shopping centre last week. Boy, I wouldn't want an old dragon like that as my mother in law," he commented.

Willy could only agree, until the notion of one day marrying Petra made him pause and reconsider. *Do daughters really turn out like their mothers?* he pondered. It was a sobering and worrying thought as Petra just seemed so nice.

At that moment, Noddy hastily stood up. Willy saw he was staring along the path to the next building and that he looked quiet scared. His gaze followed and as his brain registered what his eyes saw his own stomach contracted with fear. Walking towards them were Scranton and his cronies the Dru brothers and another Year 10 boy. They all looked hostile and were heading straight for the group.

"What's wrong Noddy?" he asked.

Noddy started to back away and glanced around, obviously seeking a way of escape. "They are gunna bash me! Save me!" he wailed.

Bloody hell! Willy thought. He did not know what Noddy had done but he did feel the pressure to stand by a mate in a crisis. *What do I do?* he wondered as the fear churned in his stomach.

Chapter 24

TROUBLE AGAIN

As the bullies got closer Willy stood up as well. His heart sank into his boots but he felt compelled to stand by his friend.

They will despise me if I don't, he thought. *And I will despise myself.* Better a bit of physical pain, he decided. So when the bullies came to a stop facing them, Willy took position on Noddy's right.

Scranton stopped a pace from Noddy and stood hands on hips. "What were you doing at my bike, Parker?" Scranton demanded to know.

"I wasn't at your bike," Noddy replied. "I was fixing something on my own."

The mention of people doing things to bikes instantly aroused Willy's suspicions. *Is Noddy my secret enemy?* he wondered.

But Scranton wasn't satisfied. "Wally here saw ya. Now what did ya do?" he snarled.

"Nothing," Noddy answered. But he did not sound very convincing and to Willy he looked shifty and ready to run. "When was this?" he asked.

Scranton turned to glare at him. "Piss off Williams or you'll get more than a rocket up your arse!"

Willy felt his stomach churn but he stood his ground. "Let's all go and have a look and settle this," he suggested. But what he actually wanted to do was have a look at his own bike. Hoping there wouldn't be a fight he glanced around to see if any of their other friends were supporting them. To his relief he found John on his right facing Ernie Dru and Stick was ranged up on Noddy's left.

Scranton shook his head and glanced along the line. "Nah! I got a better idea. The bike racks have video surveillance now. We will go to the office and get them to check who's been there and when."

There was nothing to be said to that and the bullies turned and headed towards the main office. As they moved out of earshot Willy turned to Noddy.

"So what was that all about, Noddy?"

Noddy shrugged and looked sheepish. "I just let one of his tyres down," he admitted.

"You bloody drongo! Did you let one of mine down too?"

Noddy shook his head. "No! Why would I do that?"

"Because somebody has been tampering with my bike and I'd like to know who," Willy replied.

"Well it wasn't me!" Noddy cried.

John stepped between them. "OK, let's save our fighting for when Scranton and his cronies come back," he suggested.

Willy had to agree to that but he really wanted to go and check his bike. But he decided now would not be a good time with the office staff possibly watching the video monitors at that moment.

The friends settled back down and waited for the return of the bullies. But they did not re-appear and the bell went for the next class. This was science and in a laboratory so the problem of being beside Petra did not arise. All Willy could do was exchange occasional glances with her.

Halfway through the lesson Mr Fitzgerald appeared at the door and asked for Noddy. Noddy turned a shade paler and reluctantly went with him to the office.

The lesson resumed and Noddy did not return. Then the bell went for the next class and they made their way back to their normal classroom. This time the problem of who to sit beside became important. Willy still wanted to sit beside Petra and made his way to his normal seat. But when she came in and saw him a frown crossed her face and she turned and walked across to where John was sitting on his own. She spoke to him and John turned to look at Willy and then nodded.

A moment later John stood up, collected his books and began walking towards Willy. Petra slid into the vacant desk and sat on her own. Willy was hotly aware of the faces of many classmates showing interest and on some of the girl's even bitchy enjoyment. A wave of behind-the-hand whispering went round and Willy burned with embarrassment.

John stopped and gestured to the seat Petra used to sit at. "OK if I sit here Willy? Petra told me to ask," he said.

Willy could only nod as he found his throat suddenly choked up. He had to fight to hold back tears which welled into his eyes. The arrival of the teacher eased the situation but Willy was left feeling both rejected and dejected.

That set the pattern for the day. Petra sat on her own or with another girl and John sat beside Willy. And during the breaks Petra stayed with other girls. The only good thing was that she often gave Willy wistful looks and he was sure she really wanted to be with him. The other thing that annoyed Willy was that almost all of his friends believed he had somehow been involved in the drone incident with Mr Burgomeister. When he vehemently denied this they had just shrugged and looked knowing.

His mood was not improved when Callum appeared. He and Vincent had been suspended for 3 days but now he was back. He and Willy met on the steps. For a moment they eyed each other, Willy with hostility and Callum with guilty anxiety. "Thanks a lot Callum!" Willy snapped.

Callum shrugged. "You should have run, not stood there like a dummy," he retorted.

For a moment rage rose to almost engulf Willy and he felt an almost overpowering urge to punch at Callum's smirking face. With an effort of will he mastered the urge and gritted his teeth instead. *Is Callum my secret enemy?* he again wondered.

After school Willy yearned to walk with Petra but when she saw him looking at her near the school gate she shook her head and gestured towards another girl nearby.

Willy nodded. *She is this Tania who will dob,* he remembered. Sadly he went to his own bicycle and then rode with John to his house.

There they talked model aircraft and looked at magazines until it was time for Willy to go home. At home he did his homework and then worked on his model triplane. He had hoped to get it completed for the weekend but realised there was no chance of that.

That set the pattern for the remainder of the week. Willy and Petra would exchange wistful and loving glances but they did not sit together. Each afternoon Willy went to one of his friend's houses and in the evening he studied, did homework and worked on his model triplane. At night he fantasised about Petra, and then had dreams full of raunchy scenes involving Marjorie.

On Wednesday afternoon he went to John's, but on Thursday he went to Stick's, driven by what he hoped was the secret urge to see Marjorie. In this he was unsuccessful as she wasn't home and instead Stick bored him with tales about what teachers had done.

Friday bought more problems. The first was in class. As Willy walked to his chair and pulled it out a tiny noise caught his attention. He glanced down and saw a thumb tack on his seat. It had rolled off its base because of the force with which he had pulled the chair back. *I wouldn't have heard it otherwise*, he thought, remembering how painful it was to sit on one.

At that moment John arrived at his seat from the other aisle. He pulled his chair back while chatting cheerfully. Willy glanced down and saw a thumb tack on John's seat as well. Pointing he said: "Look out John, there's a pin on your chair."

John looked down and then swore softly. "Bloody hell! Another one." Then he looked suspiciously around the room before turning back to Willy. "Someone doesn't like us," he muttered. "But who?"

That was what Willy was wondering as well and once again the notion that he had a secret enemy sent a surge of distressing emotions through him. On top of the rejection by Petra it made him thoroughly depressed.

For the next hour or so he kept glancing at the other people in the room, trying to detect if any were looking at him and John. Both Callum and Vincent were back in class but there was nobody he could see doing anything suspicious.

Or nothing related to me anyway, he thought as he noted Vincent and Sean busily setting Boyd up for a fall. Sean distracted Boyd while Vincent bent under the desk and tied his shoelaces together. *Should I warn Boyd?* Willy wondered.

But he didn't, not wanting to attract any unwelcome attention to himself. The resulting trip and crash caused a small drama which was not dealt with very effectively by the teacher, Mrs Ramsey.

She is too nice and too soft, Willy thought. *That pair of noddies wouldn't have tried that trick if it was Miss Hackenmeyer or Mr Burgomeister teaching the class.*

More trouble came out of the blue during the lunch break. Seeing Petra sitting with Tania sent Willy's morale lower and not wanting the other boys to see how upset he was he walked off down to the far end of the oval. There he found himself confronted by the Year 10 bullies.

Scranton appeared with the two Dru brothers and another Year 10 whose name Willy did not know. As soon as he saw Willy Scranton changed direction and walked over to face him.

"Well, hello shitface rocket man. How's the drone business?"

Willy felt his anxiety level shifting towards fear and he swallowed. Trying to keep a brave face he shrugged. "It wasn't me," he replied.

"Oh poop! Half the school saw ya!" Wally retorted. "So don't try to lie to us."

"I'm not. It wasn't me," Willy replied. A quick glance showed that none of his friends was close by and no teacher was visible on playground duty.

Scranton wasn't satisfied. "That's not very friendly, Little Willy," he said.

Wall Dru chortled at that. "Little Willy! That's all he's got."

At that his brother Ernie grinned. "How do you know brother? Have you been peeking in the dunny?"

"Bite yer bum!" Wally retorted angrily. "It's what they all say."

"Who's they?" Scranton asked, still eyeing Willy malevolently.

"All the girls," Wally replied, also giving Willy unfriendly glances.

Scranton nodded. "You mean he finally got to show it to Little Miss Passion Pants?" he queried.

Wally gave an evil grin. "Yeah, that's what Tania the Troll told me. That's why Petra the Porn Star dumped him. She likes big ones," he answered.

The comment really stung Willy, but confronted by four big boys and with no friends or allies in sight, he was reluctant to defend Petra's honour. But his cheeks burned and inside he felt both angry and ill.

Scranton escalated the situation by suddenly reaching out and cuffing him over the right ear. "Well, Year Eight wart? Is that true?" he demanded to know.

"Petra's not like that," Willy hotly. "She's a nice girl."

Scranton scoffed. "Oh crap! She is so! Why do you think she's always sneakin' out of school?" he said.

"She's doesn't!" Willy cried.

"She does. Look, there she is now, her and Tania the Tart. Where are they off to?" Scranton said, jeering and pointing.

Willy's gaze followed the bully's pointing finger and his heart gave a sickening lurch. Walking along the street outside the school were Petra and Tania.

Oh no! he thought. *Where are they going?*

Scranton sneered. "See, there she is, going off to meet some bloke probably."

Ernie Dru nodded. "She does that all the time," he added.

It can't be true! Willy thought, doubt and disbelief warring with memories and the evidence of his own eyes. "She might be just going home sick," he replied. "She hasn't been well recently."

"Too much pork," Scranton retorted.

The other boy interrupted. "Never mind this little turd you blokes, are we gunna go and have a smoke or not?" he interjected.

"Yeah," Scranton replied. He gave Willy a threatening look. "And don't you dob, Williams, or we will know who to come after." With that he lashed out, striking Willy in the face.

Willy had been expecting it and was able to avoid the worst of the blow but it still hurt and he stumbled as he took a pace back. Wally Dru stepped quickly forward and pushed him in the chest, sending him back another pace. With that Willy was caught behind the knees by one of the bench seats which were placed around the perimeter of the oval and he lost his balance, pitching over backwards. He landed hard on his back, getting 'winded' in the process.

The bullies all laughed and then turned and walked away. Willy lay there gasping for breath and anxiously watching them as they moved towards the far end of the oval. But it wasn't the bullying that was distressing him, it was the rotten thoughts that were creeping into his brain to squirm like maggots. Doubt and suspicion swirled in a sickly mixture to make his stomach nauseous.

Surely what they are saying can't be true? Willy told himself. *I haven't seen Petra even flirting with any other boy.*

After struggling to his feet and recovering his breath he blinked the tears from his eyes and looked for Petra. But she and Tania had now gone out of sight along the street. Sick at heart and upset at himself for even doubting her Willy forced himself to walk across the lawn to the fence beside the street they had gone along. But there was no sign of either girl.

Where have they gone? he wondered. Almost against his will his mind also formed the question: And what have they gone to do? But that was too painful to dwell on.

The whole incident deeply upset Willy. Through eyes misted with tears he looked around, noted Scranton and his cronies now sitting in a huddle in the far corner of the oval. Not wanting them to see him crying he turned and walked back towards the buildings of the school.

Pride helped him to wipe his eyes and blink back more tears before he arrived near other students. Only then did a teacher appear on playground duty. *Where were you when I needed you Miss Thatcher?* he thought resentfully. Feeling safer he stopped at the seats nearest the school but away from others. For a few minutes he sat there composing himself and brooding.

What do I do? How can I find out the truth? he wondered. He hated himself for even asking such questions and for doubting Petra.

No answer had come to him before the bell went to return to classes. And once he was back in the room Willy's sickening doubts returned. Petra was not in her seat and when the teacher asked the class where she was Willy said nothing, masking his misery with feigned indifference.

Petra did not return that afternoon. For a while Willy waited at the school gate after the last bell but there was still no sign of her. John saw him and came over.

"What ya doin', Willy?" he asked.

Willy shrugged. "Nothing," he replied. Again he had to fight back the tears that prickled in his eyes.

"Want to come over to my place?" John asked.

Willy shook his head. "I don't feel well," he answered. "I think I'll go home and go to bed."

"Hope ya ain't sick tomorrow," John replied. "We are still going to Townsville for this Model Aircraft Fly-in thing aren't we?"

Willy had completely forgotten. He nodded. "Yes. So I want to be well for that. I'll see you in the morning." As he said this he noted disappointment on John's face but he was too upset to really care. Unlocking his bike he mounted it and set off home.

At home Willy was so upset he hid in his room and cried. Only when his parents came home did he calm down and then force himself to act naturally.

His mother came to his room. "Have you packed ready for your trip to Townsville?' she queried.

Willy shook his head. "Not yet Mum."

Then his mother delivered another jolt. "Have you ironed your uniform for cadets?" she asked.

Cadets! Willy had completely forgotten cadets. For a moment he was tempted to say he wasn't well and did not want to go. But then he realised that might put his selection for the Drill Squad in jeopardy and he really wanted to do that. So he got up and kept himself busy for the next hour packing and polishing boots and preparing.

But at cadets he wished several times that he hadn't. The reason was Sgt Branch. Branch seemed to pick on him from the moment he arrived and then every few minutes after that. It was so noticeable that several other cadets commented to Willy during the breaks between lessons.

"What have you done to upset Branch, Willy?" Noddy asked.

"Don't know," Willy answered, his mind turning over possible reasons.

Towards the end of the evening he found out. During the second period, a drill lesson in preparation of the Annual end-of-year Passing-Out Parade, Branch delivered constant blistering criticism of every movement Willy made. It went on until Willy was goaded to respond.

"Stop picking on me sergeant!" he cried.

Branch exploded in anger. "Picking on you! I'm not picking on you. Your drill is so sloppy you need to be corrected. Now pick your feet up and move faster."

Willy opened his mouth to deny he was moving slowly or that his drill was sloppy but a glance at Branch's angry face made him just utter, "Yes sergeant." Sweating with stress and effort he concentrated on doing perfect drill. But inside he seethed. He was both angry and depressed.

So upset was he that he determined to have it out with Branch so after the squad was fallen out for a break he marched over and confronted him. "Why are you singling me out Sgt Branch. What have I done to hurt you?" he asked.

Branch looked at him, first with surprise and then with contemptuous anger. "You, you dirty little worm! You aren't fit to even look at Petra, let alone speak to her, or to do the things you are doing," he replied.

"I haven't done anything to her!" Willy cried. "I haven't even spoken to her all week and we don't even sit together anymore."

"Not what I've been told," Branch retorted angrily.

"Whatever it is it's a lie," Willy shouted. "I haven't done anything to her. What are people saying?"

Branch bristled and he stepped closer to Willy, yelling in his face:

"That you have been sneaking out of school at lunch time and going off to... to... to do things, you disgusting, filthy little beast!"

"That's not true! Who told you that?" Willy cried angrily.

But Branch did not reply as a furious Flight Lieutenant Comstock thrust himself between them. "Stop that shouting! What's going on here?"

Willy opened his mouth to reply but Branch beat him to it. "Williams is back answering me, sir. He is being insubordinate," he said.

"Oh, I was not!" Willy cried, stung by the injustice of the remark.

Flight Lieutenant Comstock turned a baleful eye on him. "Stand to attention when speaking to an officer! And you too Sgt Branch. And use correct titles, Sgt Branch. You mean Cadet Williams."

"Yes sir," Branch replied as he hastily came to attention. "But Cadet Williams was being insolent."

Flight Lieutenant Comstock raised an eyebrow. "Describe the incident," he ordered.

Branch's eye flickered as he glanced at Willy and at the other cadets. "Will... er... Cadet Williams was doing very poor drill sir, so I corrected him and he got angry and shouted at me."

On hearing this Willy seethed with indignation but he managed to stand to attention and keep silent.

Flight Lieutenant Comstock turned to face Willy. "Well Cadet Williams, what is your version?"

"Sir, Sgt Branch was picking on me and saying insulting things about a girl I like," he replied.

Inside he was churning with anger and anxiety as he knew that standing up for himself could make Branch an even worse enemy, but felt he had nothing to lose. *If I get a bad name I could get chucked out of cadets or never get promoted,* he told himself.

Light Lieutenant Comstock again raised an eyebrow. "Is this girl a cadet? Is she here?"

Willy shook his head. "No sir. She goes to our school."

"Did anyone else see this incident?" Flight Lieutenant Comstock asked, looking around at the watching cadets and staff.

Stick's hand went up. "I did sir," he replied. "Sgt Branch was picking on Willy... er... on Cadet Williams all lesson and then he spoke to him about a girl at our school, saying bad things about her and about what Willy has done to her."

On hearing that Willy's estimation of Stick went up considerably. *He has more guts than I thought. He obviously isn't my secret enemy if he is willing to risk making Branch an enemy.* But he was also annoyed at the assumption that he had done something to Petra.

"I haven't done anything to her sir. I just think she is nice," he said.

Flight Lieutenant Comstock shook his head. "I think we had better investigate this properly. Flying Officer Turnbull, you take Sgt Branch and get a statement from him. Pilot Officer Lowe, you take Cadet Williams to the office and get his statement and Flying Officer Lacey, you get statements from everyone in this squad. Have it done in twenty minutes please."

As the officers answered with 'sir' Willy glanced at Branch and received a very hostile glare in return. *He is really angry at me now. I will be in even more trouble,* he thought unhappily.

Chapter 25

TO TOWNSVILLE

Pilot Officer Lowe was a chubby female who worked in an accountant's office in her civilian job. Up till now Willy had barely noticed her, other than being aware that she was one of the adult staff. But she seemed efficient and neutral and she took him to the Admin Officer's office and sat him at the desk with pen and paper.

"Write down your version of events. And make sure you put in details like names, dates, times and where these things happened," she instructed.

"How far back do I go Ma'am?" Willy asked, his mind a-swirl with all the times Branch had given him grief.

"Just tonight. We will go back if we find we need to."

"Yes Ma'am. But it does need a bit to explain that it started at school," Willy replied. He was now feeling scared and anxious and could see his cadet career in jeopardy and wanted to put the best case he could.

"Yes, alright, but only a short introductory paragraph to explain the background," Pilot Officer Lowe replied.

That was the hardest bit. Making a summary was always a bit of a challenge to Willy and would much rather have written for an hour telling the whole story. But he bit his lip, chewed the pen and thought hard before starting. In a few sentences he described how Branch had spoken to him about Petra at school and on previous cadet parades.

'I believe that he is jealous because Petra likes me and as a result he has been harassing me. He continually singles me out and tells me I am doing poor drill or that I am no good and he says this in front of the other cadets. I find this very upsetting and have thought of not coming to cadets,' Willy wrote.

Then he paused, considered the words and shook his head. *I won't say I have thought of leaving cadets,* he told himself.

Bending to the task he wrote on: 'Sgt Branch is a good sergeant and knows his stuff but this is a personal ...' *Personal what?* Willy wondered, several possible words flitting through his mind. 'Vendetta' he considered too strong but seemed to fit. In the end he settled for 'thing'.

Having described the incident Willy signed his name and dated the statement. Then, barely able to keep the tears from starting, he handed it to Pilot Officer Lowe. *This could end my cadet career anyway,* he thought miserably.

By then the third period of instruction was well under way so Willy was told to wait out in the hall. He did this, noting Branch sitting on his own at the other end and several of his own section looking unhappy near the door. The whole situation made Willy feel ill and he had to struggle with his self-control to avoid public tears.

Pilot Officer Lowe took the statement into the CO's office and then went back to her own. Knowing that Flight Lieutenant Comstock was weighing the evidence caused Willy's stomach to churn with apprehension. *Who will he believe, me or the sergeant?* he fretted.

The other cadets were sent off to their lessons and then the WO(D) called Sgt Branch and marched him in to the CO. That sent Willy's heart into more flutters of anxiety and he felt he needed to go to the toilet, badly.

Then Branch came out and flicked a brief glance full of dislike towards Willy before marching off outside. Seeing Branch's body language sent a tremor of fear through Willy. But then he shook his head and felt better.

Branch looked like he has been ticked off, he mused.

And now it was his turn. CDTWOFF Mathieson called him over and checked his uniform, then called him to attention. "When I say halt you halt. I salute, you don't. Wait for my orders. Got it?"

"Yes sir," Willy replied, his stomach churning with apprehension.

"Cadet Williams, Quick March! Left, right, left, right, left, right. Cadet Williams, halt!" came the sharp commands. Willy halted in the CO's office facing the big desk. Flight Lieutenant Comstock sat behind the desk looking stern and wearing his cap. On his left stood Flying Officer Turnbull and on his right stood the adult Warrant Officer, WOFF Colley. They all looked very serious.

CDTWOFF Mathieson snapped a salute beside Willy. Flight Lieutenant Comstock sat to attention then looked hard at Willy. Frowning, he picked up a sheet of paper. "I have your statement here Cadet Williams and I found it very interesting to read. Luckily for you four other cadets corroborate your version of events. There are no essential discrepancies so I accept that you are the victim of some bullying and harassment."

As the import of what the CO was saying sank in Willy felt his spirits lighten. It seemed as though the steel fist that had been squeezing his chest and stomach was easing its grip. But there was still churning apprehension.

"Yes sir," was all he could answer.

Flight Lieutenant Comstock went on: "Insubordination is serious and can lead to demotion or discharge. But so is bullying and harassment. You will make sure you do not back answer anyone senior in rank or I will consider serious consequences. Shouting at a sergeant is not acceptable. Do I make myself quiet clear?"

Willy swallowed and felt his stomach turn over the need to do a pee became even more urgent. "Yes sir," he croaked, his throat dry with anxiety.

Flight Lieutenant Comstock eyed him for a moment and then went on. "But harassment and bullying are also not acceptable. Sergeant Branch has been advised on how to improve his leadership skills. There will be no repetition of the incident. Is that clear?"

"Yes sir," Willy replied. *So I was right, Branch has been ticked off!* But that just meant he would dislike him even more, so the problem could just shift to school.

"What you must do Cadet Williams, is take any complaint to an officer, not yell back. It is important that we, the adult staff I mean, know about any bullying or harassment as it can have serious consequences for the unit. Now, I appreciate that you will not be very popular with Sergeant Branch so do you wish to transfer from 3 Section to One or Two?"

Willy's mind raced. *Do I want a transfer to another section? Will that solve the problem?* Then he shook his head. "No sir. I would like to remain in 3 Section," he said. *Running away won't solve anything and most of my friends are in 3 Section.*

Flight Lieutenant Comstock gave a thin smile. "Good. Alright, let's have no more trouble. Carry on WO(D)."

CDTWOFF Mathieson saluted. "Sir! Cadet Williams, about turn! Cadet Williams, Quick March! Left, right, left, right. Cadet Williams halt! Cadet Williams, fall out!"

As Willy did a right turn CDTWOFF Mathieson hissed at him. "Go back to your squad Cadet Williams, and don't give us any more trouble."

"Yes sir," Willy replied, wooden-faced but bubbling with relief inside.

So he did, saluting the CUO who was instructing the class on aircraft recognition before sliding into a vacant seat. Nearby were Branch and the Flight Sergeant, Cliff Barnet. Both gave him sour looks when he glanced in their direction. *Oh well, that is to be expected,* Willy told himself.

After the lesson was over Willy avoided looking towards the sergeants but he did seek out Stick. "Thanks Stick. That was gutsy and I appreciate it," he said.

Stick nodded but looked glum. "Thanks Willy. But now I suppose Branch and his mates will make our lives a misery."

Willy hoped not and said so and instead diverted the talk onto the trip to Townsville which now popped up to the font of his consciousness. "See you in the morning then," he said as they marched off the parade ground after dismissal.

While waiting in the car park for his mother to pick him up Willy spotted Branch marching in his direction. *Here it comes, pay back!* he thought. His stomach churned and he steeled himself for another confrontation.

But Branch just marched by, not even glancing in his direction. Instead he went to his parent's car and got in. Willy let out a long sigh of relief. *He must have got a real warning from the CO not to keep picking on me,* Willy decided.

That was a heartening thought but did not ease the lingering anxiety about the longer term problems he might encounter at cadets. But it was a very relieved boy who was driven home and then offered supper by his mother. During the drive Willy considered whether to tell her about the incident and finally he decided he had better. *If they find out later they will be hurt and will lose trust in me,* he thought.

So he waited until his father came into the kitchen to make some hot chocolate and then recounted the incident. Both parents listened, looking very thoughtful. Then his mother frowned. "This is over some girl isn't it?"

"Yes Mum."

"Was it young Marjorie that you went skinny dipping with?"

At that Willy squirmed with embarrassment and blushed. "Mum! No," he cried, noting the shocked and amused look on his father's face as he did.

"Oh piffle! Your father has to know," his mother retorted. "If you are starting to play those sorts of games we need to be able to help with advice. We don't want you or them getting into any trouble," his mother said.

His father met his eyes. "This swimming, was that at the farm?"

"Yes Dad," Willy mumbled, hot and ashamed.

To his surprise his father grinned. "Down at the creek?"

"Yes Dad."

But before his father could ask another question his mother cut in. "You take that grin off your face Mr Williams! This is potentially serious stuff."

Willy's father looked contrite and blushed. "Yes dear, but I'm sure it was just kids being inquisitive. It is not end-of-the-world stuff. Anyway, I like young Marjorie. She's got spirit."

His mother frowned. "Is she going on this trip to Townsville over the weekend?"

Willy's father shook his head. "No. Just boys."

"Good! Now get to bed William and be up at six," his mother snapped.

Willy fled. In a flash of insight he realised that his father had been imagining Marjorie swimming nude. His own mind was suddenly filled with such images and he wished Marjorie was coming with them.

Poor old Dad, he's in trouble with Mum now, he thought.

Only after he had switched off the light and slid into bed did Willy remember Petra. *Not Marjorie. It is Petra I love,* he told himself. But the images of Marjorie would not go away and he became very aroused and very confused.

The following morning he saw Marjorie when he and his father drove to the Morton's to pick up Stick. Marjorie came out in a silk wrap and leaned on the car door. "I wish I was coming with you," she said.

Willy could only nod, hotly aware that his father was next to him. He couldn't even warn Marjorie that his parents knew about their aquatic antics. "See you next week," was all he could say.

Stick placed his luggage in the back of the Range Rover and then climbed in the back seat and they set off. As they drove away Willy waved to Marjorie and so did Stick. Willy then risked a glance at his dad and to his surprise saw that he was smiling.

Dad's OK, he decided. *He understands a boy's needs.*

They drove around and picked up Scott and John. Willy did not really want Scott to come as he knew he didn't like him but he also knew that John liked Scott so he said nothing. With the three boys and their gear in the back the vehicle was turned south onto the Bruce Highway.

Five hours later, much delayed by numerous sections of road works, they arrived in the city of Townsville. Slightly larger than Cairns it is a completely different city. Where Cairns is green and surrounded by jungle-covered mountains, Townsville appeared dry and parched and the few hills and distant mountains had only a thin covering of savannah woodland. Townsville also has a completely different economic situation being a government and mining base. The largest army barracks in Northern Australia was there: Lavarack Barracks.

Willy had glimpsed the barracks before when he had passed through Townsville on family holidays but he had never paid much attention. Now, his interest sparked by the stories from Stephen and Graham, he looked carefully at the kilometres of manicured lawns and seemingly endless rows of barrack and office buildings as their car drove past just after midday.

Stick pointed out the window. "Is that where we did our GST Camp?" he queried.

Willy was astonished. "No Stick. This is an army base. We were at the RAAF base at Garbutt," he replied.

"You sure?" Stick asked.

"I'm sure!" Willy answered. "See that big mountain with the TV towers? That is Mt Stuart. There is no mountain like that near the RAAF base. It is beside the airport."

Stick frowned and stared at the rugged slopes of Mt Stuart. "Well there was some sort of rocky hill near the air base we were at," he grumbled.

Willy shook his head and pointed out the car window to the left. "You mean Castle Hill. That is that hill over there," he explained. Even though the camp had only been a week long he had made the effort to learn the names of the surrounding hills and mountains. They were important features for a pilot to know and avoid and Willy wanted to be a pilot.

But Stick had spotted an armoured vehicle in the army barracks and pointed to it. "Look, a tank!" he cried excitedly.

It was actually an eight-wheeled armoured car, but Willy only grunted and nodded. He studied the machine and then a small group of soldiers wearing webbing and carrying weapons who were practicing some drill or manoeuvre out on an open area of lawn.

A few minutes later they were past the barracks and turned right. "Flinders Highway," Willy's father explained. "This road goes all the way west to Charters Towers, Mount Isa and on into the Northern Territory."

They drove southwards through the suburb of Wulguru and on into the semi-industrial area of Stuart. On the left was a railway line and beyond that a collection of buildings surrounded by a high wall.

Stick pointed at the place. "What's that joint?" he queried.

Willy's father chuckled and then answered. "Stuart Prison. That's where you and Willy will end up if you do the wrong thing."

Images of a naked Marjorie in the creek with him and Stick flashed into Willy's mind and he felt a stab of anxiety and guilt. To hide his shame and anxiety he snorted. "Huh! You usually tell me it will be Lotus Glen, Prison Dad," he replied.

His father laughed. "One or the other. So be sensible about what you do. Life's a lot easier if you stay out of trouble," he commented. Then he turned his attention back to the GPS Navigator he was using to find his way.

They drove on south over the tail end of the Mt Stuart Range through a series of light industrial and transport yards to another small range of hills cloaked in savannah woodland. As they went through a cutting and across an overpass over the railway Willy's father gestured out to the right.

"Nearly there. This is a suburb called Oak Valley we're are coming to and the Fly-in is there."

Willy looked out and saw only open bush and a few scattered houses on both sides of the road. *Suburb!* he thought. But a kilometre further along they turned right off the Flinders Highway and crossed the railway line and he saw that it really was a suburb. There were many houses, all on large allotments and scattered among trees and bushland.

Turning left they drove south beside the railway. After making their way through some hills with a scatter of houses on them, they came to the end of the bitumen and drove on along a gravel road. Three kilometres into the bush they came out of the trees at a large grassy clearing.

"This is it," Willy's father explained. Not that it was necessary as there were dozens of vehicles parked there and a long row of tents and shade structures and what looked like hundreds of people. The buzz of small petrol engines reached Willy's ears and he looked out and saw tiny dark specs flitting across the sky.

The vehicle was parked and they climbed out into hot dry air. Nearby were several portable toilets and the noise of buzzing model aircraft became the dominant sound. One came roaring low overhead and Willy glanced up and saw that it was a gleaming silver, low wing, propeller driven monoplane.

"What's that?" Stick asked.

Willy opened his mouth to reply but Scott beat him to it. "A Skyraider, an American World War Two fighter," he explained.

Two more large models flashed past: a bright blue Corsair fighter and a red painted twin engine model that Willy thought was one of the racing types from the 1930s.

I'm going to enjoy this, he decided.

Chapter 26

FLY-IN

Willy's father led the boys over to where a dozen people, mostly middle-aged men, were seated on folding chairs under a shade structure. A grey-haired gentleman with a moustache rose to meet them and introduced himself as Greg, the Club President. Feeling very self-conscious and very much the outsider Willy shook hands and then stepped back to let the others in. Only much later did Willy learn that Greg was actually a retired colonel from the Army Reserve and a much respected local leader and administrator.

It was obvious from the conversation between the adults that they were expected and that made Willy nod and admire his father even more. *Dad is good like that,* he thought. *He plans and thinks ahead and organises things.*

One aspect of this was immediately apparent when they were led over to where several officials sat under another shade structure. They had a program and booking sheet and Willy learned that their models were already entered in various events. That sent his anxiety level shooting up as he could see that other people had copies of the program and would expect his model to take part. He had been nursing the thought that if he got too anxious he could just sit and watch and not risk making a fool of himself in front of these obvious experts.

Once they were registered in Willy's dad led the boys back to the car and they unloaded another small shade structure and spent fifteen minutes erecting this and pegging it firmly down. While they were doing this Willy kept glancing at a large yellow and black, low wing monoplane model of a type he could not identify doing laps and loops and other aerobatics. Seeing how well it performed added to his nervousness.

Folding chairs and a folding table were added and then the boys sat in the shade to have 'afternoon tea' while watching the model aircraft fly.

The next event was a race between two almost identical models, a yellow, blue and white, low wing monoplane and a black and red one. This was a followed by a model that so got Willy's interest that he forgot his shyness and moved to get a closer look as the model was fuelled and prepared. It was a Bristol Boxkite model with a wingspan of about a metre.

This is fantastic! Willy thought as he watched the model take off. It was of a type that he often daydreamed he had made himself at home and which he used for various heroic exploits such as rescuing damsels in distress and so on.

The next series of events also fascinated Willy. These were performances by jet powered models. Willy was so intrigued he had to go and have a close look. One of the models was a silver MiG 15 fighter with Chinese markings and it looked so impressive Willy several times spontaneously clapped as it screeched past on high speed, low level passes.

But the next model jet had him in awe. It was a grey F18 and it did such a spectacular climb Willy thought that it looked exactly like the real thing. These was even a huge model of a C17 transport with 4 jet engines and when it landed with a faulty engine Willy and his friends went over to look at it. The model was so big it came up to the owner's waist and had a wing span longer than a man could reach.

Even more fascinating was the 'jet' engine. The man unscrewed it and carefully took it out to find the fault and Willy could only stare in amazement and admiration. The motor was a black and yellow cylindrical shape with silver mounting brackets and it looked so compact and neat that he shook his head in wordless admiration. He also shook his head at the price, although he had already worked out that real model aircraft flying was a hobby for people with plenty of money and ample spare time.

That was shown even more obviously when they moved across to the side where four men were assembling their biplane and triplane models. These were, to Willy's eyes, absolutely perfect examples of the model builder's art and seeing the quality of them thoroughly demoralized him.

I will never be able to make anything that good, he thought. One of the models was of a World War 1 German Fokker DR1 but instead of being painted red it was painted grey and green with yellow dapples. To further add to Willy's discomfiture, he noted that the markings were the straight black crosses, not the Maltese crosses he planned to put on his.

When he mentioned this to the man who was busy very carefully tensioning the bracing wires, the man explained that by the time the Red Baron was shot down the Germans had changed to their markings.

"March 1918, von Richthofen was shot down in April," he explained.

That embarrassed Willy and gave him a bit of a worry. *Do I change mine or not?* he thought.

The other biplanes were a Sopwith Camel, an SE5A and a French Nieuport. These were flown with grace and wonderful manoeuvrability and Willy could only listen with embarrassed fascination to the technical chatter about 'Rolling Moment' and how to correct yaws and skids and directional stability and lateral stability.

I don't really know very much at all, he decided and therefore resolved to keep his mouth shut and his ears open. Thus he learned a lot about dihedral, and oscillation and on keeping control to avoid stalls and spins.

The biplane models were joy to Willy, even if they made him feel inferior. But the next batch on the program he watched with mixed emotions. These were the UAVs and Drones. Most were quadcopters but a few had six or eight rotors.

Some of the drone designs looked really good, with streamlined fuselages and bright colours and many had their rotors mounted in protective covers. The largest Hexacopter, looking to Willy like a collection of black and red pipes or tubes with bits clipped on underneath, did not appeal to him at all. He was amazed when its rotor arms were all folded out and locked in position. The machine was wider across than he could reach.

And that doesn't include the rotor blades, he noted.

When the huge Hexacopter was started up all the spinning rotors made a most impressive blur and when it lifted off and buzzed across to hover in front of them, its camera traversing left and right Stick laughed and called, "Boy! If Callum had that one he could have given old Buggermaster a haircut!"

Willy experienced a wave of flashbacks and the chief thing he remembered was the look on the old man's face, the shock and obvious upset he had suffered. So he just shook his head and pursed his lips.

But Scott looked at him and said, "What about that one Willy! Would Callum like it?"

"Bugger Callum!" Willy snapped. "He dropped me right in it!"

The other two boys laughed and Willy was aware his father was giving him an odd look. That reminded him that his parents did not know about the drone incidents. *Or I don't think they do.* But now there was anxiety they might find out!

Despite that the technicalities of the drones interested Willy. He particularly liked a sleek, white quadcopter called a 'Phantom 4' that had a camera attached. He also liked a yellow and black one that he overheard was quite cheap. John asked how much it cost and a man replied, "Real cheap, only a few hundred dollars."

Only a few hundred dollars! thought Willy as he considered all the money he had recently spent on models. *And on tubes, valves and pumps!*

A tiny black quadcopter came buzzing past the audience and Stick nudged Willy again. "That's about the size of Callum's," he commented. "That would be good to fly at school."

"You do it then!" Willy snapped back and again he was conscious of his father glancing towards them.

The Club President strolled over and stood with them. "How do you boys like the drones?" he enquired.

"Super!" Stick answered. "We had a kid flying one in class the other day."

Willy stared at Stick, willing him to stop but Stick did not see his warning look and went on: "He flew it around the quadrangle at lunchtime chasing one of the teachers. It was so funny!"

"It was not!" Willy snapped. "Poor Old Mr Burgomeister nearly had a heart attack."

Stick looked at him in surprise and then shrugged. To Willy's relief John asked if the drones were the same as UAVs.

"They are," the Club President replied.

Scott made a face. "I don't like UAVs," he said. "They aren't real planes."

The Club President looked hard at him and shook his head. "Too bad! You'd better get used to the idea because they are the future and they already do thousands of jobs."

Willy agreed with Scott but said nothing. He had read a lot about Unmanned or Uninhabited Aerial Vehicles and secretly they worried him as he feared they might make pilots obsolete.

The Club President nodded and pointed to a large, black quadcopter. "These are UAVs. This one is not a very big one, in fact it only cost about

$3,000 but it is still very capable. People use them for surveying farms and so on. It is not just a toy to play with."

Then he pointed to where another man held what looked like a large boomerang. "That is also a UAV. It is a flying wing and it is really good for surveying and aerial photography of large areas."

"What's its endurance?" Willy's father queried.

"About forty-five minutes I think," the Club President replied.

They were then given the opportunity to stand beside one of the drone pilots and have the radio transmitter controls explained. They were similar to his father's so he had no difficulty understanding it all. They were all computerized with a touch screen and tiny levers and buttons but looked simple enough to Willy. As he and his father were already using a laptop computer to program the flight profiles for their models he easily understood what the man was saying. The only thing he did not like was that the screen showing what the drone was doing was very hard to see in the sunlight.

Other operators had shade screens attached to help limit the reflection but Willy still found them hard to look at. The man then popped out an SD Card and held it up. "It can record the video onto this," he explained.

As Willy had an SD Card in his own controller programmed with his flight profiles he nodded and watched as the drone was set moving. The drone then lifted up and simply screwed itself vertically upwards and Willy saw his own image shrink on the control screen. The drone was sent off to orbit the field and at each corner it did what looked like a little dance before continuing on.

Stick turned to Willy's dad. "Did you bring your drone Mr Williams?" he asked.

Willy's father shook his head. "No. It hasn't been repaired yet," he replied.

"Bloody Noddy!" John added.

Willy could only agree. If nothing else the drone would have been fun to fly. *And easier.*

They discussed drones some more and then all watched as the flying wing was put through its paces. By then Willy was becoming quite anxious as the time on the program for people like himself to fly their models approached.

But he could not see any way out of it so when the others made their way to the car to collect their models and controllers he went with them, pretending to be keen and cheerful.

Now I am glad dad made us do some flying practice, Willy thought.

And it paid off. When it was his turn to fly his plastic kit Spitfire, he was able to take it off and land it without crashing and he thought his loops and rolls were good enough not to disgrace him. He was even gratified when the watching club members politely clapped as he taxied his model in at the end of his turn.

Then he watched anxiously while his father flew the model Feisler Storch, but it was a real hit when it was flown very low and very slow and then landed in a few metres and did a take-off in a few paces. Most of the audience clapped with genuine appreciation.

That showed then! Willy thought, well aware by now that most serious model aircraft enthusiasts held a low opinion of kit models and particularly ones with electric motors. *They mostly like the loud roaring and buzzing petrol motors,* he mused.

Then Stick, John and Scott each flew their model in turn and that was embarrassing as Stick and Scott both did a bad job and both did crash landings at the end, luckily without causing serious damage.

The final event of the afternoon was a fly past of all the smaller petrol-powered models, the Mustang, Skyraider, Corsair, and the twin-engine red racer of the 1930s. To Willy it was a joy to watch and he wished his model was good enough to take part.

Next time maybe? he thought.

There was then a period of relative confusion as models were cleaned and packed up. Some of the shade structures came down and chairs were folded while others were left up. Most of the people attending the 'Fly-in' were locals so they put their models and chairs in their cars and drove off. About a dozen remained. A few had caravans parked back among the trees and there were a couple of tents.

Putting up their tents was the next task for the boys and Willy thoroughly enjoyed that. There were two tents, the boys all sharing the large square one the William's family used for holiday camping trips and Mr Williams having a small bubble tent to himself.

Erecting the tent and putting bedding and belongings inside led to a good deal of good natured horseplay and a little bit of tension as they settled who was to sleep where. Willy ended up against the left wall with

Stick beside him, then John. Scott went on the far side. That suited Willy as he still did not like Scott or trust him.

The evening meal was next. They had camping gear but Mr Williams bundled them into the vehicle and drove back to the shops at Stuart. A fish shop provided fish and chips and other goodies, and the group then climbed back into the vehicle and drove back to the airfield just as the sun was setting.

There was a proper campfire area so they carried their chairs to that and sat with some other people, an elderly couple from Mildura and a man from the Sunshine Coast. The fish and chips were shared out and Willy sat and ate, feeling happy and content.

That was a good day, he thought. *I hope tomorrow is just as good.*

Bedtime was all jokes and horseplay and that put Willy in an even better mood. The only little niggle he had was when they finally climbed into their sleeping bags and Stick nudged him. "I'll bet you wish it was Marjorie and not me next you," he said with a leering chuckle.

That annoyed Willy and made both John and Scott turn to look. Seeing that Willy shook his head. "Petra is my girlfriend," he replied.

"You hope!" Stick replied. "But you'd get more out of Marj. She thinks you are the bee's knees."

Scott snorted at that. "Huh! Can't imagine why," he cried.

"She's seen his weapon," Stick commented.

Willy blushed and saw John frown but Scott jeered. Then Willy's father called from the next tent. "That's enough of that 'Boy Talk' you fellas. Go to sleep."

That silenced them and they snuggled down but Willy was unable to sleep, his mind now full of images of Marjorie down at the creek. He became so aroused he could only wish the other boys weren't there.

At last he drifted off into an uncomfortable sleep full of dreams where he kept trying to kiss Petra but kept finding Marjorie there.

Dr Williams had them up at 0600 and insisted they get dressed immediately and then took them for a run around the airfield in the cool of the morning. "You lot all think you are tough cadets, let's see if you are," was his comment.

Then it was the less enjoyable task of rolling up bedding and packing their gear while Dr Williams cooked sausages and fried eggs on his portable BBQ.

261

They then sat around on the folding chairs, balancing their plates on their knees while they ate and joked. Willy was in a very good mood and kept taking deep breaths and relishing the open air and camping experience. He noted that the air was crisp and clear and that the visibility was so good that the trees stood out individually on the large mountain range ten or so kilometres to the east. It was good to be alive!

One at a time cars began arriving and club members and visitors began setting up shade structures or assembling and preparing models.

People began flying models even before the Club President and other officials arrived and Willy and his friends were allowed by Willy's father to fuel up their models and do a test run each. To Willy that was a joy and he thrilled to see his Spitfire zoom past and then bank and turn to go around again.

What a beautiful aircraft! he thought. *What a great design.*

And then he had a heart-in-mouth moment as Stick's model flashed past and almost collided with it. "Stick! Watch where you are going," Willy cried.

"Yeah," agreed John whose own model had been forced to climb to get clear. "Go the same way around as everyone else."

"Sorry," Stick answered. "I didn't notice."

Bloody hell! Willy thought. *Every other model is flying clockwise around the field and Stick hasn't noticed!*

Soon after, at 9am, the loudspeaker boomed to announce the start of the day's Program. All the models were brought in to land and collected. Willy picked up his Spitfire and carried it almost lovingly to their table. Here he checked it over and dusted it, rubbing his hands over the smooth, shiny plastic.

It might be only a cheap kit model, but I like it, he told himself.

After refuelling his model, he moved to sit watching the field as the day's events got under way. First was a demonstration of a new model, a large, orange painted 'sports' aircraft that was put through a series of dramatic aerobatics that drew applause and approval from the crowd and which made Willy quite envious.

Then there was a race between all the biplanes and the triplane, even the Bristol Boxkite. That was fun to watch but the next race between the big, low wing monoplanes of the Club members, was more thrilling. It was enlivened by a large blue painted 'Hellcat' suddenly slowing as its engine spluttered. Then the motor abruptly cut out and the owner frantically tried to being it down before it lost too much speed to glide. He was almost successful but the wheels obviously hit some rough turf on the far boundary of the field as it suddenly bounced and cart wheeled.

Willy saw a wing fly off. *Oh! Poor man! All that work!* he thought, now very aware of the labour and effort involved in making scratch built models.

There was a pause while the wreckage was collected and Willy joined the group crowding around to look. The model had lost a wing, one undercarriage oleo was badly bent and the propeller was clearly out of true. "Not as bad as it looked," he muttered.

The flying was resumed. Five model helicopters of various designs were put through their paces and again Willy was amazed at the skill and quality of the flying. He was astonished when one of the models even flew upside down for a short distance. He did not particularly like helicopters and had no desire to become a helicopter pilot but he did appreciate their value and how vital they are for rescue and policing.

At the request of Willy's father, the boys were next on the program so they could leave early to drive back to Cairns. This time Willy was not nearly as nervous, and he happily prepared his Spitfire and lined it up ready for a race with the others.

Each boy flew their model around the course, one at a time against the clock. Willy was last and he was confident his Spitfire would prove the fastest. He was now really enjoying himself and he carefully adjusted the control radio settings and then had Stick start the engine and hold the model.

Satisfied everything was ready Willy glanced at the control screen and then nodded. "OK Stick, let her go!" he called.

The Spitfire model leapt forward and within a few metres had lifted off. Willy smiled and was pleased with what looked like a good start, and when he was satisfied he had control and the trim was correct he prepared for the first turn. Judging the moment as the model approached the corner post of the field, he pushed the levers to bank and turn, and nothing happened.

The model kept flying straight. "What's wrong?" Willy muttered as a stab of anxiety went through him. Not wanting to look foolish in front of such an audience, he again manipulated the controls to turn the model.

Again nothing happened.

Willy tried again, now sure there was a problem, his anxiety level shooting right up. Mouth open with surging dismay he stared at his rapidly departing Spitfire. Almost frantically he again toggled the controls but the model kept flying steadily away, heading on a straight line for the distant range of mountains.

What's wrong? he fretted.

John waved his hands and reached across towards the control console. "Check the settings, Willy. Have you bumped the radio frequency setting or something?"

Pulling the console sharply out of John's reach Willy lifted it and stared at the setting in the dial. "31.60, that's right," he mumbled. *That's the correct setting for the rudder controls so what's gone wrong?* he wondered.

By then the model was so far away it was just a speck, and because the rugged mass of the Mt Elliott Range was the backdrop it was very hard to see. Tears began to prickle in Willy's eyes as he became more and more concerned. Again and again he worked the control console but still nothing changed.

By now other people were aware there was a problem and Willy was embarrassed to have the adults looking at him and at his fast vanishing model.

The Club President walked over. "Is there a problem?"

Willy was so choked up with emotion that he could only nod. His father answered for him, pointing to the now almost invisible model. "It isn't responding to the controls," he explained.

"Channel settings correct?"

"Yes," Willy croaked, hotly aware that a big tear had formed and was about to trickle down his left cheek. He did not want the added shame of crying in public!

"Are the batteries flat?" the Club President asked.

Willy hadn't thought of that and cursed himself as a fool, but a quick check of the console screen revealed that the batteries had plenty of power remaining. Shaking his head in bafflement he looked up to again try the controls.

But to his dismay, he could no longer see the model.

Chapter 27

UPSET

Where is it? Has it crashed? Willy wondered.

Again he worked the controls to get the model to turn but although he strained his eyes there was no sign of any distant speck that might be the model. His hopes of seeing it reappear began to crumble and with them went his self-control.

Sobbing and turning his head away to hide the tears that began to stream unchecked down his cheeks he thrust the control console at Stick and hurried away. Hardly able to see for the tears and burning with shame he hurried towards their tent, stumbling several times and nearly tripping over a box someone had left on the ground.

On reaching the tent Willy fumbled with the flaps, hotly aware that dozens of people could see him. Sobbing with emotion he managed to untangle the tent flap from around him and get inside. There he flung himself on his air mattress. And now the tears really came.

For several minutes Willy wept. He sobbed and felt both angry and ashamed. But slowly he calmed down. He was helped in this by his own mind which kept asking why. Then he was too embarrassed to come back out of the tent. *People will think I am a real weakling, blubbering that like,* he thought.

Now thoroughly ashamed of his breakdown he sat and wiped his face then wondered what to do. *I can't go out. People will be laughing at me,* he thought. But then it occurred to him that he could not hide in the tent forever either. *They will despise me for running away and hiding,* he told himself.

But he knew that what he really meant was that he would despise himself. So, reluctantly, he crawled back out of the tent into the bright sunshine and strolled back to where the others were. To his added discomfiture he saw that nobody was even looking his way. Everyone appeared to be watching the fly past of a huge model with four engines.

A Lancaster, Willy noted, his aircraft recognition instantly kicking in. Jealousy and resentment mixed to make him feel quite upset again. It was a most impressive model and it flew really well. Despite his mood, Willy could not help watching and admiring it.

As the Lancaster model came in to land another model took off and it also held his attention. It was jet powered and silver in colour and had red stars on the wings, tail and fuselage. *A MIG, one of the 1950s types,* Willy thought. But was it a MIG 15 or a MIG 17? He could not remember but was impressed when the model screamed low overhead at what seemed like a fantastic speed for a model aircraft.

Still watching the model as it climbed and turned in the distance, Willy re-joined the others. To his relief and annoyance hardly anyone even glanced at him. Only his father and his friends seemed to take any notice of his arrival.

His father looked at him with concern but then nodded and turned to the others. "There was a loose wire, Willy. That might have been the problem," he said.

Stick nodded and turned to show him the control console. The back cover had been unscrewed and opened and Stick pointed inside. "There," he said. "It is just off its terminal."

Willy peered at the maze of circuitry and wires and saw that the end of a blue wire was indeed just loose. He noted that it should have been held to the terminal by a tiny piece of solder but that was broken.

How did that happen? he wondered. He could not remember dropping or hitting the console or even bumping it hard. *Is it just an accident? Or is it sabotage?* Then he shook his head. *I'm getting paranoid,* he told himself. *My secret enemy isn't here. Only my friends.*

And there was one of his friends, John, offering his sympathy. "It was a good model, Willy. Sorry you lost it."

"Thanks Johnno," Willy replied. But even just mentioning the incident made him feel upset again and he had to battle to hold back more tears.

Stick helped. "Maybe we can find it?" he suggested.

Willy shook his head and gestured towards the distant mountain range. "No chance. It will have crashed into those mountains," he replied.

But later that idea of locating the model was mooted by the Club President. He pointed towards one of the eight rotor helicopter models where the rotors were contained in a solid frame.

"We have found several lost models with one of those," he suggested.

"What is it?" Willy asked, his curiosity aroused.

"It's a DJL 500 Hexacopter," The Club President replied. "It can hover and circle and it has a GPS and computer on board and also a camera which can relay back real time video. We can program it to fly a search pattern and send it off and it will come back."

But Willy shook his head. "From the way my model was flying it was heading off in a straight line for those mountains."

The Club President glanced at the distant mountains. "For Mt Elliot? How much fuel did you have on board?"

"A full tank, enough for about half an hour's flying," Willy replied. He had already done that calculation. His model could fly at about 40kph and would be 20 kilometres away by this.

"Hmm. Yes, that might be too far," the Club President conceded. "Sorry about that."

Willy's father nodded. "Even if your hexacopter could fly that distance and back, we don't have the time. We have to start back for Cairns in about half an hour," he said.

The Club President nodded again. "Well, if we find it we will let you know," he said.

Willy's father put his hand on Willy's shoulder. "Sorry son, but it is gone. Now let's go and pack up the tent."

Willy felt another sickening lurch in his stomach and again tears threatened but he had to accept that. He nodded, cast one last sad look at the distant mountains and then turned and walked towards the tent. Stick and John walked with him, collecting bits and pieces as they went.

It was a miserable boy who helped pack up the camping gear and load the vehicle. All the while he could see in his mind's eye the tiny spec dwindling into the far distance. *It was a good model, and it was a good weekend until then,* he thought sadly.

During the five hour drive back to Cairns both John and Stick tried to cheer him up. Even Scott was sympathetic but he was still upset when they got home just before dark. The other boys were dropped at their homes and then Willy's father drove the car home.

At the front door they were met by Lloyd. "Where's yer plane, Little Brother?" he queried as Willy struggled up the steps with his bag.

"Lost it," Willy mumbled.

"Lost it! How did yer lose it?" Lloyd cried.

"A loose wire on the controller. It just flew off," Willy answered.

At that Lloyd burst out laughing. "Just flew away! Like one of those planes in a science fiction movie. Hah! Hah! Hah!"

The jeers brought tears to Willy's eyes. "It's not funny!" he cried, then fled to his room before his brother saw the tears and teased him over them as well. He was saved from further trouble because his mother had overheard the exchange and sharply told Lloyd to stop teasing his little brother. Then she came to his room.

"Sorry about that, Willy. Your father told me what happened," she said.

Willy battled to hold back more tears. He sniffled and nodded. "It was a good model too, Mum. It flew really well," he managed to reply.

"Well, it's not the end of the world. It was only a model and you can always make another one," she said.

That stung. "Yes," he retorted, more sharply than he had meant. "But I haven't got the money!"

"There is always your birthday and Christmas, and you can save your pocket money or get a part time job," his mother replied, her voice still calm but concerned.

"Sorry Mum. It's just that I felt such a fool when it just kept flying away and then I got all upset," Willy replied.

As he said this, he suddenly foresaw more teasing when he went to school the next day. *Scott and Stick and Johnno will tell other kids,* he thought unhappily.

And they obviously did, as the hurtful comments and teasing began as soon as he arrived. A Year 10 boy Willy didn't even know called loudly: "Hey Jack, how does that nursery rhyme go? Is it Fly Away Peter, or Fly Away Paul?"

The laughter caused Willy to burn with anger and embarrassment. As he walked quickly on he glanced at the group and noted Branch was among them. The sight of his smirk caused Willy another spurt of annoyance.

Who told Branch? he wondered. *Stick,* he decided. *I thought Stick was a friend,* he thought resentfully. It was only later the more worrying idea came to him. *Is Stick my secret enemy?*

When he found Stick sitting with Noddy and a few others he gave him a hard look and then hesitated over sitting near him. But Stick gave a big smile and a cheery welcome so he did, unable to make up his mind.

Stephen, who was with the group, also gave him a welcoming smile. "I hear you had a bit of trouble with your model plane," he commented.

Willy nodded. "Yeah. I lost control. There was a wire loose in the radio control console," he replied.

Noddy snorted and chuckled. "Huh! More a like screw loose in the operator," he suggested.

That hurt and Willy glared at him. "Bite your bum!" he retorted. *Is Noddy my secret enemy?* he wondered. Then he shook his head. *No, he couldn't be. He wasn't even around when half the things happened.*

Willy's mood wasn't improved by the discovery that Petra wasn't at school. He had been looking forward to seeing her, even if they weren't sitting together. Just seeing her vacant chair made him feel more dejected.

The day dragged by and only got better in the afternoon when Stick suggested he and John come over to his house after school. Willy was about to say no but images of Marjorie flashed across his mind and he nodded, "Yeah, OK. But only for a while."

So the friends made their way to Stick's. When they arrived John just dumped his bike against the fence but Willy wheeled his in the gate after Stick's. Then he knelt and began to securely chain it to the fence on the inside.

John stopped and scoffed. "Gawd Willy, yer getting paranoid," he commented.

Willy blushed but then shrugged and completed locking the chains. "Maybe," he agreed. "But leaving your bike out on the footpath like that is inviting trouble," he added.

"She'll be right," John answered.

They went into the house and Stick offered afternoon refreshments. As he prepared some cordial and biscuits Willy looked hopefully around for Marjorie but there was no sign of her and there did not seem to be anyone else in the house. Not wanting to be teased Willy did not ask where she might be.

The friends settled in Stick's room talking, telling jokes and leafing through model and aircraft magazines. Willy wasn't too keen on that as the loss of his model still hurt too much but he pretended things were OK.

Then Marjorie and two other girls came in. All still wore their school uniform. The sight of the girls got him all hopeful and he hoped nobody would notice how interested he was.

269

Marjorie began to ask questions about the weekend and about the way Willy's model aircraft had flown away out of control. Willy didn't really want to discuss it and thinking about it made him upset again. Worse still tears again threatened and he didn't want to cry in front of his mates and the girls.

But Marjorie was so sympathetic and interested that he could not help responding. She was also very nice to look at, even in her school uniform. She listened intently and nodded. "So who did win the competition?" she asked.

Willy glanced at his friends and shrugged. "We didn't really decide."

"But you are going to make another model plane aren't you?" Marjorie asked.

Willy shook his head. "Oh, I don't know," he muttered.

Stick raised his eyebrows. "What about the Air Cadet's model competition, Willy; aren't you putting your Red Baron's triplane in that?"

Willy blushed at the mention of the triplane. Then he shrugged. In truth he had forgotten about the competition. "Oh, I don't think so. It isn't finished," he replied.

John sat up. "What sort of plane is it, Willy?"

"It's a model of the Red Baron's Fokker DR1," Willy replied. "But I've got a lot of work to do."

"You should," Stick said. "I'm putting in a diorama of a Hurricane in a dispersal bay."

Marjorie nodded vigorously. "Yes Willy, you should."

Seeing her smile, Willy had to smile back. "Aw, maybe," he answered.

"Oh please, Willy!" Marjorie pleaded.

At that Willy changed his mind. "OK," he replied.

So when he got home Willy went into the workshop and studied the triplane model. Running through his mind were comments by his father about not giving up too easily and not letting little setbacks defeat him. *I'll do it,* he decided.

Fired by determination he sat at the workbench and did a careful check of what he had completed. Then he made a list of things to finish and matched them against the calendar. *It's only two weeks away and there is a lot to do still,* he mused.

So he set to work. The horizontal and vertical stabilisers were made but needed the linkages for the control wires to be added and also the hinges for the elevators and rudder. Also they needed to be covered and painted. By tea time several of the linkages were attached and it was with reluctance that he placed down his tools and went upstairs to eat.

After dinner Willy was not allowed back downstairs. Instead he had to do homework and study and then he was too tired to even play computer games so he lay in front of the TV.

That set the pattern for the remainder of the week, except that on Tuesday Petra was back at school. Willy gave her a big smile, but she just nodded and went to her seat looking tired and unhappy.

Something's gone wrong, Willy decided. *Probably in trouble with that horrible mother of hers.*

So all he could do was watch from afar and yearn and daydream. Being part of a group of friends helped as there were always amusing little incidents, jokes and stories to hold his interest and it gave him some protection from the bullies.

It was after school on Wednesday that the next bullying incident occurred. Willy had watched Petra and Tania walk out through the gate near the hall and was walking back towards the bike racks when his attention was drawn to the army cadets. They were beginning to collect under B Block ready for their weekly parade.

As Willy studied them, a voice hissed in his ear, "You should join them Williams. You're a jerk and being an A.J. is about all you are good for."

It was Branch. He sneered and Willy felt his stomach churn with anxiety and resentment. The term A.J. was a nasty nickname meaning 'Army Jerk' and it upset him even more to have the label attached to him. With an effort of willpower he resisted the urge to back answer.

But his silence seemed to goad Branch into more nastiness. "What's wrong, Williams? Haven't you got the guts to say anything?" he snarled, standing close and pushing his face close to Willy's.

Willy opened his mouth to reply but before he could Graham Kirk, now in army cadet uniform, stopped beside them. "Stop picking on Willy, Branch. Pick on someone your own size," he said.

Branch turned, surprise and anger showing clearly on his face. "Piss off Kirk and mind your own business!"

Stephen, also in army cadet uniform, appeared beside Graham. "It is our business when you pick on our friends," he said.

Branch looked flustered and glared at them. "This is cadet business, Air Cadet business. I'm just reminding this cadet to do the right thing," he replied angrily.

"Sounded like bullying and intimidation to me," Stephen replied evenly.

More army cadets began to gather. Willy recognised Peter Bronsky and Roger as they ranged up on either side of Graham and Stephen. He wasn't sure if their intervention was a good thing or not. *It will make Branch even madder and he will pick on me even more when they aren't around to save me,* he thought bitterly.

Branch sneered and stood up straight. "I'm a sergeant. You can't talk to me like that. You are only a cadet," he retorted.

Graham snorted. "Huh! You aren't in uniform and you aren't acting like a proper sergeant." Turning to Willy he added, "You should join us Willy. You will get fair treatment then."

But that sparked a different reaction in Willy. Shaking his head emphatically he replied: "No thanks. Air Cadets are better, and this is an Air Cadet matter we are discussing if you don't mind." He didn't know why he said that but as he did he noted the look of surprise that crossed Branch's face.

Graham raised an eyebrow but nodded. "OK. If you say so. See you later then. Come on you guys, we have a Passing-Out Parade practice to do."

With that the army cadets walked on, leaving Willy and Branch on the path near the bike racks. Branch turned to him. "What's that all about Williams?" he snapped.

"I thought we could settle this ourselves. I don't need anyone else to fight my battles for me," Willy replied evenly.

He was now determined to settle the issue whatever it cost. He braced himself for a real fight.

Chapter 28

SHOW DOWN

Branch stared at Willy in astonishment. "Don't get too full of yourself. You are only a First Year cadet," he snarled. But as he did, he glanced around.

He is checking no-one is going to help me, Willy thought. It was something of a revelation. *He's actually scared. That's why he's full of bluster.* Encouraged by this Willy shook his head. "No, you said it. We aren't at cadets and we aren't in uniform."

"Doesn't matter," Branch snapped. "You are still a stupid First Year and I'm a sergeant. So why don't you leave?"

That really annoyed Willy. "Because in spite of you I like Cadets and I am very proud to be an air cadet. And whatever you say, my drill isn't that bad. They haven't put me off the Drill Team yet."

"Huh! They will," Branch retorted. But he looked anxious and again glanced around.

Suddenly it came to Willy and he nerved himself and said what he thought. "This isn't about me and my drill. This is about Petra."

Branch went red and appeared to puff up. "Yes, it's about Petra! Now you leave her alone!" he shouted.

"She can choose for herself who she goes around with," Willy retorted.

"Yes, but you stop doing... stop... stop doing things to her!" Branch cried.

At that moment Willy got a glimpse into Branch's real emotions. *The poor bugger is in love and is really hurting. He is really jealous!* he thought. But the accusation nettled him. "I'm not doing anything to her. I never have. The most we have ever done was a quick kiss in the library," he replied.

"That's not what I hear," Branch snarled. He looked very upset, and to Willy's astonishment tears began to form in the corner of the sergeant's eyes.

"Well whoever is telling you that is lying!" Willy cried. "I don't even talk to her at school and I don't sit next to her anymore. And she won't let me walk her home. Her mother won't allow her to have a boyfriend."

Branch looked doubtful. "So why are people saying you are doing... doing things?"

That got Willy's brain racing. "Who is 'they'? Who is saying we are doing things?" he demanded to know.

Branch looked uncomfortable and shrugged. "People, some of the Year Tens."

"Who? They are lying and I'd like to know who. I can guess why. They are jealous," Willy snapped. Suddenly it was terribly important that he have that information. *It might unmask my secret enemy,* he reasoned.

But Branch shook his head and mumbled. That angered Willy. "Who has been saying things, Sgt Branch?" he asked. He was angry but sensed that not antagonizing the other boy might be better tactics.

"Oh, Scranton and Carstairs," Branch replied.

Willy nodded. "That figures. They are both bullies who have been annoying me," he replied. "Anyone else? Who told you about my plane last weekend?"

Branch shrugged. "Not sure. One of the Year 9s I think. I just overheard them telling Scranton."

"Which Year 9? Was it Stick?"

Branch looked puzzled and then frowned. "Oh you mean Cadet Morton. No, it wasn't him."

That both bothered and helped Willy. He had been wondering if Stick might be his secret enemy but now struck him off his mental list. But he still wanted to know.

"Who was he? What did he look like?" he asked.

Again Branch shrugged. "Not sure. All I am asking is that you leave Petra alone and don't.. don't do any of the things they are saying," he replied. Then he sniffled and went red before blurting out: "I love her!"

The tone of his voice was so close to pleading that it convinced Willy that Branch really was in love with Petra. "Well I like her too," he replied, "And there is no way I would do anything to hurt her."

But even as he said this Willy was aware that he had substituted the word 'like' for 'love'. *Do I love her?* he wondered. A flood of images crowded his brain to confuse him and he was hotly aware that he had lusted over Marjorie and pushed thoughts of Petra aside while he did.

And I did things with Marjorie and never even thought about Petra, he thought. That really bothered him. *Am I just an immoral weakling?* he wondered.

To add to his doubts more images of Marjorie, mostly of her naked, flashed across the screen of his brain. He bit his lip and felt very uncomfortable. *What do I do now?* he wondered. He was sure he still liked Petra a lot but conceded it was really a crush. *And one that is going nowhere if she isn't allowed to have a boyfriend,* he mused.

But what to do about Branch? Despite his doubts Willy was reluctant to admit that he wasn't totally smitten by Petra.

Branch helped him by saying in the same anxious tone, "Well, promise me you won't do anything to her."

That was easier. Willy was sure he would never try to do any of the things he longed to do with Marjorie and her friends, or with several other girls at the school. He nodded. "I promise. She is too nice and I like her too much. Anyway, as I said, she isn't talking to me anymore, so it is all academic."

"So who does she go to meet when she sneaks out of the school?" Branch asked, the distress so plain in his voice that Willy felt a surge of sympathy for him.

He shook his head. "Not me. I didn't even know she was leaving the school until the other day when Scranton taunted me with it," he replied.

A look of pain crossed Branch's face. He bit his lip and shook his head. "So who is she going to meet?" he said.

"No idea," Willy replied. But the idea bothered him too. "It might be a quite innocent reason," he added. "Maybe she goes home to look after her mother or something."

"Hmm, maybe," Branch said, but he looked doubtful and upset.

Willy now saw a chance and decided to risk it. "Look Sgt Branch, I promise I haven't done anything to Petra and I promise I won't."

Branch met his eyes and nodded and Willy again noted that tears had formed in the corners of his eyes. Not wanting to make the situation worse by humiliating Branch in public he hurried on, "And I promise I won't give you any trouble at Cadets. I will try my hardest so that Three Section is the best in the Flight."

Again Branch nodded and he glanced away to hide his distress. "And you can leave my bike alone too," he said.

275

"I haven't touched your bike," Willy said. "I thought it was you who was doing things to mine. What has happened to it?"

Branch gestured towards where his bicycle was still locked in the bike racks. "Someone's been letting down my tyres or taking my valves nearly every day."

"That's what happened to me!" Willy cried. He was surprised and it must have showed on his face.

Branch nodded. "I know. I heard about it. I thought it was Scranton and his mates but they denied it and I've been watching them. I don't know who it is."

"Are they down now?" Willy asked, wondering if his own were as well.

"Yes," Branch replied. "Both of them."

They walked over to the bike racks and Willy saw that both of Branch's tyres were flat and that the valves were missing. Quickly he glanced at his own bike and to his annoyance he saw that both of his tyres were also flat and that both valves were gone. "Bloody hell! Not again!" he cried.

Quickly he walked to his bike to check and then he looked around. But the bike racks were now deserted. There wasn't another student in sight. *Who did it?* he wondered. *Who is my secret enemy?*

Then an idea came to him. In his bag he had two valves and his bike pump. *If I offer them to Branch he might ease up on me,* he thought. But then doubts flooded in. *Will he?* The best thing seemed to be to try it.

So he opened his bag and dug out the two valves and then held them out on his hand. "Here, I've got two spare valves. You take them," he offered.

"What's this?" Branch queried suspiciously. "You trying to bribe me or buy me off?"

"No! It's a peace offering," Willy replied. "One each is no good as we still couldn't ride our bikes."

Branch still looked doubtful but he was no longer hostile. "So how will you get home?"

"Walk to the shop and buy some more valves," Willy answered.

"Why don't you ring your parents?"

"I haven't got a mobile phone. They won't let me have one until I am in Year Eleven," Willy replied.

"Me neither," Branch said. "You could ask the office to phone. They don't close till four."

Willy shook his head. "I've been in too much trouble at the office. I don't want Mr Fitz getting involved," he commented.

For the first time Branch grinned. Then he looked at the valves. "You sure I can have them?"

Willy nodded. "Yes. And I've even got a pump so you don't have to walk to a service station to find a pump," he explained.

So Branch took the valves and inserted them and then began pumping up his tyres. While he was doing that martial music began to sound in the distance. He paused in the pumping and looked up. "What's that?" he asked.

Willy stared in the direction the music was coming from. "I think it is the army cadets practicing for their Passing-Out Parade down on the oval," he said.

Branch grunted. "Huh! They need all the practice they can get."

Willy was seized by a desire to see how the army cadets did things. "I'm going to watch," he said. "I have to walk that way anyway."

Branch nodded. "I'll join you. Here's your pump."

He unscrewed the pump and handed it back to Willy. The pair then wheeled their bikes out of the gate and walked along the grass footpath past the hall and swimming pool. When they had a clear view of the oval they stopped and leaned their bikes on the fence and then leaned on it themselves.

The music had stopped by then and Willy saw that the school's army cadet company was now standing in three ranks out on the grass oval. They were formed up 'in line' in two platoons side by side and facing towards the school.

He noted that there was a Year 11 boy standing out in front giving orders and that the company had just completed a 'Right Dress'. "That's Warwick Grey isn't it? Is he their Warrant Officer Drill?" he asked.

Branch shook his head. "No. He is a warrant officer but he's called the CSM, the Company Sergeant Major," he explained.

CSM Grey did an about turn and faced the front then stood at ease. Almost immediately he came back to attention and called the company to attention. Willy saw one of the Year 12s, Garth Grant, come marching on from the front edge of the 'Parade Ground'. Grant was carrying a sword and the sight of it quickened Willy's interest. The afternoon sunlight glittered on the sword's blade and that made it look like a magic weapon.

Branch gestured towards him. "That's CUO Grant. He must be the parade commander," he commented.

Willy opened his mouth to say that he was aiming at being a CUO but then he closed it. Better not to give Branch a reason to ridicule him. The fragile truce seemed to be holding so Willy kept his silence. But the sight of the glittering sword flashing in salute fired his own determination to become a Cadet Under-Officer.

I will command our Passing-Out Parade when I am in Year 12, he told himself.

CUO Grant called the platoon commanders to march on and two more CUOs, both with swords, saluted and marched on. Then the flag party was marched on. This involved more marching music and Willy now saw that it was coming from a sound system beside a vehicle parked on the side of the oval. A female OOC sat at a table nearby operating it.

Seeing the flag party marching on Willy wondered if they should be standing to attention but then he noted that the flag was just a practice one made of light green cloth. Watching the wheeling and forming he said, "They certainly do different drill."

"Not as good as ours," Branch muttered scornfully.

"No, not as good as ours," Willy agreed. *But it still looks good,* he thought. What also niggled at him was that all of the cadets standing in the ranks had rifles. His gaze ran along the lines of cadets who were standing rigidly at the 'Present Arms'. *There's Graham in the front rank and there are Stephen and Peter Bronsky,* he noted.

After the flag party were on parade Capt Conkey acted as the Reviewing Officer and coached the CUOs through their orders and actions during a ceremonial inspection. To begin with he was surprised that the whole parade was not called to attention but then saw that the commander of each division was doing that. The division was then stood ate ease when the Inspecting Party moved on.

That's a good idea, Willy thought, remembering how hard it was to stand at attention during a long inspection. During all of this more music was played. Willy recognised these tunes as slow marches.

As the inspection came to an end, Branch stood up and moved to his bike. "I'd better get home," he said.

Willy nodded. "Yeah, see ya," he replied in a carefully casual tone. He did not want to presume any sort of friendship but felt considerably easier. But he was also puzzled.

If Branch isn't my secret enemy then who is?

He stayed there for the next half hour watching the whole rehearsal. The many differences in drill and procedure fascinated him and he was sure that the Air Cadets drill was better.

Then he walked to a shop which sold bike valves, wheeling his bike the whole way. This took him another hour. It was a tired and quite confused boy who finally arrived home. He hoped that he had resolved something with Branch but was still upset over being targeted by a person who disliked him.

But who?

By then both his parents were home and his mother wanted to know where he had been. Willy had to admit that the valves had been stolen again. That caused both parents to frown. His father shook his head.

"Did you tell the school office?" he asked.

"No Dad."

"Then do it tomorrow or we will. And see if their video surveillance shows anything."

"Yes Dad."

Willy then fled down to the workshop to continue work on his model triplane. But then he found he could not focus. He kept worrying about who his secret enemy might be and about how he really felt about Petra.

I almost told Branch he could have her, he realised. But he shook his head. *No. Petra can choose. May the better man win,* he thought. With that resolved he settled to model making until dinner time.

The following day at school he mentioned to Stephen that he had watched the Passing-Out Parade rehearsal. Stephen nodded and then shook his head ruefully. "And we certainly need the practice," he admitted.

"Air Cadets do better drill," Willy replied with a grin.

"Maybe, but not much else," Stephen retorted. "We are much better in the bush."

"Were they Steyrs you guys had?" Willy asked.

Stephen nodded. "Yeah, but they aren't live firing. Those ones are only innocuous, for drill."

But they still look good, Willy thought enviously. "When is your parade?" he asked.

"In about three weeks' time. First week in November. Gives us time to practice," Stephen answered.

"You'll need it," Willy teased.

"We will," Stephen admitted, "particularly as we are going to do it in front of the whole school."

That surprised Willy. "Are you?"

Stephen nodded. "Yes. On a Wednesday afternoon. The whole school is coming down to watch. It will be a very public event."

"Ours is on a Friday night at our depot," Willy replied. "Are you guys taking part in the drill competition in a couple of weeks' time?"

Stephen shook his head. "No. Capt Conkey says it would take too much out of our normal program. We don't do much drill during the middle of the year. Most of our training is for field work."

They talked cadets for a bit longer and then were interrupted by Noddy who was full of malicious gossip about a Year 10 girl named Sonja and a Year 12 boy named Evans.

During the day Willy only got to observe Petra from afar and he was left with many doubts. *Do I love her?* he wondered. He could not decide but he was sure that he was interested in other girls as well because he found he could not help looking at them or thinking about Marjorie or Barbara. It was all very unsettling.

He also made himself go to the office and report the bike sabotage to Mr Fitzgerald, mentioning Branch's problem at the same time. Mr Fitzgerald went and studied the video records but was unable to find anything.

"This is becoming a bit of a problem," he muttered. "We might have to reposition the cameras and you should park your bike where it can be very clearly seen by the camera."

So Willy was left wondering who his secret enemy was. Feeling vaguely unhappy he made his way back downstairs to join his friends.

While they were talking Willy spotted Petra walking off towards the back of the school with Tania. Excusing himself he slipped away and began to follow them, taking care to keep out of sight. *I don't want to stress her out by making her think I am so obsessed I am stalking her,* he thought.

Then what he had feared happened, both girls went out of the side gate near the hall and walked off across the road and away along a side street. *Where are they going?* Willy wondered. He decided to follow them but a quick glance revealed a teacher walking his way on playground duty.

"Drat!" Willy muttered.

So he had wait, pretending to be strolling around. But by the time the teacher had gone out of view Petra and Tania had turned a corner and were out of sight and Willy had not seen whether they had gone left or right.

Even though he knew would get into trouble from the office if he was caught Willy decided to follow the girls. He made his way to the gate and then looked around, his heart beating fast with fear and excitement.

But to his annoyance the teacher reappeared. *Oh bugger it! Go away sir!* Willy thought.

But the teacher didn't, and all Willy could do was grit his teeth in frustration. And then the bell went and the teacher began shepherding the students in that area back to their classrooms. Willy had no choice but to obey. All the way his mind was in turmoil.

Where are they going? he wondered.

Chapter 29

WHO IS THE BEST?

A ll afternoon Willy was consumed by doubt. *What are Petra and Tania doing?* he fretted. Against his will he found some of the doubting thoughts slipping in. *Is she up to some sort of mischief? Surely not!*

He kept hoping she would appear but she didn't. When the teacher, Mrs Ramsey, asked the class where Petra was Willy just bit his lip and remained silent. *Now she is marked absent on the roll and will be in trouble at the office,* he thought. *If her mum finds out she will get what for!*

Images of Petra's mother made him quite anxious for Petra, but there was nothing he could do so he tried to focus on the schoolwork. That was difficult and it was made harder because he kept worrying about whether his bicycle had been sabotaged again.

It hadn't been, so when school ended he was able to ride off on it. First he went along the street that Petra and Tania had vanished along, hoping to see them. But there was no sign of either girl so Willy sadly made his way home. There he settled to model making. This time he set to work making and painting all of the markings.

Remembering what the man had said in Townsville, Willy hesitated. He knew that at some stage during the First World War the Germans had changed their markings from the black 'Iron Crosses' edged with white to simple straight edged black crosses but he wasn't sure when. To check he referred to several books with illustrations of what the markings should look like and he even turned on his computer and studied the computer images of the Red Baron's triplane. The result was conclusive, straight crosses.

Very carefully he drew and then painted 8 black crosses of 2 different sizes, each with the white edging that made the German markings so distinctive. The end result he thought looked very good and he went to bed well pleased with his efforts.

That night Willy had trouble sleeping. For a long time he lay awake worrying about Petra and puzzling over what strategy to use. Then his thoughts drifted to fantasies and into them slipped images of a naked Marjorie. Annoyed with his weakness he tried to banish the thoughts, but they kept sliding back in.

Bloody hell, I'm weak! he told himself.

Hardly able to hide his emotions Willy hurried early to school, hoping to see Petra. As he arrived at the bike racks, he remembered what Mr Fitzgerald had said and made sure his bike was locked in a rack that was in clear view of one of the surveillance cameras. Then he loitered near the gate.

But Petra had not appeared by the time first bell went, so feeling quite distressed and emotionally drained Willy reluctantly made his way to class. He slumped into the seat beside John and managed a weak smile.

John raised an eyebrow. "What's the matter, Willy? You look a wreck," he said.

"Just... just didn't sleep very well," Willy replied.

He wanted to confide in John but felt too inhibited. Instead he forced himself to do the schoolwork and to pretend that everything was alright.

Then Petra appeared at the door. She knocked and gave the teacher a note and then made her way to her seat. As she did, her eyes met Willy's and she gave him a sickly sort of smile and then looked quickly away.

Oh! That didn't look good, Willy thought. For the remainder of the lesson he wrestled with the question of whether to ask her where she went or not. Finally he decided not to. *She might resent it if she thinks I am watching her every move,* he decided.

During the morning break Willy noted Petra sitting with Tania under the next building, but he was careful not to make his observations obvious. Instead, he sat with his mates and told jokes or laughed at their stories.

As the day wore on other worries began to crowd concern about Petra to the side of his consciousness. Being Friday, that meant cadets. *Will Branch still pick on me?* he worried. And there was anxiety about whether he would be selected for the Drill Team. At the bottom of his concerns was whether his bike had been tampered with or not.

It hadn't been, so he was able to ride home. There he had afternoon tea and set to work on his model. *Only a week to go. I must get this finished,* he told himself. A check revealed that he had now made all the main pieces and had mounted the servos and wiring for the rudder and elevators so now he concentrated on securing the servos for the ailerons in the upper wing.

After an early tea he made sure his uniform and the brim of his hat were both ironed and that his boots were well polished. *No point in attracting attention by being lazy,* he reasoned.

His mother drove him to cadets and to his relief Branch just glanced at him and then seemed to ignore him. It was a busy training session. First the whole unit did a talk-through rehearsal for the Passing-Out Parade. Willy had no real role to play just being one of the cadets in the ranks, but he observed everything with a keen interest.

As the rehearsal moved along, Willy compared it to the army cadet's parade and found many similarities but also some quite different aspects, particularly in where the officers stood and in some of the drill movements. He found it all fascinating.

In particular he observed CUO Penrose, who had been chosen as parade commander. *That will be me in four years' time,* he told himself.

The other Cadet Under-Officer, CUO Bergman, had the honour of carrying the banner and Willy was very impressed by his drill as well. *That would be nice to do too,* he considered.

Another aspect that intrigued him was that the two flights or wings were both commanded by Flight Sergeants and they carried swords. *I thought the army cadets said that only officers carried swords?* he wondered. *I must ask.*

After the rehearsal the Drill Team was formed up for practice while the others went inside to lessons. Now Willy became quite anxious. He badly wanted to be selected and tried his hardest. It surprised him to learn that the group had fallen from 20 to 18, one having been removed and one having dropped out because his parents said he could not attend that weekend for family reasons.

It would have to be a pretty serious family reason for me not to turn up, Willy thought, *like a death in the family or something.* He was sure he would win an argument over any normal family event like birthdays or relations visiting.

At the end of the night a Joining Instruction with Permission Form attached was handed to all the cadets who had volunteered for the weekend in Mareeba. *That is next weekend. I had better get my model finished,* he thought.

That became his priority over the weekend, resulting in a few snappy words from parents about chores and assignments. Grudgingly Willy gave up time to the housework and yard work and then to completing assignments.

"I'm only in Year Eight," he grumbled, "They aren't that important."

"They are!" his mother snapped. "This is when you lay the foundations for later success by developing the right attitude to work and to self-discipline."

"I've got plenty of self-discipline!" Willy snapped back.

Before his mother could reply Lloyd chuckled and said, "Tell that to Stick's little sister!"

"Lloyd!" their mother snapped. "That will be enough of that sort of talk."

Willy burned with embarrassment and tried to pretend he wasn't blushing but he was bothered by the suspicious and anxious look his mother gave him. *How does my big brother know about Marjorie?* he wondered. *Who has been telling him?* Names like Scott and Stephen and even Stick flitted across his mind.

Not having an answer was worrying but he shrugged and got on with his work. Then he hurried to the workshop and resumed model making. During Saturday afternoon he assembled and glued on the undercarriage and then tested it to ensure it was on square and true.

If it is out of alignment the model will run skew-if on take-off, he reasoned.

Satisfied with that he painted the model seat and other cockpit furniture and then the instrument panel was glued in. By evening he was feeling he had made real progress.

Sunday was even better. Willy devoted nearly the entire day to assembling the cockpit and then to carefully gluing the paper covering over the frames of the wings and fuselage. When that was done he felt very pleased.

It is starting to really look like a plane now, he congratulated himself.

At school on Monday Willy was pleased to see that Petra was there and she seemed her normal friendly self. But she still did not want him to sit with her so he stayed away and chatted to his friends. During the morning break he discovered from Stephen that the army cadets had spent the weekend at Porton Army Barracks at Edmonton.

"What did you do there?" Willy asked, hiding his jealousy.

"Our Section Competition weekend and another couple of rehearsals for our Passing-Out Parade," Stephen answered.

"Section Competition?"

"Yeah, each section goes around a bull ring of stands and at each stand they get tested at something," Stephen explained.

"What sort of things?"

"Oh you know, safe rifle handling, navigation, First Aid, signals, fieldcraft, pioneering and general military knowledge and some drill," Stephen said.

The mention of safe rifle handling caused Willy a minor spurt of jealousy but then he shrugged. "We have a weekend in Mareeba next weekend," he replied, anxious to make the Air Cadets look good.

"What's that about?" Stephen asked.

"The Tri-service Drill Competition and flying model aircraft."

Stephen looked interested. "Are you flying a model?"

"Yes," Willy answered, but the idea now filled him with anxiety. Not only was his model unfinished it was untested. *I will look a prize idiot if it doesn't fly or crashes!* he thought.

So after school he hurried home and continued working on his model. He set to work fitting the wings. This was something he had been putting off because he was worried about doing it wrong but now he forced himself to concentrate. The real problem was to get the dihedral, the upwards tilt of the wing tips, at the same angle on both sides.

"If I don't get this right the plane won't fly," he muttered. "It will tip over and crash."

To make sure the dihedral was correct Willy firmly secured the fuselage on the bench top between two marble book ends. Then he placed books on either side, adding to the pile with thin volumes until he had the correct angle and so that both were exactly the same height. Satisfied he was ready and after several 'dry runs' he glued on the bottom wings.

For the next half hour he kept anxiously checking and making minute adjustments so that both wings were firmly in place and, as far as his eyes and a ruler could tell, at exactly the same angle. In between each check he busied himself with ensuring that the fuel lines were ready and in checking his motor.

Before fitting the motor Willy secured it to the work bench and then attached a fuel line and tank and gave it a test run. To his relief it started without too much trouble and then began to run smoothly. But the noise was very loud and the fumes began to fill the workshop so he only ran it for a few minutes.

The little radial engine was then placed in position in the nose of the fuselage and locked in place with the end of the fuel line attached. That was all he got done that day as homework took up most of the evening.

Willy also made sure his parents were still Ok for providing transport for the weekend. Lloyd wasn't too happy but was told he had to join in as a family weekend.

On Tuesday afternoon and evening Willy fitted the battery which provided the power for the servos and radio control mechanism. That done he very carefully picked up the model by its wingtips. One of the books he was referring to advised checking the balance of the model by its wingtips to see if the fore and aft weight distribution was correct.

If it isn't the attitude will be wrong, Willy thought, attitude being the way the aircraft 'sat' in the air while flying. *I don't want it nose down or dragging its bum.* That would be shameful. And he certainly didn't want it to get out of control and crash!

To his relief the model was close to a balance but as there were a few parts to add yet he wasn't too worried. The worry that he might be setting himself up for public humiliation and ridicule caused him to bite his lip with anxiety.

So on Wednesday afternoon Willy did not linger to watch the army cadets practising for their Passing-Out Parade but instead he hurried home and settled to painting the model. He used a small brush and bright scarlet Humbrol brand model paint. With each brush stroke he began to like his model more.

It is really starting to look good, he told himself. He considered that he might win a prize just for the quality of model, even if it didn't fly. "But a test flight would be good," he muttered.

His anxiety got him to switch on the battery and to test the controls. To his relief all the controls worked. The elevators went up and down on command and the rudder moved from side to side. One of the ailerons seemed to be a bit slow but he was sure he could cope with that.

Most of the painting was completed by tea time. Only some under surfaces were still unpainted as he did not want to risk trying to do both sides at once and then having the paint stick to the newspaper he had spread against accidental spillage.

By Thursday morning Willy was starting to get really anxious and his nervousness affected his mood. He barely noticed Petra and only realised she was not in her seat after lunch when John mentioned it. Willy's reaction was to glance at the empty seat and then shrug. *It doesn't feel like the relationship is going anywhere anyway,* he mused. It was sad but there did not seem to be much he could do about it.

After school he hurried home and completed the painting

That evening he began the intricate and awkward job of putting on the middle wings. The tricky part was getting the inter-plane struts secured and at the correct angle and then of using very fine craft wire to do the bracing between the wings. It was such a fiddly job that he began to lose patience after half a dozen failures. But by persevering he managed to get it done.

In the process he had another argument with his mother. She came down and shook her head. "Stop that and go and do your homework," she said.

"No Mum. I've only got tonight and tomorrow afternoon and I've got a lot to do," Willy replied.

"Your schoolwork is more important."

Willy felt a spurt of annoyance. "I can do my schoolwork standing on my head!" he replied. "But this is important to me."

"Not so important that you can lose marks by handing in an assignment late," she replied.

"I won't lose marks, Mum. It is only a History assignment and Mr Conkey will understand. Please Mum, I will work much better at school if the rest of my life is in balance and if I feel good about myself."

At that his mother almost gaped. Then she smiled and shook her head. "Who told you that?"

"Miss Fisher," Willy replied, naming his music teacher.

"Oh did she! Well you listen to me young man, if I let you do this tonight you must promise me you will work extra to make up time."

"Yes Mum."

So Willy was allowed to keep working. It was difficult as some of the paint was not completely dry, but he set to work positioning more inter-plane struts and then gluing on the top wing. As he placed it in position he felt a surge of triumph. *Oh yes! This is starting to look really good!* he thought.

His father thought so too. He came down to look after obviously having a discussion with Willy's mother about schoolwork and models. "It looks really good William. From a distance it looks like the real thing."

That pleased Willy enormously. He smiled and nodded. "It will look even better when the markings are glued on," he added.

But rigging the bracing wires between the middle and top wings proved to be very difficult. Several times Willy made the tension wrong on one so that the wings were pulled slightly out of alignment or were warped. Swearing softly to himself he made himself try again.

Then his mother was at the door telling him to get to bed. "It's after ten o'clock and you've got school tomorrow," she added.

"But Mum, if I don't get this finished I won't be able to sleep. I will be worrying too much. It has to be ready by Saturday morning and tomorrow night is cadets,"

His mother wasn't happy but finally gave in, with much shaking of the head and tooth sucking. "One more hour. That is all," she told him.

So Willy applied himself to the task. But to his own annoyance he had now become so anxious that his nerves transmitted themselves to his hands and fingers and he began to make little slips and mistakes.

Oh calm down! How can you be the fearless fighter pilot if you get so het up over a mere model, he chided himself.

It was slightly over an hour before he had the top wing securely on and braced. He was just packing up and moving to turn the lights out when his mother called to him from the back stairs. Willy locked the door and called back, "Coming Mum!"

Even after that effort sleep was hard to come. Over and over in his mind Willy kept thinking about the model and what could go wrong. In his mind he planned the final finishing touches to be done the next afternoon. *Or is it already this afternoon?* he wondered, twisting his head around to look at his radio clock.

When he finally did drop off, it was into a series of dreams that melded into nightmares: romance with Petra turning into horror stories where he was flying a homemade Bristol Boxkite but kept getting trapped below the power lines or among high rise buildings.

Then the engine stopped and he began to plummet!

Chapter 30

STRESS AND TEMPTATION

Friday went by in a blur of nervous anticipation. Willy was aware that Petra was at school and looking vaguely unhappy, but she gave him no hint that she wanted to talk so he left her alone. He also noticed that John was a bit moody.

"What's the matter mate?" he asked.

John shrugged. "Oh, nothing really. Are we doing anything this weekend?"

Willy shook his head. "Sorry. I will be in Mareeba this weekend," he replied.

"What for?" John asked.

"Air Cadets," Willy explained.

John looked quite annoyed. "Oh them!" he said.

"You should join. It's great fun," Willy enthused.

John shook his head. "No thanks. Is this the thing you are flying your new model at?" John asked.

"Yes," Willy replied, "That is if I can get it ready in time."

"Isn't it finished yet? You've been working on that for weeks," John said in a tone that made Willy aware that he wasn't happy.

That afternoon after school at the bike racks as Willy wheeled his bike out the gate he waved to John. "See ya!"

John nodded but looked quite sulky. That bothered Willy a bit. *I should spend more time with my friends,* he told himself. But he also had a model to get into flying condition in a few hours so he hopped on his bike and pedalled quickly home.

For the next two hours he worked, anxiously aware that the minutes were flying by. During that time he carefully positioned and glued on the markings and then tested the controls. With the gleaming new red paintwork and all the markings complete he thought the model looked superb.

It is really good! he told himself. But would it fly? That was the real worry. Willy filled the fuel tank and then tested the balance of the model.

To his relief it was only slightly down by the tail. *That should be alright,* he decided.

Then he took the model out onto the front driveway to test the motor. What he really wanted to do was take it to a park and test fly it but he was out of time. His uniform still wasn't ironed and he knew his boots needed a final polish. With these niggling anxieties to spur him on he crouched and wound the propeller around to build up the compression.

With a smart twist of the wrist he flicked the propeller. To his dismay the engine just coughed twice and did not fire. Embarrassed and worried he knelt and checked it, making sure all the wires were connected and that the fuel line was open. Then he rewound the propeller and gave it another hard flick.

This time the motor started and it quickly built up its revolutions to top speed. Blue smoke filled the still, evening air. Willy gripped the fuselage to stop the model from moving and then realised he needed the controller to adjust the throttle speed. The controller was lying nearby and he had to stand up and hurry across to it while holding the model horizontal.

He was just fiddling with the controller's on-off switch when he heard his mother's voice. She was at the top of the front steps. "Turn that blasted thing off and come and have your tea. You will be late for cadets otherwise," she shouted above the roar of the motor.

"Yes, Mum," Willy replied.

Regretfully he switched the motor off and then stood there holding the model till the engine spluttered to a stop. Then he began coughing and his eyes watered.

His mother was not impressed. "What about the neighbours? What do you think they will say about all this noise?" she snapped. "Now get up here and eat. Have you ironed your uniform yet?"

"No Mum," Willy replied, the anxiety hitting him in the stomach again. *If my uniform is no good I might not get chosen for the Drill Team,* he thought.

Quickly he hurried in under the house and placed the Triplane on the work bench. Then he scurried back outside and scooped up the controller and other items and placed them near the model. A few minutes later he was upstairs eating his tea.

His mother watched for a minute and then shook her head. "And you can slow down and eat like a civilized human being instead of wolfing your food down like a pig!"

The thought flashed across Willy's mind that wolves did the wolfing, not pigs, but he resisted the temptation to say it. Instead he nodded and scooped up another fork full.

Then it was ironing, boot polishing and into the shower. Even so he was five minutes later than usual getting to cadets. As his mother stopped the car in the depot car park Willy saw that the cadets were already formed up on the parade ground. Feeling very conspicuous and anxious he quickly climbed out, put on his hat and adjusted it then started marching across to where CDTWOFF Mathieson was standing at the front of the parade.

As he marched across the bitumen Willy felt so self-conscious and anxious that he seemed to lose control of his limbs. He was aware that his marching gait was probably awkward and he became both embarrassed and slightly flustered.

Halting in front of WOFF Mathieson Willy went to salute, then remembered that he shouldn't salute a warrant officer. Just in time he stopped the jerky motion of his arm, but he still felt very self-conscious and foolish.

"Cadet Williams reporting sir. I am late," he said.

WOFF Mathieson raised his eyebrows. "I can see that. Fall in and make sure your sergeant marks you present on the roll."

"Yes, sir."

Willy did an about turn, and again felt embarrassed as he did it so quickly he almost lost his balance. *I am not doing very well,* he worried. Aware that everyone was watching he started marching, once again feeling like his arms and legs were made of wood and moving like a puppet's. *But at least I didn't start square gaiting,* he told himself.

As he marched around to the rear of the flight Willy noted Sgt Branch watching him. Their eyes met briefly and Branch made a wry face to show he wasn't impressed. That caused Willy to blush with shame and to try even harder. He moved into the blank file in the rear rank and stood at ease.

Once in the ranks Willy was able to relax a bit. But not much. The unit commenced an hour of ceremonial parade rehearsal and all imperfections of drill were quickly pointed out by the sergeants and WO(D). Willy made sure he wasn't one of the names called out and hoped his late arrival had been forgotten.

This rehearsal included more marching practice and when Willy stepped off to the music of *Eagle Squadron* he felt uplifted and very proud. *What a great tune!* he thought. And it was good to be alive and to be allowed to wear the uniform!

Then the real test began, the final practice for the Drill Team. The candidates were first inspected by the CO, Training Officer, adult WO(D) and CDTWOFF Mathieson and then they were put through the whole sequence of the competition twice: forming up in threes, dressing, turning, marching, wheeling, forming, turning on the march and marching past to give an eyes right and then an advance in review order.

By the end of the first practice Willy was perspiring heavily but was sure he hadn't made any mistakes. *But I'm glad the dress inspection was first,* he thought, very aware that trickles of perspiration were now running down his back and soaking his shirt.

At the end of the second rehearsal the sweating and puffing squad were halted and the staff added up scores and consulted with each other. Only then did Willy learn that there were only 17 on parade. Another cadet had dropped out. *So they only need to get rid of one of us,* Willy thought. But who?

Flt Lt Comstock took the list from WO Colley and went to the front. "We need a team of 15 plus the CUO in command and we have 17. We also need a couple of reserves. So we have just enough. After some discussion, we've decided that the person to be the reserve should be the person who most recently joined as the fairest way to do this," he said.

As he heard this Willy's heart sank. *That is me. I am the newest recruit,* he thought.

And that is how it was. Flt Lt Comstock looked at him and continued: "So Cadet Williams, you will be the first reserve. Now please don't think this was because your drill was not good enough. I am simply trying to be fair. But be sure we still want you to be there this weekend. Are you allowed to come?"

"Yes sir," Willy croaked. He was so upset that he had trouble getting the words out and he had to struggle to avoid tears. He was sure that Branch would be smirking and that added to his sense of disappointment and shame.

It was hard telling his mother but she took it philosophically. "They want the best team and the people who have been in longer should be the ones to go in the competition," she said.

Willy could see the logic of the decision but it still hurt his feelings. *Bloody Flora Finlay has only been in cadets a week longer than me and her drill isn't as good as mine,* he thought resentfully. He even wondered if she had been selected because the team had to have a certain number of females.

So he went home deeply disappointed and even more concerned that his model aircraft might not be good enough either. He was so cast down that he was tempted to tell his parents that he did not want to go on the weekend but a residual spark of pride held his tongue. Instead he set to work ironing his good uniform.

Despite his upset Willy managed to fall asleep almost at once but later was tormented by the recurring dream of not being able to get his home-made biplane up past the electricity wires or away from all the tall buildings.

In the morning the family loaded their gear into both vehicles and Willy dressed in his camouflage uniform and then carefully carried out his ironed blue dress uniform and hung it in his father's vehicle. Then he went back under the house and picked up his triplane model. As he did he felt a surge of satisfaction at how good it looked. But this was quickly replaced by an even stronger spurt of anxiety. *Oh, I hope it flies alright!*

The family climbed into the two vehicles, Willy going with his father. They then drove around and picked up Stick and Marjorie and their gear. Stick also had a large cardboard box containing his diorama.

Just seeing Marjorie got Willy feeling excited, aroused, but also guilty. *I should be thinking of Petra,* he chided himself.

Marjorie was very demurely dressed in jeans and long sleeve shirt and she climbed into the back of Willy's mother's car. That eased the tension a bit and Willy relaxed and chatted to Stick, who was also in his camouflage uniform. They then went and picked up Noddy.

They then drove north and up the Kuranda Range. From Kuranda they continued on westwards along the Kennedy Highway until they had crossed Davies Creek. Soon after that they turned off to the farm. That got Willy's mind surging with heated memories and he became quite aroused until they pulled up and got out.

Willy had suggested a short stop so he could test fly the Triplane but his mother had looked at him askance and pursed her lips. "We are stopping for a little while anyway. You don't think we would just drive past and not call in to see Aunty Isabel and Uncle Ted do you?" she had commented.

Willy felt guilty at being so focused and could only nod. So when they did reach the farm he made a point of being very friendly with both Uncle Ted and Aunty Isabel. Luckily Uncle Ted was aware of the purpose of the expedition. He turned to Willy after greeting his brother. "So let's see this new model then young William," he said.

Willy felt a flutter of anxiety and embarrassment but this was pushed away by pulsing pride when he took out the model and Uncle Ted's eyes opened wide and his face showed evident appreciation. "Why this is great!" he cried.

The triplane model was admired and examined then the controller collected and a fuel can. They made their way to the machinery shed. But first Uncle Ted had to start up the tractor and drive it out and then Willy had to sweep a runway before he could test the model. As he refuelled it the flutters of anxiety made his fingers shake slightly.

Then the motor wouldn't start. He had three goes, getting more stressed each time. The others all crowded round to study the tiny engine. Willy blushed with shame and bit his lip. *I hope this doesn't happen when we get to the competition,* he worried.

Uncle Ted made some adjustments and carefully dried the outside of the motor and then tilted it twice before winding the propeller. He gave the prop a strong, sharp flick and to Willy's relief the engine roared into life. The model was then placed on the concrete 'runway'.

Stick was detailed to hold the model by the fuselage while Willy turned on the controller and checked the channel settings. By this time his stomach was fluttering with nervousness. *If I muck this up and crash the model I won't even get to go in the competition,* he thought. Then his eyes met Marjorie's and she grinned and nodded. That calmed him, even as he thought she was very desirable.

Nodding to Stick to let go Willy eased the throttle to increase the engine revolutions. By then Stick had let go and by the time Willy looked back at it the model was already rolling forward. To Willy's astonishment the tail came up off the concrete after a run of only a few metres and even as he looked down at the controller, intending to increase the revolutions some more, the triplane lifted off.

It was so sudden and after such a short run that it caught Willy by surprise. As the triplane climbed to head height he saw the wings wobble and he quickly adjusted the climb so that the model did not stall. *It flies!* he thought, satisfaction flooding his emotions.

Feeling very anxious but at the same time thrilled Willy got control of the model and made it level out. Then he cautiously increased the speed and aimed it to fly down the paddock. Satisfied he had sufficient control he gently put it into a wide turn to port. As the model turned into a graceful banking turn he experienced another spurt of pleasure and satisfaction. He grinned at his father.

His father grinned back. "It flies really well," he commented.

That was balm to Willy's battered feelings and he breathed deeply and savoured the moment. Then he used the controls to straighten the model out on a course that brought it straight back towards them. As it got closer he eased back the engine revolutions and put it into a gentle descent.

He was aiming to land it on the concrete apron in front of the shed but as it got rapidly closer it suddenly dawned on him that the model was flying much too fast and was holding its altitude better than he had expected. Hastily he shut off the power and concentrated on setting it down.

For a few moments the triplane looked like it would continue to glide and it even began an upwards swoop which could have resulted in a stall before it sank to ground level and the wheels touched. It came down in an almost perfect 'three point' landing and slid to a stop at Willy's feet.

Amazed and delighted, Willy stared at the shiny red model in a state close to joy. *It works!* he thought, astonished and pleased at his own achievement. Grinning at the others he picked the model up and held it so he could study it.

The others crowded in. Stick reached forward. "Can I have a go Willy?" he asked.

Willy didn't want him to and his mind raced to try to come up with a polite way of refusing. But his father saved him. He shook his head. "No. It is Willy's model for the competition. He is the only one to fly it until after the judging is completed," he said in a very firm voice.

The others accepted this and Willy felt real relief. Then he put the model down and started the engine again. This time it roared into life at the first spin and he was able to release it and get control before it had left the shed. A few seconds later it was airborne and heading down the paddock again.

For twenty minutes Willy practised, gradually getting more and more daring. He experimented with speed and rate of climb and then with increasingly sharper turns before finally attempting some aerobatics. But his one attempt at a roll brought his heart into his mouth when he thought he had made a potentially disastrous miscalculation. The model went zooming over the top of its climb and seemed to rocket towards the ground.

"Pull up, pull up!" he muttered.

It looked like the model would just drive itself into the ground in a splintering crash but at the last second it did pull up and then went zooming up above the trees. At that Willy's father looked serious. "OK William that is enough. Bring it down before it runs out of fuel or we have an accident," he instructed.

Willy did so, his second landing being another almost text book job. Feeling very pleased with himself he picked the model up, and promptly burnt his forearm on the hot motor.

"Aaargh!" he cried.

"Serves you right," his father commented. "That will teach you to be careful. Now, it is time we were on our way. It is after eleven already."

The model was placed in the back of the car along with its fuel can and controller and spare batteries. Farewells were said to Uncle Ted and Aunty Isabel and then Willy and his family and friends climbed into their vehicles and set off for the location of the flying competition.

The venue was a large open paddock near Emerald Creek about 10 kilometres east of Mareeba. As they drove in the approach road Willy was surprised to see that about thirty cars were parked along the side of the field and that five shade structures were standing amid a crowd of what looked like hundreds of people. Most were in camouflage uniform but there were many civilians including children. The sight of so many people sent Willy's anxiety shooting up again. Any mistake with his model would be a very public disaster!

There was a model Mustang buzzing and zooming around overhead and after getting out of the vehicle Willy stood and looked at it for a few moments before looking around at the crowd.

"I didn't expect so many people," he commented.

Leaving his own model in the vehicle he followed the others across to where several officers sat behind a table under one of the shade structures. They appeared to be the officials or judges. One was Flt Lt Comstock and Willy hastily put on his hat and wondered if he should salute.

As he did a tall girl in camouflage uniform walked over and stood beside him. "Hi!" she said. "I'm Melissa. What's your name?"

Willy looked at her and was immediately impressed. Melissa had sparkling white teeth and a very pretty face below a mop of brown curls. He managed a flustered smile back.

"Hi. I'm Willy, and this is Stick," he added, gesturing to his friend.

"This is Ashlee," Melissa said, indicating another girl in camouflage uniform who had joined her.

Willy glanced at Ashlee and then stared. *She is the most beautiful girl I have ever seen!* he thought. He was instantly smitten.

To add to his confusion, Ashlee gave him a brilliant and very friendly smile. She looked to be about his age; and when Willy tore his eyes from her heart shaped face and ever so kissable lips and glossy black hair, he noted that she appeared to have a very curvy shape under the camouflage uniform.

Heavens she is not just pretty! She is heartbreakingly beautiful, he thought.

And she was friendly. Instantly his male mind clicked into gear. *I wonder if I have a chance with her?*

Chapter 31

MAREEBA

As Willy studied Ashlee, he realised he was staring. He also became conscious that Marjorie had moved next to Stick. Willy glanced at her and noted that she was giving both female cadets a frosty smile that did not reach her eyes. At that Willy was torn. Here was the most beautiful girl he had ever seen being friendly to him, but he was being unfaithful to Petra.

God I'm a weakling! he chided himself. *But God she is beautiful!* And her friend Melissa was also very pretty and also very friendly.

She smiled at him. "We are from 106 Squadron. Are you from Cairns or from Innisfail?" she asked.

"Cairns," Willy replied, his emotions still in whirl.

Ashlee gave him a brilliant smile. "Are you here for the flying or the drill?" she asked.

"Both," Willy croaked. He flicked a guilty glance at Marjorie and resolved to try to get to know these two girls.

A large male cadet sergeant with the name JONES on his shirt came over to them. Looking at Ashlee and Melissa he said, "You two girls go back over to the unit."

"Yes Dave," Ashlee replied. She then gave Willy another heart stopping smile and said, "Got to go. See ya! Bye!"

She then gave a little wave that set Willy's heart all a flutter. Melissa also said goodbye and reluctantly turned and walked away. Willy's gaze took in how tight her trousers were over her behind. *Nice bum!* he thought, noting her long legs and graceful walk.

As he did the male sergeant stepped closer. "You buggers keep away from our girls," he hissed.

Willy was stung by that. He was about to retort that the girls could talk to whoever they liked but he managed to check himself. "Yes sergeant," he replied woodenly.

Dave eh? he thought wryly.

Cadet Sgt Jones gave them both a hard look and then turned and followed the girls. Stick waited till he was out of earshot and then huffed. "Huh! He must be the jealous type," he commented.

"Very insecure," Willy agreed.

Then he noted a hurt look cross Marjorie's eyes and he experienced another little spurt of guilt. *Why do I care? She isn't my girlfriend,* he thought.

Willy and the others, having signed the visitor's register, moved to watch the models flying. By then the Mustang had landed and a bright yellow Acrobat took its place. Willy watched it flying with some dismay. It was both impressive in speed and in its manoeuvres. Seeing how well it performed set his anxieties on the boil again.

So did frequent glimpses of Ashlee and Melissa. From time to time he got glimpses of them further along the side of the airfield. They looked so happy and natural that his heart kept leaping with hope. *They are both very attractive,* he thought, noting how Ashlee's shirt pulled tight across her bosom when she twisted round.

Lunch time came and they sat in the shade of the trees along the side of the field and ate their sandwiches, washed down by cordial. After that there were more flying displays, formation flying and aerobatics. Then two large models, a Sea Fury and a Kittyhawk, did a pretend dog-fight. Willy enjoyed that but did not feel he was ready for such a competition yet. After that the cadet flying competition began. A model Cessna was first, made and flown by a corporal from 106 Squadron. It was good but not as good as the model JU87 Stuka fielded by a sergeant from 105 Squadron. Willy thought it was really impressive and watching it dive and swoop made his hopes plummet with it. He started to worry that his model would look sad and that he would make a fool of himself.

Then it was his turn. Feeling quite stressed and anxious Willy carried his triplane out to where the starting judges stood. Stick carried his controller and Marjorie brought the fuel can. As he did Willy noted Branch watching and then he also noted Ashlee and Melissa. They both waved and smiled and his nervousness shot up another notch. He did not want to muck it up with them watching!

Carefully he fuelled the triplane and then he knelt to start the motor. *Oh please start first go!* he thought. To his relief it did. At the first flick the motor burst into life and he had to hold the model in place on the short grass while Stick switched on the controller and handed it to him.

His next concern was with the airfield. It was stubbly short grass but looked much rougher than the neatly mowed field in Townsville or the smoothed dirt at the farm. He worried that the longer clumps of grass might trip up his model. Biting his lip and fretting over whether the wheels were large enough he carefully lined the model up and let it go.

The triplane began rolling across the grass, bumping and jerking alarmingly. Quickly Willy stood up, checked the controller and then began to increase the engine revolutions. The humming sound became a loud buzz and the speed of the model increased. Then, as on the test flights, the tail just rose up and before he was really ready the model lifted off.

Pleased but trembling slightly with anxiety Willy steered the model away and set it to gain height. Only when he was confident that it was above the tops of the distant trees did he increase speed even more and start to make the model perform.

First he flew the triplane in a slow, low circuit of the field. He found it a real pleasure to watch the way everyone's head turned in unison as they followed the model's progress overheard. Feeling confident he had mastered the basics of the controls he started the model doing some aerobatics. After getting the model to climb to what looked like an extraordinary height he put it onto a steep dive and then pulled it back into a loop.

This time, with plenty of altitude in reserve, Willy managed to get the model to perform very well. The loop was good. So were some rolls he then executed. He followed this up with a series of zooming dives towards the crowd and then pretend dive bombing or strafing attacks on other models parked out on the edge of the runaway.

As he did, his father nudged him. "No more dives towards the audience, Willy. It is a safety problem and the judges are frowning."

"Yes, Dad," Willy replied.

Now he was really enjoying himself and with each successful manoeuvre his confidence increased. He made the model do a very low, fast pass along the airfield and then another swooping roll before getting it to twist and turn in sharp jinks that drew several murmurs of appreciation from the people near him.

Then his father nudged him again. "Time's up, Willy. Bring it in to land."

Feeling some regret that he had to end his display Willy did as he was told. He aimed the model to stop at his feet, attempting to show off even more. To his embarrassment that plan almost failed. The speed was right, the angle of descent was good, the wheels touched well and without bouncing, but then the grass interfered. The model suddenly stopped and jerked up onto its nose, the propeller digging into the turf.

"I hope I didn't damage it," Willy muttered as he and Stick hurried out to where the model stood on its nose. Carefully he picked it up and switched off the fuel. To his relief the model did not appear to have suffered any damage and he carried it proudly over to the table where the judges were seated.

As he did he noted Ashlee and Melissa both smiling and waving and he felt sure he had done alright. Then he noted Branch nodding approval and almost smiling. To Willy's surprise Branch spoke as he went past. "Well done Willy," he said.

That was a surprise. Willy began to glow inside. *Now, let's hope the judges like the craftsmanship,* he thought.

They did. The triplane was awarded First Prize for a scratch built model in the craftsmanship category. But it only rated as 3rd in the flying competition. Only then did Willy discover that there were only five models in the competition and two had been made by one of the adult staff, a corporal Instructor of Cadets from 105 Squadron. The other models all belonged to the local model aircraft club and were there for show or to fly.

As he made his way back towards the vehicle Willy felt a touch on his arm. It was Ashlee. She was smiling and kept glancing at the model as she walked beside him. "That is a great model," she said. "What is it?"

"The Red Baron's Fokker Triplane," Willy answered, not sure if he should bore her with all the technical details or not.

"Oh, I've heard of him. He was a German in World War One wasn't he?" Ashlee replied.

At that moment Willy noted Marjorie watching them from near the vehicles. She had a sour smile on her face and was obviously not happy with Ashlee. He shrugged. "Yes," he replied. "He shot down eighty British and French planes."

"Did you make the model yourself?" Ashlee asked.

"Yes," Willy answered. But by then they had reached the vehicle and Marjorie stepped forward and put her hands out. "I'll take the model thank you Willy," she said, her eyes glinting a challenge at Ashlee.

Willy was both nettled and amused. *Marjorie must really like me,* he decided. *But she's just a Year 7 kid. And besides, it is Petra I love.* But then he glanced at Ashlee's beautiful face and experienced a sharp stab of doubt.

Ashlee was called away by Melissa. "Come on Ashlee, never mind boys," she called. "We have to go to the depot to practice for the drill competition."

"Bye, see ya later," Ashlee said, smiling and waving again, her eyes dancing with flirtatious mischief.

Willy would have liked to watch her walk away, but with Marjorie there he felt compelled to pretend he wasn't interested. So he busied himself carefully placing the model in the back of his father's vehicle.

WOFF Mathieson appeared and informed them that they now needed to go to Mareeba to do drill practice. Willy, Stick, Marjorie and Lloyd climbed into the vehicles which then waited for a gap in the line of departing cars before starting off.

Ten minutes later they were in the town of Mareeba. The two boys were dropped off with their models and gear at the front of the Air Cadet Depot in Abott Street. As they did Marjorie gave Willy many wistful glances. "I wish I was staying with you," she said.

Stick snorted. "You can join the cadets next year when you are old enough," he replied.

"See you tomorrow morning, William," Willy's father said. His mother kissed him and wished him well and the two vehicles turned and drove away. They would be spending the night back at the farm.

Willy had never been to the Mareeba depot so now stood and looked at it. The depot is located on a small ridge which slopes down to Granite Creek on one side and to Abott Street and the Bi-centennial Lakes Park on the other. A bitumen parade ground 50 metres by 25 takes up much of the area. Three buildings butted together to form an 'L' shape are located at the northern end of the parade ground. At the other end are a store shed and fence and then a private house. On the creek side of the parade ground is a concrete retaining wall, the ground beyond that is all lawn that slopes down to a line of trees and a fence. There is a public walking track beyond the fence.

The larger buildings had a veranda and comprised two lecture rooms, one of which also doubled as the canteen. The smaller building contained two offices, the armoury and male and female toilets. This building was flush with the ground beside the parade ground but was held up by a row of concrete stumps on the creek side and had more rooms underneath. A wire link fence surrounded the whole yard, including an area of lawn on the north side of the buildings.

Other cadets were already there. One of the teams (105 Squadron Innisfail?) was marching around on the parade ground. A few cadets stood or sat on the veranda or on folding chairs watching them. CUO Penrose was among these and he waved to them and told them to come in. Feeling quite self-conscious Willy picked up his model and did so. Stick carefully picked up the large cardboard box containing his diorama. Noddy collected their bags and followed.

CUO Penrose pointed through a door on the right. "Put the models on the big table at the far end and you gear against the wall at this end then come and help put up some stretchers," he instructed.

Willy made his way through the doorway, taking care to keep the wings of his model clear of any obstructions. He saw that the room was a large lecture room that could be divided into two. There were more cadets in there and as he made his way towards the large table at the rear he saw among them Ashlee and Melissa. His spirits shot up at once.

Ashlee and Melissa quickly made their way over to join them as Willy carefully placed his model triplane at the back of the table next to the model Cessna. Stick then placed his cardboard box down beside it.

Melissa pointed to the box. "What's in that?" she asked.

"My model," Stick answered, blushing.

"Show me," Melissa asked.

"You show me yours too then," Stick quipped.

Willy held his breath, waiting to see what how the girls would react to the innuendo. To his relief and excitement they both gaped and then burst into giggles. Melissa shook her head but laughed. "Oh you are naughty!" she cried.

Stick grinned back and Willy returned Ashlee's smile. *We might be in luck here,* he speculated. Then he noted a sour, faced male cadet standing behind the girls and that made him glance around. Cadet Sgt Jones was nearby and glowering at them. *And then again, maybe not!*

It was obvious to Willy that the local male cadets were very possessive and jealous. Looking at Ashlee's vivacious and beautiful face and figure, he could understand why. *If she was my girl I'd be jealous,* he thought.

To defuse a possible clash Willy urged Stick and Noddy to move back outside. At the back of the second large building on the north lawn they found WOFF Mathieson and Sgt Branch organising the erection of 'Cots Folding'. This was a new skill for Willy and his friends and kept them busy for the next hour.

As they worked Ashlee and Melissa came and watched, making giggly comments to each other as they did. Willy smiled and made what he hoped were witty comments back and so did Stick. While collecting the rope ties, Willy went to talk to the girls.

The conversation was interrupted by an angry Cadet Sgt Jones. "You girls get out on the parade ground for a rehearsal!" he bellowed.

Melissa and Ashlee both gave Willy and Stick amused and impish grins before hurrying off. Before he followed Cadet Sgt Jones glared at both Willy and Stick before turning and stamping away.

Cpl Wellington, a male NCO from Willy's flight, who was helping with the stretchers sidled over and grinned. "I see you two have met the Teeth with Legs and the delectable Ashlee."

Teeth with legs! Willy was surprised and then he wasn't. When he brought Melissa to mind it was her brilliant smile and long, graceful legs that he pictured. But it was Ashlee he considered the prettiest. "Delectable alright," he replied.

Cpl Wellington grinned. "Be careful or you might get your face rearranged. The local lads seem a bit possessive of those two," he commented. Willy could only nod and agree, and then feel guilty about being disloyal to Petra.

Once the stretchers were assembled and arranged in three rows along the walls and centre of the room the boys placed their gear on them. They then moved to wait their turn doing a rehearsal for the Drill Competition.

Warrant Officer Colley called the Cairns cadets aside and then called the names of the team, telling them to form up to one side. But two of the team were not there. "Has anyone seen Cpl Lendel or Cadet Timmson?" he queried.

I might get to be in the team, Willy thought, his hopes rising.

Nobody had. WOFF Colley quickly consulted with Flt Lt Comstock and CUO Penrose and they nodded and WOFF Colley turned to look at the small group of other cadets who were also present. "Cadet Williams, you are First Reserve, do you have your dress uniform with you?"

"Yes sir," Willy replied, his hopes going even higher.

"Good. Join the team. Now, we are still down one. We are willing to give a volunteer the place if they have their good uniform and we think they are up to it. Who would like to volunteer?"

To Willy's surprise Stick put his hand up. So did Leading Air Cadet Carpenter. WOFF Colley looked at both and then back at the group. "What about you Cpl Bourke?"

But Cpl Bourke shook his head. "Sorry sir. I only came for the model competition and didn't bring my dress blues."

"You were supposed to! It is the laid down dress for tomorrow," WOFF Colley snapped. "Oh well, let's try you two out and see who is the better."

So Stick and Carpenter were taken around the other side of the building. A few minutes later a smiling Stick and a sour faced Carpenter returned. Stick gave Willy a grin and a thumbs-up. "I'm in!" he said

Willy was pleased for his friend but anxious. *Stick hasn't done all the rehearsals. I hope he doesn't muck it up!*

While they waited they watched the local 106 Squadron Drill Team go through their paces. As both Ashlee and Melissa were in the team Willy found it a pleasure to watch. *Even in cams they look really curvy,* he thought.

Stick, who was standing beside him watching, shook his head gloomily. "They are good," he commented.

They were. Willy bit his lip and hoped their own drill was as good as that. While he watched he tapped his foot in time with the marching tune being played on a sound system.

"That's a good tune. I wonder what it is called?" he said.

Flora Finlay answered. "Aces High," she said.

"Thanks," Willy grunted. *Bloody Finlay! What a know-all!* he thought. Then he shifted his interest back to admiring Ashlee as she marched past. *God she is beautiful! I could fall in love with her.*

Then it was his team's turn to do a rehearsal. Luckily by then the afternoon sun had sunk below the trees lining the creek so it wasn't as fierce but being October the air was still very hot, about 32 degrees. For thirty minutes the squad sweated up and down the parade ground. To Willy's relief (and no doubt CUO Penrose's) Stick did not make a mistake, even during the turns on the march and the more complicated marching manoeuvres.

As the team practiced Willy was conscious that Ashlee and Melissa were both watching but he tried to ignore them and concentrated on his drill. He was very aware, having been constantly reminded of the fact, that the Cairns Air Cadets had won the competition for the last four years.

"And we intend to prove we are the best again!" CUO Penrose told them. Willy was fired by the same aim.

There were about 50 cadets and 10 adult staff from three units at the depot and as the sun went down they were fed at a barbeque. This was done out of doors at the front of the building and involved the usual sausages, steak, onions and bread rolls to which were added salads and cheese slices as desired. The cadets filed past and were handed a plate to which they added first a buttered bread roll and then the other fillings.

As they weren't called to line up by units Willy worked it so that he ended up in line behind Melissa and in front of Ashlee. They both seemed happy with that and quickly struck up an animated conversation. Willy decided that he did have a chance and made a maximum charm effort to impress.

Having collected their food the three moved to the side of the group. Willy began to speculate on how he might persuade Ashlee to meet him somewhere private. Just looking into her achingly lovely face and sparkling eyes made Willy feel weak at the knees. Slowly he edged them around to the side of the building where they were just outside the crowd.

By this time he was feeling really good about life. His model had flown and won a prize, he was with two lovely girls who were responding to his flirting, and he felt very proud to be a cadet and to be with such a group.

Melissa frowned, opened her burger and then shook her head. "This needs more sauce. Just a minute," she said. Then she turned and walked back through the crowd. Willy's mind raced. *I am alone with Ashlee. Now is my chance,* he told himself. Glancing around he noted that the corner of the building on the north lawn were just nearby and the lawn was in darkness.

Licking suddenly dry lips, he took a deep breath. "I'd like to kiss you," he blurted.

Ashlee's eyes opened wide, but to his relief she smiled. "That's nice," she said. "But we aren't supposed to kiss while we are in uniform."

Before he could stop himself Willy replied: "We could always take the uniforms off."

Again Ashlee's eyes opened wide and for a second Willy feared he had overstepped the mark. But then her face transformed into a mischievous grin and she giggled. "Oooh! You are naughty!"

"How about it then?" Willy queried, his heart now hammering with excitement and his body staring to become aroused.

"You are a bit fast!" Ashlee complained, but not very convincingly. "Where could we go?"

I'm in! Willy thought, his hopes shooting up.

Chapter 32

JEALOUSY

Ashlee smiled and Willy's heart thumped with hope. His body surged with desire. He knew it was wrong to do any fraternising at cadets, but he had never met such a beautiful and apparently willing girl.

"I have to be fast," he answered. "I've only got a few hours to get to know you."

As he said this, he turned and they both began strolling towards the corner of the building. Ashlee pouted and looked anxious. "You just want to love me and leave me," she replied.

Willy's mind exploded with images of Ashlee with no clothes on. "That's nice to think about, but no. I want to love you for sure, but I would never leave you," he replied.

By then they were at the corner. Willy kept walking and, to his relief, Ashlee followed. She still looked doubtful. "But I don't know anything about you. Besides, you live in Cairns so how could we be friends?"

Across Willy's mind flashed the old saying: *Love will find a way,* but he resisted the temptation to use it as being too melodramatic. Instead he said, "I often come up to Mareeba. My uncle and aunty have a farm near Davies Creek. If we find we really like each other I would make the effort."

That caused her to look at him in a new way. "Would you? Oh, that's so sweet!" she purred.

"I would," Willy replied in his most sincere tone.

Ashlee smiled, stopped walking and turned to face him. "But I don't know anything about you other than your first name and that you are an air cadet. What school do you go to?"

Willy knew exactly what she wanted to know. *She is worried I will be too young for her,* he thought. And it was also what he badly wanted to know as well. "I'm in Year Eight at Cairns State High School," he replied.

At that Ashlee nodded and then smiled. "I'm in Year Eight too, here at Mareeba State High."

Willy almost sighed with relief. It was alright. He looked at her in wonder, trying to decide whether her eyes were hazel or green. *Bright and beautiful anyway,* he decided. Where they now stood was still brightly lit by the security light at the rear of the buildings and he really wanted to get her somewhere more private. He glanced around to try to find a place that might be suitable.

Then the sound of footsteps made him look around in annoyance. He found himself confronted by the angry looking male air cadet he had seen earlier. The youth looked to be a year or two older and he was bigger and obviously in a bad mood. He glared at Willy and then turned to Ashlee.

"I thought we were going together," he said.

Ashlee bit her lip and looked worried. "It's alright, Kevin. We are only talking. Don't be so jealous."

"Jealous!" Kevin exploded. "You sneak off around the corner with this jerk and say don't be jealous!"

"We didn't sneak anywhere!" Ashlee said. "And I will do what I like."

At that moment Cadet Sgt Jones appeared at the corner. When he saw them his mouth tightened and he strode over. "Cadet Greenway, you get back with the others!" he ordered.

Ashlee pouted but nodded, "Yes sergeant," giving Willy a wistful look she turned and walked away.

Willy went to follow but as he did Kevin grabbed his sleeve, spun him around and slammed him against the wall. "Keep away from my girl!" he snarled. "Or I will beat you to pulp!"

Willy was caught off guard but reacted quickly. Angered by being manhandled he struggled to get free. "Huh! You and what army?"

Cadet Sgt Jones stepped closer. "This army!" he hissed. "You and your mates keep away from our girls or we will smash you." As he said this he shook a fist in front of Willy's face.

"You can't hit me. Sergeants aren't allowed to do that," Willy replied, but under his bluster he was feeling very unsure and now a little scared.

"Can't I!" Cadet Sgt Jones hissed. With that he drove his fist into Willy's stomach. As Willy began to double up Jones drew back his fist. Willy tried to straighten up to defend himself but Kevin kept a tight grip on Willy's right arm and kept him pushed against the wall.

"What's going on here?" called a voice.

Through eyes misting with tears Willy looked. It was WOFF

Mathieson. With him was Branch. Cadet Sgt Jones looked and then lowered his fist and straightened up. "Nothing sir," he answered. "Just clearing up a little misunderstanding."

WOFF Mathieson looked sceptical but nodded and jerked his hand toward the front of the building. "All of you go back and join the others," he ordered.

"Yes sir," Cadet Sgt Jones answered loudly. He let Willy go and turned away. Kevin also let him go but as he did he leaned closer and hissed, "Leave my girl alone, or else!" Then he moved off as well.

Willy straightened up and tried to calm his breathing. His racing thoughts suggested that he not make a complaint so he pretended he was alright although the surging waves of pain made that hard to do. Adjusting his shirt he strolled towards the corner where WOFF Mathieson and Branch both waited.

WOFF Mathieson stopped him. "Keep out of trouble, Cadet Williams, or you will be out of cadets," he said.

"There was no trouble, sir," Willy answered, hoping his rapidly beating heart and hunched posture weren't obvious.

"Oh yes there was, and I don't mean the fighting. If they had punched your lights out you would have deserved that. I meant slipping off into the night with girls. Remember you signed the Cadet Code of Conduct. Your honour and self-respect are at risk."

"We were only talking," Willy replied sulkily, resenting the word 'slipping' but burning with shame as he knew it was accurate.

"Only talking, SIR!" WOFF Mathieson snapped.

"Sir," Willy responded.

"From the look of it, you are lucky Sgt Branch saw them follow you and told me," WOFF Mathieson said. "Now go and stay with the group and no more sneaking off. I don't care how pretty she is."

"Sir."

WOFF Mathieson turned and marched away. Branch gave Willy a sardonic smile and Willy didn't know whether to thank him or not. It was obvious that Branch had been watching him.

Did he dob to try to get me into real trouble, Willy wondered.

Branch chuckled. "You are a glutton for punishment, Williams. Don't go around flirting with the local chicks. They have jealous boyfriends and we might not always be around to save your hide," he said.

"Yes sergeant. Thanks sergeant," Willy mumbled.

They walked back to where the barbeque was still in progress. Stick saw him and raised an eyebrow. "What was that all about Willy?" he asked.

Willy shrugged. "Just a little disagreement," he replied. Now that the pain had subsided, he was feeling aggrieved. Glancing around the area, Willy saw Ashlee standing with Melissa and Kevin. Briefly their eyes met and she gave a half smile and a shrug and then looked back at Kevin.

Stick made a face. "Serves you bloody right, you bloody flirt. What about Marjorie?"

"What about her? She's not my girlfriend," Willy retorted, stung by the accusation and by guilty images of Petra.

"She's in love with you and she thinks you like her," Stick replied.

Willy shrugged and wanted to say he didn't like her but then he realised he did. "I haven't promised her anything. I'm going with Petra remember."

Stick grunted with annoyance. "You are the one who needs to remember, sneaking off with that Ashlee like that. Don't you hurt my sister or you won't be my friend anymore."

With that Stick turned and began talking to Cpl Wellington. Willy stood there burning with embarrassment and shame. *Was it that obvious?* he worried. *I hope none of the officers saw us.* Then the shock hit him as he realised just how silly he had been and what risks he had run. This was followed by guilt at also risking Ashlee's reputation and cadet career. *You are a selfish shit Williams,* Willy chided himself.

For the remainder of the evening Willy sat quietly at the back and kept away from the girls. But he could not help glancing frequently at Ashlee. *But she is beautiful,* he thought.

After the barbeque was a movie: *Those Magnificent Men and their Flying Machines.* Willy had seen it before but he still enjoyed it. And then it was time for supper and for bed. As he made his way outside he glanced back and his eyes met Ashlee's. She gave him a cheeky smile and he could only smile back and then quickly turn away.

Bloody flirt, he thought, but aimed the idea more at himself than her.

To sleep that night the male cadets were accommodated in the first large classroom and the girls in the second lecture room. The adults slept in the various offices or a couple of tents which had been erected along the side of the parade ground. For safety and security there was a piquet and Willy was rostered on this, from 0230 to 0330hrs. He had never done piquet before so found it an interesting experience. He was rostered with a corporal from Innisfail for the first half hour and then with Cpl Wellington for the second.

Would have been nice to be rostered with Ashlee, he fantasised. Then he stood and considered who he really did like. As cadets on piquet were forbidden to talk except when required for duty thinking was all he could do. But his thoughts soon wandered off girls to noting how cool the night air had become. *And how quiet it is!* he marvelled.

Mareeba was asleep and only the sound of a distant vehicle in the main street disturbed the silence. Even the sound of his boots crunching on the sand as he walked on the edge of the parade ground seemed very loud. To pass the time Willy began to fantasise about saving the depot from a terrorist attack. That led to daydreams about rescuing Ashlee.

But then his mind filled with conflicting images: Petra, Marjorie, Ashlee, even Barbara. *What am I?* Willy wondered. *Am I just a disloyal weakling?*

He had not resolved this when he had to go and wake Stick to relieve him. That done Willy lay down and tried to calm his thoughts. For a long time sleep would not come, the effort made worse because Stick started talking to Cpl Wellington and the murmur was both annoying and distracting.

But he did slip off to sleep, to be roused at 0600 for Check Parade. This was done by units with the Cairns cadets lined up on the north lawn and the other two units on the parade ground.

Breakfast was another barbeque with more sausages and bacon and fried eggs. Willy was tasked with setting up two tables with cereal packets, plastic bowls and spoons and milk. During this he briefly glimpsed Ashlee but her smile was fleeting and she hurried off to do something inside the buildings.

When he met her again at breakfast time Ashlee again gave him a smile, but it was just a normal one with none of the 'come hither' hinting she had previously used. Then she went and sat with her back to him and facing Kevin. Willy was left feeling puzzled and a little hurt.

She has obviously changed her tune in the night, he decided.

After breakfast Willy was detailed as part of a work party tasked with bringing chairs out of the lecture rooms. These were lined up along the side of the parade ground, mostly in the row of tents that now had their sides rolled right up so that they became shade shelters instead. Next he helped pick up litter and then Branch told him to get a broom to sweep the parade ground.

Willy stared at the expanse of bitumen in disbelief. "Sweep the bitumen!" he cried.

"Yes, you and the rest of your section. Now get to work and work fast. We want it done by nine," Branch replied.

Feeling quite grumpy and put upon, Willy obeyed. But he also saw the sense in it. Small pieces of gravel had ended up on the bitumen from vehicle tyres or people's boots and he understood that a perfectly smooth surface would be better for the drill. So he set to work. It kept him and Stick and several others busy for nearly an hour.

Between 0830hrs and 0930hrs each of the Air Cadet Drill Teams did two rehearsals. As he watched the 106 Squadron team Willy was struck by the extra moves that they had included in their performance. As they were marching past 'in line' they changed into 'slow time' and then they did an 'open order march on the march' and then after their 'eyes right' and 'eyes front' they did a 'close order march on the march' before breaking into quick time again.

Willy watched with something close to awe. "That is really good," he commented. "Why don't we try something like that?"

"Because we haven't practiced it and would just muck it up," CUO Penrose replied. But he looked worried too.

After morning tea the Drill Teams went to change into their best uniforms. By then parents and friends and the Army Cadet and Navy Cadet Drill Teams were arriving. When Willy emerged from the room after dressing he was astonished at the number of people that now crowded the fence and sat in the chairs.

Among them was Marjorie and she waved and then ran across to say hello. "How was your barbeque?" she asked, anxiety and jealousy plain in her face and tone.

"OK," Willy answered as sharp images of Ashlee and of being punched crowded his mind. And there was Ashlee! She was standing on the veranda adjusting her shirt next to Melissa. And she was looking. *She will think Marjorie is my girlfriend,* he thought.

But there was no strategy he could think of for making Marjorie go away until it was time for the competition to begin. So Willy stood and chatted to her and to his parents and to Uncle Ted and Aunty Isabel. Willy was both pleased and embarrassed to see them there. *I hope I don't let them down,* he worried.

Then he chatted to his father and a very nervous but pleased Stick while they studied the cadets from the Army and Navy Cadet teams. Willy noted that the Navy Cadet team included both Andrew Collins and his big sister Carmen. They looked very smart in white uniforms with white gaiters which had polished black straps and shiny gold buckles and white belts with gleaming brass buckles.

The Army Cadet teams were from the Cairns regional unit, 134 Army Cadet Unit, and from 144 Army Cadet Unit (Atherton) and Willy did not know any of them. They all wore the DPCU as a ceremonial uniform, the shirt tucked in behind a black belt and the sleeves rolled up. They also wore their Hat KFFs with the left side clipped up, the 'Rising Sun' badge twinkling in the sunlight. *They look pretty good,* Willy conceded, giving his own pressed blue uniform another anxious check.

Willy was particularly struck by the scarlet sash worn by an Army Cadet sergeant. It added a splash of bright colour and really looked good. It made the pale blue sashes worn by the Air Cadet sergeants seem very bland by comparison.

He also noted the shiny leather Sam Browne belts worn by the Army Cadet Under-Officers and was again mildly jealous. *They look really good,* he thought.

As the time drew closer Willy felt himself grow more tense and he made a point of going to have a big drink and then of visiting the toilet for a nervous pee. He then joined the team where they were forming up off the north edge of the parade ground. As he did he noted that the Navy Cadets were in front and then the two Army Cadet units. His own team was the first one of the three Air Cadets teams.

For the first time Willy learned about the laid down protocols of seniority. He asked Cpl Wellington why the Navy and Army Cadets were in front.

"Navy is the Senior Service," Cpl Wellington explained, "So they always lead or stand on the right on parade. Then army, then us."

"Why?" Stick whispered from behind them.

"Because the navy and army have been around for hundreds of years and the air force is only new," Cpl Wellington replied.

"What happens now?" Willy asked.

"We all march on and the Regional Wing Commander will arrive and get saluted and then inspect us. After that each team will perform for the competition," Cpl Wellington explained.

"Who's this wing commander?" Stick queried.

"Commander One Wing, Wing Commander De Boom. He was our CO last year," Cpl Wellington answered.

"Is he an Air Force officer or an Air Cadet officer?" Willy asked.

"Air Cadet, now shush!"

At 1030 Flt Lt Avolio, the CO of 106 Squadron, moved to the microphone at the 'saluting base' and began a speech of welcome. The competition had begun!

At the command of CUO Penrose all of the teams came to attention and marched on to be welcomed by loud applause from the spectators. Once on the parade ground and halted they did a left turn to face the official party and the spectators.

After another 'Right Dress' to tidy the ranks they were stood at ease until a white car was driven onto the edge of the parade ground. It halted between two Air Cadet door openers and out stepped the Regional Wing Commander, resplendent in his dress blues and peaked cap. Flt Lt Avolio saluted and greeted him and then moved him to a small box on the edge of the parade ground. By then CUO Penrose had called the parade to attention and now ordered the officers to salute.

Standing there in the ranks Willy felt very proud and pleased and stood stiffly at attention. He tried to ignore the sweat now trickling down his face and back. *The perspiration will ruin my shirt for the inspection!* he fretted. To keep aware in the heat Willy focused on the Regional Wing Commander, who stood at the front resplendent in dress blues and with peaked cap, medals and sword. *I'll be a wing commander one day,* he told himself.

Wing Commander De Boom returned the salute and then CUO Penrose marched over to him and saluted. The Wing Commander then marched with CUO Penrose to do the inspection. This seemed to take a long time and Willy sweated and hoped he wouldn't faint in the heat. First the Navy cadets were inspected and then the two army cadet units.

C.R. Cummings

Willy found it a relief when the inspection party reached his group. As the Wing Commander walked past, Willy studied him and mentally nodded with approval as he looked the part. *If I can't get into the RAAF I will volunteer to be an Officer of Cadets in the AAFC,* he decided. At that moment he was strongly motivated to serve and to be a useful Australian.

After the other two AAFC flights had been inspected CUO Penrose conducted the Wing Commander back to his dais and then saluted again before marching to his position at the front. He then ordered a right turn and quick march and the whole parade marched past the Wing Commander, giving him an 'Eyes Right' as they did. They were halted on the grass beside the buildings and then stood at ease.

According to the agreed rules for the competition each team had to then perform the same laid down sequence of orders and actions but were allowed to make variations as long as nothing was left out. The order they would perform in was chosen by drawing names out of a hat. That put Willy's team on first.

The other teams were marched off and fallen out and Willy's team stood on the parade ground and waited. Beside him Stick fidgeted.

"I wish we were last," he muttered.

Willy shook his head. "No. Better to get it over with," he whispered.

From behind him Branch hissed. "Stop talking in the ranks!"

And then it began. First they marched back onto the parade ground, halted and did a left turn. There was a 'Right Dress' followed by 'Open Order March'. A team of six assessors then moved slowly along the ranks, clipboards and mark sheets in hand as they inspected the uniforms. There was one adult assessor and one cadet assessor from each service.

As each assessor looked him over Willy had to use willpower to stop his nervousness showing but he felt like he was trembling. To help take his mind off his anxiety he studied the girls in the audience, even catching Marjorie's eye. She grinned at him but he did not dare smile in reply.

The inspection over the assessors left the parade ground and CUO Penrose moved to the front. Then it began, ten minutes of hard drill, sweating and trying to do their best. The presence of their rivals and of family and friends added an extra dimension of anxiety which Willy tried to ignore.

The team did a right turn at the halt then started marching in quick time. A left turn on the march followed by a right turn and an about turn had them all sweating but still holding together in their formation. Willy tried to ignore the lines of faces watching and instead concentrated on the arms of his neighbours to keep the rhythm.

As they passed back across the parade ground the team did a left wheel and then a left turn into line. In this formation they passed along the back of the parade ground. Two left forms on the march brought them to the front of the parade ground and they marched back across towards the saluting base.

From behind Willy both WOFF Mathieson and Sgt Branch were muttering, "Keep in line" and "Dressing by the right."

Willy kept glancing out of the corner of his right eye to stay beside Cpl Wellington. His own arm swing he thought was just right. The marching tune was again *Eagle Squadron* and Willy decided that was his favourite marching tune and he puffed out his chest with pride.

CUO Penrose gave the command "Eyes right!" and Willy swung his head to the right and focused on getting the line straight and then on looking at the Wing Commander who was again standing on the small dais and returning the salute.

Then it was 'Eyes front' and 'Left Form', followed by another two left forms. This placed them at the halt back where they had started from facing the saluting base. Here they halted. After a 'Right Dress' they did a 15 pace 'Advance in Review Order' and CUO Penrose saluted the Wing Commander again.

The audience clapped and Willy felt relieved. *Phwew! That is over. I hope we did alright,* he thought.

Chapter 33

ARMY CADETS

The squad was fallen out and the 144 ACU team took their place on the parade ground. Willy was handed a cup of cold cordial by Marjorie and she beamed at him.

"That was really good Willy," she praised.

Willy glowed and remembered to congratulate Stick. Then he watched the next performance. What he saw filled him with consternation. The Army Cadets from Atherton did an apparently faultless performance.

I think they were better than us, Willy thought gloomily.

But the performance by the next Army Cadet team, the 134ACU group, reversed that opinion. During the turns on the march several members of that team made mistakes. On one occasion the whole team turned right except one person who turned the other way and went marching off on their own until they realised their mistake. Red-faced the cadet scurried back to re-join the ranks. Willy shook his head and felt a surge of sympathy.

Oh, poor bugger! I'm glad I didn't make a mistake like that!

Unfortunately that seemed to throw that team's confidence and they did badly after that. Even from a distance Willy could hear the muttered recriminations and see the glowering looks at the cadet.

Then the Navy Cadets, who started very well and looked very good, suffered an even worse disaster. When they did their about turn on the march a couple did a right turn instead and that resulted in others colliding with them. Then one cadet tripped and in a moment half the team were sprawling on the bitumen in a struggling heap.

Willy saw Andrew Collins disentangle himself and struggle to his feet. His white uniform was now smudged and he looked quiet dismayed.

Poor buggers! Willy thought with another spurt of sympathy.

Not so Noddy. He chortled and called out, "Like a mob of drunken sailors!"

That annoyed Willy. "Fair go Noddy! Be thankful we didn't make a mistake like that," he chided.

Noddy looked puzzled but not abashed but he stopped laughing. "They should have practiced more," he replied.

"You weren't even in the team so don't criticise," Willy retorted.

By then the Navy Cadets were all on their feet and Willy saw Carmen Collins, her face beetroot red with embarrassment as she urged others back into line. The Cadet Midshipman in command, looking very smart in his white uniform and dress cap but also looking both furious and ashamed, gave the command 'Quick March!' and the team resumed its performance.

After they came off Willy was tempted to go and offer his sympathy to Andrew but seeing how unhappy the group looked he decided not to. *They haven't a hope of winning now,* he thought.

The two remaining teams then performed. The 105 Squadron team were alright but had several members out of step and out of line during the march past in line but the 106 Squadron team did what looked to be a flawless performance. *They are the best,* Willy decided., *They will probably win.*

And they did. Second were the 144ACU team and Willy's team were ranked third. *Oh well, better than last,* he thought. "We will do better next year," he commented to a dejected looking CUO Penrose.

CUO Penrose nodded but still looked bleak. "We might have done better if our whole team had turned up. Having a couple of ring-ins didn't help."

"Oh sir, fair go! Stick did a good job," Willy replied.

"Yes, yes he did. But we might have done better with more practice," CUO Penrose conceded.

The team leaders were called to the front to receive the trophies and then the teams were all grouped for photos. As they milled and jostled Willy found himself near Ashlee.

"You guys were great," he commented.

Ashlee gave him a dazzling smile and then thrust out her boobs and put a hand up to her hair. "That's because we are the best!" she boasted.

"You certainly are," Willy replied. Then he caught sight of Kevin's angry face just behind her and he quickly moved away.

As soon as the photos of each team were completed Flt Lt Avolio again moved to the microphone. "I would now ask that everyone move into the lecture room for the awards in the model competition," he announced.

It took five minutes to move everyone into the lecture rooms. As people crowded in the model makers were called to the front. The others stood around the walls and in the middle of the room. Flt Lt Avolio then announced the place getters in the model awards. To his pleased embarrassment Willy had to go with the others to collect his model. He then had to march out in front of everyone with his Fokker Triplane model, salute the Wing Commander and then shake his hand. He was then handed a red ribbon which he carefully placed over the top wing.

As Willy moved to the side he glanced around and saw his smiling parents and he smiled back. Then his eyes took in both Ashlee and Marjorie and he tried to give each a smile without making it too obvious. From the look on Marjorie's face, he did not think he succeeded.

And certainly Mister Jealous Kevin thinks I am still flirting!

There were also prizes for non-flying models. These were all plastic kits and while they were all very skilfully assembled and painted Willy still felt himself to be superior as a 'scratch builder'.

Next the dioramas were judged. Stick won third prize for his Hurricane in a dispersal bay. It did look good, but the 'Kittyhawk refuelling from petrol drums at Milne Bay in 1942' was obviously better and so was the 'B17 loading bombs'.

Then it was lunch and packing up. Willy was not allowed to go until the tents had all been pulled down and rolled up, stretchers rolled up and placed in the Q Store, and the area cleaned and the lecture rooms restored. This all took an hour and he was kept so busy that he had little chance to talk to anyone.

During this time the coaches full of Navy and Army Cadets drove away and most of the parents and families departed. Willy's parents went off to the main street to buy lunch, taking Lloyd and Marjorie with them. They returned at 2pm and waited until the Air Cadets were all dismissed. There was a short parade and the Wing Commander thanked them all and again congratulated the winning team.

As he did Willy glanced around to look for Ashlee and was annoyed to see her beaming at Kevin. Miffed, he looked away and when the group was dismissed he made no attempt to go and say goodbye. Instead he collected his gear and model and along with Stick and Noddy made his way out to where the vehicles were parked.

Two hours later he was at home and in the shower. *It was a good weekend,* he decided. *And that Ashlee is very pretty, but she is a real flirt.* His thoughts then shifted back to Petra and he wondered what, if anything, he could do to recapture that feeling of blissful emotion and sense of intimacy.

Those thoughts were still very much at the front of his mind when he went to school the next day. Petra was there but she just gave him a perfunctory smile and then went to her desk. Willy was left feeling deflated and baffled.

But school also meant mates and rivals. During morning break Willy sat with Stick, Noddy, Scott and John at their usual seat. While they were discussing the weekend Noddy suddenly pointed and then called out: "Here come the belly button cadets. Hey navy! Hard a port!"

Willy looked and saw that Andrew Collins and his two mates, Luke the Torres Strait Islander and Blake, were passing. The three navy cadets all glanced at Noddy and a scowl appeared on Blake's face. Luke suddenly veered across and halted with his clenched fists on his hips. He glowered down at Noddy and stood over him.

"What you say?" he growled.

Noddy blanched and goggled up at Luke, who was nearly twice his size and obviously much stronger. "N... n... n... nuth... nothing," he stammered.

"Yes you did. You insulted us," Luke snapped.

"J... just a... just a joke," Noddy replied. He licked his lips nervously and looked to Willy for support.

But Willy wasn't amused either. *The poor old Navy Cadets got enough humiliation yesterday,* he thought. Shaking his head he said, "Your problem, Noddy. You started it so you finish it."

Noddy scowled but then Luke reached out and grabbed the front of Noddy's shirt. "Well Space Cadet, what'd you say?"

"I... I'm not a space cadet. I'm an air cadet," Noddy replied.

Luke snorted. "You is a space cadet. You got a big empty space between ya ears where ya brain is supposed to be. Now apologise."

"S... sorry," Noddy replied. He was now half standing and had his lower legs caught under the bench.

"That better," Luke answered, shoving Noddy back onto the seat. "So no names or we not call you names back, we just thump ya, eh?"

Noddy could only nod. Willy met Andrew's eyes and he was tempted to speak but Andrew looked so unhappy he just gave a sympathetic smile. The Navy Cadets walked on towards the tuck shop.

As they left Noddy turned on Willy. "Huh, some mate you are!" he cried.

That stung Willy. "You didn't need to rub salt into their wounds," Willy replied. "You started it. They hadn't done anything to you."

Stick now joined in from the other side. "Yeah Noddy, and anyway I nearly did that same mistake yesterday so it could have been us they were crowing at. And you weren't even in the team so shut up!"

Noddy did but was obviously unhappy. Scott and John both exchanged glances and then Scott nudged Noddy. "Here come some of the army cadets; why don't you tease them too, Noddy?"

Noddy scowled but said nothing. Willy looked up and saw that Stephen was approaching with his mates Graham, Peter and Roger. This time there was a brief exchange of greetings but no name calling. *Wrong team anyway,* Willy thought. *Our school unit didn't take part in the drill competition.*

The four army cadets stopped and Stephen grinned. "I hear you guys did well in the drill competition yesterday," he said.

Willy nodded. "Came third," he agreed.

"But you got beaten by army cadets," Stephen added.

That rankled. "Yeah, that mob from Atherton, but we beat your mates from the Cairns unit," Willy retorted.

The army cadets laughed and Stephen grinned. "You wouldn't have beaten us if we'd been in it," he commented.

That brought a round of derisory jeers and cries from the air cadets. "So why don't you go in it and prove it?" Willy said.

Stephen shrugged. "That's up to Capt Conkey. We would have to drop out some other training to make time for it."

Noddy now joined in. "We are better than you lot any day," he cried.

There was a distinct change on the mood. A look of anger crossed Graham's face and he stepped forward but rather than confronting Noddy he looked at Willy. "I hear you won a prize with a model plane."

Willy seized on the opportunity to ease the sudden tension. Knowing that Graham made model ships and that they were all 'scratch built' he nodded. "Yeah, Third in the flying section and First in the 'scratch built' section," he answered.

"I'd like to see it," Graham said.

Willy nodded. "OK, and Stick got third in the diorama section."

They discussed models for a few minutes and then the army cadets went on their way. And the subject of models came up in the very next lesson. It was History and Mr Conkey mentioned to Willy that he had heard about his model. "I hear that your team came third in the Drill Competition. Congratulations."

"Thank you, sir," Willy mumbled, a bit embarrassed to have the achievement publicly discussed in class as most students were very negative about Cadets.

Mr Conkey continued: "And I hear you did very well in the model competition."

"Yes, sir," Willy replied, blushing even more as he did not want his classmates (Especially the girls!) to think he was still a little kid who played with toys. Feeling quite coy he described his awards.

Mr Conkey nodded. "That sounds very good. I would very much like to see this model," he said. "You could bring it and use it in your lecturette that you are all due to present this week."

Willy was both pleased and embarrassed. "But you said the lecturettes have to be on Australian History sir," he replied.

Mr Conkey nodded. "So they are. But you do know that the Red Baron was shot down by Australian troops and we provided the firing party at his funeral, don't you? That is Australian enough for me," he said.

"I'll have to ask my mum if she can bring it to school," Willy replied. "I can't bring it on my bike."

And that is what he did that night. She at once consented. "But you must make sure it is safe during the day," she added.

"Mr Conkey said I could leave it in his staff room," Willy answered.

So it was arranged. Tuesday came and went with no dramas and that night Willy researched the death of the Red Baron. On Wednesday morning Willy carefully loaded his model Fokker Triplane into the back of his mother's car. As she closed the back she said, "Now you get to school early and be there to meet me. Get going."

Willy got going. After riding to school and parking his bike and chaining it up in the bike racks he hurried to the side gate and waited. He was nervous and embarrassed and kept glancing around. *I hope that*

Scranton and the other bullies don't see me, he fretted. He knew he would get teased by all his enemies who would sneer and call him a little kid who played with toys and now he regretted agreeing to bring the model.

And he was not wrong. Even as he lifted the model triplane out of the back of his mother's car he noted student's faces looking at him with what he thought were disdainful and sneering looks. Blushing with embarrassment he thanked his mother and hurried in the gate.

I need to get this to Mr Conkey's staff room as quickly as I can, he told himself.

Holding the model firmly he hurried around the buildings. That wasn't the quickest route but there were now so many students under the buildings that he did not want to risk getting it damaged by accident. All the way he kept looking around for any sign of the bullies.

Then, what he dreaded, happened. He was seen by Larsen, Carstairs and two other Year 11 boys who saw him and detoured to block his path. "What's this Rocket Rectum? Did your rich daddy give you another toy?" Larsen said with a sneer.

Willy broke into a sweat of anxiety and glanced around hoping for help. "No. I made it," he replied.

"Made it!" Larsen jeered. "Don't lie to me you little turd. You couldn't even make a good shit. Now give it here," he snarled.

As Larsen reached out Willy stepped quickly back and swung the model away. "No. Leave it please! It is only balsa wood and tissue and it is very fragile," he cried. His heart was now hammering with what he did not like to admit was fear.

"Larsen!" bellowed Mr Fitzgerald from under a nearby building. "Stop bullying the Year Eights."

"I'm not bullying him sir. I just wanted to admire his model," Larsen replied.

"Just keep your hands to yourself and let him go. Come here Williams," Mr Fitzgerald ordered.

For once Willy was happy to see the deputy and he hurried over, leaving the muttering and scowling bullies behind. Mr Fitzgerald studied the model. "You know it is against school rules to bring toys to school? They cause jealousy and fights and we have enough problems without that," he said.

Willy was stung by the word 'toy'. "It's not a toy sir. It is a flying model and Mr Conkey asked me to bring it so show during my talk in History today. I am on my way to his staffroom with it."

Mr Fitzgerald nodded. "Alright. But take care. Did you make the model?"

"Yes sir," Willy replied. Blushing with pride and hoping he did not sound too boastful, he described the prizes he had won on the weekend.

Mr Fitzgerald looked impressed. "Very good! Now get going while I have more words to these lads," he said.

Willy did, hurrying on and not looking back. At the bottom of the steps he met John. John studied the model with interest. "Hi Willy! Gee, is that your model that won the competition?" he asked.

"Yes," Willy replied, blushing with a mixture of pride and embarrassment. Wanting to get the model to the staffroom as quickly as he could he continued walking.

John fell into step beside him. "Are you going to fly it? Did you bring a controller and fuel?" he asked.

Willy shook his head. "No, it is just for the History talk to the class," he replied. To change the subject he asked what John was going to give his talk on.

John shrugged and muttered he was going to talk about how horses were important in the early settlement of North Queensland.

Willy smiled. "You should have brought a horse to illustrate your talk," he commented.

John scowled and obviously wasn't amused. "I did bring some stuff," he muttered, his eyes flicking to the model with a look that appeared to Willy to be filled with resentment or jealousy.

The model was safely placed in the staff room and Willy and John went off downstairs to find their friends. The school day then began. During Period 3 Willy gave his talk, hotly aware that Petra was among the audience. Blushing with embarrassment he kept hoping the other class members weren't thinking of him as a little kid. *Particularly the girls!* He wanted them to consider him a mature man.

The talk went well but Willy found it a relief to finish. The model was then placed on the teacher's table and Willy thankfully sat down. As he sat through the next lecturette, on old farmhouses by Fiona, his gaze kept wandering to the model.

It is a good model, he thought.

The end of the period meant the morning break. Willy asked if he could show the model to some friends. Mr Conkey nodded. "Alright, but then bring it along to my staff room," he commented.

Willy turned to John. "Johnno, will you mind my model please while I go and find Graham Kirk please?"

John nodded but did not look happy. "Don't be long. I don't want to miss my lunch."

Willy hurried down stairs and soon found Graham. He and his friends followed Willy back to the classroom where the model was admired. While they were doing this several other students who were passing along the veranda came in to see what the fuss was about. Then Mr Page, the Geography Head of Department, appeared in the doorway.

"What are all you people doing here? You know students aren't supposed to be in rooms during the break," he bellowed.

"Just showing my model to my friends," Willy replied. "Then I have to take it to Mr Conkey's staff room."

"Take it there now and the rest of you get downstairs," Mr Page ordered.

Carefully Willy picked up the model and made his way out of the room. John walked with him while the others all hurried off downstairs. At the staff room John knocked as both of Willy's hands were in use holding the model.

Mr Feldt, the Science teacher, looked at them. "Yes?"

Willy answered. "I have to leave this here for Mr Conkey," he explained.

"Mr Conkey's not here. He is off organising for the Army Cadet parade," Mr Feldt replied. "Now put it on that table inside the door and go downstairs."

Willy did as he was told and then hurried off with John. "I forgot the Army Cadets are doing their Passing-out Parade after lunch," he commented.

"Huh! Army Cadets suck!" John replied with a sneer.

That nettled Willy, who suspected that John meant that all cadets sucked.

"Well I hope it goes really well for them," he answered.

Chapter 34

STUNNED AMAZEMENT

John made no answer to this. The two boys moved downstairs. The school day then ground on, English, Maths A and then German. Willy had no trouble with any of it and was able to chat happily to John when it was safe to do so. He was feeling very good about himself.

I am starting to get good at things, he thought. *Now, if only I can get my love life back on track!*

With that he cast a wistful glance at Petra but she was head down and working hard. When she did look up she gave him a sad little smile. Willy smiled back but was secretly shocked. *She looks awful,* he thought, noting her pale complexion, dark rings under her eyes and generally dejected appearance.

The lunch break came and Willy went out to get his lunch. He expected John to sit with him but as he took his lunch out of his bag he glimpsed John hurrying off. Assuming he was just going to the tuck shop Willy made his way downstairs and sat with his other friends.

An hour later, along with the remainder of the school, and hundreds of parents, Willy made his way down to the oval to watch the Army Cadet's 'Passing-Out' parade. The students moved in class groups. John walked beside him on his left, grumbling. "What a waste of time this is. A thousand students waste an hour and a half watching military morons perform," he said.

Willy wanted to refute this, feeling quite annoyed. All sorts of arguments about nations needing people trained and willing to defend their freedoms and rights and so on flitted across his mind but he held his tongue. Then he forgot about John when he realised that Petra was walking on his other side.

When they arrived at the oval the class was led to the area allocated for them to sit. To Willy's satisfaction this was at the front and just to the right of the VIP area. For seating the teachers and parents had chairs and there were the bench seats which circled most of the oval but even so there were not enough so the remainder had to sit on the grass in front.

Luckily, Willy was able to get a place on the bench seat. John sat down on his right and as he did Petra stepped in front of them.

"I sit here plis?" she asked.

John reacted first. "You can sit here," he said, shoving Vincent further along the seat to make room.

But Petra moved and sat on Willy's other side, squeezing in between him and Stick. Willy was thrilled and turned to give her his full attention

"Sure," he agreed. "But won't Tania dob on you?"

"Dob?"

"Tell your mother," Willy explained.

Petra shook her head. "Tania, she not here today. She... er... she sick."

Willy didn't care what was wrong with Tania. He turned to face Petra and began to devote all his attention to her, being only vaguely conscious of Stick's disapproval.

A hush then fell on the assembled audience as the loudspeaker began to boom. Miss McEwen, now transformed into Lieutenant McEwen, was the narrator. She welcomed them all and then explained the sequence of events. As she did Willy leaned forward to look past Petra so he could study both her and the layout. He saw that a small dais just big enough for one person had been placed in front of the row of chairs for the VIPs. On either side were tables covered with brown cloth. The table furthest away was a gleaming mass of trophies and prizes.

A group of VIPs was now led out to the chairs by Mr Conkey, now Captain Conkey and resplendent in his ceremonial uniform complete with Sam Browne belt and medals. The VIPs included the Principal and Deputy Principal, a naval officer in a most impressive white dress uniform and his own CO, Flight Lieutenant Comstock in his dress blues. Also among the VIPs were the local state and federal members of parliament and the mayor.

Quite a gathering, Willy thought, impressed in spite of himself.

Crisp commands from behind Willy caused him to turn his head to look. A platoon or army cadets with rifles had formed up there and were now ready to march on, led by a CUO with a sword. The CUO was one of the Year 12s. Willy eyed the rifles with more envy than he cared to admit.

I wish we could have rifles on our parade, he thought.

The CUO gave the command 'Guard, by the left, Quick...!' Willy expected him to give the order 'March!' but instead from the sound system came three drum rolls and then the platoon began moving as a march tune began. The platoon passed through a gap in the seats and then wheeled left to halt in front of the dais. After a left turn and dressing their ranks they were stood at ease.

Two cadets wearing white gloves marched out into the space between the dais and the platoon and the furthest one did an about turn so that they were facing each other. *Door openers,* Willy thought, remembering how they had acted at Mareeba. He became absorbed in studying the drill, only half aware that Petra was pressing against his side.

The platoon was suddenly called to attention and everyone looked to the western side of the oval. Curious as to why Willy also looked that way. Into view came an army staff car. It drove slowly across the lawn and came to stop between the two cadets. They now stepped forward and opened the doors and both saluted at the same moment. It looked very smart to Willy and he was both jealous and impressed.

Out of the car stepped an army colonel in his ceremonial uniform with red tabs on his lapels, Sam Browne, sword and medals. Capt Conkey was there to meet him with a salute and handshake and then a salute and bow for the colonel's wife who had emerged from the other side of the car. The pair were ushered to meet the VIPs by Capt Conkey.

While the VIPs exchanged greetings Willy studied the medals on Capt Conkey's shirt. He had known that Capt Conkey had once been in the regular army and that he had been overseas on active service but until now he had not really payed any attention to the details. He had seen Capt Conkey in his cadet uniform back on the school Anzac Ceremony in April but then he had only been a new recruit and had been standing off to one side among a group of air cadets. Now he felt a glow of pride that his teacher had such a proud record.

After the colonel's wife had been shown to her seat the colonel was placed on the dais. The CUO commanding the platoon ordered 'Present arms'. As the cadets in the ranks moved their rifles the CUO saluted with his sword in time with their movements. A bugle tune which Willy recognised as the 'General Salute' was played. The colonel returned the salute and the CUO ordered 'Attention' and then 'Move to the left in threes, left turn'. Willy had expected the colonel to go out and inspect the guard but instead Capt Conkey ushered him to a seat while the guard marched off.

Puzzled by this Willy turned to comment to John but found he had gone. With a shrug Willy turned the other way and leaned past Petra to talk to Stick. "This is different from what we do," he commented.

Stick nodded and they began to chat. As they did Willy became very aware that Petra was pressing against him and turning her head from side to side to watch them in turn. Now hotly conscious of Petra's bare leg pressing against his own Willy began to become aroused.

More shouted commands and movement from behind him caused Willy and the others to turn to look. In the process Petra twisted the other way and her right breast pressed hard against Willy's left arm. That sent his pulses racing and when she put her hand up on his shoulder he became even more aroused.

The audience was then treated to a series of displays. The first explained the organisation of the unit. The company sat in line in platoon groups and Capt Conkey explained what a section was and then what corporals and lance corporals did. Then he had all the corporals stand so the students and parents could see them. The corporals were then seated.

The rank of sergeant was then explained their place in the organisation and their duties. The sergeants were already very obvious because of their scarlet sashes and the sight of them elicited another little niggle of jealousy in Willy.

They look very good, he admitted. *Better than our blue sashes.*

The roles of the Company Sergeant Major and Company Quartermaster Sergeant were next described. During this Willy noted that the CSM was positioned to the right of the right marker of the company.

Our parade warrant officer stands out front as part of the Command Group, he thought.

The Cadet Under-Officers were then introduced and once again Willy vowed that he would one day get to be a CUO.

The whole company then moved to sit in section lines behind their corporals and the CUOs and sergeants moved aside. For the next ten minutes each of the sections in turn put on a short play act to show the types of training activities the army cadets did. The first section showed a drill lesson, the next a navigation lesson. This was followed by one doing First Aid and another doing camping skills and one learning knots. Field cooking, Radio work and fieldcraft were demonstrated and also rifle shooting and observation.

Throughout it all humour was added by the section Barbara was in walking around in a big figure of 8 pretending to be lost navigators. Every time they reached the front of the crowd they stopped and argued about which way to go and which way up the map was.

Petra thought this very funny and clutched at Willy. "Oh Villy, how silly! Zey not know vere dey are," she cried.

Willy smiled but also studied Barbara intently, regretting that she had never shown any interest in him. *And her corporal is the prettiest of all,* he thought as he studied beautiful blonde Gwen Copeland.

The whole cadet unit then moved off. After a few minutes of preparation a platoon group marched back on and made its way to the far end of the oval. To his astonishment Willy saw that all the cadets were carrying brown painted broom sticks, the top 30centimetres of which had been painted silver.

What on earth is this? he wondered.

Once again Capt Conkey began talking on the public address system. "Ladies and gentlemen, you are now going to be treated to a display of 18th Century battlefield manoeuvres. This is how the battles were fought back when Captain Cook was a boy and it is the origin of the movements the army still uses on ceremonial parades," he explained.

That caught Willy's attention. He had been vaguely aware that Capt Conkey had an interest in military history but now his admiration grew as he gave simple and clear explanations of each of the manoeuvres.

For the next ten minutes the army cadets put on a display that Willy found fascinating. The painted broom sticks were now revealed to be imitation 'muskets' with bayonets fixed and the cadets did old-fashioned drill with them.

The platoon marched across the far end of the oval in column of twos and suddenly all turned on the march and advanced towards the audience. "That was good!" Willy commented.

Stick jeered but Willy could tell that he was also secretly impressed. The next manoeuvre was even better. The platoon did a right turn on the march and were then back in column of twos. Then they did a left wheel and marched toward the audience. In the centre of the oval they halted and demonstrated 'forming a platoon'. This placed the platoon in line facing the audience.

At the command of CUO Grant, who was leading, they suddenly did a half turn to the left and did a manoeuvre that Willy recognised from his Drill Team training as a Left Form at the halt. This placed the platoon in line facing the flank.

More orders had the platoon do a right form and they ended up back facing the audience. They then began marching forward until they were about 50 paces away. They then showed how to 'Prepare to repel cavalry'.

As the front rank knelt and placed the butts of their 'muskets' on the ground and the rear rank went to the 'present' spontaneous clapping broke out.

Willy joined in. "That was really good!" he said. By now he was so interested in the display that he was only half aware of Petra. For the first time he got a real appreciation of how poor drill and poor discipline could have led to disaster on the battlefield in the age of the sword and musket.

More commands got the platoon standing up. As they did Willy admired CUO Grant with his polished Sam Browne belt. The CUO's sword shimmered in the afternoon sunlight and he presented the very image of the ideal heroic leader. *I am going to be a CUO,* Willy again vowed.

As the applause died down Capt Conkey went on to explain how attacks were done in the age of the musket. The platoon then demonstrated. At CUO Grant's command all the muskets suddenly went to the 'make ready' and then to the 'Aim'. Willy found himself staring at a platoon who all seemed to be aiming straight at him. There was some fumbling with the cadet's hands and then the cadets went still.

"Fire!" CUO Grant cried, sweeping his sword down as he did.

BLAM! Blat! Pop!

Willy jumped with surprise as a volley of small explosions burst from the 'muskets'. A cloud of smoke formed and began wafting away. "Reload!" shouted CUO Grant.

"Huh! Only 'Party Poppers'," Stick commented with a sneer.

Noddy chuckled from beside him. "Still made you jump though," he teased.

"Made me jump too," Willy agreed. "That was good!"

As the audience all chatted excitedly at the noise the cadets dropped the butts of their 'muskets' to the lawn and pretended to reload them.

Captain Conkey explained. "After firing a volley there would have been a thick cloud off smoke from the gunpowder, so they used to reload under cover of the smoke, then advance through it. Carry on CUO Grant."

CUO Grant glanced to check that the cadets were ready and then gave the command 'Platoon will advance in line of battle. By the right, fifteen paces, quick march'. The platoon started marching towards the audience and again Willy got a glimmering of what all those history books might have been saying. It certainly looked impressive and he even felt a twinge of anxiety as they got closer.

But the platoon all halted after counting the 15 paces and CUO Grant just gave the commands; 'make ready', 'aim' and 'fire'.

Blam!

Smoke billowed then CUO Grant screamed 'Charge!'

Willy stared in amazement as the whole platoon began charging towards the audience, bayonets levelled. Just as he thought they were going to crash into the watching crowd the cadets stopped and put the broom sticks back to their shoulders. The audience burst into enthusiastic applause.

The grinning red face of Stephen appeared just in front of Willy. "Got you then Willy!" he cried. Then he grinned again and added, "But not you, Petra the Perfect. We wouldn't shoot you."

That peeved Willy, and when Petra rewarded Stephen with a smile he was even more annoyed. But instead of responding with an insult, he nodded and said, "That was really good Steve."

"It would want to be. We did enough bloody practice!" Stephen replied.

Without further commands the cadets filed through the gaps in the audience and made their way to the rear. Capt Conkey explained that was the end of the display and that the cadets would now have a drink and then march on for the formal ceremonial parade.

While waiting for the cadets to march back on the audience broke into animated conversation. Petra put her hand on Willy's arm. "Zat vos ver good," she said. "I not like soldiers but zat vos interesting. I see now how Napoleon he do it."

Stick leaned across. "And Wellington. He beat Napoleon at Waterloo remember."

Willy didn't want Stick butting in but sensed he was doing it to annoy him because of Marjorie. Feeling his position threatened he took hold of Petra's hand. To his immense relief she did not try to take it away and instead leaned against him, sending both his hopes and his desires soaring.

After a ten minute break during which the army cadets handed back their broom sticks and were issued their rifles they reformed and were ready to march on. Willy kept looking back to watch how they did things. Jealousy was one of his motives. As a person he wanted everything to go well for the army cadets but as an air cadet he was envious and a little concerned that his own parade might not be as good.

The commands and music began again and the company marched back onto the oval, this time in two divisions with sergeants beside them. The platoons wheeled and halted in line facing the VIPs. The CSM, WO2 Grey, gave them a 'will advance, left turn'.

Our WO(D) would say 'Into line, left turn!' Willy thought.

This time the army cadets were in three ranks and now did an 'open order march' followed by a right dress. This was done with the full ceremony of sergeants dressing each rank in turn from out to the right flank of their platoons with all the shouted 'steadies' and boot stamping drill. The right dress went on for nearly five minutes and Willy could see the weaker cadets in the front rank all leaning to their right as their muscles began to complain at holding their left arms up so long. After his experiences on the Drill Competition he could sympathize with them.

'Eyes Front!' was called and the sergeants then made their way to the front of the divisions. By then two CUOs had lined up along the front of the parade ground with their swords drawn. CUO Madden, another Year 12 boy, stood only a few paces to Willy's left front and he was able to study the details of the sword and Sam Browne belt with the scabbard slung.

WO2 Grey called the company to attention and CUO Grant marched on. Salutes were exchanged and once again Willy jealously admired the process of saluting with a sword. Once again he told himself he would one day be a CUO. CSM Grey then marched off to the right flank of the company, taking post one pace to the right of the right marker.

Once the CSM was in position CUO Grant did an about turn to face the front and then stood the company at ease. But then he called it to attention again.

"That was dumb!" Stick commented. "They were already at attention.

Why did he waste time standing them at ease and then calling them back to attention?"

To Willy's surprise his Chemistry teacher, Mr Feldt, answered from over to the left. "Because he is symbolically demonstrating that he now has the responsibility, that he is in command," he explained.

How does old Mr Feldt know that? Willy wondered. *Was he in the army once?*

On the parade commander's command the two CUOs saluted and then marched forward. As they did the sergeants in front of each division did a right turn and marched off around the right markers to take position at the centre rear. The CUOs halted at the front of the divisions and did an about turn.

Lt McEwen now called on everyone to stand and CUO Grant gave the command 'present arms'. Then he ordered the flag party to march on. Music began and from over the other side of the VIPs a flag party of five cadets marched into view. The front rank was made up of three cadets: a CUO carrying the Australian flag and two sergeants, one either side. Behind the two flag escorts marched two more sergeants.

The flag party did a right turn and marched right across the front of the parade. As the flag party passed the VIPs all the people there in uniform saluted. Willy wished he could salute as the flag passed him but contented himself with standing to attention. As he did, he let go of Petra's hand.

I hope she understands, he thought.

As the flag party crossed his front, Willy studied them very carefully. Having seen an air cadet Banner Party he had been fired with ambition to be part of such a group. Now he watched somewhat enviously as the white gloved hands all swung in unison and the various manoeuvres were executed without any obvious mistakes.

With the flag party in position between the two centre platoons the parade was ordered back to the attention and then stood at ease. The audience were told to sit. As he did Willy fumbled for Petra's hand and to his relief she eagerly took it and then gave him a shy little smile and leaned against him.

At that Willy cast a guilty glance in both directions. *I hope a teacher doesn't notice,* he thought, well aware that physical 'frat' was against the school rules. But with such a crowd he thought he was safe.

Movement among the VIPs caused him to look that way and he saw that Capt Conkey had requested the colonel to stand. The colonel was now ushered onto the low dais. CUO Grant called the parade to attention and ordered 'present arms'. The colonel saluted and a bugle tune was played. CUO Grant returned the parade to the 'at ease' before marching out to halt facing the colonel.

Salutes were exchanged and then the colonel stepped down and began walking towards the company with CUO Grant. Capt Conkey and the Principal both followed them. This was all normal to Willy.

They are going to do the inspection now, he told himself.

Music began playing, a slow march that Willy really liked. The commander of the right hand division was CUO Broughton, another Year 12 boy that Willy admired. He called his division to attention and then saluted the colonel when he arrived. The colonel began slowly inspecting the front rank with CUO Broughton beside him on his right and the others members of the Inspecting Party close behind.

As they made their way slowly along, the colonel stopping to talk to almost every second cadet, Willy searched the ranks for people he knew. First he picked out Peter Bronsky who was in the middle rank and then he noted Graham Kirk standing stiffly and proudly in the front rank.

At that moment a familiar sound reached Willy's ears. It came from behind him and he frowned and then looked around. *That sounds like a model aircraft engine,* he thought.

To his astonishment a model aircraft flew low overhead, so low that most people ducked. As it did Willy's eyes focused on the model. It was a red painted triplane. *That looks like my model of the Red Baron's Fokker DR1,* he thought.

As the triplane model skimmed low over the ranks of army cadets and then swung around and dived back at them Willy stared at it in stunned amazement.

Chapter 35

SHATTERED

As the red painted model triplane skimmed low over the parade and then zoomed up Willy stared at it in a state of bewilderment.

From the way Capt Conkey and those cadets are behaving I don't think this is part of the display, he thought.

The model triplane then came screaming down in a dive so steep Willy felt sure it would drive straight into the ground. A gasp went up from the audience and many of the cadets glanced nervously up. At the last moment the triplane pulled up and then rolled and came racing towards the audience where Willy was sitting.

Willy stared in horror. *It is going to fly straight into us!* he thought.

As an instinctive reaction he began to duck and threw up his arms to shield his face. But the model aircraft put its nose up and just skimmed over the crowd. Another collective gasp went up and all heads turned to follow the flight of the model. It went into a climbing turn and headed back towards the oval.

Stick pointed at it. "That looks like your model, Willy," he cried.

It does, thought a now thoroughly alarmed and bewildered Willy. *But how? Who?* He had not brought a controller to school, nor any fuel. But the odds of anyone else at the school having made a flying model of the Red Baron's triplane were so long as to be most unlikely.

To Willy's annoyance, he heard several people call out: "Willy's plane" and he wanted to refute it. But his attention was still on the model. Its progress was easy to follow as the angry snarl of its engine kept the ears tracking it. It now went into a long dive from the side of the oval.

It will crash into the cadets, he thought, his heart rate shooting even higher with anxiety.

But it didn't. The model triplane zoomed down so low it almost touched the grass and then it roared along between the centre and rear ranks of the cadets. The cadets were now reacting. Some were trying to ignore the interruption and were standing stiffly at attention but with their eyes swivelling to follow the model. Others were gaping at it, their heads turning to follow its course. A few even stepped hastily out of the ranks to avoid being hit.

Willy groaned. "Oh, it is spoiling their parade," he muttered.

Petra clung to his arm and gaped at it. "Villy, vot it do?" she cried.

That was exactly what Willy was wondering. He watched the model climb again and then turn and circle around the area of the parade just above head height. Capt Conkey, the colonel and the principal, who had just passed Graham Kirk, all stopped and watched it.

Then the model triplane came swooping down again, curving in from the left hand end of the company. For a moment Willy thought it might crash into the flag but then it roared past just in front of it. The CUO with the Australian flag jerked it back in alarm as it did. The model dipped to below head height as it raced along the front of the parade.

Capt Conkey cried a warning and grabbed at the colonel, dragging him aside. The principal flung himself to the ground, as did CUO Broughton. A furious looking CUO Grant stood his ground and slashed at the model with his word as it flashed past. The whole front rank of cadets either jumped backwards or threw themselves to the ground, except Graham Kirk who stood rigidly at attention.

Cr... unkle!

The model triplane flew straight into Graham's left side. A wingtip hit and then wings went fluttering in all directions. With an audible splintering sound the now shattered model spun away and crashed to the lawn. The motor stopped with a *bang!* Graham staggered and winced but then glanced at his arm and rubbed it before straightening up again.

Willy stared in horror at the crumpled wreckage on the lawn. *Oh no! I hope that wasn't my model,* he thought. But then he knew it was because more people were calling his name and heads were turning to look at him.

As the obviously shaken principal was helped to his feet by Capt Conkey, and as the whole crowd burst into an excited buzz of conversation, Willy sat there appalled. The parade was in disarray with cadets talking to each other or getting to their feet and dusting themselves down. The whole dignity of the event was gone.

Capt Conkey looked calm but angry. The colonel was looking bewildered and outraged and the principal was obviously shocked. CUO Grant was furious and walked over and slashed at the shattered model with his sword.

Willy's mind raced. *It must be my model,* he decided. *But who was flying it?* From his limited knowledge of flying model aircraft he made a few quick deductions. *Whoever it is must be able to see the oval clearly.*

Aware that many people were looking at him, even pointing at him, Willy stood up and scanned the people sitting around the oval. As he did, he was vaguely aware of the cadets milling around out on the lawn and then of the VIPs all standing. Among them was Mr Fitzgerald and he was looking in Willy's direction. Miss Hackenmeyer was with the deputy and she was pointing at him.

But Willy was more concerned with finding out who had flown the plane. *They must have a good view and be high up,* he decided. There was no way anyone would have been able to have done it from down among the seats he was sure. *And if they had people would be looking at them and teachers would be moving,* he reasoned.

Willy now turned and looked. Behind where most of the school were sitting were a row of basketball courts and tennis courts and a small shed. Beyond them were an entrance road and then the first of a series of large workshops that were part of the technical education section. There were windows in that building but they looked to be all closed and were of frosted glass so did not offer a clear view.

Then movement higher up at the end of the building closest to the swimming pool attracted Willy's eye. There was a second row of windows just under the eaves to allow extra light into the workshops and the movement was at one of them. Willy looked and caught a fleeting glimpse of a face. For a moment the face seemed to stare back at him and then vanished.

That's him! Willy thought.

At that moment, Mr Fitzgerald's very loud voice penetrated Willy's consciousness. "Williams! Come here!" he ordered.

Willy glanced over his shoulder and saw that a very grim looking Mr Fitzgerald was walking towards him. But that was of small concern to Willy. *That person who flew the model is my secret enemy,* he thought.

Ignoring the deputy principal's repeated commands to come to him Willy pushed his way through the people behind him. A few students made half-hearted attempts to stop him but he just brushed them off or thrust them aside and began running.

As he did, he glanced up and again saw the face at the top windows.

A mouth in the face opened and shut and then the face vanished. But not before recognition had burst in Willy's brain.

John!

John is my secret enemy! But? But..?

Willy was so shocked that he faltered in his determination but then a spurt of white-hot anger lanced through him and he gritted his teeth and pushed himself to run faster.

I have to know! he told himself.

From behind him there came loud shouts to stop from Mr Fitzgerald and other teachers, as well as a rising volume of cheering, jeering and comments from the student body. "Run Willy, run!" screamed a voice he thought was Noddy's.

But what was bothering Willy was how he could catch the perpetrator. There were doors at both ends of the workshop and on both sides. The ones facing him were closed and he suspected were locked. For a few moments he considered trying a double bluff by going to the far end but then he just kept running towards the end closest to where he had seen the person (He still did not want to admit to himself that it might be John!).

What was goading Willy to make such a determined effort were not only his shattered illusions about friendship but also the sickening knowledge that his own future might be in jeopardy. *It might not only be my model that is wrecked,* he told himself. *Flight Lieutenant Comstock saw it all so my career in the Air Cadets might be finished too!*

What puzzled Willy as he ran was how the person had been up at that window. From his memory of the building from doing Manual Arts lessons it was just a big shed with no second floor. *He must have climbed up? Or maybe there is a landing or ladder or something?* he thought.

There were more loud and angry shouts from behind him but Willy did not even glance back. *I have to know!* he told himself. So he ran on. By then he was gasping for breath as he was not very athletic.

He reached the corner of the building and dashed around it and then came to a skidding standstill at the end door. It was slightly ajar so he wrenched it open and hurried inside. But the transition from the bright sunlight to the relatively darkened interior caused him to stop while his eyes adjusted. Blinking and gasping for breath he looked around, absolutely determined to grapple with the person so he could learn the truth.

There was a person striding towards him from one of the offices at the far end of the building but Willy saw he was one of the Manual Arts teachers. The teacher wore a grey work apron and was hurrying between the rows of work benches. As he did, he called angrily: "What are you doing here? What was that crash?"

For a moment Willy thought he meant the crash of his model aircraft, but then he saw that the teacher was frowning and looking over towards the side wall. Willy glanced that way and his heart skipped a beat. A person was lying on the concrete floor amid a litter of tools, wiring and other objects.

The teacher saw the person at the same moment and turned towards him. Willy felt his heart leap into his throat with anxiety. *John has fallen and hurt himself,* he thought. Apprehension instantly replaced anger and he also started hurrying across to him. As he did the guilty thought crossed his mind that John might have lost his grip while climbing down. *Hurrying to get away from me!*

It was John and he lay on his back in a crumpled heap. *He's not moving,* Willy noted. *Oh no! I hope he isn't dead.* That was an appalling thought and Willy felt nauseas from dread.

The teacher, Mr Duncan Willy remembered, obviously had the same concern as he knelt and felt for John's pulse. Then he looked up at Willy. "What the devil is going on? Who are you and what are you doing here?"

"Looking for him," Willy answered, gulping and gasping and feeling faint. "Is he alive sir?"

Mr Duncan nodded and got to his feet then frowned. "Never mind that. This boy needs an ambulance and fast. I will phone for one. Wait here," he said. With that he hurried off along the aisle towards his office.

Willy stood and shook his head and stared down at John. He wanted to help but did not dare touch him or move him in case he had a neck or spine injury. John lay very still. His face had gone very pale and he did not appear to be breathing.

A creaking noise and the sound of a small object falling down the wall made Willy look up. He saw that a large set of wooden shelves was bolted to the wall and that a bolt or screw had just fallen from them.

John must have been standing on top of the shelves and when he tried to climb down he slipped and fell, Willy deduced.

Then John groaned and Willy felt a gush of relief. He glanced down at him and saw that he was lying on some tools and small boxes of screws or bolts.

That must be uncomfortable, Willy thought. To try to ease John's pain he knelt and gently moved several screws away from under his outflung arm. There were more bolts, screws and nails scattered on the concrete floor so he brushed them to one side. As he did his eyes took in the model aircraft controller lying near John's hand.

A model aircraft controller. So it was him! Willy thought. He reached down and picked up the controller. *It looks like mine,* he thought. Turning it over he scanned it for his name. But it wasn't his. In black felt pen was printed JOHN RHUDDOCK.

Willy stared at the name in shock and then glanced at his unconscious friend and shook his head. *So he did do it. But why?* he wondered.

At that moment, three male teachers came hurrying through the doorway: Mr Elms the PE Teacher, Mr Page the Geography Master and Mr Ritter, his Maths B teacher. Mr Elms glanced around. "What's going on Williams? What have you done?"

By then Willy had straightened up and he gestured to John. "He fell sir," he began.

"Fell? Or did you knock him down?" Mr Elms snapped, his face darkening with suspicion.

"No sir!" Willy gasped. "He was lying here when I got here."

But then he realised he was standing there with the model aircraft controller in his hand. *They will think I did it and was trying to get rid of the proof.* Then his mind made another deduction and his heart gave a sickening lurch. *And like a fool I have picked the controller up and now it has my fingerprints on it!*

"What's wrong with him?" Mr Elms queried, stepping forward and brushing Willy aside. He knelt to check John's breathing and pulse and the other two teachers, both of whom were big fit men, stood close to Willy.

Willy was really shaken and felt ill. "He fell and got knocked out," he answered, pointing to the shelves as he did.

"Or did you hit him?" Mr Page asked.

Willy shook his head. "No sir. He was lying on the floor when I got here. Mr Duncan was here too. He saw it. He has gone to phone for an ambulance.

Mr Page pointed to the controller in Willy's hands. "What's that thing?"

"A model aircraft radio controller sir," Willy replied, his spirits sinking as he did. "John had it," he added.

"No need to implicate your mate," Mr Ritter growled. "He can do his explaining for himself."

"If he lives," Mr Elms commented.

That made Willy feel even worse. At that moment Mr Fitzgerald came panting into the workshop and dozens of students crowded the doorway behind him. "What's going on? What's happened? You caught him then?" he asked.

Mr Page gestured to John. "Rhuddock here is hurt and Williams was standing over him holding this radio control device," he said.

Willy was aghast. "But sir! It wasn't like that."

"Be silent boy! Speak when you are spoken to," a livid Mr Fitzgerald snapped. "Now Mr Page, what happened?"

Again Mr Page explained what he had seen. Then Mr Fitzgerald turned to Willy. "So what is your version Williams?"

Willy felt queasy. He gestured to the prostrate John and then he choked up and tears filled his eyes. "You saw sir!" he sobbed. Shame engulfed him as the tears began to trickle down his cheeks. He wanted to turn away from all the faces peering in and did not want the teachers to witness his humiliation either.

For a few moments he was so choked up he could not speak. Mr Fitzgerald glanced over his shoulder and his face clouded with anger at the sight of the gawking spectators crowding in the doorway. "Mr Ritter, send those people back to the oval please," he instructed.

Mr Ritter quickly did, he being one of the teachers the students actually respected and obeyed. By then Willy had regained some self-control. Between sniffles and sobs he began again. "You. (sniff) saw sir. I was down (sob) down on the oval and then my (sniffle)..my model plane flew around and (sob) crashed – crashed into the .. the cadets (sniffle). Then I saw a person's face up at that window and I ran here to see who it was."

Mr Fitzgerald frowned and glanced up at the row of top windows then back at Willy. "So it was your model plane that wrecked the Army Cadet's parade?"

"Yes sir (sniffle)," sobbed Willy. "I think so."

"So how did it get here?"

Willy shook his head and wiped both his eyes and his nose. He had been wondering the same thing. "I suppose John took it from the staff room sir."

"And you are telling me that he was the one who used that radio control device to fly it?" Mr Fitzgerald asked.

"Yes sir," Willy answered, holding up the controller as he did.

"Is this yours?"

"No sir. It's John's. It's got his name on it," Willy replied, holding it so the teachers could read the name.

"So why would he do something like that? He's your friend isn't he?"

"Yes he is sir," Willy replied, before he realised what he was saying. *Is John really my friend or is he actually my secret enemy,* he wondered.

Mr Fitzgerald frowned. "So why?"

"I don't know sir," Willy replied miserably.

Mr Fitzgerald shook his head. "Well, you are in big trouble now so you had better be telling the truth," he said.

"Yes sir," Willy muttered. As the full realization that John must have planned the whole thing and then carried it out struck Willy he felt his emotions churn.

Has John been deceiving me about our friendship? he thought. Willy suddenly felt as though his whole mental framework of good and bad was shattered. Tears began again, quite uncontrollably this time.

But why?

Chapter 36

THE TRUTH

The next couple of hours were among the most miserable of Willy's young life. A very grim-faced Mr Fitzgerald pointed to the doorway. "To the office! Make sure he gets there please Mr Ritter," he ordered.

Escorted by Mr Ritter Willy was ushered outside. As he walked out into the sunlight the sound of military music attracted his attention and he turned his head to look. To his satisfaction the army cadets had resumed their parade. *Good!* he told himself. But inside he was churning with apprehension over what might happen to him next.

At that moment the ambulance arrived and Mr Page met the paramedics at the door and led them inside. Willy was led away to the office. Sick at heart he sat on the seat outside the main office and waited.

I hope John doesn't die, he thought. *But why did he do it? And did he do all those other things to me?*

His mother arrived first, all concern. "Willy, what has happened?" she asked.

Willy opened his mouth to answer but couldn't. Instead he burst into tears. Mortified at such weakness in front of the office staff he tried to turn away and hide his shame. His mother didn't help by hugging him. But he could not bring himself to tell her to stop it.

The other kids will tease me for being a little sook if they see, he fretted.

At last his sobbing subsided and he was able to give his mother a more or less coherent account of the incident. He was almost finished when his father arrived.

"What have you done this time William?" he asked.

Willy was hurt by the assumption that he had done something wrong. "Nothing!" he snapped back. But then the tears began again and Willy felt even more embarrassed and ashamed. Crying in front of his mother was one thing but not in front of his dad!

With an effort he managed to ease the flow of tears. But his chest was still heaving and tears were still trickling down his cheeks when he was even more upset by the arrival at the principal's office of the principal and some of the other VIPs who had been invited to the parade. Among them was Flight Lieutenant Comstock and he gave Willy a very searching and hard look.

Willy desperately wanted to call out that he hadn't done anything and it wasn't his fault but he managed to restrain himself. *I hope he believes me when the truth comes out,* Willy thought. But the incident distressed and depressed him even more.

His father raised his eyebrows. "So what happened? All the school would tell me was that you had been involved in an incident and that another boy was seriously injured and has been taken to hospital."

Willy was appalled at the distortion. "It was nothing like that, Dad! John used my model plane to buzz the Army Cadet's Passing-Out Parade and then he fell and got hurt," he explained.

His father was shocked. "Used your model plane to *buzz* the Army Cadet's parade! Did you tell him to do it? What was your part in this?"

Willy was even more hurt by his father's doubts but had to admit that some of his exploits over the past year had not helped his reputation. Vigorously shaking his head he said: "No Dad! I had nothing to do with it. John took my plane without permission and then used it to strafe the parade. He was trying to get away when he slipped and fell."

Saying that made him feel guilty, wondering if John had slipped in his haste to get away from him. Then he shrugged and went on: "He had his own radio controller and I was down at the oval with my class just sitting watching when the model flew over the parade." He went on to describe the subsequent debacle and then how he had seen John at the window and had run to try to catch him.

His father listened and then shook his head. "I'll bet the army cadets aren't impressed," he commented.

That made Willy feel even worse. *The army cadets will hate me now,* he thought. He was feeling thoroughly miserable and worn out by the time Mr Fitzgerald arrived along with Mr Duncan. Mr Fitzgerald was carrying the wreckage of Willy's triplane model and seeing the splintered and broken pieces upset him so much he almost burst into tears again. *All that work wasted,* he thought bitterly.

The VIP guests had been taken into the principal's office for afternoon refreshments and Mr Fitzgerald went in and said a few words to the principal and then came over to the unhappy group. "Thank you for coming Mr and Mrs Williams. I wish we were meeting under more social conditions," he said.

"So do we!" Willy's father replied grimly, making Willy feel even worse.

Mr Fitzgerald held up the wrecked model. "Is this yours, William?"

Willy stared at the mangled wreckage. It was almost a ball of broken pieces. Splintered balsa protruded from torn red tissue paper. The propeller dangled from a grass and dirt encrusted motor. Only the back half of the fuselage and the tail were recognizable. Once again tears prickled but he blinked and controlled them.

"Yes sir," he croaked.

Mr Fitzgerald shook his head. "Alright, let's get to the bottom of this," he said. "We will use the conference room."

Mr Fitzgerald led the way into a nearby room with a long table in it. The smashed triplane model was placed in the centre of the table and everyone seated themselves and the door was closed. Mr Fitzgerald then said, "We will start with Mr Duncan first so he can go about his duties if you don't mind."

Willy's parents agreed and Mr Duncan then related what he had seen. Mr Fitzgerald took notes while he did and then asked a couple of questions. To Willy's immense relief Mr Duncan made it clear that Willy had come into the workshop after he had and that he was nowhere near John when he fell.

Mr Duncan left the room and then Willy was asked to give his version of events. As he did the principal came into the room. As the door opened and closed Willy glanced out and saw that school had been dismissed and that both Stick and Noddy were sitting outside. That cheered him slightly.

After Willy had been questioned he was told to write out his version of events and was then escorted to another room. As he went from one room to the other Willy looked hopefully at Stick and Noddy and Stick gave him a thumbs-up and a heartening nod. Mr Ritter then led Stick in for questioning.

Stick will tell the truth, Willy thought, feeling much more hopeful.

He did. The investigation went on for another hour and by then Willy was feeling quite drained. Having written out his version of the incident he sat with his parents outside the principal's office while the principal and Mr Fitzgerald conferred. They were all then called into the principal's office.

The principal looked sternly at Willy. "Well, it seems that all the witnesses corroborate your version of events William," he said.

Willy felt his chest ease and he took a few deep breaths. The principal continued: "It seems it was all done by another boy but until he can give his version we cannot complete the investigation."

At that Willy felt his chest and stomach tighten up again as dread clutched at them. "Sir, is John alright? Is he going to die?"

"I don't know. We have not been told. I will call the hospital and find out. If you'd like to wait?"

The principal phoned the hospital and by his nods and facial expressions Willy could tell that John was still alive. This was confirmed. The principal looked grave and added, "He is still unconscious and he possibly has a serious head injury. They do not think he will die but he may have brain damage."

That was a horrible thought to Willy and he felt ill and guilty at the same time. *If I hadn't gone to catch him maybe he wouldn't have slipped,* he told himself.

The principal went on: "He has also broken his wrist and fractured his lower arm and there are some bruising and contusions so he may not be back at school for some time. We will interview him when it is appropriate and until then we will suspend judgement and give Willy the benefit of the doubt. I have always found him to be a truthful boy, even if he does seem to get involved in some... er... er... in some unusual happenings, and as I said the witness statements all support his version."

Willy's father nodded. "Thank you sir."

Willy went to speak and then choked up. All he could do was nod and then battle to hold back the tears again. In this he was successful and he was able to get out of the room and away from his parents before the misery engulfed him.

His father picked up the smashed model and followed him out. "I will take this home in the car," he said. "Do want to get your bike and put it in the back as well and come home with me?"

Willy could only blink back the tears and nod then shake his head before hurrying off. To his relief his father did not call him back and a glance over his shoulder showed his parents going out the front entrance.

Willy made his way to the classroom to collect his bag and then sat in a corner and howled.

Only when a cleaner appeared at the other end of the veranda did he pull himself together and take himself downstairs. Luckily the school was almost deserted by then so he was able to recover his dignity as he walked to the bike racks. As he got closer he saw that his was the only bike still in the racks.

As he approached his bike the awful thought crossed his mind that it might have been sabotaged again. To his relief it hadn't been but for a few minutes he stood and looked at it, his thoughts churning with doubt. *Did John do all those things to my bike? And if he did, why?*

Once at home there was more embarrassment and unhappiness. Big brother Lloyd of course had been a witness to the whole event on the oval. "Well done, little brother!" he cried as Willy came up the back stairs. "The Army Cadets won't forget that parade in a hurry!"

Willy gave him a sour look. "I didn't do it," he retorted.

"Everyone said you did," Lloyd replied. "They said that you and Rhuddock ran away and tried to hide the evidence and that Rhuddock slipped and fell while he was trying to hide the controller."

Willy was appalled at this distortion of the story. "That's not true at all!" he cried. "I didn't have a controller and John wasn't with me. I knew nothing about it until the plane appeared."

Lloyd laughed. "And didn't it appear! I reckon those army cadets all crapped themselves when it zoomed down on them and then flew in among their lines."

"Ranks," Willy corrected angrily.

"Whatever!" Lloyd sneered. "And didn't the old colonel look funny when it flew straight at him! I nearly wet meself laughing."

At that Willy's mother interjected from the kitchen. "Stop teasing Willy Lloyd. And don't spread rumours."

Willy gave Lloyd a baleful glare and went off to his room, just in time to hide the tears as misery engulfed him again.

It did so after tea as well. His father commented that he had put the model on the workbench downstairs. Images of the crumpled, splintered wreck caused Willy to choke up with bitter anger. "You can just throw it in the bin!" he cried.

But his father shook his head. "It was a really good model and you weren't responsible. Besides, even if you can't fix it there are a lot expensive parts that can be salvaged and used in other models," he said.

Willy wanted to retort that he would never make another model aircraft as long as he lived but held his tongue. He spent the remainder of the evening in his room, brooding over how his life had turned out and dreading going to school the next day.

He had a terrible night with little sleep. For hours he tossed and turned worrying about John and puzzling over whether he was really his secret enemy. Willy was even tempted to get up and phone the hospital to ask if John was alright but, from overheard conversations of his parents he doubted if he would be told. Sleep, when it came, was restless and punctuated by nightmares of an aircraft he was flying ending up so low it got caught in among high buildings and then, when he tried to land, among the powerlines.

The next morning he tried to summon the courage to ask to be allowed to stay home. But his pride and speculation of what his parents would say got in the way. *Mum and Dad will just think that is cowardly,* he told himself after breakfast, at which he ate almost nothing. *I have to face the music sooner or later so I may as well get it over.*

The ordeal was made worse by the knowledge that he had History with Mr Conkey first period. Sick at heart, he made himself pedal to school.

And it started even as he wheeled his bike in the gate. Willy saw heads turn and then heard words like, 'Willy willy', 'rocket', 'mad' and 'cadets'. There was a lot of sniggering and as he walked towards his part of the school after chaining his bike into the rack voices called, "Williams, ya jerk!" and "Give it to 'em Willy."

Larsen and Carstairs both jeered and laughed as he went past. Larsen shouted: "Stick it up 'em Rocket Man!"

Willy ignored them, but he felt embarrassed and upset. But he couldn't ignore his friends. Noddy shouted out as soon as he saw him. "Here's Willy! Hey Willy, that showed those bloody army cadets who's best."

Already feeling bad about having ruined the army cadet's parade Willy glared back and made no reply. Stick then joined in. "Just as well your plane wasn't rocket propelled Willy. It would have knocked Kirk arse over if it had been."

"How is he?" Willy asked, holding in his temper with an effort.

Stick shrugged. "Dunno. There he is there with Stephen," he replied, gesturing to a group further along under the building.

Willy looked and saw Graham Kirk with Stephen and his other friends Peter and Roger. For a few seconds Willy hesitated then he shook his head. *Don't be a coward. Go and say it now,* he told himself.

Excusing himself, he continued walking towards where the other group were seated. As he got closer his eyes met Stephen's and Stephen nudged Graham and nodded towards him. Graham lifted his head and looked and his face went all stony. Inside Willy quailed but he forced himself to keep walking.

Stopping a couple of paces from a now grim-faced and standing Graham, Willy swallowed and nerved himself to speak. "Sorry," he said. "I didn't know that my model was going to be used to spoil your parade."

For a few moments Graham glared at him and Willy thought he might strike at him. But then Graham's face eased and a rueful grin spread across it. "That's OK. We heard it wasn't your fault. Capt Conkey told us. Anyway, it made it a parade to remember," he replied.

Willy could only nod. He began to tremble as the tension flowed through him. He also noted that some of the other army cadets did not look so forgiving. "Did you get hurt?" he asked.

Graham shrugged. "A few bruises."

Stephen laughed. "Which is more than you can say for your model plane, Willy. It looked a complete write-off."

"It is," Willy replied.

As images of the shattered wreck flooded his mind his emotions welled up and he felt tears begin to prickle in his eyes. Nodding he continued on his way, not wanting to go back to his friends. *I wonder if Petra is alone?* he thought.

She wasn't. She was sitting beside Tania. Willy silently cursed and went to the library to be out of everyone's way. But that was impossible and everywhere he went people made comments or teased him. With dismay he realised that he was now something of a notorious celebrity.

Then the bell went and another meeting he was dreading was upon him: that with Capt Conkey. As usual the class lined up at the door with their books and waited for the teacher. When Capt Conkey appeared he told the class to move in and then stopped Willy and fixed him with a hard stare.

Willy faltered and stopped. "Sorry sir," he croaked, desperately hoping he wouldn't burst into tears in front of his class mates.

Capt Conkey shook his head and gave a rueful smile. "I did tell you that it was the Australians that shot down the Red Baron," he said. "And now we have brought his plane down again."

Willy didn't know if Capt Conkey was making a joke or if this was just the precursor to a real blast. All he could do was nod and then repeat that he was sorry. Capt Conkey then gave a wry smile. "I know it wasn't your fault. I have spoken to the principal. I gather that John was the instigator of the outrage."

"Yes sir," Willy replied. "Sir, is John alright?"

"I don't know," Capt Conkey replied. "I will find out and let you know in Geography. Now move in and get to work."

Feeling much better Willy did. In the period after morning break Capt Conkey informed Willy that John was alive but in a coma. That sounded awful to Willy and he became quite dejected.

And the teasing continued during the lunch break. Two Year 10s: Zeigler and Carmody, who were also army cadets, glared angrily at him. "You wait Red Baron!" shouted Zeigler.

"That's right," Carmody added. "You mucked up our parade. Maybe we will muck up yours."

Another Year 10 boy whose name Willy did not know grinned and nodded. "You should drive a tank through the Air Cadets parade."

Willy tried to ignore them but they kept calling out as he walked past. Zeigler laughed and said: "We might. One of those remote controlled model tanks. That would be fair."

"With a cannon that shoots caps," Carmody suggested.

"Nah! One that shoots darts and you could drive it up behind Williams and hit him in the arse with a dart," the other boy suggested. They all laughed and Willy blushed and shook his head but did not reply.

Another boy shook his head and called, "Nah, not with darts. Get one of those paint ball guns and it can shoot that."

"Or a 'gel blaster' gun," suggested another.

The images appalled Willy and made him feel even worse.

Five minutes later Branch stopped him and laughed. "That showed the Army Cadets who's best!" he said.

"Made them pretty angry," Wellington added.

Willy could only nod. Once again the possible effects on his Air Cadet career sprang to the front of his concerns.

But while he was brooding about this another incident quite pushed those thoughts out of his head. As he walked past the end of the workshop where the incident had taken place he saw Petra. She was looking miserable and Tania was pulling at her sleeve. With obvious reluctance Petra turned and went with Tania. Willy watched from a discrete distance and was surprised to see the two girls leave the school.

Where are they going? The bell for classes is about to go.

The two girls walked across the street and vanished around the corner of the next block. Intrigued and more than a little concerned, Willy looked quickly around to check if any teachers were in the area and then hurried through the gate himself. As soon as he was on the footpath he broke into a run and sprinted after them.

But when he arrived at the corner of the next block there was no sign of the two girls. *Where have they gone?* Willy thought. Puzzled he looked both ways along the street but they were nowhere to be seen. For a minute or so he stood there feeling anxious but then shrugged and made his way back to school.

But as he crossed the street towards the gate he saw Mr Ritter waiting just inside it. "Where have you been Williams?" the teacher demanded to know.

All Willy could do was shake his head and say, "Just up the street sir." There was no way he was going to say anything that might get Petra into trouble.

"You know it is against school rules to leave the grounds without permission?"

"Yes sir."

"Do you have a note?"

"No sir."

"Then it is the office for you."

Willy silently cursed to himself but took the note Mr Ritter wrote and reluctantly made his way up to the office. Mr Fitzgerald was already busy with some Year 10s who had been fighting and when he saw Willy and read the note he was incredulous.

"What's this? Are you on a self-destruct mission or something, Williams?"

"No sir," Willy mumbled.

"So what were you doing?"

"Just went for a walk, sir," Willy replied.

"I don't believe you."

"I just went for a walk, sir," Willy replied stubbornly.

"Well, you can just have a detention tomorrow at lunch time," Mr Fitzgerald answered. He made a note in his book and sent Willy on his way.

During the afternoon classes Willy did his school work but he was miserable and depressed. *Where do Petra and Tania go?* he worried. Remembering some of the names others had called Petra caused some dark thoughts to niggle suspiciously in his brain but he resolutely thrust them aside. *Petra's not like that,* he told himself.

When he got home Willy took himself to his room and wept. Then he lay and brooded on life and fate and his future. His parents came home and said hello and he pretended everything was normal. *They don't know about the detention,* he thought, deciding not to tell them.

At ten to six the telephone rang. Willy heard his mother answer it and then, in a surprised voice say, "Oh, alright. We will come."

Her footstep sounded in the hallway and she put her head around his door. "You friend John has regained consciousness and he wants to see you," she said.

Relief and anxiety both surged in Willy. "Oh good!" he said.

Maybe now I will learn the truth.

Chapter 37

CONFESSION

After dinner Willy's parents drove a very anxious Willy to the hospital. He was dreading the meeting but equally was consumed by the desire to know why John had done what he had. Feeling distinctly nervous Willy walked along the hospital corridors with his parents.

Waiting in a private room were John and his parents. John lay there with the whole top of his head bandaged and plaster on his left arm. He looked miserable. When he saw Willy his face crumpled even more but he tried to smile and nodded a greeting. The parents exchanged civil greetings but it was obvious that John's mother and father were not happy.

"John won't tell us what happened," his mother explained. "But it is obviously something he wants to get off his chest."

Willy moved forward, unsure what to say or how he felt. Emotions warred in him from concern about John to resentment and anger at being deceived and hurt. Finally, as he stood beside the bed, he nodded and licked his lips.

"How's the head?" he asked, hoping to ease into it.

But John shook his head irritably. "Fine! But that's not why I asked to see you. I owe you an apology," he muttered.

"That's alright," Willy replied. Despite everything he felt distinctly sorry for John.

"No it's not! I got you into trouble," John exclaimed.

Willy could only shrug. "Not much. What happened? Did you go and get my model?" he asked.

John nodded and looked even more miserable. A tear formed and trickled down his right cheek. "Yes. I went home at lunch time and got my controller and some fuel then took your plane from the staffroom," he explained.

Willy nodded. "I guessed that. But why?"

John looked even more miserable. "Because... because I wanted to hurt you!" he cried. Then he did cry, big tears streaming down both cheeks.

Willy felt very uncomfortable and embarrassed and John's mother suggested they leave but John shook his head vigorously. "No! I have to explain," he almost shouted.

"Explain what?" Willy asked.

"It was me! I did all those things! I put the pins on your seat and threw the paper planes and did all those things to your bike," he cried. Then he began to blubber so much his chest heaved.

Willy shook his head in puzzlement. "But... but you mean even things like my model plane in Townsville?' he asked.

John wiped his tears and nodded. "Yes! That was easy. I just tampered with your controller and then set my own on the frequencies you had chosen and took the plane off and flew it away," he explained.

"But... but why?" Willy cried. "I thought you were my friend. What did I do to make you want to do that?"

John glanced at his parents and then back at Willy. His face twisted to display real anguish and he went bright red. "Because I love Petra!" he cried.

Willy was stunned. "Petra!" he gasped. "But... but you never said."

"I was too... too shy," John answered. Then he sobbed some more and between sniffles continued. "I love her (sniffle) but she doesn't even (sob)... even know I exist! And you... you just (sniffle) walk up and chat her up and then she sits next to you. And you don't appreciate her. You flirt with all those other girls and do things to them. It is so... so disgusting and unfair!" he shouted.

Willy blushed bright red as images of naked Marjorie flooded his mind. Out of the corner of his eye he saw his mother give him a sharp glance. His father nodded and tried to look serious.

Willy swallowed. "They don't mean anything. They are just being friendly," he replied.

"Well, Petra means something to me, even if she isn't important to you!" John snapped. His face changed to anger and he scowled at Willy.

Willy's mind race and his emotions went into turmoil. *Do I love Petra?* he thought. *Or is it just a crush because she is so pretty?* With a shock he realised he was not really in love at all and that his relationship with Petra was only based on her being such an ideal girl. *I actually relate to people like Marjorie more,* he decided.

The other problem was whether he and John were now to be enemies or not. But that was too hard. Willy shook his head to try to clear his thoughts. As he did John burst into tears again and turned his head away. John's mother now stepped forward. "I think that is enough. I think you should go," she said.

Willy could only nod. He was now feeling so confused and emotional that he was choking up as well. *John, my secret enemy,* he thought. *And all because of jealousy over Petra!*

"See you then," he mumbled. Hot with embarrassment and anxiety Willy turned and hurried from the room, followed by his parents.

As they made their way back along the corridor his mother came up beside him. "What's this about doing things to girls?' she queried.

"Oh Mum! We were just... just playing," he replied, flaming again with shame.

"It had better be!" his mother snapped.

Willy's father now spoke. "I will take this situation in hand I think mother," he said firmly.

His mother looked doubtful but agreed. Willy cast a grateful glance at his father. *Good old dad,* he thought. It dawned on him that his father was not really angry at him. *I think dad is rather proud of me,* he decided.

They made their way home and Willy then excused himself and made his way to his room. He was feeling quite emotionally drained and was also extremely puzzled. Now all of the little disasters and problems of the last few months made sense and he could fit together how John had managed to do things while appearing as though he was not there or as a friend. Willy was left with a sneaking sense of admiration for John's cunning even while he smarted at the hurts to his pride and pocket.

Poor bastard! he thought, *And all the while burning up over Petra!*

It was more trying to decide how he felt about his relationship with John than over what he felt about Petra that kept him awake until far into the night. Each time he remembered one of the hurtful incidents, Willy felt little stabs of anger and injured pride at being so easily fooled. But he also felt sorry for John and wondered how to treat him next time they met.

There was also resentment at being falsely accused of things and of people not believing his version. This was brought home to him at school the next day when Arthur Blake teased him for spoiling the Army Cadet's parade.

"You did a bloody good job at making them scatter, Willy. It certainly upset their drill," he commented.

Luke Karaku snorted. "Huh! Their drill ain't all that flash anyway," he commented.

Andrew Collins made a face. "That mob from Atherton beat us remember."

"Yeah well, but not this mob," Luke agreed.

Noddy, who had been listening to this laughed. "You should have put little rockets under the wings, Willy. You could have really blasted them off the oval then," he suggested.

"I didn't do any of it!" Willy retorted hotly.

"It was your plane," Noddy pointed out.

Willy opened his mouth to explain that John had done it but then shut his mouth and shook his head.

Blake looked at him hard. "You'd better not do anything to muck our parade up," he retorted.

"I won't!" Willy snapped.

Stick now spoke. "When's that?" he asked.

"In a couple of weeks' time," Andrew answered. "On Saturday the twentieth, in the afternoon."

"Can we come and watch?" Willy asked, genuinely interested.

Andrew looked at him hard. "I suppose so, but don't spoil it for us."

Stephen had been listening and now leaned forward. "When's your passing-out parade Willy?" he asked.

"Next Saturday afternoon, in a week's time," he answered.

Stephen nodded and grinned. "We have been invited. We will see you then."

The look on Stephen's face sent a shiver of apprehension through Willy. *Are Steve and his mates planning revenge,* he thought. He became distinctly anxious at the notion that the army cadets might be planning something to upset his own parade.

But all concerns about cadets were swept aside when he encountered Petra outside the classroom at the start of the next lesson. She was standing with her back to the class while she dug in her bag and her shoulders were heaving.

She looks like she is crying, Willy thought.

He made his way over to her and said quietly. "Petra, are you alright?"

Petra did not turn but nodded. "Yes. I alright," she replied.

But the sniffles told another story. She was crying. Then Willy glimpsed her face and he was shocked. She had red eyes rimmed with dark shadows and she looked pale and haggard. She was trembling and obviously upset.

"What's wrong, Petra? Can I help?" he asked.

"I alright! (sniffle) Liv me plis," she replied, wiping her nose and then her eyes.

"But..."

"Go avay, plis! I alright!" Petra snapped. Then she began to cry again.

Embarrassed but very anxious Willy retreated. He itched to help her but equally did not know what to do and did not want to annoy her further. So he shrugged and made his way into the room and sat down. When she came in she did not look at him but he certainly studied her. And what he saw shocked him more. *She is really thin,* he noted. *She has lost a lot of weight. Something really serious must be wrong.* The word 'gaunt' flitted across his mind.

All he could do was worry. *If she won't let me help there isn't much I can do,* he decided.

But that didn't make him feel any better and he sat there puzzling over how to help and what to do about John. Luckily the school work was easy and he could just do most of it mechanically.

At lunch time he was again teased about his model aircraft. He gave up trying to explain that it had not been his doing. In fact he began to enjoy his newfound fame, until he passed a group of male students he knew were all army cadets. They glowered at him and muttered threats.

"You'll get yours!" growled 'Pigsy' Pyne, a thug of a Year 9 with a reputation for bullying.

The veiled threat reawakened Willy's fears that the army cadets might do something to spoil his parade. And that reminded him of another ordeal to come. It was Friday and that meant Air Cadets that evening.

I hope I'm not in trouble, he fretted.

He became so anxious about what might happen to his Air Cadet career that he became nauseous during the last period. By the time he got his bike from the racks he was almost hyperventilating with nervousness.

Oh! I hope I am not in trouble, he told himself.

He was even tempted not to go to cadets but then scorned himself for even thinking it. *Running away won't solve things,* he told himself. *Face up to it and get it over.*

So he did. At home he took special care to prepare his uniform, polishing his boots obsessively in an attempt to get a glass-like shine. But he was so anxious he felt ill. He did not want any dinner but his mother insisted he eat. Not wanting her or Lloyd to think he was scared or worried he hid his feelings and did so. And it helped. By the time he had to get in the car he was feeling calmer.

But the nervousness continued to afflict him as his mother drove him to cadets. It took him a real effort of willpower to talk to her without betraying his state of anxiety.

On arrival, Willy got out of the car and stood in the darkness on the side of the car park after his mother had driven off. He could see other cadets over at the depot and it all looked quite normal. Taking a deep breath to calm his nerves he walked across to the building and stepped inside.

Almost at once Willy sensed the atmosphere change. People who normally ignored him turned to look and he noted a lot of whispering. *They are talking about me,* Willy decided. That caused him to burn with self-conscious embarrassment and he remembered something he had read to the effect that if people were talking about you, you could be sure it would not all be good.

It wasn't. A few senior NCOs from 1 Flight cast him baleful looks and shook their heads and then Branch stopped him. "I hope your antics at school don't cause us any grief," he said.

"But I didn't do anything," Willy protested.

"It was your model plane."

Willy was stung by the injustice. "But I didn't fly it and I didn't give J... er... er... anyone permission to use it," he replied hotly.

"Huh, that's your story," Branch retorted. "So let's hope there are no pay backs."

"Why should there be?" Willy asked. But he knew

Branch confirmed his worries. "If the army cadets do anything to get their own back by wrecking our parade you will be sorry," Branch growled.

"Yes sergeant," was all Willy could reply. But inside he felt sick and wondered what he could do to make sure nothing did happen.

Then what he had been expecting and dreading happened. CDTWOFF Mathieson beckoned him over. "The CO wants to see you Cadet Williams. Stand to attention. Head up! Shoulders back! Get those thumbs in line with the seams of your trousers. Cadet Williams, quick march!"

Willy was marched into the CO's office. A serious looking Flight Lieutenant Comstock sat behind his desk with his cap on. Behind him, one on each side, stood Flying Officer Turnbull and Warrant Officer Colley.

After CDTWOFF Mathieson had saluted Flt Lt Comstock looked Willy hard in the eyes. "Cadet Williams, I was a guest at your school for the Army Cadet's Passing-Out Parade on Wednesday afternoon."

Willy swallowed. "Yes sir. I know sir," he replied, striving to keep the quaver out of his voice.

Flt Lt Comstock fixed him with a steely stare. "I was appalled when that model aircraft ruined their parade. It was the most embarrassing and outrageous thing I have ever seen on a parade in all my career. I gather the model belonged to you," he stated.

"Yes sir," Willy answered.

He badly wanted to deny he had anything to do with the incident but found he was loath to use John as an excuse. *They won't be impressed if I dob in a mate,* he thought. He knew he would despise himself as well so he said no more.

Flt Lt Comstock looked hard at him. Willy tried to hold his gaze without being defiant or insubordinate. After a painful silence of many seconds Flt Lt Comstock nodded. "If you had anything to do with it I would now be handing you a 'Show Cause' Notice to dismiss you from the AAFC. Do you understand?"

"Yes sir," Willy replied, swallowing again and feeling his stomach churn with near despair. It sounded bad.

"So what happened?"

"It was my model sir but another person used it without my permission," Willy answered. To his dismay he had trouble forming the words and his eyes began to water.

Flt Lt Comstock gave him another hard look. "Actually, I know what happened. Luckily for you, Captain Conkey phoned me and explained it all."

"Yes sir."

"So you aren't in trouble. What I wanted to say to you is that you should take this as a warning. Choose your friends wisely. Remember the American saying: 'If you want to soar like an eagle, don't associate with a pack of turkeys'."

"Yes sir," Willy replied, his pride smarting at the implied insult to both him and John. *I thought John was my friend,* he thought, *and a good person.* But he saw no point in trying to explain it.

Flt Lt Comstock glanced at Flying Officer Turnbull then went on: "What now concerns me is that a rumour has reached us that some of the army cadets might try to disrupt our Passing-Out Parade in revenge. That is a real worry."

It was. Willy swallowed again and felt even more anxious. His mind raced, wondering what, if anything, he could do to avert such a disaster. "None of them have actually said that sir but there have been a few hints," he replied.

Flt Lt Comstock shook his head. "I hope nothing happens. It will do a lot of long term damage to relations between the AAC and AAFC if it does. There is enough unpleasant rivalry as it is," he commented.

"Yes sir."

"Right, keep your nose clean. Don't react to any teasing from army cadets and keep doing your best," Flt Lt Comstock said. "March him out W. O. D."

Willy was ordered to about turn and marched out. Outside CDTWOFF Mathieson called 'Halt!' and then said, "If those army cadets do spoil our parade you aren't going to be very popular around here."

Willy's stomach turned over. "No sir," he replied. Again he saw no point in trying to explain it had been none of his doing. As soon as he was given 'Fall out!' he moved to join Stick and Noddy who were watching from over near the door.

"What was that all about?" Stick queried.

Willy told him. When he explained about the rumour of army cadets taking revenge Noddy nodded. "I heard that. Some of the Year 10s told me that was what they were going to do."

"Oh, I hope they don't!" Willy replied. Feeling sick at heart he considered how he might avert such a happening. That he was not popular with many other cadets was also very obvious both from their looks and muttered comments.

But his worries were cut short by bellowed commands to form up on the parade ground and for the next hour nearly all his focus was on trying to do good drill while the unit went through a complete rehearsal for their Passing-Out Parade.

It was a very anxious boy who went to bed that night. Lying there in the darkness he reviewed the events of the previous week and puzzled over what he might do.

"I must make sure there is no revenge attack," he muttered.

But how?

Chapter 38

MONDAY

It was an ordinary weekend but felt like a long one to Willy. Saturday was chores and homework. The only event of note was when he went into the workshop under the house and was confronted by the crumpled wreck of his model triplane. It was such a mess he was again almost overwhelmed by emotion.

All that work! All that effort! What a waste! he thought.

Tears formed and his mood became even more dejected and he was tempted to just smash the wreck even more. Trembling with anger and upset he clenched his fists. Then he shook his head. "No, it wasn't a waste," he told himself. After all he had won two prizes in the model competition.

And I got a lot of pleasure from making it, and it was fun to fly.

So he sat and began to carefully salvage the motor, servos and control linkages. Even the wheels were in good condition although the axle was badly bent. As he stripped away torn tissue paper and sliced off parts which had been glued to balsa he also realised he had gained a whole range of skills.

It was worth it, he decided.

But what to do about John? In spite of being angry at the hurt John had caused him Willy had to admit that Petra was a suitable subject for jealous obsession.

Do I love her? he thought. It was a hard thing to decide because pride was involved but finally he decided that he really only had a crush on her, even though he admired her very much.

It was the constant images of a nude Marjorie and other girls that kept flitting across the screen of his mind that helped him reach this decision. *Petra is just the most perfect girl but I won't just give her up. She is down at the moment and I don't want to depress her anymore,* he reasoned. *She can decide.*

But it was the other problem, of the possibility of some of the army cadets disrupting his squadron's Passing-Out Parade that nagged at him the most. After deciding to speak to Capt Conkey about it Willy also considered speaking to Stephen and his friends.

They might be able to do something. Willy decided. The image of Graham Kirk being struck by the model kept recurring. *If anyone was hurt by my model it was him,* Willy thought. But he had doubts about whether Graham was the sort of person to hold a grudge. *I hope not,* Willy thought, suspecting that Graham might be an implacable enemy.

When a tired and anxious Willy got to school on Monday, the first thing he did was go to the staff room and ask to see Capt Conkey. Capt Conkey came to the door and raised an eyebrow. "Yes Willy?"

"Er... er... sir. it's... it's something about cadets," Willy mumbled, embarrassed and now very anxious.

"What about cadets? Don't tell me you have seen the light and want to transfer from the Air Cadets to the Army Cadets?" Capt Conkey queried, obviously tongue-in-cheek.

"Oh sir! I've got some pride!" Willy retorted. But the joke helped steady him. "No sir, it's about something Flight Lieutenant Comstock said. Thank you for speaking to him sir. I would have been chucked out of the Air Cadets if you hadn't assured him it wasn't my fault."

Capt Conkey shrugged. "That's alright. I am never going to allow someone suffer an injustice if I can help it," he replied. "Now what did your CO say?"

"Sir, he heard there was rumour that some of the army cadets plan to disrupt our Passing-Out Parade next Saturday afternoon."

Capt Conkey frowned and nodded. "Yes. I have heard the rumours and Flight Lieutenant Comstock has spoken to me about it. I assure you that I will be speaking to my people on parade next Wednesday. I will be a guest at your parade and if any of my people do anything to disrupt it they can kiss their cadet career goodbye," he said.

"Thank you sir," Willy said, impressed in spite of himself. "Er... sir, er... do you think I should speak to any of the army cadets myself."

"Who did you have in mind?"

"Graham Kirk sir. The model hit him really hard," Willy answered.

Capt Conkey shook his head. "No. Graham understands it wasn't your fault. Talk to him by all means but don't make a big deal of it. He has assured me he won't do anything and I know he is very touchy about his honour. He has promised so I am sure he will stick to his word."

"Thank you sir," Willy replied, mentally agreeing with Capt Conkey in his assessment of Graham. *But not Stephen. I think he might hold a grudge,* he thought.

Capt Conkey smiled. "And I will tell your CO that you have shown real loyalty and moral courage by coming to speak to me. Now I have essays to mark so you run along."

"Yes sir," Willy replied, his heart swelling at the praise.

Feeling much better he hurried downstairs to look for his friends, and was immediately confronted with a dilemma.

The first person he met at the bottom of the steps was John. John stood there with an anxious look on his face. He still had a plaster cast on his left lower arm but apart from a small dressing on a shaved patch on the back of his head he looked quite normal.

Before Willy could formulate a planned response, he found himself smiling. He blurted out: "John! You are out of hospital. How are you?"

John gave a weak smile in return but appeared to visibly brighten. "OK, it was only a whack on the head and the scans showed no sign of swelling or of bleeding inside the skull so they let me go home yesterday afternoon," he explained.

"I didn't expect to see you at school for a week or so," Willy answered. He was also very relieved as he had half dreaded that John might die.

John then swallowed and looked at his feet before looking up at Willy. He licked his lips. "Er... Sorry about your model plane, Willy. I will make it up to you," he said.

Tears began to form in the corners of John's eyes and that embarrassed Willy too. *I don't want the poor bugger to cry,* he thought. To spare John the humiliation and shame of crying in public, Willy said: "It flew really well, didn't it?"

John nodded and mumbled 'yes' so Willy hurried on. "And you did a great job at flying it. I couldn't have controlled it as well as that. Those aerobatics were just fabulous."

John's face softened to a small grin. "It was very manoeuvrable," he said. "It could turn on a wingtip."

"It certainly made those army cadets jump," Willy added. He then managed a rueful smile. "When you flew it through the ranks I was amazed. That was really good flying."

"Is it badly smashed?" John asked.

Willy nodded. "Totally wrecked. It ran into Graham Kirk and that caused it to shed a couple of upper wings and to cartwheel into the ground. Then CUO Grant slashed it a couple of times with his word."

"CUO Grant?"

"The Cadet Under-Officer commanding the parade, that big, good-looking bloke in Year 12," Willy explained. It dawned on him that because John wasn't a cadet he did not know the meaning of CUO.

As Willy explained this Stick and Noddy joined them. Noddy obviously overheard him as he called, "What's this Willy, you given up on girls and started to admire the blokes?"

"Get stuffed, Noddy!" Willy retorted. He wasn't in the mood for any of Noddy's nonsense.

Stick asked John how he was and then got John to turn around to show his dressings on the back of the head. "They did some scans and they showed there wasn't any brain damage," John explained.

Noddy chortled. "Huh! More likely the scan showed there wasn't any brain there to be damaged," he commented.

John looked hurt and Willy was annoyed. "Stop teasing everyone, Noddy," he snapped. As he said this his future policy towards John formed in his mind.

I will just act as though nothing has happened and over time it will be forgotten, he told himself. It came to him that all of the things John had done to hurt him simply did not matter. *Character building, that's all,* Willy decided. Now they just seemed irrelevant and trivial and as though they had happened to someone else a long time ago.

But Petra was another matter. As soon as they went up to the classroom the tension between them increased. Petra was on the veranda unpacking her bag, but she only glanced at them and then nodded before making her way inside to her seat.

John watched her go with eyes that looked hungry, even haunted, to Willy. Then John turned to face him. "She is just so beautiful," he said.

Willy nodded and agreed but privately he thought that Petra had lost her bloom over recent weeks. *She looks pretty stressed out,* he thought.

John faced him, his face drawn and his eyes pleading. "It was... was because she is so wonderful, such an angel, that I wanted to stop you," he said.

Willy nodded but had to control his own emotions. John continued:

"She is so pure and innocent, and I couldn't bear to think of... of you... of you doing things to her, things like you do with other girls," he muttered.

Both were deeply embarrassed. Willy shook his head. "I would never do anything to hurt Petra. She is just too nice," he said.

"Do you love her?" John asked, his voice husky with emotion.

Again Willy shook his head. "No, I just admire her and like her a lot," he replied.

"Do you mind if I... if I...," John croaked.

"Not at all," Willy answered. "Who she goes out with is up to her. She can choose."

As he watched how John took this, Willy felt very sorry for him. *Poor bugger! He is really eaten up by her,* he thought. Privately he did not think John had a chance. *She doesn't even know he exists.*

John could only nod and then turn away to hide the tears that formed in his eyes. Sniffling and nodding he dug out his books. The boys then made their way inside. As he walked to his seat Willy's eyes met Petra's and she gave a sad little smile.

Something is wrong alright, he thought. Wondering how he might be able to help her, he seated himself next to John and settled to his work.

The morning lessons dragged but slowly the tension between Willy and John eased. Willy several times made a deliberate attempt to help this along by making small jokes and by allowing John to use his ruler and eraser.

The morning break arrived and Willy made his way downstairs, determined to speak to Stephen and his friends. At the bottom of the stairs he turned left. John, who was with him stopped. "Where are you going to Willy?" he queried.

"I just need to speak to the army cadets for a minute," he explained.

"Oh them!" John answered, curling his lip.

"I'll be with you in a minute," Willy answered, nettled by John's attitude. *If it is going to be a choice between cadets and friendship with John it will be cadets,* he told himself as he hurried away.

He found the army cadets in their usual place under the school. But as he approached them Willy's resolve faltered as both Roger and Stephen gave him hostile looks. He heard Roger say, "Here comes the Red Baron."

Both Graham and Peter Bronsky turned their heads and Graham gave Willy a hard stare. "What do you want Rocket Man?" he asked.

This time Willy did not beat about the bush. "I've come to ask for your help," he replied.

"Oh yeah! To do what, put a rocket to the moon?" Graham answered.

"My CO has heard a rumour that some of the army cadets plan to disrupt our Passing-Out Parade next Saturday afternoon," Willy answered. "I'd like you to help persuade them not to do that."

It was Stephen who answered. "Why should we? You mucked our parade up."

"No I didn't, and nor did any air cadet," Willy replied heatedly. "Anyway, I was just hoping you would help."

Stephen smirked. "If you really want help then you have to beg."

Willy made a face but stood his ground. Stephen smirked and went on: "You have to admit that the Army Cadets are better than the Air Cadets."

At that Willy bristled. He stiffened and stood up straight. "Never!"

Graham nodded. "That was the right answer kid. Now buzz off and let us study," he said.

Willy wasn't sure if he had understood. "I'm only asking so the other kids in my unit won't have their parade spoiled," he explained.

Peter now spoke. "We believe you. Now we've got exams next session and need to study so go away."

"So you won't upset our parade?" Willy asked, anxious to be certain.

Stephen grinned. "We've been invited. We'll be there," he replied.

Peter made a face. "Steve means yes, we won't do anything Willy, now bugger off!" he said.

"Thanks," Willy replied, noting for the first time that all of them had text books open on the table in front of them. Accepting that they would not now do anything, even if they had contemplated it, he turned and walked away.

He re-joined John and sat to eat his 'little' lunch. Stick and Noddy were with them and Stick was explaining about a model helicopter with eight rotors that he had seen on TV. Willy remembered the one they had seen at the 'Fly-in' at Townsville and began to describe it. As he did he also remembered that it had been John who had caused his model to fly off into the mountains. A little spurt of resentment made his emotions surge but he restrained himself and pushed the incident to the back of his mind. The boys then discussed other model helicopters and how difficult they were to fly.

When the bell went, they made their way back to the classroom. Roger joined them there. Willy noted him putting away a Science text book. Curious he commented on Graham actually studying during a break. "I didn't think he was the studious type," he added.

Roger nodded. "He wasn't, but since the cadet annual camp he has experienced an epiphany," Roger replied.

"Epiphany?" Willy queried, embarrassed that he wasn't sure what the word meant but knowing it was something religious.

"Like St Paul," Roger explained. "He was a Roman official from Syria or somewhere and his real name was Saul. For years he gave the Christians a hard time, this was just after Jesus and before the Romans became Christian. He persecuted them badly. Then, one day while travelling across the Golan Heights on the way to Damascus, he went through a storm and during it he saw the light and became a devout Christian."

"Has Graham taken to religion?"

Roger shook his head. "No, he goes to church sometimes but this is over cadets. He wants to be promoted in the Army Cadets. Apparently they run a ten day Promotion Course in December and he wants to go on that but there are only limited numbers allowed from each unit and he wants to be selected."

Willy understood that. *I want to be promoted in the cadets too,* he thought, his ambition to one day become a CUO coming to mind. "He has been in a lot of trouble at school. Does he have a chance?" he asked.

Roger nodded. "He has been but he is the First Reserve and apparently Capt Conkey has told him that his schoolwork needed to pick up as well."

Amazing! Willy thought, remembering seeing Graham at the office on several occasions and hearing stories about his exploits all year.

Further discussion was then ended by the arrival of the much feared Miss Hackenmeyer and the class moved in for Maths. The next two periods were full-on. Willy did not mind. He was good at Maths and knew he needed to get top marks to have any chance of being selected to be a pilot in the RAAF. The only distractions were provided by noting John staring wistfully at Petra and with studying Petra himself.

She looks fairly normal today, he thought. *I wonder what is bothering her?*

Lunch time came and Willy and John went down under the school to sit with their friends to eat and talk. During this John excused himself and got up. As he walked away Willy at first thought he was going to the toilet but when he saw him detour away from that he frowned.

Where is John going? he wondered.

He had a good idea and a niggle of jealousy caused him to excuse himself as well. Stuffing the last of his sandwiches into his mouth he hurried to keep John in sight. Not wanting John to think he was being followed or watched Willy was careful to stop at the next corner and to peek around. That revealed John also peeking around the next corner. Even as Willy watched John hurried on out of sight.

Curious now about what John was doing Willy sprinted across to the corner he had just left and looked around it. He saw John at once, standing near a group of Year 10 boys under one of the trees with seats around it. Beyond them were two girls who were walking the other way: Petra and Tania.

Petra. I was right, Willy congratulated himself.

He stood and observed as the two girls turned right around the far end of the hall and then waited until John had run to the corner where they had vanished from view. As soon as he went around it out of sight, Willy ran after him.

Puffing with the unaccustomed exertion, Willy paused at the corner of the hall and saw John standing at the side gate of the school. The two girls were just visible across the street.

They've left the school again, Willy thought with surprise. *Where are they going?*

John looked around and Willy hastily pulled his head back out of sight. Then he risked a quick look. To his surprise he saw that John was now outside the gate and hurrying across the street.

That's asking for trouble. That's not like John, he thought. But then he remembered how obsessed with Petra John was. *If I was in love I'd take risks for her too,* he decided.

Curious to see what happened next, Willy made his way to the gate. By the time he got there John was across the street at the corner of the side street and the girls were no longer in sight. Then John went out of sight as well.

He is following them, Willy thought, remembering how he had done exactly the same thing the previous Friday.

He went to follow but then hesitated. *And I was caught out of bounds by Mr Ritter and will be in deep shit if I get caught again,* he thought.

But he felt he had to know. Biting his lip with anxiety, he glanced in both directions to see if there was a teacher in sight. There wasn't. Taking a deep breath and resigning himself to fate he stepped through the gate and hurried across the road.

A minute later he was at the corner and a quick peek revealed John at the next corner and looking around it. Then John went out of sight again and Willy started running. Another minute later he was at the next corner. Panting and wiping perspiration from his face, he bent forward and peeked around.

As he did, he almost collided with John. He had come running back the other way and looked quite agitated. Skidding to a stop he looked at Willy in surprise. "Willy! What are you doing?"

Willy thought it was obvious and he coloured with embarrassment. "Following to see if you need any help," he answered lamely.

But John seemed not to notice. "Where have they gone?" he cried, waving his arms distractedly.

Willy straightened up and shook his head. Glancing the other way along the street he caught a glimpse of school uniforms passing between two cars on the other side of the street. "There!" he cried, pointing.

John looked and they both stared as the two girls walked into the driveway of one of the big international hotels which lined that street. As the girls went out of sight, John stared at Willy again. "What are they doing there? Where are they going?" he cried.

Willy did not know but was now consumed by the urge to find out. "I think her mother works there," he answered.

"Works there?" John queried as he began hurrying towards the hotel. "Doing what?"

"Cleaning the rooms and making the beds I think," Willy replied, remembering what Petra had told him.

"But why are they going there now? It is school time," John answered. He stopped and waited for two cars to pass then dashed across the road. Willy followed, his mind full of questions and niggling, suspicious thoughts about what Petra's mother might actually do.

The two boys arrived at the driveway to the hotel. The building stood twelve stories high, a massive tower of glass, concrete and steel. A semicircular driveway ran in to a reception area and down the side was another concrete driveway to what looked like a car park and service area. The two girls stood at a small door set in the side wall.

Willy was now regretting following John and he wanted to leave, but even as he tried to formulate the words an incident happened that drove all such thoughts from his mind. Tania pressed a button and spoke into a speaker beside the door. A few moments later the door opened. Willy saw Petra shake her head and turn to walk back but as she did Tania grabbed her and held her. Petra protested and tried to shake Tania off. But then a man's arm shot out of the door and grabbed Petra as well. Petra cried out and struggled to break free.

The man stepped into view, a big, burly man with a bull neck and short cropped hair. He was wearing a grey suit and dark sunglasses and had the look of a bouncer or bodyguard about him. His left hand suddenly lashed out, slapping Petra hard on the side of the face. She cried out again and then the man stepped back and she was dragged inside.

Tania followed and the door slammed shut.

Chapter 39

WHAT THE HELL?

John stared wide-eyed at Willy. "What the hell? What's going on?"
Willy was shocked. "It looked like Petra just got abducted."

Suspicion and anxiety whirled in his mind and he felt anger. Concerned that Petra was in some sort of real trouble, he hurried forward.

John followed. "That man hit her!" he cried. "We must save her!"

Willy could only nod, so choked up with anxiety did he feel. But he was also confused. *What is Petra doing here? And where does Tania come into this?* he wondered. There were elements to the situation he did not understand and which caused him niggling doubts.

Reaching the door he grabbed the handle and tried to open it. But it was locked. Turning to the wall just inside the recess he studied the speaker system. It was a key pad with a small speaker below it. *How does this work?* he wondered.

John jostled him. "Talk into it! Ask them what is going on. Tell them we want to see Petra," he cried. He was highly agitated and kept waving his arms.

Willy studied the speaker system and then shook his head. "I don't know how it works," he replied.

"Try it!" John cried. Stepping forward he began shouting into the speaker. "Open up! Open up! We want to see Petra."

Willy shook his head. He had seen his father use a speaker like this at a hotel resort in the Whitsundays but had not really paid attention. Now he wished he had. "I think you have to punch in the room number and then press the talk button," he commented, pointing to the keypad.

"Then do it!" John cried.

Again Willy shook his head. He stepped back and looked up. The wall rose sheer with row upon row of windows. "This place must be ten stories or more high," he answered. "There must be hundreds of rooms. We don't know which room she has been taken to."

John also looked up. "But.. but.. there must be a way in," he said. He was so agitated and anxious he kept dancing from one foot to the other.

Willy looked up and studied the windows but none were open. Nor were there any external balconies. The wall was just smooth concrete. Annoyed by what he felt was John's overreaction he answered sarcastically. "There is, there is front door and there is sure to be other doors."

"What about a fire escape or something?" John almost shouted.

"Calm down!" Willy cried. "If she is in trouble we don't want to warn them we are here."

John glared at him but then seemed to slump and he nodded. Willy pointed to the door. "I reckon this might be the fire escape."

"Aren't they on the outside?" John asked.

"Only on old buildings," Willy replied, memories of several hotels he had stayed in with his parents coming to him. At the time he had been amused by his father insisting they walk up the stairs for fitness rather than use the lift but now he was grateful. He gestured to the door. "Most fire escapes now are concrete steps in concrete stair wells. And you can only open the door from the inside unless you have a key or unless someone opens it for you electronically."

"I think she was kidnapped. We must get help," John cried.

The idea of calling the police had already occurred to Willy but he frowned. "I don't think we should call the police yet. We need a bit more proof that something is wrong. She might just have not wanted to work and that man might be her father or her uncle or something."

"What can we do?" John asked, still glancing up and around and trying again to open the door.

"Ask at the front desk," Willy replied with a shrug.

He could see that might cause them difficulties but then he shrugged again. *Getting into trouble doesn't matter if Petra needs help,* he told himself.

John immediately headed towards the front entrance. Willy followed, caught up and walked beside him. They strode in under the covered entrance road and among the potted palms to where a large glass door opened onto a porch area. There was no one at the door which slid open electronically as they approached it.

Inside was the hotel lobby, a vast atrium with a very high ceiling. On the right was a small open office with the usual stands and racks of tourist information. Two elderly people stood there leafing through brochures.

The man wore a Hawaiian shirt and baggy, knee-length shorts and the woman had purple rinsed hair and long chequered trousers.

American tourists, Willy thought.

On the left were some lounge chairs but ahead were the reception desk and a wall with four elevator doors set in it. To the right of that was a corridor and some more doors. Behind the reception desk was a male of about 30 wearing the usual white shirt and dark tie. He looked up and a frown crossed his face as the boys walked across the marble floor towards him.

Willy felt very conspicuous and self-conscious as he crossed that vast open space. He had been in such places before but always with his family. Now it was just him and John and he was aware they must really stand out because of their age and school uniforms.

The man raised an eyebrow. "Yes?"

"We are looking for two girls from our school. They came in here," Willy said.

"I don't think so. I didn't see them," the man answered.

"They went in the side door," Willy explained, pointing in that direction.

The man shrugged and frowned. "So a person who knew them and was expecting them has let them in," he answered.

Feeling distinctly at a disadvantage, Willy bit his lip. "Then can I speak to Mrs Pantovitch please?" he asked.

"What is your name please?" the man asked.

"Willy Williams," Willy answered. "Her daughter Petra is in my class. I was told that her mother worked here."

The man shook his head. "I'm sorry. I cannot give out any information on staff or guests to strangers. If you give me a contact number and they are here I can pass them a message and if they wish they can call you back."

Willy bit his lip and wondered what to do next, but John suddenly leaned forward on the counter. "She is here! Tell us what room she is in," he cried.

At that the man raised both eyebrows and began talking apparently to himself. Willy had noted that he wore an earpiece and microphone and knew it connected to the telephone network. The man then glanced to his left and Willy's eyes followed the movement. From around the corner came a very big man in a dark suit. The man had 'security' or 'bouncer' in every line of his body language.

"Yes, Mister Craigs?"

"Please escort these children off the premises, Jacob," the man said.

John then got angry and shouted, "Let us in! We know Petra is here. We want to see her."

The security guard stepped across and reached out but Willy moved quickly away and John stepped back. The man behind the counter gave them a hard look. "Stop disturbing the guests please and leave the premises. If you don't go immediately I will phone your school."

That annoyed Willy but also seemed a good idea. "Good, do that!" he snapped. Then it occurred to him that such a course of action might get Petra into even more trouble so he grabbed John by the arm and pulled him away. "Come on, John. Let's go," he said.

John did not want to but the security guard was so large and so threatening that he backed away. Muttering and casting angry glances back he followed Willy back to the front door.

Once outside, John stopped and glared back in. "That man knows something!" he cried.

"Maybe," Willy answered. "Come on, let's move away so that that guy doesn't phone the school. That will get Petra in trouble for sure."

At that moment, a bus drove up the entrance driveway and stopped, blocking their view of the door. Out of the bus climbed a dozen of more Asians. *Japanese or Chinese tourists,* Willy thought. Uncertain what to do next, he led John out onto the footpath.

John looked up, his face a mask of angry misery. "We should get someone to help," he said as he shielded his eyes against the sun's glare.

Willy had been thinking the same thing but was very undecided. "Do you mean the police?" he asked.

John shrugged. "Maybe, but some adult anyway."

That was what Willy was feeling but against that were his own doubts. "But if Petra is just here to help her mother work in the hotel then we will be left looking silly and will get into trouble for leaving the school grounds," he said.

"So what! I don't care. As long as Petra is safe," John cried. He leaned back and scanned the windows and balconies on the front of the high rise.

"Nor do I, but what if... what if she is here for some other reason?"

Willy answered, finally summoning the courage to voice his own doubts. "Then Petra could be in real trouble with her parents as well as the school."

"I think she is in real trouble anyway," John replied, his distress evident in his voice.

Willy also turned and looked up. The morning sun was behind the building so that the front was in shade but there were high rise buildings on either side and the sunlight was reflecting from them to make it very glary. Squinting and shielding his eyes, he stared up and tried to count how many stories there were.

Suddenly, John gasped and cried out. "There she is!" He grabbed at Willy's arm with his left hand and pointed up with his right. "There, right up on the top floor."

Willy looked and saw movement on one of the glass fronted balconies. It was Petra. She was leaning over and looking down.

"Petra!" John shouted. "Petra!"

The shout sounded very loud to Willy but several cars drove past behind him and Petra did not look in their direction. "I don't think she can hear you," he said.

John cried again and began waving his arms. To make himself more visible he stepped backwards between the parked cars. Willy looked around and moved to follow then dashed across and grabbed John's shirt. Just in time he stopped him steeping back in front of a truck. The truck driver tooted his horn and only then did John became aware of his danger.

"Oh! Thanks Willy," he replied. Then he checked both ways before running across the street between cars. He then stood on the other footpath and began jumping up and down and waving his arms. "Petra! Petra!" he yelled.

Willy waited for another car to go past and then also crossed the street. As he did he saw heads turning to look at them from along the street and a face peered out of a nearby doorway. *We are attracting some attention,* he thought with embarrassment.

Safely across the street Willy turned and stood next to John. Shielding his eyes he peered up and saw a tiny arm movement. John yelled again and waved and the arm waved back. Very faintly Willy heard what might have been Petra's voice but it was lost in the traffic noises and the sound of the breeze in the trees and around the buildings.

John stared at him and then upwards. "She heard me. She is calling."

Willy nodded. "Yes, but we can't hear her," he replied.

"I'm sure she is trying to tell us something," John said. He was so agitated that he danced on the spot. "I am sure she is in trouble." Cupping his hands around his mouth, he yelled upwards, "Are you in trouble? Do you need help?"

But it was obvious that Petra could not hear properly and that she could not call out loud enough to make herself heard. Very distinctly Willy saw her turn her head to look back over her shoulder several times. He shook his head.

"Maybe she can't call out in case she attracts attention to herself," he suggested.

"Oh, what can we do?" John cried.

Willy bit his lip and studied the situation. Petra was on the end balcony at the highest level of the building. For a few seconds he considered going back inside and trying to go up in the lift or by the internal stairs he knew must be there. But then he shook his head. *No chance of crossing that big lobby without being seen by the man at reception,* he decided.

So what to do? He now felt sure that Petra was in trouble but did not want to act without more information. *I don't want to cry wolf and then look like a fool,* he thought. And then he was ashamed of being a coward and not acting. *What sort of trouble and how could we help?* he wondered.

Then his gaze noted that the neighbouring building on his right was an even higher hotel. It looked to be set a few metres further forward. *If we can get onto the roof of that hotel next door we should be able to speak to her,* he decided. The distance across between the two buildings he estimated to be only about 20 or 30 metres.

He pointed this out to John who at once agreed it was worth a try. He stared forward but Willy grabbed him. "Wait! Don't rush into this. Let's do a bit of a reconnaissance first," he suggested.

So the two boys waited for a break in the traffic and then hurried across the street. As they did Willy glanced up and noted that Petra was still on the balcony. He gave her a wave and pointed to the next hotel but then she was lost to view as he and John went in under the overhang outside the hotel.

Once on the footpath they turned right and hurried along the footpath until they reached the front of the next hotel. It was another luxury high rise with a curving covered entrance way and a wall of glass fronting the lobby. This had the advantage of allowing them to look in as they strolled slowly past. To Willy's satisfaction he noted that the reception desk was semicircular and set in the centre of the lobby and that there was a grand stairway to the right of what looked like the lift doors in the rear wall.

If we can pick our moment we should be able to get up those stairs without being seen, he decided.

Once past the building the two boys stopped and Willy explained his idea to John. "What we need are some guests who divert the receptionist's attention for a minute or so," he said.

Even as he said this a mini-bus with the words 'Airport Shuttle' on the side pulled up the driveway and stopped at the entrance. The driver and half a dozen middle-aged tourists climbed out.

Germans? Willy wondered as he overheard snatches of their conversation. He nudged John. "This is our chance. Wait till they reach the reception desk and then I will just stroll in and go up the steps. You follow when I am out of sight. We will meet up on the first floor and then use the lift."

"No. I go first," John insisted.

Sensing John's determination, Willy gave in and nodded. "OK, off you go then," Willy replied. The guests were busy collecting suitcase and bags from a trailer at the era of the bus by then and the first ones began moving in through the front door.

The boys walked up to the now open door and looked in. There was a very attractive and well-dressed young lady at reception and she was smiling and nodding to an elderly couple as they approached her. Willy saw that she was half facing away from him and the moment she took some documents off the couple and began to study them he nudged John.

"Off you go!" he hissed.

John did not hesitate. He strolled in through the doorway with four more tourists and then stayed over on the right of the group, keeping them between himself and the stairway. Halfway across the lobby he deviated away to the right and walked quickly across to the stairs.

Willy watched this heart in mouth and with his mouth dry with anxiety. Then he realised he must move as the last of the arriving guests were making their way inside. Taking a big gulp of air to steady his nerves he walked quickly through the doorway and headed for the stairs. Out of the corner of his eye he kept glancing to make sure he had the group between him and the receptionist. To his satisfaction he noted that she was engrossed in conversation over some documents. Nobody paid him any attention but he forced himself to walk normally.

Don't hurry. It will attract attention, he told himself.

The bottom of the stairs got closer and closer with every step and became the whole focus of his vision. And then he was on them and out of sight. Letting out a big sigh of relief he hurried up the carpeted stairs, taking them two at a time.

John was waiting at the top and he pointed to the left. Four lift doors lined the wall and one of them was open. Without hesitation Willy followed John into the lift. His eyes then scanned the control panel. A glance revealed that there was a basement car park, then the ground floor with numbers above that. They went up to 12. Then his eyes fixed on the top words: Rooftop Garden

"That's what we want," he said.

Firmly he jabbed his fingertip on that button. The doors slid shut and the lift began to move. Willy watched the numbers lighting up to indicate their upward progress and found his heart hammering rapidly. He was still worried that they might just come to a top floor with no outside access.

But when the lift stopped and the door slid open he saw at once that they were in luck. They were on the roof. Directly in front of him were some deck chairs and lounges under beach umbrellas and beyond them a small swimming pool.

Stepping out of the lift, Willy looked quickly around. To his relief there was nobody there. To his right beside the pool was what looked like a small bar but it had its shutters down and apart from the potted palms and greenery of a roof garden the place was deserted.

"This way," Willy muttered, turning left and hurrying across the tiled flat roof. John followed and behind them Willy heard the lift doors close automatically and then a whirring sound indicated the lift going down.

Made it! he thought. But would they be able to see Petra?

Chapter 40

HIGH RISE

Heart in mouth, Willy strode to the concrete balustrade at the side of the building facing the hotel Petra was in. As he did, he was half aware of a spectacular view out over the city and the encircling mountains to the west, but he only had eyes for the immediate problem.

The balustrade was chest high and 20 centimetres thick. Even before he reached it, Willy noted that the roof he was on was higher than the level Petra was on. As he reached the balustrade and stopped, he saw that this impression was correct. Better still, he noted that the front of the hotel he was on was a few metres closer to the street than the main structure of the other hotel.

Moving quickly to his left to the corner of the roof, Willy saw that he could now just see the front of the other hotel. "Aah! Good!" he muttered. For there, only about 30 metres away, was Petra. She was standing on the balcony in front of a glass-fronted room and was staring down at the street.

Willy glanced over the edge, and even though he was not normally afraid of heights he experienced a sharp spurt of vertigo. The wall dropped sheer to the driveway. It looked a *long* way down! Hastily he looked up.

John joined him and let out a little cry. Then he began waving and called loudly: "Petra!"

Petra at once heard him and her head jerked sharply around. Her mouth opened in surprise and then she waved back.

John gripped the concrete. "Petra, do you need help?" he shouted.

At that, alarm showed plainly on Petra's face and she glanced anxiously towards the room she was standing outside. Then she shook her head and put her finger to her lips.

Willy noted the look of what he thought was stark terror on her face and, as John sucked in a deep breath to call again, he grabbed him. "Sssh! Don't call out!" he hissed.

"Wh... Why not?" John answered, looking from him to Petra and back.

"Because she is scared witless. Look at the look on her face. And she is trying to tell us not to call out," Willy replied.

"But... But why not?" John queried. Once again he was becoming agitated and angry.

Willy tightened his grip on John's arm as he saw Petra shaking her head vigorously. "Don't call out! I think she is scared that the people in the room might hear you and then she will get into trouble," he said as forcefully as he could.

"But... but if she is in trouble, she can tell us and she will then be safe," John answered. He gave Willy a bewildered and anxious look.

But Willy's mind was now racing. "Not necessarily," he replied. "If they know we know, then that man who grabbed her will be warned," he answered.

"So what? He won't harm her then," John cried.

"Oh yes he might!" Willy retorted. "He can be out of that building and in a car in a few minutes and be long gone well before the police can arrive. And he would take Petra and Tania with him."

"Oh he wouldn't!" John said.

"Oh yes he could!" Willy snapped, remembering news reports about girls who went missing and of their bodies being found later. "If she is a witness to some crime he might kill her to shut her up," he added.

John was aghast and stared at Willy in horror and then looked at Petra, who now stood silently staring at them while frequently glancing over her shoulder into the room. "But.. but what can we do?" John queried.

"Call for help first," Willy replied. He turned to go but John gripped his shirt sleeve.

"Shouldn't we try to find out what the trouble is first?" he said. "We don't want to get her into more trouble."

"I'm sure she's in some sort of trouble, Willy replied grimly. "Anyway, how can we find out exactly what the problem is without calling out?" In his own mind the only course of action now was to go down to the lobby and telephone the police.

"By phone?" John suggested. He dug in the pocket of his shorts and dug out a mobile phone and held it up.

Willy was astonished. He knew many students had mobile phones but did not know that John owned one. "Good idea. But how will you call her? Does she have access to a phone and does she know your number?"

John looked crestfallen. He shook his head. "No, she doesn't know my number," he muttered.

Willy thought hard. "I think if she had access to a phone she might call for help herself," he suggested.

"Aren't there phones in hotel rooms?" John said.

Willy nodded. "Usually, but there may not be one in that room or she may not be able to use it without people knowing," he answered. Ideas of printing John's number on something big and holding it up for her to see flitted across his mind. "Hold your phone up and see if she can get to a phone," he said.

John did and he then used his other hand in the little finger, thumb hand signal to mean 'telephone'. Petra watched carefully and then made the same hand signal but then shook her head vigorously.

"She can't get to a phone," John said. He began to dance in agitated frustration again.

Willy leaned over the balustrade and studied the gap. For a moment he considered trying to make a paper plane with John's number written on it and try to fly it across but then he shook his head. *Too windy. And a silly idea anyway. If she has access to a phone, she will know to ring triple 0 for the police.*

Biting his lip with anxiety, Willy carefully studied the other building as an idea formed in his mind. He saw that the balcony Petra was on had a steel-framed glass balustrade but that there was then a 10-metre expanse of sheer wall across to the next balcony. There were more balconies directly below her and the notion of her making a rope from bedclothes and sliding down it to the next balcony to escape crossed his mind. But another glance down made him shudder and suspect that Petra might be too terrified to attempt such a thing, even if she really did want to escape.

But does she? What is the real problem? Willy wondered. Then another idea came to him. "I wish we had a model helicopter. We could fly the phone across to her and she could tell us," he suggested.

"A drone would be even better," John said.

"A drone!" Willy cried, instantly thinking of his father's. He pictured the quadcopter silently buzzing across with a mobile phone attached. "Maybe we could get one," he suggested.

"She still wouldn't know the number," John answered.

"We just tape it to the phone," Willy replied.

"Who would she call?" John queried.

"She could either just phone the police or we could go home and she could phone us there," Willy suggested.

John nodded and chewed his bottom lip. "It would be even better if we had another mobile phone. We could just fly one across to her and use mine to talk to her. Have you got a mobile phone?"

Willy shook his head. "No, my mum and dad won't let me have one yet." Then another idea came to him. "But my brother has one."

"Where is he, at school?"

"He's at school but his phone is at home. Mum and dad won't let him take it to school," Willy answered.

"So where do we get a drone from?" John answered.

"My place. Remember my dad's?" Willy had been studying the balcony Petra was on and was certain he could land a drone on it.

"Didn't it get broken when Stick crashed it?" John asked.

That gave Willy a jolt. It had, but he distinctly remembered his father working on it to fix it. "I think he fixed it," he replied.

"But that man might hear it," John objected.

Willy shook his head. "It has an electric motor. And even if he does she might still have time to phone us. It's worth a try," he said. Now that he had thought about using a drone it seemed a practical plan. "I'll go and get it and Lloyd's phone," he said.

"How?"

"I'll get my bike from school," Willy replied.

"What if the teachers see you?"

Willy shrugged. "Then I tell the principal the story and he can phone the police. Now you wait here and I will be as quick as I can."

"How long will you be?" John asked.

Willy bit his lip and did a quick calculation. He was about say half an hour but then he realised he was being unrealistic and also that he must not fool himself by any wishful thinking. "Could be an hour or so. If I am not back in an hour then go down to the lobby and phone the police," he said.

With a quick wave and a thumb's-up to Petra, Willy turned and hurried across the roof, leaving John standing facing Petra. A minute later he was in the lift and less than another minute after that the lift doors opened at the lobby.

Willy was now gripped by feverish anxiety. Now that he had a plan the last thing he wanted was to be detained by any security staff. He determined to make a run for it if queried but a quick glance showed only a few guests sitting around the lounge and one speaking to the girl at reception.

Oh well, nothing ventured, nothing gained, Willy told himself and he took a deep breath and just strolled out of the lift and headed across the lobby.

At every step he expected a voice to demand to know what he was doing and he tensed, ready to run. But nothing was said and he reached the large glass doors without trouble. The doors slid open when he walked into the photoelectric beam and he hurried through.

Outside he breathed out and sighed with relief then hurried down the driveway without a backward glance. He was half afraid that if he was seen they might suspect he was a thief and that the hotel security might detain him. But no-one called out or followed and he made it to the street without incident.

After a quick check for traffic Willy ran across the street. On the other footpath he paused to look back up and he was just able to make out John's head and waving arm against the glare as the sun was now right overhead and starting to shine down on the front of the building. He waved back and glanced towards the hotel where Petra was and was just able to make her out still standing on the balcony. She did not wave and appeared to be staring off into the distance.

Now gripped by the worry that he might take too long, Willy broke into a run. A minute later he was around the next corner, and another minute after that he was at the corner across from the school. Here he paused but only for a few seconds. He knew that the lunch break must be over so all the students would be back in class and he doubted that any teacher would be still out in the playground, other than the PE teachers, and it was with them in mind that he looked towards the school swimming pool.

But no teacher was visible there so Willy broke into a run, heart hammering with excitement and apprehension. He raced across to the side gate of the school and in and then along between the library and the fence to the bike racks.

Now his anxiety increased and he glanced up at the security camera at the side of the bike racks before telling himself he shouldn't have done that. Putting his head down, Willy hurried across to his bicycle, wiping his sweaty hands on his shorts as he did. For a few seconds he was assailed by the anxious thought that his bike might have been sabotaged again, but then he remembered that John had been the one doing that.

His bicycle was undamaged and he quickly bent to unlock it. Twenty seconds later he was wheeling it towards the gate. Again he was gripped by tension as he anticipated some teacher calling out, demanding to know where he was going.

But again nothing happened and once outside Willy jumped on his bike and began to pedal as he had never pedalled before. Within a block he was panting but he pushed himself on. *Petra is in danger. I mustn't take too long,* he told himself.

As he pedalled he fretted about his father's drone. *Did he fix it? Will it fly?* he worried. And what about the battery? Was it charged? It all added to his distress and made him wonder if he shouldn't just go to any phone and call the police.

He even considered going to a Hobby Shop to buy a drone but then shook his head. "I would also need a controller and I don't have the money," he muttered. So he aimed for his home.

Forcing tired legs to work, Willy pedalled on as fast as he could. His chest began to heave and perspiration poured out of him in the tropical heat. After four blocks his breath was coming in great gasps and he had to continually wipe sweat from his face and out of his eyes. But it was the traffic which slowed him more and twice he nearly had accidents with cars at intersections.

Barely aware of the tooting horns and screeching brakes, Willy just glanced irritably at the cars with their angry drivers and pedalled on. Fifteen minutes later and with his breath now laboured and his legs feeling like lead, he reached his home.

As he rode, Willy had thought through the details of his plan and after throwing his bike on the front lawn he acted on it with rapid moves. First he went upstairs to get Lloyd's mobile phone. That had been a weak point in his plan, but he had carried an image of it lying on Lloyd's bedside table in his mind and that is where it was. Snatching it up, Willy checked it was on. Satisfied it was working, he grabbed notepaper and pen and then a roll of sticky tape. His piggy bank was then robbed for cash.

Then another idea came to him. He had been worrying about trying to carry the controller and the drone on his bike so now he made a decision. Picking up the home phone he quickly dialled for a taxi. Satisfied that one was on its way, he continued his preparations. From his own room he collected money and then quickly made his way down the front steps.

"Now for the drone," he muttered, silently praying that it would work.

In the workshops under the house he hurried to where he had last seen his father's drone was lying on a work bench. And there it was! But even as Willy picked it up he saw that it was missing one of its rotors.

Oh no! he thought, dismay and despair flooding through him. He suspected that it would not have the balance to fly with only three rotors and knew he could not risk failure. *I will just have to phone the police and risk looking silly if it is all a false alarm,* he thought.

And then his gaze noted his father's model Feisler Storch standing on a shelf. *That might do!* he thought. In his mind's eye he estimated the possibilities of flying a fixed wing model to a safe landing on the tiny balcony. *I think I can do it,* he decided. For almost a minute he stood there, agonizing over whether his plan was stupid or not. *The Storch is a STOL after all,* he told himself, visualizing the landings he had watched. But the only other choice seemed to be to involve adults (the police!) so he decided to try it.

That got him all in a flustered frenzy of doubt and preparation. He rushed around looking for the controller (and fretting over whether it or the model's batteries might be flat!).

Despite his urgent desire to hurry, Willy forced himself to find a battery charger and to test the model's battery. To his relief, it had plenty of power, but just in case he snatched up a spare battery and slid it into a carry bag. His father's controller was added to the bag and then Willy carefully picked up the model aircraft to check it.

As he did, he heard a vehicle stop on the street. Glancing through the window he saw it was the taxi. Quickly he made his way outside, pulling the door shut behind him. He was aware that he should lock up properly and that he shouldn't leave his bike just lying on the front lawn, but he was now so focused on saving Petra that he just did not care.

When he walked down the driveway the taxi driver gave him a surprised look. "Where to kid?' he asked as Willy opened the back door.

Willy named the hotel and then carefully slid into the back of the taxi, making sure that the model's wings and tail did not touch anything. The driver looked even more surprised but started the taxi moving.

"Seatbelt on kid," he said.

That was tricky to do without damaging the model but Willy achieved it, aware that the driver was studying him in the rear vision mirror.

The driver met his eyes. "Shouldn't you be at school?" he asked.

"Yes," Willy answered. "But I have to deliver this first."

The man made no more enquiries so Willy was able to sit back and plan his next moves. The first problem he could foresee was getting the model through the lobby and up to the roof.

I will be very obvious, he mused.

He was. Five minutes later the taxi stopped at the front of the hotel. After paying the driver and climbing carefully out with the model Willy slung his carry bag over his shoulder and headed for the door. From the taxi he had been unable to see if either John or Petra were still up at the top of the building so he could only hope all was well.

But as he walked through the door he saw that a different receptionist was on duty, a middle-aged man and he looked at Willy at once. "Where are you going kid?" he called.

Heart hammering with anxiety Willy kept walking towards the bottom of the stairs, his mind racing to formulate a suitable answer. Gesturing upwards he replied, "Just up to show my model plane to my dad."

"Who's your dad?" the receptionist queried, obviously not happy.

"Doctor Williams. He's in Room 316," Willy replied. He chose the number because his family had once stayed in a hotel room with that number and he fervently hoped that this hotel had a similarly numbered room

A frown crossed the man's face and he bent to look at a computer screen. Then he began tapping on the keyboard. Willy kept walking and at that moment a lift door opened almost in front of him and young couple came out.

The man at reception looked up. "Hey! Just wait!' he called.

But Willy didn't. He ducked around the young couple and hurried into the lift. With fingers that trembled with excitement he pressed the roof button and then stood fretting while waiting for the doors to close. At every moment he expected the man to appear and to haul him back out.

But the doors slid closed and the lift was whisked rapidly upwards. Nothing happened to stop it and a minute later Willy was out on the roof. Thankfully, he noted that there were still no patrons or staff there and he hurried across to where a mightily relieved looking John was standing.

But Petra wasn't on the balcony!

"Where is she?" Willy croaked, his breath coming in gasps.

"She got called inside about ten minutes ago," John answered, anguish clear in both his voice and his face.

"Bugger!" Willy swore. Now he was afraid that the hotel security would find them before they could act. *Too bad. Better get ready just in case,* he told himself.

Quickly he wrote a note and then asked John for his number. This was added and he taped the piece of paper to the back of John's mobile phone. Then he taped John's mobile phone to the underside of the model. Anxious that he had the balance right Willy stood up and held the model up by his fingertips under the wingtips.

John watched anxiously. "What are you doing?" he asked.

"Checking the balance," Willy answered. "If the centre of gravity is wrong the plane could just crash instead of flying."

And he wasn't happy so, with trembling fingers he ripped the tape off and moved the mobile phone a centimetre forward. Then he checked the balance again. While it wasn't perfect he felt he could control it. He was now consumed by anxiety about being caught by security and he kept flicking glances towards the lift.

But no-one appeared so Willy took out the controller and tested it. As he did John's finger's twitched. "Let me fly it," he pleaded.

But Willy shook his head. "No. It is my dad's plane and I will do it," he replied firmly.

"Don't muck it up!" John cried as Willy stood up with the model in hand to study the next building.

No, don't muck it up William, Willy told himself.

Chapter 41

RESCUE FLIGHT

To his dismay, Willy found that he was trembling and that his fingers were fluttering and wet with perspiration. With an effort of will he calmed himself and then he wiped his hands on his shorts. Next he bent to the controller and made sure it was switched on. He then set the radio channels needed.

I think that is right, he thought, screwing his face up with the effort of remembering what his father had set it on in Townsville. Carefully he switched everything on and then gingerly tested the controls and then the motor. To his relief the propeller purred into silent motion and the model began to roll forwards across the concrete. Quickly he stopped the motor and wiped sweaty hands on his shorts.

With everything ready Willy stood up, holding the controller and leaving the model aircraft facing across the roof into what little breeze curled down over the concrete balustrade. *How should I launch this?* he wondered. The two options were to hand launch and or use the roof as a runway.

To check the strength of the wind Willy leaned out over the railing and was dismayed at how strong the breeze was. The wind was being channelled between the high rise buildings and felt quite strong. *That could throw the model right off course or even send it out of control.*

But the real problem was that Petra was nowhere to be seen. There was no point in flying the phone across otherwise. *Some other person might find it then,* Willy thought. *We would look a right pair of nongs then!*

And every passing second meant that the chances of being apprehended by security got higher. *It won't take them long to work out we must be on the roof,* he thought. Anxiously, he glanced over his shoulder towards the lift door.

John followed his glance and frowned. "What's wrong Willy?"

Willy described the incident in the foyer. "So the hotel security should locate us soon," he concluded.

Feeling quite defeated, he turned to face the other hotel and leaned his elbows on the balustrade. But the other balcony stayed empty and Willy felt his hopes sliding. *All that effort and to fail when we are so close!* he thought.

Once again he looked around and tested the strength of the wind. He was still unsure which method to take-off to use but he was inclined to favour taking-off from the roof. *That way I have a chance to get the aircraft under control before it hits the real turbulence,* he reasoned.

And there was Petra!

She had walked out onto the balcony, and even as Willy spotted her she turned to speak to someone inside. To Willy's surprise, he saw that she was no longer in her school uniform but was wearing a very short towelling wrap and her bare legs looked very long. At the sight of that wrap, ugly suspicions coalesced into stomach churning thoughts.

What has she been doing? he thought, his memory dredging up all the hurtful little comments and innuendos about what sort of girl Petra might be. To him it looked like she had been crying. She certainly looked unhappy.

John gaped and obviously wondered the same thing. "Why has she changed out of her school uniform?" he queried. He looked both baffled and anxious.

Willy's mind raced in an attempt to find an answer that did not shatter John's illusions, but he was unable to find a suitable explanation. His own thoughts were now full of disgusting notions of sex. Instead, he grunted and made no reply and he found he felt profoundly sorry for John.

She's not a goddess, he thought sadly. *She's just a girl.*

Petra nodded to the person inside the room and then reached out and drew the curtain and sliding glass door across. Only then did she look towards the boys.

By then John was dancing with excitement. He waved and pointed down then grabbed at Willy's right arm and pointed. "Quick!" he cried. "Show her the plane."

Willy at once bent down and lifted the model aircraft up. To make certain she understood their plan, he held it high above his head and side on so she could clearly see what it was. Then he pointed to the mobile phone and message taped underneath and used his left hand to mime talking on a telephone. To his relief, Petra nodded and a brief smile showed on her tear-streaked face. Then she glanced fearfully towards the room.

Now the tricky bit, Willy thought. *How to get this aircraft airborne and across there without losing control or crashing it!*

The stakes suddenly seemed so high that he was almost overcome by nervousness. His whole body shivered and his eyes went briefly out of focus.

Willy blinked, swallowed and took a deep breath. *Get a grip on yourself,* he berated himself. *Now isn't the time for nerves. There is too much at stake. Just focus on the task.*

So he did. He switched on the controller and then the electric motor of the model aircraft. The model's propeller began to rotate and Willy stared at it anxiously, still undecided as to whether to hand launch or use a take-off run.

"Willy!" John cried.

Willy looked up and the cause for John's anxious cry was at once apparent, a thin man wearing a white shirt, black trousers and black bow tie had come out of the lift doorway and was looking towards them with a quizzical expression on his face. He began walking towards them.

Bloody hell! Is he Security or what? Willy thought.

"Stall him John!" Willy cried.

Without further debate he bent down and grabbed the model and flicked it up so he could grab the fuselage just behind the undercarriage. With his other hand he braced the controller on the narrow ledge and used the fingers of his left hand to push the throttle lever forward. The tiny electric motor began to whine and the propeller became a blur.

By then John had walked halfway across the roof to meet the man and was gesticulating and blocking his path. Willy glanced at them and decided that ploy would only last for a few more seconds. With no more time for niceties, he pulled his right hand back and then thrust forward, letting the model go as he did. The direction of launch was into the wind, which meant across the side of the roof.

At once the wind caught the model and it swooped steeply up and then began to roll over. Willy quickly moved his right hand to the controller and centred the controls and then watched, heart in mouth, as the model went spinning down between the two buildings.

For a few seconds he feared that it was just going to spin down and crash, but then the wind being funnelling between the buildings caught it and it was swept out from between them. By then Willy had gained some sort of control and the model stopped spinning. He wanted it to face into the wind, but before he could get proper control it was halfway across the street and in danger of crashing into a block of units on the other side.

"Bloody hell!" Willy muttered.

Then he sighed with relief. He had managed to turn the nose of the model into the wind and it began to fly slowly back against it. As it did, he put it into a gentle climb. For a few seconds, the pressures all cancelled each other out and he saw that the model was climbing but making no headway over the ground.

To add to his dismay, he saw that it was down among the powerlines strung along both sides of the street. "Oh no!" he muttered, frantically trying to keep control in the gusty conditions.

He managed that and also managed to keep it facing into the wind and in level flight but then he had to fly it slowly up. What bothered him was that in his nightmare he was in the cockpit and could see more clearly where the powerlines were but here he was a long way above and was having great difficulty in judging whether the model was above or below the powerlines it was heading for.

"Go down and then come up over the street," he told himself.

It was still a risk as he could not accurately judge if the model really was below the powerlines, but to his immense relief he saw it pass just under them. Heart hammering with anxiety he sent it down a bit more, and as soon as it was clear from under he set it to climb. To his relief, he noted that the model was soon well above the power lines.

But by the time it was above the powerlines on his side of the street, it was also clear to Willy that the model would run into a hotel unless he made it circle back.

I need to circle it back to gain altitude, he thought. For a few seconds fear of failure caused Willy to pause. Then he took a deep breath and moved the controls.

To his relief, his touch was sure and the model swung smoothly around but he was then appalled at how fast it flew back across the street with the strong tail wind. There were buildings there and he feared it might crash into them. Just in time he managed to turn the model around again and got it facing back towards the hotel Petra was in. Then he set it climbing again, trying to keep it on the lee of the building but also conscious that there must be back eddies and turbulence caused by the structure.

There was turbulence but by circling above the street well away from the building, Willy got the model safely up to almost his own level.

Sweating profusely and biting his lip with concentration, he sent the model to edge over into the lee of the other hotel. In this he almost miscalculated as a swirl of turbulence set it almost tumbling. But he had been expecting that and quickly regained control and then flew it back away from the other hotel in a wide, climbing turn. Gnawing at the back of his mind was anxiety about whether the battery would last.

This time he was more confident and he even let the model fly right back across the street before aiming it back at his objective. Carefully he set it to climb and then watched, totally focused on his minute adjustments. The model aircraft then did exactly what he wanted and began to climb slowly forward and upwards until it was at the same height as Petra's head and aimed at the centre of the building.

Movement next to Willy caused him to briefly glance that way. The man was at the balustrade, John just beyond him. The man watched the model for a few seconds then frowned and turned away. Willy had expected him to say something but instead the man just walked back towards the lift.

Willy watched for a moment then refocused on his flying. "Who is he? What did he want?" he asked.

John glanced back at the man. "He didn't say but I think he is a waiter or bar attendant," he replied. "He just asked what we were doing."

A glance showed the man unlocking the door to the bar area. "There will be a phone there," Willy commented before turning back to concentrate on his task.

"Sorry Willy, I couldn't stop him," John cried.

Willy nodded, relieved that the rescue attempt had not yet been thwarted. By then he had the model flying close across the front of the other hotel. As it reached Petra's balcony, he gave a twitch of the controls and it banked and flew in above the balcony. Another quick twitch just in time stopped it crashing into the glass sliding doors of the room.

Petra stood back, hands held up in fear of being struck. Willy pulled the throttle back and the model eased down and he jiggled carefully to lower the speed and it sank below the level of the glass balustrade and landed lightly on the balcony. The model then veered into the glass screen and Willy remembered to switch off the motor as it began to career along the side of the balcony.

"Did it!" he muttered. *Come on Petra, pick it up! Get that phone before someone comes out of the room!* he thought, clenching his fists as he did. He found he was dancing with nervous tension and he again made a telephone signal with his left hand.

But Petra was already bending to act. She scooped up the model aircraft and looked at it. For what seemed like many seconds, Petra scrabbled at the sticky tape with her fingernails and then she tore the phone and note free. Dropping the model plane, she turned the phone over and read the note. Twice she glanced towards the room and even from that distance Willy could see that she was shaking.

After another glance at the room, and then at them, Petra punched in the number of Lloyd's mobile phone. By then Willy had placed the controller on the balustrade and had the phone in his hand. Moments later it rang and he pressed the 'Accept Call'.

"Hello Petra, it's me, Willy," he said.

"Villy!" Petra answered. Then her voice choked up and she lifted her eyes to look at him while holding the phone to her ear.

"Petra, are you in trouble? Do you need help?"

"Yes plis. I in trouble. Help me," Petra replied, her voice cracking with emotion.

Willy went to speak but was distracted by John pulling at his shirt. "Willy, what did she say? Let me talk to her" he cried.

Willy shook John off and frowned. "Trouble," he muttered, then he spoke into the phone again. "What sort of trouble Petra?"

The reply was a mixture of sniffles and sob and then, quite distinctly, Petra said: "Zey make me do the disgusting things I not like and they..." The rest was lost in more sniffles.

Willy felt his stomach churn and gritted his teeth. "Do you want us to call the police?" he asked.

"Yes... polis," Petra replied, accenting the word to emphasize the 'S'. She began sobbing and turned her back to the room.

"What sort of trouble, Petra? The police will want to know," Willy asked.

Petra stared across the gap at him and he saw tears streaming down her face. "My... My mother... she (sob!) she... she sell me for sex to horrible men... (sob)."

Willy was stunned. *Her mother! Selling her for sex!* "Petra, can't you escape?" she asked.

Petra shook her head. "No. My mother's man, he watch me and he tell me he do horrible things to me with knife if I do not do vot zey say," she explained.

Willy was shocked and also instantly afraid for her. Biting his lip his mind raced. "What about Tania?" he asked.

"She also," Petra explained.

Willy wasn't sure if Petra meant that Tania was also threatening her or whether she was also being forced to be a prostitute, but he realised he was wasting time.

We have to call for help without the man knowing or she might get hurt and he might escape, he thought.

Lifting the phone to his ear, he spoke rapid instructions. "Petra, throw the model aircraft over the side. Then put the phone in your pocket and pretend nothing is happening. I will get help. Quick, do it now!"

To his intense relief, he saw Petra nod. She slid the mobile phone into the pocket on the wrap and then bent forward and scooped the model aircraft up and launched it over the side. For a second Willy considered switching the motor on and trying to fly the model but then he shook his head.

It doesn't matter if it gets wrecked. It has done its job, he told himself. *Petra is more important than any model plane.*

Even so he leant over the balustrade and watched with real regret as the model aircraft struck the wall and then spun out, helicoptering down to crash onto the driveway between the two buildings. "Oh well!" he muttered.

Then he lifted the phone and ended the call to Petra. John had also watched the model as it spiralled down but now he grabbed at Willy. "Willy, what did she say? What does she want?" he cried.

"The police," Willy answered. In his heart he knew that when John learned the truth about what Petra had been doing in the hotel he would be emotionally devastated.

It will shatter him, poor bugger! he thought.

Pressing the buttons to call 000 he put the phone back to his ear.

The operator's voice came through almost immediately. "What service please?" she asked.

"Police please," Willy replied.

After being asked what city or place he was in, Willy was connected to a police operator. That was the easy bit. The hard bit was to convince the man at the other end that he was serious. He had to give his name and then his address and then, as the man did not seem convinced he named his school.

"Why aren't you at school? Is this a prank?" the police operator asked.

A feeling of frustrated desperation began to assail Willy. "No!" he cried. "This is an emergency. A girl's life is at stake!" After naming the hotel Petra was in he went on: "My friend and I are on the rooftop. She is on the top floor of the next hotel and has just called us on a mobile phone," he explained.

"Oh yeah? What's her name?"

"Petra, Petra Pantovitch. She is being held prisoner by some man and her mother and they are forcing her to have sex with men for money," Willy cried.

Then he saw the shocked look on John's face and wished he hadn't said that. Anxiously, he glanced around and noted that the man who had come onto the roof was now inside the small outdoor bar area. He had pushed up the shutter and was talking into a telephone while looking back at him and John.

He's calling security now, Willy thought.

Knowing that he might be interrupted lent a sense of almost desperate urgency to Willy. Quickly he described the location and again gave the name of the hotel Petra was in and the floor she was on.

The police operator now sounded more businesslike. "And where are you?" he asked.

"On top of the next hotel, on the roof," Willy replied, naming the hotel.

"And why are you involved? Are you a relation?"

"No. She's a girl in my class at school and we followed her," he said. "You can check with the school if you like."

"We will. Just remain where you are please and stay on the phone. Do not hang up," the police operator ordered. From the sound of his voice he was at least half convinced and Willy began to relax slightly.

A minute went by during which he glanced across at Petra and then back at the man in the bar. The man was still watching them and Willy suspected he had instructions to stop them leaving. He didn't care. *We need adults to help now,* he thought.

But would they be in time? Willy began to fret and chewed his lip while he stared across at Petra. Then, to his horror, the curtains and glass sliding door to the balcony were slid open and a very large, fat Asian wearing only a pair of underpants stepped out and gestured to Petra to go back inside.

Oh no! Willy thought, his mind suddenly a mass of swirling maggots of disgust and, he realised to his shame, jealousy.

John was aghast. He grabbed at Willy and gabbled. "Willy! She... She... They... We must stop him!" he cried, anguish and desperation clear in his voice. He opened his mouth and took a deep breath.

Willy realised John was going to yell out, so he sprang at him and clamped his hand over John's mouth. "Sssh! Don't call out!" he hissed.

John tried to shake him off and clawed at the hand and forearm. "We... muffft... we... can't... Leff.. me go!" he spluttered.

"No! Keep quiet," Willy snarled, wrestling John aside so that they both tumbled onto the concrete roof. That hurt as knees and elbows stuck hard but he ignored the lancing pains and kept a tight grip.

If John alarms those men Petra will be in real trouble, he thought. Mentally he had now magnified the man into men and he dreaded them harming Petra and Tania. *They are now inconvenient witnesses,* he thought. *They could take them away and dispose of them.*

It was a heart and gut-wrenching choice, but he knew that leaving Petra at the mercy of the man's lust was the lesser of the two evils. "The police must be able to get here and catch them before they can harm Petra," he hissed in John's ear.

"Let... let me go!" John cried while struggling violently. But then he stopped and seemed to slump.

For a few moments Willy kept gripping him tightly, suspecting it was just a ruse to lull him into easing his grip but then John began to sob.

"She... They... She.. Oh no!" he muttered, evidently in deep distress.

At that moment, Willy saw movement out of the corner of his eye. A quick glance showed that it was another man and he was coming towards them from the lift doorway. This time the man was big and burly, and even though he wore a grey business suit Willy was sure he was hotel security.

Damn! Another problem, he thought.

Catching John's eyes he gestured with his head. "Here comes more trouble. Let's hope he doesn't muck things up," he said.

Chapter 42

QUICK TALKING

Willy struggled to get up as the security man approached. As he did, his mind raced. *How can I persuade this bloke to do what we want?* he fretted, fearful that the man might not listen to explanations and might then blow the police operation.

As he regained his feet, Willy decided on what to say. *The simple truth is the best option,* he told himself.

By then the man was looming over them and looking hostile. His sheer size and physical presence was so intimidating that Willy felt his resolution waver and he understood fully what the expression 'weak at the knees' meant. The man placed his hands on his hips and glared at them. "What are you bloody kids up to? What are you doing on the roof?" he demanded.

"Waiting for the police," Willy answered, his heart now beating with a mixture of apprehension and determination.

"The police! That's who I'll be calling if you give me any trouble. You are trespassing," the security man snapped.

"Please mister," Willy began, acutely conscious that every moment was precious. To his dismay his mouth went dry and he seemed to choke up with emotion. Swallowing and moistening his lips with his tongue he looked the man in the eye. "We are trying to save a girl in the next hotel."

The security man turned to look that way and then back at Willy and John. "What girl? I don't see any girl. What do you mean save?" he snapped.

"She is being held prisoner in that end room there," Willy said. "Please don't make a lot of fuss. That might attract the men who are holding her. True mister. Please believe me. She is in real danger."

The man hesitated and looked astonished. "What sort of danger?" he queried, again casting suspicious looks towards the other hotel.

Inspiration came to Willy. He held out the phone and said, "We have called the police. You can talk to them if you like."

The security man looked even more doubtful. Behind him was the bar steward, his face alive with interest. The security man then frowned and reached out for the phone. Willy had doubts about handing it to him in case he kept it but he reasoned he had to take that risk to convince the man quickly. The security man took the phone and raised it to his ear. "Hello, this is hotel security. Who am I speaking to please?" he asked.

As the police operator replied, the security man's eyebrows shot up and he nodded, then said, "I am on the roof with two boys." He then turned to Willy. "What is your name?" he asked.

"Willy Williams," Willy replied. "Please mister, we need to move away from the edge of the roof so the men don't see us," he said.

But the security man was again focused on what the police operator was saying. The security man then nodded and again looked at Willy. "The police say they are on their way and we are to move back out of sight and to wait here," he said.

Willy felt immensely relieved and nodded but then anxiety again welled up. "Tell them no sirens or they might warn the men," he cried, reaching out for the phone.

The security man held the phone away from Willy and relayed this suggestion. Then he listened and nodded before gesturing for Willy and John to move with him. Willy cast a last glance over the balustrade but there was no sign of either Petra or the man. Feeling very tense, he followed the security man to the small outdoor bar.

The security man told them to wait there and the barman positioned himself to block the lift door. Then the security man went into the bar and picked up the phone on the counter and dialled a number. For the next minute or so he carried on a conversation with someone while continually looking at either Willy or John. Then he nodded, said, "Yes sir," and placed the phone down.

When he came back out, Willy put out his hand. "Can I have my phone back please," he asked.

The security man shook his head. "Not till the police arrive," he replied.

That annoyed Willy. "It doesn't belong to you," he said. Amazed at his own temerity and boldness he went on, "If you keep it I will get my parents to have you charged with theft. It is my brother's phone and you have no right to take it."

To his surprise, the security man shrugged and handed him back the phone. Willy tried to hide his relief and then held the phone up so he could hear if the police operator spoke.

But he didn't. The minutes ticked by and it became very hot in the sun. Willy looked around for some shade and then moved in under the awning around the small bar. John followed. They sat on the bar stools and waited. While they did, Willy repeated what he knew to the security man. The man now looked both convinced and serious. John just looked crumpled and sat with drooping shoulders and misery on his face.

Poor bugger! Willy thought. *His dreams have been shattered.* It made him feel sad but also made him aware that he had also worshiped Petra when he first met her. It was all very depressing.

"Oh, where are the bloody cops!" he muttered in anxious frustration.

And there they were. The lift door slid open and two men in long grey trousers and white shirts and ties strode out and over to them. The men both had radios and wore pistols in holsters on their belts. They did not have to show their ID cards to convince Willy they were police, they just looked it!

One of the plain clothes policemen was a Detective Inspector and Willy told him the story. The man asked a few questions but mostly just listened. "And you used a model airplane to fly a mobile phone over to this Petra?" he queried.

"Yes sir. It was John's idea," Willy replied.

The two policemen both shook their heads in amazement and then the Detective Inspector asked for more details. These were noted down and then he nodded. "Thanks," he said. "Now wait up here." He then called on the radio and listened to the reply. "All in position, Frank? Good. OK, go!"

Knowing that the police were now acting, Willy felt excitement, apprehension and relief all surge. He itched to watch but got no chance. The other plain clothes policeman made sure he and the hotel staff stayed away from the edge of the roof while the Detective Inspector walked over to where Willy and John had been. From there he directed the operation by radio. Willy fretted with anxiety but could do nothing. Then he saw the Detective Inspector raise his right hand and give a thumbs-up to someone over in Petra's hotel.

Is that it? Willy wondered. *Is it all over?*

It was. The Detective Inspector walked back to them with a grim smile on his face. "Got them!" he said.

"Is Petra safe?" John cried.

"Yes. Now you two come with us and we will organise for parents to be present while we interview you," the Detective Inspector replied.

Parents! Willy had forgotten about them and now his stomach turned over with anxiety. *Poor old mum and dad! They will start to lose any trust in me,"* he thought.

But they didn't. Instead, when the full story had been explained, they were full of praise. Willy's father shook his hand. "Well done young William! Bloody good effort!"

"I wrecked your Feisler Storch, Dad," Willy replied.

His father just made a dismissive gesture. "All in a good cause. We can always get another model plane but people are precious. That was a good decision son," he replied.

"A drone would have been better," Willy commented. He explained how he had planned use his father's but had found it unserviceable.

His father made a face. "Hmmm! Well I thought you didn't like drones, so I didn't hurry to fix it. They aren't real aircraft you said."

Willy squirmed but nodded. "Drones have their uses," he replied. "It would have been a lot easier to manoeuvre one over that balcony."

"Well done, son! I like a man who learns from experience and who has the courage to admit when he is wrong," his father said, sticking out his hand. Willy blushed and shook it, a warm feeling of being loved and valued flooding through him.

There were several hours of interviews at the police station before Willy's parents were allowed to take him home. By then it was dark. A very worried Lloyd met them, all agog as he knew something serious had happened but not the details.

"I was real worried," Lloyd said, "and don't you leave the house unlocked and your bike just lying on the lawn next time, little brother. It could have been pinched or we could have been burgled," he added.

Willy's mother cut in. "There had better not be a next time! That is enough excitement for this family."

Lloyd then mentioned that there had been a brief news item on the TV news of two girls being rescued from a hotel that afternoon. "Is that what you were doing, Willy?" he asked.

Willy nodded. "Yes. I used dad's Feisler Storch to fly your mobile phone from one building to the other," he explained.

"My mobile phone! You little toad! Who said you could take my mobile phone? Where is it?"

"The police have it. It is now evidence," Willy replied. "Don't worry, you'll get it back."

Lloyd wasn't happy and grumbled a bit. "The news never said anything about that or about you being involved. It just said that two girls had been kept as sex slaves. Were they?"

Willy's mother now intervened. "That is enough questioning Lloyd. You can get the smutty details later. Now leave Willy alone. Willy, go and have a bath while we organise something to eat."

That night Willy slept badly, tormented by the discovery that his innocent little Petra, who looked and acted so pure, was actually the victim of revolting abuse. As he considered what she might have had to do with disgusting men, his stomach churned with nausea and jealousy. "Poor little Petra!" he muttered. "How could her own mother force her to do things like that?"

And poor John! He had obviously been more devastated by the revelations than he was. But then Willy decided that he had much more experience with girls than John had. *I actually like them, and I'm not scared to talk to them,* he thought.

It was John he was worrying about next morning when his parents drove him to school. But to begin with he got no chance to look for him. Instead Willy had to explain to the Principal and Mr Fitzgerald what he and John had done and why. They were astonished, annoyed and then admiring and both shook Willy's hand. "Very brave and very ingenious," Mr Croswell said.

Mr Fitzgerald nodded and also put out his hand. "There's hope for you yet, young William, but next time tell the adults first."

"We wanted to be sure what the problem was first sir. We didn't want to cry wolf and waste everyone's time and make ourselves look foolish," Willy replied.

Mr Croswell nodded. "Well you have saved those poor young girls so well done. Now run along to class while we talk to your parents. And don't discuss any of this with your friends. It is legal stuff and we need to minimise the damage to Petra's reputation," he ordered.

Willy did so after saying a quick goodbye to his parents. As he walked along the veranda towards his classroom, he found his emotions in turmoil. He felt glad and sad at the same time.

On reaching his classroom, Willy was tested even further. Class had begun and he had to explain to Mrs Ramsey that he had been at the office.

She raised an eyebrow. "In trouble again?"

"No Miss. Just.. just something I saw," Willy replied.

He then looked around the room and was more put out than he wanted to admit to: almost nobody was paying him any attention. He certainly wasn't the celebrity of the hour. Feeling quite miffed but relieved, he looked towards where Petra usually sat but her seat was empty. Willy had not expected her to be at school but seeing that vacant seat sent shivers of emotion through him.

And John wasn't present either. Sadly, Willy made his way to his seat and sat down. After finding out what work to do, he sat and brooded while making a perfunctory effort to do it. All the while his mind went over the whole incident and he was satisfied he had done all he could. But he felt very upset about Petra.

Poor kid! Her life will be wrecked, he thought.

That brought tears to his eyes and he had to struggle to hold them back and to hide them. Bending over his books, he did the best he could. Slowly his churning emotions subsided, and he settled to the mundane routine of education.

During the break he expected to be asked where he'd been the last afternoon and had a suitable off-hand reply ready, but nobody did.

Surely they noticed! he thought. Now his ego was hurt and he studied his friends and wondered if they really were.

Despite this he was astonished to find he had a compelling urge to tell everyone what had happened. It took all of his willpower to resist. *How can I not say anything?* he wondered. And then he knew. *I have lots of little guilty secrets already and can keep my mouth shut about them. I'll just pretend I am a secret agent in enemy territory and play act.*

So the day dragged on and each bit of time placed another layer of new memories over the events of the previous day until by mid-afternoon Willy felt as though it had been something he had seen on TV or read about or which had been done by another person a long time before.

But he knew it had been real and he sat alone during the lunch break and relived every moment. He also brooded on what he might have done if he had learned earlier that Petra was in that situation.

I got enough hints, he thought gloomily. Now all the clues seemed to drop into place to form a picture, a horrible set of images that caused him to burst into tears.

But other people soon jolted him out of that. To his dismay, Larsen and Carstairs came walking past and saw him. "Look, there's little shitface rocket man. What ya blubbing about ya big baby? Did ya last rocket go fizz?" Larsen jeered.

Willy wiped the tears from his eyes and stood up. As he hurried away jeering taunts and laughter followed him, Carstairs calling him a bloody sook. "Petra the Poke must have turned him down," he added.

That really stung and caused another flood of tears. There were so many Willy could hardly see and he blundered along, blinking and trying to hide his face from other students.

To his dismay, he encountered four girls from his own class. He tried to detour but Barbara came over to him. "Willy, what's the matter?" she asked.

Her tone was sympathetic and she even put her hand on his shoulder. Willy could only lean against the wall and try to hide his face and sniffle. Barbara patted him. "Is it because of Petra?" she asked.

"W... What (sniffle) about (sob) Petra?" he wailed.

"We heard she had left school," Barbara answered.

"Don't know," Willy replied, wondering and worrying about how much the girls knew. More sobs and sniffles came as he choked up with emotion.

But Petra had. Willy never saw her again. All he learned was that she had been forced into prostitution by her mother and her mother's boyfriend and that was so distressing he tried not to think about it.

And worry about John rose to bother Willy. *I hurt him badly,* he thought. But what was really gnawing at Willy was the lurking fear that John might be so shattered and disillusioned that he might decide that life wasn't worth living.

He might commit suicide! Willy fretted. But what to do about it? In the end he decided he had to take some action and he plucked up the courage to take the problem to his father. It took him a bit to get started but then he found himself pouring out the story and his concerns.

"John is absolutely shattered, Dad. I think he worshipped Petra and I am worried that he might... might do something drastic if he gets too depressed."

His father at once grasped the seriousness of his worries. "You are worried about your friend's mental health are you son? That is good. But this is where professionals should take over. You can support your friend by just staying his friend but his parents need to know. And he probably needs to be referred to a professional counsellor."

"How do I do that, Dad?" Willy asked.

Willy's father reached out and patted his shoulder. "You are a great son! I am proud of you. But relax. You do not have to do it; in fact, I don't think you should," he said.

Willy glowed at the praise but was still puzzled and anxious. "But... but how do we help him?"

"I will do that son. I am a doctor and that sort of thing is part of the job. Leave it to me. We will make sure your friend is looked after and gets the help he needs."

"Thanks Dad," Willy croaked, choking up with emotion.

"And what about you son? You thought the sun rose and set on this Petra, didn't you?"

Willy nodded, but then said, "I did, Dad, but I think I have a lot more experience of girls than John. I am sad about Petra and care what happens to her, but I also understand that girls are only... well... girls. And it wasn't her choice."

Willy's father grinned and nodded, and again patted his shoulder. "We will keep an eye on you too mate. And you be a good man. And remember, women are a lifelong study, but you need to be careful. Just remember to be honest and loyal and to be caring and considerate, and you will get on fine. So just talk to us if you really have a problem."

"Thanks Dad."

So his parents were very supportive during the next few days and only on Friday morning did his misery start to abate. His mother reminded him that he had cadets that night. "And you have your Passing-Out Parade tomorrow. You need to buck up," she said.

Passing-Out Parade! I had forgotten. Oh, I hope those army cadets aren't going to muck it up, he thought anxiously.

The following afternoon at 1700 hours, Willy was still very anxious.

He was standing in the ranks in his best blue uniform at the Air Cadet depot ready to march on to the parade ground. Off to his left were what looked like hundreds of people. Seated at the front were a row of dignitaries including a navy officer in dress whites and Capt Conkey in his Army Cadet ceremonial uniform with Sam Browne belt, sword and medals.

Standing off at the side of the crowd were half a dozen army cadets in their camouflage ceremonial uniforms and with them were five navy cadets, including Andrew and Carmen Collins, and both Blake and Luke Karaku. Among the army cadets Willy recognised Graham Kirk and his friends. *Oh I hope they aren't going to spoil the parade,* he thought, breaking into a sweat of apprehension as he did.

Then Warrant Officer Mathieson called the air cadets to attention and Willy stiffened, determined to do the best drill he could. *Even if someone does muck our parade up we will still show the Army and Navy Cadets that our drill is better than theirs,* he resolved.

The air cadets marched on and were halted. A left turn into line had them facing the audience and then they were right dressed and stood at ease. The ceremonial parade continued according to plan: Attention, officers on parade, then the banner was marched on. As the Banner Party crossed in front of him Willy admired how good their slow march was and silently determined that one day he would have the honour of carrying the banner.

Next came the reception of the Reviewing Officer, a RAAF Wing Commander. Willy stood rigidly to attention and watched every move. By now he was feeling very tense. *If there is going to be a disruption it will be next,* he told himself. That was during the inspection and as CUO Penrose marched over to salute the wing commander Willy looked around.

That was hard to do without moving his head. First he scanned the army cadets for any sign of them looking elsewhere or of them doing something unusual. But they just seemed to be standing and watching. Graham Kirk in particular appeared to be focused on the details of the ceremonial and his eyes were on the Inspection Party.

As the Wing Commander, CUO Penrose and Flight Lieutenant Comstock marched across to begin the inspection Willy remembered the comments about a remote controlled model tank and he squirmed with the urge to look around to check. He resisted the urge but found he was breathing fast and deep.

Calm down! he told himself, *or you will faint.*

Sweat trickled down Willy's back and he knew it wasn't just because it was a humid, tropical summer night. *I'm glad I wore a singlet,* he thought. *Otherwise the perspiration would be staining my shirt.*

Then his roving gaze took in Stick's parents and beside them was Marjorie. She looked very pretty in a floral print frock and for a moment Willy admired her busty curves before an image of Petra made him choke up. At that moment the Reviewing Officer stopped in front of him.

"Are you alright lad?" the Wing Commander asked.

"Yes sir," Willy replied, blinking back tears and using all his willpower to control his voice. "Just proud to be here."

"Good show! Good show!" the Wing Commander replied. He and CUO Penrose moved on and Willy found himself looking into Flight Lieutenant Comstock's eyes.

"Good answer, Cadet Williams," he murmured.

Willy quivered with pride and took a deep breath. Flight Lieutenant Comstock continued on and only then did Willy remember the possibility of the parade being sabotaged.

But nothing happened. The Inspection Party returned to the saluting base and CUO Penrose turned to give orders. The parade turned to the right and the music began. Relieved, Willy felt elation well up and, almost bursting with pride stepped off to the strains of *Eagle Squadron.*

After the March Past and Advance in Review Order there were speeches and the awarding of prizes. Willy had harboured a faint hope that he might win a prize for Best Cadet or something. But he didn't. To his annoyance that went to Flora Finlay.

Her! he thought as the jealousy bubbled up. *I'm better than her!*

And then the parade was over and the socialising began. Willy was congratulated by his parents. Then he found his hand being pumped by Stephen while Graham, Peter and Roger stood grinning. "Bloody good parade! Well done!" Stephen said.

"Nearly as good as us," Graham added.

"Oh get real!" Willy retorted, but he had to smile. Then he found soft female arms around his neck and the waft of perfume came to his nostrils just before he was kissed. It was Marjorie.

411

"That was really good!" she whispered in his ear.

"So are you," Willy whispered back. But he experienced a series of painful images of Petra and he sighed deeply.

For the rest of his life, during moments of profound contemplation, he would sometimes think about Petra and wonder what had become of her.

I hope she is having a good life.

Did Willy make another model aircraft? Of course he did! And did the army cadets get their revenge? Well, there was certainly plenty of intense rivalry which tested Willy's inventiveness and intellect. So read on.

Enjoy more C.R. Cummings stories

The Air Cadets

The Navy Cadets

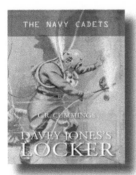

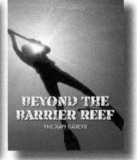

The Army Cadets

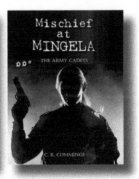

Lightning Source UK Ltd.
Milton Keynes UK
UKHW011952090720
366299UK00002B/18/J